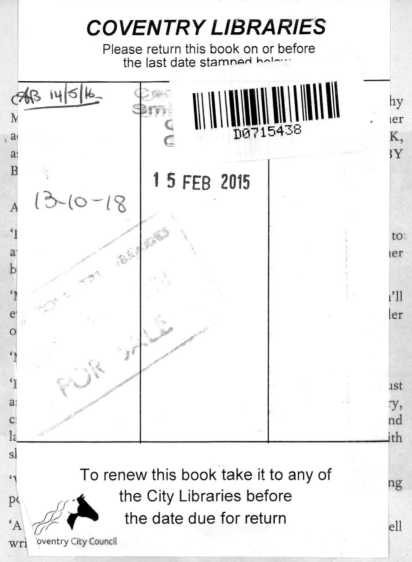
'O'Connell is a consummate storyteller – a unique talent who deserves
to be a household name' Val McDermid

'Memorable characters and blazingly original prose. Once again,
O'Connell transcends the genre' *Kirkus Reviews*

By Carol O'Connell

Judas Child
Bone by Bone

Kathleen Mallory Novels

Mallory's Oracle
The Man Who Lied to Women
(This book was published in the US under the title *The Man Who Cast Two Shadows*)
Killing Critics
Flight of the Stone Angel
(This book was published in the US under the title *Stone Angel*)
Shell Game
Crime School
Dead Famous
(This book was originally published in the UK under the title *The Jury Must Die*)
Winter House
Shark Music
(This book was published in the US under the title *Find Me*)
The Chalk Girl
It Happens in the Dark

Carol O'Connell
CRIME SCHOOL

headline

First published in Great Britain in 2002
by HUTCHINSON

First published in paperback in Great Britain in 2003
by ARROW BOOKS

This edition published in Great Britain in 2014
by HEADLINE PUBLISHING GROUP

1

Cataloguing in Publication Data is available from the British Library

ISBN 978 1 4722 1293 1

Typeset in Fournier by Avon DataSet Ltd, Bidford-on-Avon, Warwickshire

Printed and bound in Great Britain by
Clays Ltd, St Ives plc

Papers used by Headline are from well-managed forests
and other responsible sources.

HEADLINE PUBLISHING GROUP
An Hachette UK Company
338 Euston Road
London NW1 3BH

www.headline.co.uk
www.hachette.co.uk

For the Teachers

Thelma Rantilla once said, 'Every child, at the age of ten, should be dropped on its head in the center of New York City and forced to find its own way home.' Thus, this school teacher put a dull knife into the heart of every parent – and twisted it – *slowly*. For this and additional outrages, she became my personal hero. However, because she went everywhere in a rarified air of distraction, I believed she had no idea that I was on the planet.

The last time I saw her, she was carrying a carton with the year's end debris of papers and books. Her hair was a dangerous nest of sharp pencils, and her head was tucked in to avoid eye contact with anyone who might slow her quick trot to the door and flight into summer vacation.

As I pursued her down the hall, hurrying to keep up, I had no idea of what I might say beyond goodbye.

Miss Rantilla suddenly halted, then turned on me and said, 'You know, every once in awhile, you show a flash of talent – *just* a flash.'

I was stunned, stopped cold and speechless. This bought her the time she needed to make her escape.

PROLOGUE

High in the sky, apartment windows were smudges of grimy yellow, and this passed for starlight in New York City. Loud Latin rhythms from a car radio drifted down First Avenue. The sedan turned sharply, brakes screaming, narrowly missing a small blond girl with fugitive eyes. The child stood on tiptoe, poised for flight, arms rising like thin white wings.

A book was knocked from the hands of a woman on the sidewalk as the little girl sped past her in a breeze of flying hair and churning legs, small feet slapping pavement in time to the music of a passing boom box – a rock 'n' roll getaway. The eyes of the running child were not green, not Kathy's eyes, yet the startled woman saw her as a familiar wraith rocketing through space and years of time.

Fifteen years, you fool. And Kathy Mallory was not so small anymore, nor was she dead – not the makings of a ghost.

Sweat rolled down Sparrow's face. If not for the stolen book, would her mind have made that stumble? Again, the woman looked back the way she had come, but there was no sign of the man who had followed her from the bookshop. She had circled round and round, taking the long way home to lose him, and he had not hurried his steps to keep up with her. He had moved with inexorable resolve to the measured beat of a march. His body had no language, no life.

If a dead man could walk.

Sparrow's hands were clammy, a sign of anxiety, but she blamed it

1

on the weather so hot and muggy in this gray hour after sundown. And she blamed her costume for the stares from other pedestrians. The mutton-sleeve blouse and long skirt were too bizarre for a twenty-first-century heat wave. A match flared close beside her as a man, a harmless type, lit a cigarette, then passed her by. Her heart beat faster, and she rationalized away the second warning, taking it for guilt.

If not for the book—

She looked down at her empty hands and panicked – then sighed. The precious paperback lay on the sidewalk at her feet, and she bent low to snatch it back. On the rise, another figure, quiet as smoke, moved alongside her in the half-dozen mirrors of a drugstore window. She could still be surprised by these chance encounters with herself, for the surgically altered face needed no makeup to cover a history of broken bones and ravaged skin. The blue eyes of her reflection looked back across a gap of seventeen years, fresh off a Greyhound bus from the Southland.

Sparrow nodded. 'I remember you, girl.'

What an unholy haunted night.

She hid the book behind her back, as if a tattered novel might be worth stealing. In fact, she planned to burn it. But the book was not what the stalking man wanted. Sparrow looked uptown and down. He would be so easy to spot in this crowd of normal humans. Apparently, she had lost him at some turn of a corner. Yet every inch of her prickled, as though a thousand tiny insects crept about beneath her skin.

She hurried homeward, not looking back anymore, but only paying attention to a voice inside her head. Fear was a good old friend of hers, who broke into her thoughts to say, *Hello*, and then, *Ain't it gettin' dark?* And now, *Run, girl!*

ONE

Greenwich Village had lost its edge long ago, becoming a stately old lady among New York neighborhoods. One of the grande dame's children stood beneath the great stone arch in Washington Square Park. The boy wore trendy camouflage pants, all dressed up for a revolution – should one come along, the way buses do.

A guitar case lay at his feet, open to donations from passersby, though no one slowed down to drop him a dime. People marched past, sweating and cursing the heat of August, hurrying home to cold beers and canned music. It would take spectacle on a grander scale to get their attention tonight.

An unmarked police car crawled by in air-conditioned silence. Detective Sergeant Riker rolled down the passenger window and listened to a ripple of melancholy notes on soft nylon strings.

Not what he had expected.

Evidently, the teenage musician had missed the point of being young. Thirty-five years ago, Riker had been the boy beneath the arch, but his own guitar had been strung with steel, electrified and amplified, ripping out music to make people manic, *forcing* them to dance down the sidewalk.

What a rush.

And the entire universe had revolved around *him*.

He had sold that electric guitar to buy a ring for a girl he had loved more than rock 'n' roll. The marriage had ended, and the music had also deserted him.

The window closed. The car rolled on.

Kathy Mallory took the wheel for every tour of duty, but not by choice. Torn between drinking and driving, her partner had allowed his license to expire. The detectives were nearing the end of their shift, and Riker guessed that Mallory had plans for the evening. She was wearing her formal running shoes, black ones to match the silk T-shirt and jeans. The sleeves of her white linen blazer were rolled back, and this was her only concession to the heat. If asked to describe the youngest detective on the squad, he would bypass the obvious things, the creamy skin of a natural blonde and the very unnatural eyes; he would say, 'Mallory doesn't sweat.'

And she had other deviations.

Riker's cell phone beeped. He pulled it out to exchange a few words with another man across town, then folded it into his pocket. 'No dinner tonight. A homicide cop on First Avenue and Ninth wants a consult.'

The jam of civilian cars thinned out, and Mallory put on speed. Riker felt the car tilt when it turned the corner, rushing into the faster stream of northbound traffic. She sent the vehicle hurtling toward the rear end of a yellow cab that quickly slid out of the lane – *her* lane now. Other drivers edged off, dropping back and away, not sporting enough to risk sudden impact. She never used the portable turret light or the siren, for cops got no respect in this town – but sheer terror worked every time.

Riker leaned toward her, keeping his cool as he said, 'I don't wanna die tonight.'

Mallory turned her face to his. The long slants of her green eyes glittered, thieving eerie light from the dashboard, and her smile suggested that he could jump if he liked. And so a nervous game began, for she was watching traffic only in peripheral vision. He put up his hands in a show of surrender, and she turned her eyes back to the road.

Riker held a silent conversation with the late Louis Markowitz, a ghost he carried around in his heart as balm for anxious moments like this one. It was almost a prayer, and it always began with *Lou, you bastard*.

Fifteen years had passed since Kathy Mallory had roamed the streets as a child. Being homeless was damned hard work, and running the tired little girl to ground had been the job of Riker's old friend, Louis Markowitz, but only as a hobby. Lost children had never been the province of Special Crimes Unit, not while they lived. And they would have to die under unusual circumstances to merit a professional interest. So Kathy had become the little blond fox of an after-hours hunt. The game had begun with these words, spoken so casually: 'Oh, Riker? If she draws on you, don't kill her. Her gun is plastic, it fires pellets – and she's only nine or ten years old.'

After her capture, the child had rolled back her thin shoulders, drawn herself up to her full height of *nothing*, and insisted that she was *twelve* years old. What a liar – and what great dignity; Lou Markowitz could have crushed her with a laugh. Instead, with endless patience, he had negotiated her down to eleven years of age, and the foster-care paperwork had begun with this more believable lie.

Now Kathy Mallory's other name was Markowitz's Daughter.

The old man had been killed in the line of duty, and Riker missed him every day. Lou's foster child was taller now, five ten; she had upgraded her plastic gun to a .357 revolver; and her partner was not allowed to call her Kathy anymore.

The homicide detectives were speeding toward a crime scene that belonged to another man. The East Side lieutenant had sweetened his invitation with a bet, giving odds of 'Ten'll get you twenty' that they had never seen a murder quite like this one.

Revolving red and yellow lights marked the corner where police units and a fire engine blocked the flow of traffic along the borderland between the East Village and Alphabet City. All the action was on a side street, but the fire escapes were crowded with people hanging off metal rails, as if they could see around corners of brick and mortar. Cars honked their horns against the law, and hollered obscenities flew through the air.

Mallory's tan sedan glided into the only clear space, a bus stop. She killed the engine and stepped out on to the pavement as her partner slammed the passenger door. Riker's suit was creased and soiled in all the usual places, and now he loosened his tie to complete the basic slob ensemble. He could afford dry cleaning, but he was simply unaware of the practice; that was Mallory's theory.

The sidewalks were jumping, buzzing, people screaming, 'C'mon, c'mon!' Crime made do for theater in this livelier part of town. Young and old, they ran in packs, off to see a free show, a double bill – murder and fire. And these were the stragglers.

The detectives walked in tandem toward the spinning lights. The uniforms behind the police barricades were doing a poor job of crowd control. The street and sidewalks were clogged with civilians chomping pizza and slugging back cans of soda and beer.

'What a party,' said Riker.

Mallory nodded. It was a big production for a dead prostitute. The East Side lieutenant who owned this case had not provided any more details.

They had waded ten heads into the fray before the harried policemen recognized them and formed a human plow, elbows and shoulders jamming taxpayers. The uniforms yelled, 'Coming through! Make way!' One officer pulled back the yellow crime-scene tape that cordoned the sidewalk in front of a red-brick apartment building. Riker moved ahead of his partner. He descended a short flight of steps to a cement enclosure below the level of the street, then disappeared through the basement door.

Mallory waved off her entourage of cops and remained on the sidewalk. Soon enough, she would be barraged with information, some of it wrong, most of it useless. She leaned over a wrought-iron fence to look down at the sunken square of concrete. Garbage bags and cans were piled near the basement window, but the bright lightbulb over the door would not give an attacker any cover of shadows. The arch of broken glass had no burglar gate – a clear invitation to a break-in.

In the room beyond the shattered window pane, local detectives were getting in the way of crime-scene technicians as they slogged through water in borrowed firemen's boots. Riker, less careful about his own shoes, splashed toward the dead body on the gurney, and dozens of floating red candles swirled in his wake.

The corpse wore a high-collared blouse with French cuffs, and her long skirt was tangled around cheap vinyl boots – strange clothing for a prostitute in the heat of August.

Mallory recognized the chief medical examiner's assistant. In the role of God Almighty, the young pathologist lit a cigarette despite the waving arms of an angry crime-scene technician. And now he ambled across the room to finally have a look at the body. After pressing a stethoscope to the victim's heart for a few moments, completing the belated formality of declaring death, the doctor showed no curiosity about the short tufts of blond hair, evidence of a crude attempt at scalping. He seemed equally unconcerned about the clot of hair stuffed in the woman's gaping mouth.

Mallory wondered why the firemen had not removed it to attempt resuscitation; it was their nature to destroy crime-scene evidence.

A police photographer made a rolling motion with his hand, and the pathologist obliged him by turning the corpse on its side, exposing the silver duct tape that bound the hands behind the dead woman's back. The noose was removed for the next shot. The other end of the severed rope still dangled from a low-hanging chandelier of electric candles. The East Side lieutenant had not exaggerated. Beyond the era of lynch mobs, hanging was a rare form of murder. And Mallory knew this had not been a quick death. It would have taken a longer drop to break the woman's neck.

Torture?

7

She turned around to face the crowd and saw a man who had once been a uniformed cop in her own precinct. Six minutes away from losing his job, he had decided to quit NYPD, and now he was a fireman. 'Zappata? Who broke the window, you guys or the perp?'

'We did.' The rookie fireman sauntered toward her. His smile was cocky, and Mallory thought she might fix that if she had time. He would not look up at her face, for this would wreck his delusion that he was the taller one. He spoke to her breasts. 'I need you to do something for me.'

Not likely, you prick.

Aloud, she said, 'Only one engine turned out?'

'Yeah, not much of a fire. Mostly smoke.' He pointed to a young man with electric-yellow hair and a dark suit. 'See that idiot dick *trainee?* Go tell him he doesn't need statements from everybody on my damned truck.'

'He's not with me. Talk to his lieutenant.' And of course, Lieutenant Loman would rip off the fireman's head – less work for her. She turned back to the window on the crime scene. 'So your men cut the body down?'

'Nope, the cops did that.' Zappata was too pleased with himself. 'She was stone dead when we got here. So I preserved the evidence.'

'You mean – you left her *hanging.*'

'Yeah, a little water damage, some broken glass, but the rest of the scene was cherry when the cops pulled up.'

This was Zappata's old fantasy, running a crime scene, as if he had the right. Mallory searched the faces of the other firemen, a skeleton crew gathered near the truck. There were no ranking officers in sight. If Zappata had not been an ex-cop, the rest of these men would never have followed his lead. An ambulance would be here instead of the meat wagon parked at the curb. And now she understood why three departments had converged on the scene at one time. 'You made all the calls tonight?'

'Yeah, I got lucky. The meat wagon and the CSU van were only a few blocks away. They showed up before the detectives.' Zappata grinned, awaiting praise for assuming powers that were not his – *police* powers.

She decided to leave the fireman's destruction to the reporters hailing him from the other side of the crime-scene tape. Cameras closed in on Zappata's face as he strolled up to a cluster of microphones and a rapt audience of vultures from the press corps. Now he shared with them every rule and procedure he had personally violated to run the show tonight – and run it wrong.

Mallory walked down the steps to the cement enclosure and stood before the basement window. From this better angle, she could see one end of the rope anchored to a closet doorknob. The floor beneath the chandelier was clear of any object that might have been used for a makeshift gallows.

She could picture the killer placing a noose around the woman's neck and pulling the other end of the rope to raise her body from the ground. The victim's legs were not bound. She would have struggled and tried to run across the floor, then kept on running, feet pedaling the air until she died.

The murderer was male – an easy call. This hanging had required upper-body strength. And Mallory knew there had been no passion between the victim and her killer. When a man truly loved a woman, he beat her to death with his fists or stabbed her a hundred times.

She was looking at her partner's back as Riker bent down to grab something from the water. When the man turned around, his hands were empty, and he was closing the button on his suit jacket. If she had not seen this, she would never have believed it. Riker was a dead-honest cop.

What did you steal?

And why would he risk it?

Riker joined the others, and they moved away from the body. None of them noticed when a young man entered the basement room. Zappata's nemesis, the rookie detective with bright yellow hair, approached the gurney and leaned over the victim. Mallory saw a wet wad of blond hair come away in his hand as he removed the packing from the corpse's mouth.

That chore belonged to a crime-scene technician.

You idiot.

What else could go wrong tonight?

The young cop blocked Mallory's view as he leaned over the dead white face, as though to kiss it.

What are you doing?

In the next moment, he was straddling the body.

What the—

The fool was pumping the victim's chest, performing emergency first aid on a dead woman. Now he grinned and shouted, 'She's alive!'

No! No! No!

Three detectives whirled around. The horrified pathologist moved toward the gurney. Riker was quicker. Hunkering down beside the victim, he held one finger to her nostrils. 'Oh *shit*! She's breathing!' In a rare show of anger, Riker's hands balled into fists, and he yelled at the younger man, 'Do you know what you've done?' Unspoken were the words, *You moron.*

Too much time had elapsed since the woman's death. An inexperienced cop had just turned a perfectly good corpse into a useless vegetable.

The chief medical examiner broke the silence of the hospital room with a dry pronouncement that 'Human vivisection is illegal in all fifty states.' Dr Edward Slope had the physical authority of a tall gray general. This impression persisted despite the tuxedo, a physician's Gladstone bag and heavy sarcasm in the presence of a dying woman. The pale patient swaddled in bedsheets took no offense. The involuntary movement of her eyes was mere illusion of awareness. 'I say the autopsy can wait until she's dead.'

'That's just a technicality,' said Riker. 'She used to be dead.' And all the detective needed was a superficial exam by this man, whose word was never questioned in court.

'She'll die again soon enough.' The medical examiner held up a clipboard and read the patient's chart. 'Her attending physician has a note here, "Do not resuscitate." She's brain-dead. Give her another ten hours without life support. That'll kill her.' He turned to the bald man beside Riker. 'Loman, bring the body to my dissection room in the morning. But first – check for a pulse.'

Lieutenant Loman seemed close to death himself. A virus epidemic in the East Village precinct had shortstaffed his squad, and the longer duty hours were showing in his bloodshot eyes and pasty flesh. 'Not my case, Doc.' Loman clapped one hand on Sergeant Riker's shoulder. 'It's his body now.'

'No way!' said Mallory. And now, for Loman's benefit, she glared at the patient, clearly estimating the value of a comatose hooker as being right up there with a dead cat.

'It's *your* case, kid.' The lieutenant's voice was still in that cautionary zone of rumbling thunder. 'A deal is a deal. Sparrow was Riker's snitch. He *wants* the body.'

Mallory gave Riker the squad's camera, as if she might need two free hands to finish this fight. She turned to face Loman. 'So a john strings up his hooker. That's not a case for Special Crimes, and you *know* it.' As an afterthought, she remembered to say, '*Sir*,' then promptly abandoned the protocol for speaking with command officers. 'Palm it off on the cops in Arson.'

'The guy's a freaking *psycho*!' Lieutenant Loman moved away from the bed and advanced on Mallory, yelling, '*Jesus Christ!* Look at what he did to her!'

What remained of the victim's hair was a fright wig of wild spikes, and saliva dribbled from her lips. Adding to this portrait of dementia, her eyes rolled back and forth like shooting marbles.

Riker drew the curtains around the bed, closeting himself with the patient and the medical examiner. 'Just a quick look, okay?'

11

'No,' said Dr Slope. 'Tie a note to one of her toes so I'll know who won the body. I'm late for a dinner party.'

Beyond the flimsy curtain, a fast, light rapping on the door escalated to two-fisted banging, then stopped abruptly. Riker could hear muffled words of argument from the guard he had posted in the hall. When the banging resumed, Mallory raised her voice to be heard above the racket. She was telling Lieutenant Loman, thanks anyway, but he could keep the dying whore. To his credit, the man never pulled rank on her when he went ballistic, shouting that he was understaffed, that his men were stacking up corpses in a heat wave when tempers were exploding and homicide rates soared.

August was a busy season for cops and killers.

Dr Slope had formed a shrewd guess about the incessant banging on the door. His wry smile said, *Gotcha.* 'The attending physician wouldn't allow his patient to be stripped for an audience of cops. Am I right?' He stared at the camera in Riker's hand, as if he suspected the detective of being a closet pornographer.

'The doctor's a kid, an intern,' said Riker. 'Even if he did the exam – what good is his testimony in court?'

The door-banging was louder now, accompanied by shouts of 'Let me in, you *bastards!*'

Dr Slope dropped his smile. 'And that would be our earnest young doctor trying to get to his patient. Any idea how many laws you're breaking tonight?'

'Well, yeah – I'm a cop.'

Riker heard the door open. Mallory was speaking to the young doctor in the hallway, saying, 'This is a *hospital.* Keep the noise down.' The door slammed, and her bargaining with Lieutenant Loman resumed. 'I've got my own problems with manpower,' she said. 'I'd need at least three of your men to make it worth my while.'

'You're nuts! *Nuts!*' The lieutenant's voice was cracking. If Mallory had not been Markowitz's daughter, he would have slammed her into the wall by now.

Behind the thin protection of the curtain, Riker lowered his voice to plead with the chief medical examiner. 'Just five minutes? A fast exam, a few samples for—'

'Not a chance.' Slope turned in the direction of the banging. 'You have to let that doctor in.'

'Why? What can he do for her now? He'll stop the—'

'If this woman has family, you're leaving the city open for a lawsuit. So we'll go by the book.'

As Slope reached for the curtain, Mallory ripped it aside. Behind her, the door was closing on the East Side lieutenant. As a parting gift, Loman must have released his pent-up aggression on the doctor in the hall, for the banging had ceased.

'I made Loman give us two detectives for grunt work.' Mallory turned to face Dr Slope. 'Dead or alive, we need the exam. *Now.*'

The chief medical examiner was a man who *gave* orders, and he was not about to take this from her. All of that was in his voice when he said, 'The victim will be dead by morning. This can *wait.*'

Riker braced for a new round of hostilities, but Mallory surprised him. 'Maybe you're right,' she said. 'A cover-up is better.' And now she had the pathologist's complete attention.

Dr Slope folded his arms, saying, 'What do you—'

'A lot of mistakes were made tonight,' said Mallory. 'No one called an ambulance. A rookie fireman decided the victim was dead. Maybe because she didn't blink – who knows? He used to be a cop, so he preserved the crime scene.' She pointed to the hospital bed. 'And he left that woman hanging.'

Her foster father had been Edward Slope's oldest friend and the founder of his weekly floating poker game. The doctor had known Mallory in her puppy days, loved her unconditionally, and knew better than to trust her. He turned to her partner for confirmation of this highly unlikely scenario.

'It happened,' said Riker. 'It's the East Village virus. No senior men were riding on that fire truck tonight. '

Mallory all but yawned to show how little this case mattered to her. 'So Loman's detectives go along with a call of homicide – by a *fireman*. And then *your* man, a *doctor* – the only one authorized to operate a damn stethoscope – he confirmed the death.'

'If he confirmed it—'

'I hear things,' she said. 'I know all about the corpse that woke up in your morgue last month – another victim who wasn't quite dead. Was your assistant on that case too?'

'I'm sure this woman was dead at the time—'

'You'll never be sure.' She stepped back to appraise his tuxedo, then reached out to run one red fingernail down a satin lapel. 'But what the hell. It's a party night.' This was one of Mallory's more subtle insults: the fireman, the police and Slope's own assistant had all done their part to turn a woman's brain into coma soup – but why should that spoil the doctor's fun? 'No great loss.' Mallory glanced back at the door, then lowered her voice to the range of conspiracy. 'She's just a whore. We'll let the nurses wash the body and destroy the evidence. No one will ever know what happened tonight.'

She turned her back on an outraged Edward Slope, and this was Riker's cue to step forward and soften the damage, saying, 'I *need* this exam. It's gotta be now.' And last, the finishing touch, he saved the doctor's face with a bribe. 'You'll get a police escort to the party. Traffic's murder tonight.'

'You've won my heart.' Dr Slope set his medical bag on the bed, then turned to Mallory. '*Kathy*, take notes.' This was the doctor's idea of getting even, for she always insisted on the distancing formality of her surname. He smiled, so pleased by her irritation, as he pulled on latex gloves.

'No makeup.' Riker leaned over the bed to take the first photograph. 'Looks like Sparrow was in for the night. So the perp wasn't some john she picked up on the street. Any sign of drugs?'

Dr Slope examined the woman's eyes, then the fingernails. 'Nothing obvious.' There was no bruising on her arms, nor any fresh puncture wounds. He clicked on a penlight and examined the nasal passages, then pulled an empty syringe from his bag. 'She's not snorting it, but I'll get a blood work-up.'

When the sheets had been pulled away and the hospital gown untied, an old stab wound was exposed on Sparrow's left side. 'Looks like a knife was twisted to widen the cut – sheer cruelty.' Dr Slope was impressed. 'I gather this isn't the first time someone tried to kill her.'

Through the camera's viewfinder, Riker watched the other man's gloved fingers explore the scar. 'It happened a long time ago.'

'A street fight?'

'That's my guess.' Riker knew Mallory could give exact details of that fight, but she was continuing the long silence of Kathy the child. 'Sparrow was real good with a knife.'

'In that case, I'd hate to see the damage to her opponent.' The pathologist looked up. 'Or perhaps I did – on the autopsy table?'

Riker merely shrugged, for he disliked the idea of lying to this man. 'It wasn't my case.' And that was the truth. He turned the camera on Sparrow's face. Even after seeing proof of her identity, it had taken him a while to recognize those naked blue eyes undisguised by mascara and purple shadow. Two years ago, the prostitute's hair had been bleached to straw. Tonight, what was left of it was a more natural shade of blond. And there had been other changes since he had last seen this woman.

Awe, Sparrow, what did you do to that wonderful shnoze?

Once, her broken nose had been a dangerous-looking piece of damage in the middle of her pretty face, hanging there like a dare. Now the nose was remade, and all that remained of her character was a slightly prominent chin that stuck out to say, *Oh, yeah?* the bad-attitude line of a true New Yorker.

At their last meeting, Sparrow had been in her early thirties. The street life of drugs and whoring had aged her by another twenty years, but now she seemed brand-new again – so young. 'She had a facelift, right?'

'Rhinoplasty too,' said Slope, 'and dermabrasion. Her last surgery was a brow lift. There's still some post-op swelling. Nice work — expensive. I gather she was a pricey call girl.'

'No, nothin' that grand.' Sparrow had never been more than a cheap hustler with an accidental gift for making him laugh. When she was a skinny teenager, Riker had turned her into an informant.

You were soaking wet that night, too stoned to come in from the rain.

She had strutted up and down the sidewalk, shaking her fists at skyscrapers and hollering, praying, 'God! Give me a lousy break!' All of Sparrow's deities lived in penthouses, and she had truly believed that manna would fall from heaven on the high floors — if she could only get the gods' attention.

But you never did.

Over the years, she had peddled her body to pay for heroin, always vowing to kick the habit tomorrow — and tomorrow. *Lies.* Yet Riker remained her most ardent sucker. He gently touched a short strand of her butchered hair. 'What did the perp use on her? Scissors or a razor?'

The pathologist shrugged. 'Haircuts are not my area.'

'It was a razor,' said Mallory, who paid hundreds of dollars for her own salon expertise.

Riker imagined the weapon slashing Sparrow's hair, her eyes getting wider, awaiting worse mutilation as the razor moved close to her face — her *brand-new* face — stringing out the tension until she lost her mind.

Mallory moved closer to the bed. 'What about that mark on her arm? That looks like a razor, too.'

'It *might* be,' Slope corrected her. 'So be careful with your notes, young lady. I *will* read every word before I sign them.' He bent low for a better look at the long, thin scab on Sparrow's arm. 'This is days old — not a defensive wound.' He consulted the patient chart. 'Her doctor did a rape kit. No semen present. No sign of trauma to the genital area.' He glanced at Mallory. 'I can't rule out sex with a condom and a compliant hooker. So don't get creative.' After rolling the nude woman

16

on to her stomach, he examined the back of each knee, then checked her soles and the skin between her toes. There were no fresh punctures. Sparrow had beaten her addiction. She was clean again.

And young again – starting over.

Where were you going with your new face?

After reviewing the notes, Edward Slope signed them, thus completing his own hostage negotiation, and Mallory opened the door to set him free. He backed up quickly, making way for a man in the short white coat of a hospital intern. The young doctor crashed into the room with a jangling, rolling cart full of metal and glass equipment and a running nurse at his heels.

Dr Slope stayed to watch the intern and nurse as they outfitted their patient with tubes and wires. 'What's the point of this if she—'

'She's got brain activity.' The intern tracked Sparrow's rolling blue eyes with the beam of his penlight. 'I never should've listened to the damn cops. They told me this woman was revived twenty minutes after death. That can't be true.' He turned on a startled Riker. 'And you had no right to keep me out of here. Suppose she'd gone sour before I got her on life support?'

'That's enough.' Edward Slope looked down at the *smaller* doctor, then held up a wallet with his formidable credentials. Satisfied that the younger man's testicles had been neatly severed, he continued. 'Your patient was never in any danger while I was here.' He reached down to pick up the clipboard that dangled from a chain on the bed rail, then pointed to the bottom of the page. 'I see a clear order not to resuscitate.' He glanced at the intern's name tag. 'I assume this is *your* signature?'

'Yes, sir, but that was before I saw the EKG results.'

'Screwed up, didn't you.' This was not a question, but Slope's opinion of inexcusable error.

The intern had the look and the whine of a petulant boy. 'I *told* the cop my patient needed life support.'

'Nobody told me anything,' said Riker. 'I didn't know.'

'*She* knew!' The young doctor whirled around to point an accusing finger, but Mallory was gone, and the door was slowly closing.

Riker settled into a chair beside the bed. He was fifty-five years old, but feeling older, shaken and suddenly cold. Yet he managed to convince himself that no cop would leave herself so exposed to a charge of manslaughter by depraved indifference to human life – and that Mallory had *not* just tried to kill Sparrow.

TWO

The high-pitched laughter of crime-scene tourists drifted in from the street, unhampered by a bedsheet draped over the broken window. The basement floor was no longer covered by water, but the air was hot and dank. Mallory removed her blazer and folded it over one arm as she moved about the room, taking in each detail.

Beads of moisture trickled down the cheap metal cabinets of the kitchenette to make wet tracks through black fingerprint dust. A fold-out sofa made do for a bed, and wrought-iron lawn furniture passed for a dining room set. The wooden crucifix was the only wall decoration. Crime Scene Unit's airtight metal canisters and plastic bags were stacked by the door, awaiting the van's return.

Though the work of collecting evidence was done, Riker kept his hands in his pockets to pacify Heller, a great bear of a man with slow brown eyes and rolled-up shirtsleeves. The forensic expert ran a blow-dryer over a small paper box and muttered, 'Freaking clowns.' This was his least colorful name for the firemen who had broken the window and hosed down his crime scene. 'My crew didn't find a camera to go with this film box. Maybe your perp took a snapshot for a souvenir.'

A soggy cockroach was also drying out, perched on the edge of the sink and basking in the warmth of Heller's floodlights, a bug's idea of the Riviera. New York City roaches were not afraid of bright light. Nor did they fear fire, flood or cops with guns, and it would take more than all of that to kill them.

'Well, this is all wrong.' Riker stood beside the table, examining a plastic bag filled with dead insects. 'Hey, Mallory. Ever see so many flies turn out for a body that wasn't dead yet? There must be a thousand bugs here.'

'At least.' Heller switched off the blow-dryer, then turned his head with the slow swivel of a cannon. 'And the perp brought the flies with him. He carried them in that jar.'

'What?' Riker leaned down for a closer look at the evidence bag that held a large glass jar coated with black dust. 'You didn't find any prints.'

'That's how I know it belonged to the perp. He wore gloves.' Heller sorted through a stack of elimination cards marked with the fingerprints of firemen and police. 'All I got here is the victim's prints and that idiot Zappata's.' He nodded toward the plastic bags. 'The jar's got a crack in it. Either the perp dropped it, or the fire hose knocked it off the table. I skimmed those flies off the water, but I know they were all dead before they hit the floor. I can even tell you how they died.'

Riker raised one eyebrow to say, *Oh, yeah?* 'Did they drown? Or did you find smoke in their little lungs?'

Heller's glare of quiet disdain was an unmistakable message: *Don't fool with the master.* 'The inside of the jar smells like insecticide. So do the flies.' He pulled four specimen bottles from his pockets and lined them up on the table. Four dead flies floated in clear liquid. 'They're in different stages of decomposition. I'd say he's been collecting them for a week. And I got twenty bucks that says an entomologist will back me up.'

'Naw.' Riker waved him off, for he knew this was a sucker bet. In or out of court, the man from Forensics was rarely challenged.

'So he's been planning this for a while.' Mallory turned to the makeshift curtain. Was the freak just passing by when he looked down, saw Sparrow for the first time – and decided to murder her? Was that the day he started collecting his flies and hoarding them? Or maybe the whore had bumped into him on the street, a New York kind of accident, a chance collision with violent insanity.

20

Heller crouched beside his toolbox and began the work of putting away unused razor blades and cotton swabs, brushes and bottles of dust. 'Lieutenant Coffey called. He's on his way over.'

Mallory wore her I-told-you-so smile. Riker ignored her and hovered over Heller, prompting him. 'So? Was Coffey pissed off?'

'You bet. The lieutenant heard a scary rumor that you guys accepted this case for Special Crimes. How do you plan to sell him on this one? Given it any thought?'

'Yeah.' Riker glanced at his partner. 'She's gonna handle it.'

Heller nodded. 'Excellent choice.'

Mallory studied the scorch marks at the base of the brick wall, then turned to the evidence bag of ashes and paper fragments. 'Did the perp use anything fancy to start his fire?'

'Just a match,' said Heller. 'I'll test for accelerants, but I don't think I'll find any.'

A rocking chair and a small magazine rack blocked the bathroom door. The scorched wall was the only logical place for them. 'And you're positive none of the firemen moved any furniture?'

He nodded absently as he placed each aerosol can in its proper compartment in the toolbox. 'One of Loman's detectives got statements from everybody on the fire truck.'

She pointed to a couch cushion leaning against another wall. A large square of material had been cut away. 'What's that about?'

'I cut out a scorch mark and bagged it. That was the perp's first try at arson. It should've gone up like a torch. The couch must've come from out of state. New York law doesn't require fire-retardant upholstery. Lucky for you it didn't burn. Inside of four minutes, the whole place would've gone up in flames.'

'And destroyed all the evidence,' said Riker. 'You're sure that's not what he wanted?'

'Yeah, I'm *damn* sure. This guy was looking for a fast controlled burn. Lots of smoke, but no major damage. He was real careful to clear the area around his bonfire.'

Mallory agreed. The hangman had wanted to call attention to his work, not destroy it. A wet mound of bright cloth and sequins lay at her feet. 'Some of these clothes have scorch marks.'

'Another experiment,' said Heller. 'He picked them because the material's so flimsy. More bad luck. The law *does* call for fire-retardant costumes. Eventually, they'll burn – everything does. But the guy's in a hurry. So next, he collects all the paper – junk mail, magazines. He even burned the window shade.'

'So our boy's an amateur at arson.' Riker leaned down to examine the pile of wet cloth deemed unworthy of evidence bags. 'I spent four years in Vice. Never heard of a streetwalker with a costume collection like this.' He drew out a scanty garment with sequins and sewn-on wings. 'I've seen this one before. June, I think. Yeah, Shakespeare in the Park. The play was *Midsummer Night's Dream*. I *loved* the fairies.'

With a rare show of surprise, Heller turned to stare at the man voted least likely to have an up-close encounter with culture.

Riker shook his head, saying, 'Naw, must've been October – the Halloween Parade.'

The forensic expert sighed, then returned to the task of putting his toolbox in order.

Mallory looked down at the carefully labeled insect collection on the table. Heller was deluded if he thought Lieutenant Coffey would pay for an entomologist. It would be a fight just to keep this case in Special Crimes Unit. Among the evidence containers stashed near the door was a bag of votive candles. There were at least two dozen in various stages of meltdown. All were covered with fingerprint dust. 'The candles belonged to the killer?'

'Yeah. Part of his little ritual.' Heller pointed to the area beneath the ceiling fixture. 'Check out the wax.' Melted droppings had survived the fire hose, and they formed a circle on the cement. 'There were spots of red wax on the victim's skirt. So I know she was lying on the floor while the candles were burning. I used the wicks for a time frame. The last one was lit fifteen minutes before the place was hosed down. That's how much time he had to hang the woman and start his bonfire.'

'That can't be right,' said Mallory, risking heresy. 'We have to add on another ten or twelve minutes before Sparrow was cut down and revived. But she isn't even brain-dead.'

'She was starved for oxygen, but her air supply wasn't completely cut off.' Heller reached into the evidence pile and selected a canister. After breaking the seal, he pulled out a section of rope. 'With a hangman's noose, he could've killed her in a few minutes. But this is a fixed double knot. The noose didn't tighten with the weight of the body. Satisfied?'

Yes, she was. Mallory could see it now – Sparrow hanging quietly, sipping air and playing dead, waiting for the freak to leave. Cagey whore. She must have had great hopes. The window had been bare and all the lights left on. Help would surely come any moment. Then her lungs had filled with smoke, and Sparrow had blacked out. Or perhaps she had been dimly aware of her rescuers, the conversation of firemen all around her, and not one hand lifted to help a lady down from the ceiling.

'The jar of dead flies doesn't fit,' she said.

'You're right.' Heller interrupted his work to stare at the perfect circle of wax droppings. 'A very tidy job, *meticulous*. Even the scalping. You can't trim a moustache without making a mess, but there wasn't one stray hair on that woman's clothes. And the candles – each one an equal distance from the next. Your perp is compulsively neat. I can't see this guy catching bugs.'

Mallory could. She pictured a man ripping garbage bags open, then waiting patiently with his can of insecticide. He would have worn gloves to harvest the dead and dying flies, and still it would have made him queasy to touch them.

The basement door opened, then slammed with a bang. The commander of Special Crimes Unit had arrived.

Before his last promotion, Jack Coffey had been a middling man with a forgettable face, hair and eyes of lukewarm brown. Now, at age thirty-seven, the stress of a command position had widened the bald spot at the back of his head and added a premature decade of worry lines and character. Riker noticed the lieutenant's hands were balled into fists, and he counted down the seconds, waiting for the man to explode.

Coffey's gaze passed over the two men and settled on his only female detective. His tone was too calm, too reasonable when he spoke to her. 'Imagine my surprise when Lieutenant Loman dropped off the paperwork for a hooker.' His voice jumped ten decibel levels when he shouted, 'And she's not even a *dead* hooker!'

Mallory never flinched. She had the slow blink of a drowsing cat, and her serenity would cost the lieutenant one game point.

'We're tossing this case back to the East Side squad,' said Coffey. '*Tonight!* What the *hell* were you guys thinking? This is assault, not murder. Loman says it's a damn sex game gone wrong.'

'Autoerotic asphyxiation?' Heller kept his eyes on his toolbox as he shook his head. 'I've seen a few teenage boys strung up, and even some old guys, but no women. Her hands were tied with—'

'She was a damn *hooker*,' said Coffey. 'She did whatever she was paid to do. And bondage is part of the trade.'

'Sparrow was never into freaks and their games.' Riker said this so casually, an offhand line dropped into the conversation.

The lieutenant's reaction was predictable. 'We're not tying up a squad so you can keep faith with one of your snitches.'

Riker shrugged, then lit a cigarette as he leaned against the wall, leaving the fight to his partner. Coffey could make no personal connection between her and Sparrow. Mallory had been ten years old the last time she had spoken to the whore.

'The perp is a serial killer,' she said. 'Loman's squad would've botched it.'

Riker sucked in his breath. *Awe, Mallory, what are you doing?* Was she *trying* to lose this case? No cop on the force had ever heard of a serial hangman. It would have been better to run with Heller's portrait of a tidy psycho with a penchant for dead flies.

'A serial killer?' Coffey wet his lips, tasting the words. 'So, tell me.' His cursory glance swept the entire room. 'Where are the rest of the bodies?'

'In a Cold Case file,' she said. 'It's the same MO. The rope, the hair – everything.'

And now the fun begins. Or this was Riker's impression of Jack Coffey's smile. Hands on his hips, the lieutenant squared off with Mallory. 'And where *is* that file?'

'They haven't located it yet.'

Riker relaxed a little, for his partner was on safer ground now. The Cold Case files dated back to 1906, and the squad had recently moved this staggering inventory to new headquarters. What were the odds that they would rush to unpack a hundred cartons just to appease Special Crimes Unit?

Jack Coffey's tight smile never wavered. 'Then you pulled this information from the computer. Where's the printout?'

'The case isn't in the system,' she said. 'Most of the older files aren't. Just basic inventory – names and numbers.'

With budget problems and lack of manpower, it would take Cold Case Squad years to make complete computer entries for every unsolved murder of the last century. Mallory might get away with this.

Not so, said the look in Coffey's eyes. 'If you've never seen this file—'

'Markowitz told me about it,' she said.

The lieutenant's mouth dipped on one side. 'Well, how *neat*. Your corroboration is a dead man. How damn *convenient*.'

Riker was also skeptical. He knew she had the talent to tell a better lie than that one.

Heller slammed the lid of his toolbox. And now that he had everyone's attention, he rose to his feet, saying, 'I was there when she heard about the other hanging.'

Jack Coffey's smile evaporated as he faced the man from Forensics, and so he missed the stunned surprise in Riker's eyes.

'I don't know all the details,' said Heller. 'But neither did Markowitz. It wasn't his crime scene. He only got a quick look at the room and the body, but he couldn't get it out of his mind. Damn strange way to kill somebody.'

Heller would never back anyone in a lie. No one on the force had stronger credibility. And so Lieutenant Coffey's eyes rolled up, as if his concession speech might be written on the ceiling. 'Mallory, I wanna see that Cold Case file. Until I do, your hooker isn't draining resources from Special Crimes. You got that?' He was walking toward the door as he said, 'You can use that man Lieutenant Loman gave you, but that's all—'

'*Two* men,' said Mallory. 'Loman promised two.'

Jack Coffey was close to joy when he turned on her. 'Oh, did he? Well, I guess the bastard scammed you. He only came across with one detective – *half* a detective. The guy's a whiteshield, no experience. And here's the best part, Mallory – it's the same idiot who resuscitated the corpse. So Loman's squad gets rid of a half-dead hooker and a screw-up cop. What a deal, huh?'

Score one for the boss.

Riker was almost happy for the man. Jack Coffey needed these small victories to keep him going. Over time, the lieutenant had learned the value of a hit-and-run game. And now that he had scored, he slammed the door on his way out.

Heller knelt on the floor to close the snaps of his toolbox, then glanced up at Riker. 'Markowitz never told you about that hanging, did he? Naw, he'd never give up details from another cop's crime scene. That's a religion in my job, too. I was the *only* one he could talk to.' Heller aimed his thumb at Mallory. 'And Markowitz never told *her* a damn thing. She was only thirteen years old. The way I remember it, we caught her listening at the door.'

Riker stubbed out his cigarette. 'What else can you tell me?'

'The woman's hands were bound. Rope or tape – I'm not sure.' Heller stood up and mopped his brow with a handkerchief. 'So that knocked out murder dressed up as suicide. And Markowitz said the perp must've planned it. He brought his own rope to the party – just like your guy. But why plan a hanging?' The criminalist grabbed his suit jacket from the back of a chair, and only now did he notice that, despite the sweltering heat of the basement, Riker was the only one not stripped to shirtsleeves.

Before Riker could check the movement, his hand touched the button that kept his jacket closed. 'What about money? Lou always loved money motives.'

'No,' said Heller. 'On his own time, he looked into that and came up dry. He didn't see any sex angles either.'

'And the victim didn't step off a piece of furniture,' said Mallory. 'The noose was around her neck when the perp raised her from the floor – just like Sparrow.'

'But there was no fire,' said Heller. '*No* candles, *no* jar of flies.' He made this sound like an accusation against her. 'And there wasn't any hair in the victim's mouth. Your old man never mentioned any of that.'

Riker jammed his hands in his pockets. 'Mallory, why did you have to elaborate so much? You told Coffey the hair was—'

'It's not a problem,' she said. 'Without a name or a case number, no one can find the file. We don't even have a date.'

'She's right,' said Heller. 'That case was years old when Markowitz told me about it. It bothered him for a long time. Too many things didn't fit.' He shrugged. 'That's all I remember.'

The door opened, and a technician from Crime Scene Unit entered the room to pick up an armload of canisters. Heller grabbed two evidence bags and followed his man outside to the waiting van.

Riker took one last look at the departing bag of ashes and unburned fragments. He could see the charred spines of magazines, yet some miracle had preserved the brittle tinder of an old paperback novel. It had not even been scorched when he had retrieved it from the water.

Carol O'Connell

He could feel the wetness on his skin under the pressure of his holster's strap.

Mallory was attracted to the damp spot spreading across the breast of his suit. Her gaze dropped lower. 'I bet you never used that button before.'

True, he never bothered to close his jacket, but on any other night, there would be nothing to conceal.

You spooky kid. Always picking up on the oddest things.

Mallory met his eyes, and her gaze was steady. She was clearly waiting for him to say more.

To confess?

Damn her, she knew he had robbed the crime scene. But she could not pose a direct question. A cop could never ask a partner, Did you break the law?

Riker went out in search of a cold beer, and Mallory stayed behind to double-check Heller's work. On the subject of forced entry, she deferred to no one. There were no recent scratches on the outside of the lock. Even after dismantling the mechanism, she could find no sign of a metal pick.

Sparrow, why did you let the hangman in?

The prostitute had been good at reading men and sorting out the mental cases. It was unlikely that the collector of dead flies had been her customer; he would never have gotten past her radar – unless she had been dope-sick and desperate. Then she would have opened the door to any drug dealer, however squirrely. But Dr Slope had found no signs of recent addiction, and there were no syringes listed on the evidence log.

The junkie hooker had always been careful to keep a supply of clean ones. In what had passed for a childhood, Kathy Mallory had stolen boxes of needles from a local clinic – presents for Sparrow, a little girl's idea of payments for shelter from the streets.

One hand drifted down to a tear in the couch cushion and touched a

28

hard lump. Heller's crew had missed something. Her fingers dug into the upholstery and pulled out an ivory comb with delicate prongs. Sparrow had always worn it in her hair. The oriental carving was elaborate, unforgettable. This was the only thing of value that the whore had not sold for drug money. The antique comb had been stolen long ago to buy the first story hour. The whore had laid her present down with a sigh, saying, 'Baby, you don't have to *pay* for stories. They're *free*.'

No. Young Kathy had shaken her head to tell the woman that she was wrong. And the child's logic had been indisputable: All hookers would be beggars if this were true; their lies would be worthless – *if* this were true. But then, Sparrow had never understood precisely what the little girl was buying.

How long had they kept company – and why?

Mallory's early history on the streets was not linear, but called up in shattering events remembered out of order. And now her memories were so distant, they could be twisted any way she liked. She decided that, at best, Sparrow had been merely a bad copy of a dead mother.

A whore and nothing more.

She had not recognized the prostitute's new face at the crime scene. On the way to the hospital, Riker had broken the news, and he had done it so gently, as if the victim were a family member – and not the dangerous debris of the past. But soon enough, Sparrow would be dead, and only Riker would know the story, but he could never tell it.

Mallory's hand closed over the comb. It had not been dropped through the tear in the couch cushion, but buried there. So Sparrow had had some time to hide it, but when? While the hangman was knocking at the door? Perhaps he was already inside when she pushed her precious comb deep into the upholstery so it could not be stolen. Had there been time for conversation? Had Sparrow tried to talk him out of killing her?

She stared at the bedsheet covering the broken glass. Why had the man risked burning the window shade before he made his escape?

You wanted a big audience for your work — not just the cops — civilians too. Fame? That's what you want? Yes, he had even left an autograph, a signature of dead flies.

The door opened. Mallory rose to a stand, then whirled around to face Gary Zappata. The rookie fireman stood on the threshold. His sleeveless T-shirt and chinos were a size too small, the better to show off his gym-sculpted torso. His dark hair was slicked back, still wet from a shower, and he stank of cologne.

'This is a crime scene, Zappata. Did you forget the rules?' She nodded toward the door in lieu of saying, *Get the hell out.*

'Hey, I'm here to help.' He shut the door, then sauntered into the room. There was arrogance in his smile and his every move. 'So, Detective—' One hand waved about, feigning frustration, as if her name might be difficult to remember. 'How's it going?'

'I'm working here. What do you want?'

He hooked both thumbs in his belt loops and strolled over to the couch. 'Just tying up loose ends.'

'Zappata, don't waste my time. If you've got something — let's hear it.'

That made him petulant, but he forced a smile. She was forgiven. 'I can help you, babe. I know things about that fire. For instance, the candles had nothing to do with it.'

'Great tip. Thanks for stopping by.' Mallory turned her back on him to study the blackened wall of the burn area. After a moment, she glanced over one shoulder with a look that asked, *Still here?*

The fireman ignored this blatant dismissal and flopped down on the couch. 'The guy's not a pro.' He draped one leg over the upholstered arm — just to let her know that he planned to stay awhile. 'A real arsonist would've made a fuse to the door. You know, when a blaze gets hot enough, the *air* can ignite.'

'Did you learn that in fire school?'

He disliked this reminder that he was new at his trade. Even when he had been a cop, his police career had not lasted long enough to lose

30

the rookie status. 'Listen, Mallory.' This was an order. 'The guy's an amateur at homicide too. These freaks always stick with what worked in the past. So this is definitely our perp's first try at murder. 'Cause of the botched fire.'

Our perp?

Mallory looked up to the window, attracted by the silhouette of a man pacing across the makeshift curtain. His hat had the crown of a uniformed officer. Riker must have requested a guard for the crime scene. Bad move. This unapproved use of manpower would not sit well with Lieutenant Coffey.

Zappata left the couch to hover over the wet pile of flashy silks and rayon. He picked up the sparkling costume that Riker had so admired. 'I wonder what the hooker looked like in this.'

'Drop it!' Mallory strode across the room, aiming herself at the man, planning to walk over him or through him. He backstepped to the door, clutching the costume to his breast in a lame attempt to hide behind a swatch of sequins and fairy wings.

'Don't *touch* her *things!*' She ripped the garment away from him. 'Get *out!*'

His hand was on the knob when he noticed the guard's shadow rushing across the bedsheet curtain. And now there were footfalls on the cement steps leading down to the basement door.

The fireman was as nervous as a schoolgirl afraid of losing her reputation. He puffed out his chest and summoned up a bit of bravado.

The cop outside was coming closer.

Zappata opened the door, yelling, 'I'm done here, you *bitch!*' He stomped out of the apartment, as if this were his own idea.

Mallory wondered if the fire department knew that their rookie was a physical coward. But he was forgotten when she looked down at the ivory comb in her hand.

Sparrow, how did the hangman get in? Did he bring you presents, too?

* * *

31

Sergeant Riker could smell the apartment-house odors of meals cooked and eaten hours ago. His stomach rumbled as he stepped off the elevator.

The landlord's floor was divided in two. On one side was Charles Butler's apartment, and across the hall was a consulting firm of elite headhunters. And here Kathy Mallory broke the law in her off-duty hours, investigating the deluded, the grifters and other poseurs to weed them from a clientele of wildly gifted and generally unstable job candidates for think tanks. Riker called them Martians.

Lieutenant Coffey had given her a direct order to dissolve this business partnership, and tonight, Riker had his first glimpse of Mallory's response, an elegant solution. She had nailed a new brass plaque on the old familiar door. Once, this had been the entrance to Butler and Mallory, Ltd. Now it was called Butler and Company. She had become a *silent* partner.

Attracted by the aroma of a recent meal, the detective strolled across the hall to the private residence. His nose for fast food told him it was Chinese take-out. Before he could knock, the door opened, and he was looking up – and up – at Charles Butler.

The man was at least a head taller than most of the world, and his nose was also above average, a wonderful hook that could perch a pigeon. His heavy-lidded eyes bulged, and the small blue irises were surrounded by vast areas of white, giving Charles a startled look that he shared with frogs and frightened horses. From the neck down, Mother Nature had gotten it right – better than that in Riker's estimation, for the body was well made, aiming for the angels in form and power.

'Riker, *hello!*' When Charles Butler smiled, he took on the aspect of a lunatic, but such a charming loon. Over the past forty years of his life, he had learned to be self-conscious about this idiosyncrasy. The line of his mouth waffled with embarrassment, apologizing for every happy expression.

'Hey, how are ya?' Riker noted his friend's rare departure from Savile Row suits. The denim shirt screamed of money; nothing off the rack could fit so well. And apparently Mallory had introduced Charles to a tailor shop that customized her own blue jeans. The two of them were still struggling with the concept of casual dress.

'I hear you're on summer vacation.'

'Yes, Mallory's idea.' Charles pushed a curling strand of light brown hair away from his eyes. He was always forgetting appointments with his barber. 'No more clients until the fall.' And now the man looked worried. 'She's all right, isn't she? You didn't come by to—'

'Oh, no. She's fine. I should've called. Sorry.' And Riker's regret was genuine, for Charles must have thought that he was here to break the news of Mallory's premature death. 'It's late. I should leave.'

'Nonsense, I'm glad you stopped by.' Charles stood back and ushered his guest inside. 'I was only worried because we had dinner reservations, but she wasn't home when I—'

'She never called to cancel? I'll rag her about it.' And that nearly explained the reek of Chinese take-out in the home of a gourmet cook. Riker passed through the foyer, then paused a few steps into the front room. 'She rewired your stereo, didn't she?'

'How did you—'

'I'm a detective.' Perfection was Mallory's signature, and it was writ in what could not be seen. She had made the machinery, its wires and speakers invisible. And the sound was remarkably well balanced, creating the illusion of an orchestra at the center of Riker's brain. The concerto was bright and hopeful, a portrait of Charles Butler in strings and flutes.

There were never any CDs lying about in Mallory's personal car, and he sometimes wondered if she ever listened to music, perhaps something metallic with New Age clicks and whirrs.

'Can I get you a drink?'

'I wouldn't say no to a beer.' Riker sprawled on the sofa while Charles crossed the formal dining room, heading for the kitchen.

Though the detective had been in this apartment many times, he scrutinized the room of paneled walls and antiques. Books and journals

33

were piled on all the tables and chairs, the sign of a man with too much free time. Riker found what he had been looking for – food, a bowl of cashews partially hidden under a newspaper, and he had devoured them all before Charles returned with two beers foaming in frosted glass. Any man who kept his beer steins in the freezer was Riker's friend for life.

'I have to tell you—' As the detective accepted his beer, he spied a fortune cookie on a small table next to the sofa. 'This isn't exactly a social call.' He grabbed the cookie, then remembered his manners and asked, 'You mind?'

'It's yours.' Charles settled into an armchair. 'What can I do for you?'

Riker unbuttoned his suit jacket and pulled out the stolen waterlogged paperback. 'Can you fix this?'

Charles stared at the soggy cover illustration of cowboys and blazing six-guns – so far removed from his own taste in literature. His face expressed some polite equivalent of *Oh, shit,* as he attempted a lame smile. 'I think so. It might take me a while.'

'I got time.' Riker cracked his cookie open. His printed fortune fell out. He watched this sliver of paper drop to the floor and let it lie there, for he was that rare individual who ate the cookies for their own sake. And now he looked around for another.

Charles excused himself for a few minutes, then came back with a sandwich wrapped in a napkin, and Riker happily traded his wet book for the roast beef on rye. A moment later, his happiness was destroyed. The paperback lay open in the other man's hands, and the detective could see a piece of paper stuck to the back cover. If he had not been so tired and hungry, he would have thought to leaf through the book before handing it over. 'What's that?'

'A receipt.' Charles gently peeled up the paper. 'From Warwick's Used Books. Odd. I thought I knew every bookshop in Manhattan.' He closed the old novel and stared at the lurid cover. 'So this is rather important to you.' He was too well bred to ask why in God's name this might be true.

'Yeah, you can't get 'em anymore. That western went out of print forty years ago. It's the last novel Jake Swain ever wrote.' Riker wolfed down his sandwich, then drained the beer stein, stalling for time, for the right words. *Sheriff Peety rides again.* What was the other character's name? He had blocked it out of his mind long ago and hoped it would remain forgotten.

'I'll have to get started before this dries out.' Charles rose to his feet, and Riker followed him into the next room. The library walls were fifteen feet high and covered with a mosaic of leather bindings. A narrow door set into one bookcase opened on to a small boxy room. Glue pots and rolls of tape, brushes, tweezers and spools of thread lay on a long work table where the bibliophile repaired the spines and pages of his collection. Charles swept aside volumes with gold-leaf decoration to make room for a paperback that had cost fifty cents in the year it was published.

'You can't tell Mallory about this,' said Riker. 'Promise? I don't want her to know I wrecked it.'

Stole it, robbed it from a crime scene.

But his partner would never know about that if Charles believed—

'It's *hers*?' Charles should never be allowed near a poker game; his face expressed every feeling, every thought. And just now, he was thinking that Riker had lied to him. The office across the hall contained all the books that Mallory owned. Most dealt with computers; none were fiction. And, before leaving college to join NYPD, she had received two years of an elite education at Barnard. No way could he believe that this book was her property. Yet he nodded and said, 'Understood.' Charles reached up to a shelf above the work space and pulled down a bundle of blotting papers. 'You were never here. We never had this conversation.'

'Great. Thanks.' Riker imagined that he could hear the man's beautiful brain kicking into high gear and making connections at light's speed.

Charles teased the block of pages away from its paper spine, then noticed his guest's anxiety and mistook paranoia for concern. 'Don't worry. I can put it back together.' After setting the cover to one side, he peeled away a top sheet of advertising and stared at the underlying page. 'Oh.' His face conveyed that everything had suddenly been made clear. 'Well, I can't blot this one. I'd lose most of the ink. I can save the inscription, but Louis's signature is gone.'

Calmly, the detective asked, 'What?' And inside his head, he screamed, *What?*

'This *is* Louis Markowitz's handwriting, isn't it? I imagine there'll be trouble when Mallory sees the damage.'

Startled, Riker looked down at the inscribed page. An old friend's quirky penmanship trailed off in a wash of blue ink. 'No, it's okay. She hasn't seen it yet. I was gonna give it to her later – a present.'

Charles read the inscription. 'So it's a gift from Louis to Mallory. Almost poetry. I gather he wanted her to have it after his demise. A posthumous goodbye?'

'Yeah, something like that.' Untrue. On the only day when that note could have been written, Louis Markowitz had not been anticipating his own death; he still had many years ahead of him, time enough to raise Kathy Mallory. The old man must have forgotten that the book existed, and so had Riker – until it floated past him in Sparrow's apartment.

'Louis's funeral was some time ago.' Charles used clamps and cotton batting to fix the page to a board, then picked up a palm-size heater and switched it on. 'You're delivering this a bit late, aren't you?'

'Yeah.' Riker was slowly coming to terms with shock. A dead man had corroborated his lie – fifteen years before it was told.

An hour later, every surface in the room was covered with a book leaf pressed between blotting papers. Only the inscription page was exposed. The detective stared at the scrawl of blue ink, the words of a man who had loved a homeless child. The lines suggested that the book had been inscribed after the old man had seen convincing proof that the ten-year-old was dead and gone. Yet that grieving cop had obviously clung to the insane idea that Kathy *might* come back.

Riker bowed his head over the page to read the passage again.

'Once there was a little girl. No, scratch that, kid. You were always more than that, bigger than life. I could have set you to music — the damn Star Spangled Banner *— because you prevailed through all the long scary nights. You were my hero.'*

After Charles had bid Riker good night at the elevator, he saw a crack of light under the door to Butler and Company. Mallory? He had not seen her face since early June. And now he forced himself to walk, not run, as he entered the office and passed through the lighted reception area, then moved quickly down a narrow hall, pulled along by the dim glow from Mallory's room — where the machines lived.

He paused at the open doorway, staring at the back of his business partner. She sat before a computer workstation, one of three. Most of her personal office was lost in shadow, a sharp contrast to the halo, a silhouette of burnished gold made by lamplight threading through her hair.

What could he say to her? He doubted that she would regret or even recall their missed dinner date, for she was in holy communion with her machines and oblivious to human disappointment.

Years ago, he had written a rather poetic monograph on her gifted applications of computer science. Over the course of his career, he had evaluated many wizards who could force electronics to do remarkable things. But she was a creature apart, employing an artist's sensibility similar to a composer of music. She merged with the technology, fashioning effect by thought, blending the psyches of musician and mathematician to write original notes for electronic bells and whistles.

During his study of her, Charles had indulged in a fanciful, albeit unpublishable, notion that Nature had planned ahead for this new century, that some long-sleeping gene had awakened when she was made. Later, after learning more about her childhood, his vision had altered and darkened, for Mallory had been hammered into what she was – the perfect receptacle for something cold and alien. And her intimacy with machinery chilled him.

Once, he had been ambivalent about computers. Now he saw them as perverted soldiers that blurred the demarcation line between her fingertips and the keyboards. He had sought to dilute their influence with offerings of fine art and the soft edges of antiquarian objects. Mallory had fought back, encroaching on the office kitchen with ugly technology that he could not abide. Then she had invaded his personal residence, staging a surprise attack to reconfigure his stereo system. Stunned, he had been assaulted from all sides by musical perfection via enemy components that removed the necessity of human hands for turning the knobs and fine-tuning the song. The sheer beauty of it had seduced him for a time. But now, seeing her like this, he was back in combat mode, dreaming new schemes to disconnect her computers, to unplug them all – and Mallory too.

It was a good fight.

She never looked up as Charles approached. He stood beside her chair and stared at the monitor. Her only task tonight was the harmless typing of text. All that angst for nothing. Bracketed question marks pocked the glowing screen. A battered notebook lay on the metal surface of her workstation. It was open to a page of faded coffee stains and lines of blue ink from an old-fashioned fountain pen. Charles could even describe that pen; Louis Markowitz had willed it to him. For the second time in one night, he was staring at a sample of an old friend's handwriting. Mallory was deciphering her foster father's shorthand scribbles between the clearly written words, *duct tape* and *rope*.

She raised her face to his, and they exchanged grins of hello. Their technology wars had caused no hard feelings between them. They still smiled and waved at one another across the great divide.

THREE

Riker watched the sidewalks roll by the passenger window of Mallory's tan sedan. The landscape kept changing on him. Early memories of beatniks in funereal black gave way to colorful flower children, hippies with love beads, and bless the girls with diaphragm earrings who had bedded every boy with a guitar.

Rock 'n' roll. Salad days.

Nose rings were the next new thing in another parade of fearless children with hair every color of the chemical neon rainbow. Girded in tattoos and vintage corsets with cruel metal spikes for nipples, they had flung themselves into the badlands of the East Village.

This morning, he saw a girl in a white polo shirt and jeans still creased from the store hanger. Another yuppie strolled by in a similar uniform. One day, while Riker's back was turned, the kids had all gone shopping at The Gap.

He turned to his partner behind the wheel. 'Maybe I should do the interview with Tall Sally.' He might as well have added the words, *just to be safe*. It was not the size of the ex-convict that worried him, but Sal's history with Sparrow when Kathy Mallory was a child. 'It's not that you can't handle it—'

The car stopped before the light turned red. No warning! Not fair! She hit the brakes hard and slammed him toward the dashboard. His teeth were saved by a seatbelt, but it was a near thing. 'So that's a definite no,' said Riker.

After the silent wait for a green light, the car moved on, and Mallory lowered her dark glasses. 'You think I should do the old woman instead?'

Enough said. According to a police report, the elderly witness was very fragile in mind and body. Mallory might want to take her out for a drive.

The detectives pulled up to the curb in front of the crime scene. Riker stepped out of the car and watched it drive off, passing only one other moving vehicle. Sparrow's street had a tranquil character in the early morning light. There were flower boxes on some of the window ledges, a sign of gentrification, law and order, though last night's mob had made off with all the blooms, and now the headless stalks were turning brown.

The detective on loan from Lieutenant Loman was hovering near the front steps of the apartment building. All dressed up in a suit and shiny new shoes, the youngster shifted his weight from foot to foot, suspecting that he was in trouble – and he was.

Riker's gaze traveled over the smoke-stained bricks, then down to the yellow crime-scene tape lying on the sidewalk. It had been pulled aside so a man in coveralls could board up the broken window. A familiar uniformed officer stood guard over Sparrow's basement apartment. Riker smiled. 'Hey, Waller. Go grab some food. I'm gonna be here awhile.' He nodded toward the workman and the young detective. 'I'll make sure they don't run off with anything.'

After the patrolman had crossed the street and passed out of earshot, Riker turned to face the worried young cop in the dark suit. The new man was in that whiteshield limbo between a uniform's silver badge and a detective's gold. And he was too young to have been promoted without a father-in-law at Number One Police Plaza. His sole distinguishing feature was bleached hair that went beyond blond; it was yellow, the color of a baby duck.

And Riker christened him accordingly.

Department politics dictated that he handle Duck Boy with great care, and so he held up the young detective's report and crumpled it into a tight ball, saying, 'This sucks.' Riker was not usually that fancy with his critiques. The wadded-up paper should have made words unnecessary, but he was feeling expansive this morning. He looked toward the window of a first-floor apartment directly across the street, then squinted to make out a woman's head piled high with white hair.

How he loved old ladies, the watchers of the world.

He opened the crumpled ball of paper, Duck Boy's idea of an interview, and read the closing words aloud, '"Religious fanatic. Ramblings of senility." That's *it*? What the hell kind of a witness statement is this? When I send you back to Lieutenant Loman, he's gonna think I didn't raise you right.'

Officer Waller had returned with his breakfast in a brown deli bag, and now Riker crossed the street with Duck Boy following close behind, and they climbed a short flight of stairs leading up to the front door of a narrow building.

'This is a school day.' The senior detective pushed the buzzer. 'Keep your mouth shut and *listen*.'

The door was opened by a bespectacled elderly woman in a long and flowery summer dress. Her lenses were thick, and one eye was clouded with cataracts, yet she recognized Duck Boy immediately, and it was obviously not a pleasant memory. 'Oh, you've come back.'

Riker detected a trace of the Southland in her accent. 'Emelda Winston? I'm Detective Riker. May I call you *Miss* Emelda?'

'Why, of course you may.' Her eyes lit up, and even her red-painted toes were thrilled, curling and uncurling in her sandals. She belonged to him now, charmed by this old custom of address never observed in northern climes.

'Now you boys come right in.' She stepped back to open the door a little wider. 'I've got a nice breeze goin' in my parlor.'

When the two men had been seated awhile on a gigantic horsehair sofa, Miss Emelda returned to the front room, rolling a tea cart laid with white linen, glassware and a plate of chocolate chip cookies.

'So you're here about Sparrow.' She lifted the pitcher of lemonad and poured each of them a glass. 'You know, I was the one who called in the fire.'

'So that was you?' Riker glanced at the younger man. 'No one told me.' He bit into a cookie that was definitely homemade, for it lacked the preservatives to keep it from turning to stone. 'So, Miss Emelda, how well did you know Sparrow?'

'Not well at all, I'm afraid. That poor girl. She just moved in a few weeks ago.'

'Then you don't know what she did for a living?'

'Oh, yes. She was an actress. But I don't see how she made a living at it. I went to her dress rehearsal yesterday. The play was in the basement of the elementary school, and they were only planning to charge a few dollars a ticket. I suppose they'll cancel it now.'

Riker nodded. 'I wondered why Sparrow was wearing those clothes. Long-sleeved blouse, long skirt – boots. So that was her costume for the play?'

'Yes, they were doing a period piece, something by Chekhov, I think.' The old woman smiled. 'Sparrow was surprisingly good. A very moving performance.'

After consuming two more rock-hard cookies and nearing the dregs of the lemonade, they were old friends, Riker and Miss Emelda.

'Ma'am,' said Duck Boy, violating orders of silence, 'why don't you tell him about the angel.'

'Oh, yes – last night. Well, the crowd parted, just for an instant, mind you, and there was the angel floating in front of Sparrow's window.' Miss Emelda clapped her hands. 'Just *glorious*. But there was nothing about the angel in the morning papers.'

Riker continued to smile, as if she had just said something perfectly rational. 'Can you describe the angel?'

'I think it was a cherub.' She fished in the pocket of her dress and pulled out a small Christmas tree ornament. 'I showed this to the young man.' She nodded toward Duck Boy, then spoke to Riker in a stage whisper, 'But he didn't seem to understand. He thinks I'm pixilated.'

Riker shook his head in sympathy. 'Kids today, huh?' He stared at the ornament in her hand, a pair of white wings attached to the disembodied head of a child with gold curls. The detective turned to the window behind the sofa and its view of Sparrow's apartment across the street. And now he knew that the old woman's angel was a cop. Last night, Mallory's black jeans had disappeared in the dark; Miss Emelda had only discerned the blond hair and white blazer, a winged thing on the fly.

'It was a miracle,' she said, hands clasped in prayer.

Riker was satisfied that, thick lenses or no, the old woman could see well enough. He drained his glass, then leaned forward, speaking as one gossip to another, 'Just between you and me, who do you think did it? Who hung Sparrow?'

'The reporters. Naturally.'

Duck Boy rolled his eyes, then winced when his supervisor kicked him. This act was hidden behind the safe cover of the tea cart's linen. It was a clear shot to the shinbone, and Riker hoped it hurt like hell. He turned back to his star witness and smiled. 'I never trusted reporters myself.'

She nodded. 'They're everywhere. Even in the trees – watching us all the time. I saw one of them out there with his camera. And that was *before* I smelled smoke. Very suspicious, don't you think?'

'Yeah,' said Riker. 'So this reporter – did you get a good look at him?'

'I'm sorry, no, not his face. His back was turned. I remember his camera. Oh – and he wore a white T-shirt and blue jeans. He might've had a baseball cap. Yes, he did. I'm sure of it now.' She made a delicate moue of distaste. 'I remember when reporters wore suits and ties.'

Riker glanced back at the window, attempting to judge the zone of Miss Emelda's vision. She could not have seen anything across the street in great detail, or she would never have made Mallory into an angel. 'How close was this guy?'

'He was in a tree. Didn't I tell you that? Oh, yes, right in front of my building. Then that van showed up with the other news people from the TV station. The name of the news show was painted on the side of the van, but I can't remember which one it was – I'm so sorry. Well, as you can imagine, it was quite a time. The fire engines came a minute or two after that. Of course the fire didn't amount to much – thank the Lord.'

'Amen,' said Riker. 'So the guy with the camera climbed a tree *before* the news van showed up?'

'Yes, and before I smelled smoke.' Miss Emelda walked behind the sofa to stand before the window. She pointed at a nearby oak on the sidewalk. It was large, one of those rare specimens that thrived in cement. 'That's the tree.'

'Ma'am?' Duck Boy took out his pencil and notebook. 'Did the suspect's videocam have a network logo?'

A confused Miss Emelda turned to the senior detective, silently asking what language the youngster was speaking.

'I know,' said Riker. 'All cameras look alike to me.'

'I can show you mine.' The woman bustled out of the room, then returned with an old Instamatic. 'Now his was a bit smaller than this one, and maybe the brand was different. His could've been a Polaroid. But the pictures popped out the front, same as mine. They develop themselves right before your eyes. I'll show you.'

Duck Boy was blinded by the flash and caught in the act of snapping his pencil in two.

The carpenter was gone when Riker emerged from Miss Emelda's apartment and crossed the street with Duck Boy. He had one more piece of information from his witness, and – serendipity – the man he most wanted to hurt was within reach. Ex-cop Gary Zappata was starting down the steps to Sparrow's basement apartment when Officer Waller grabbed him by the arm and roughly pulled him back to the sidewalk.

'Back off! I got business here!' The shorter man puffed out his chest the better to display a fire department logo emblazoned on his T-shirt, as if this passed for credentials.

Riker guessed that Zappata had been asked to turn in his fireman's shield and identification. Soon there would be a hearing on charges of gross misconduct, the prelude to being fired from his new job.

Officer Waller blocked the entrance to the basement room.

'Get out of my way,' said Zappata. 'I won't tell you twice.'

Unimpressed, the policeman responded by tipping back a can of orange soda and draining it dry. The pissing contest was officially underway, and Waller was already winning. A true son of New York City, he bit into a bagel and looked up at the sky, ignoring the ex-cop, soon to be an ex-firefighter.

Zappata turned to see the two detectives step on to the sidewalk. He pointed to the senior man and yelled, 'Hey, you!'

Riker so rarely answered to that form of address, and he liked the commanding tone even less. He waved the man off, saying, 'It can wait.'

You weasel.

After opening the door to Waller's patrol car, Riker motioned Duck Boy to follow him into the front seat. When the windows had been rolled up, he said, 'Did you get all that?'

'All *what?*'

'Sparrow's acting gig. We just expanded her social circle. I want names for everyone at that dress rehearsal. And the reporters were on the scene *before* the fire engines turned out. Even if the old lady was slow to call in the fire – they shouldn't have beaten the engines. You're gonna find out why that news van was in this neighborhood. And I don't care who you have to sleep with. But you wear a condom when you bang a reporter. You don't know where those bastards have been.' Riker reached across the other man's chest and opened the car door. 'Move!'

The young detective was quick to scramble out, and then he was off and running down the street. The duckling was launched.

Detective Riker took his own time stepping out onto the sidewalk. Now he was looking down at the short fireman.

Gary Zappata rolled back his muscular shoulders, gearing up for a fast round of King of the Hill.

Of all the stupid kid games.

The detective made a point of looking at his watch to convey that his own time was worth a lot more. He glanced at the fireman, as if he had just noticed him standing there. 'Yeah, what?'

Zappata nodded in Waller's direction. 'He won't let me in.'

'I got orders.' Officer Waller leaned down to attach the crime-scene tape to a gatepost. 'Only Special Crimes detectives get in. Punk firemen don't.'

Riker shot a warning glance at the man in uniform. Waller had never served with Zappata, the former loose cannon of the SoHo precinct. A nutcase ex-cop was too dangerous to have for a friend or an enemy.

'Where's your damn partner?' Zappata demanded.

Right about now, Mallory should be walking into Macy's department store in search of New York's tallest whore. 'She's busy. So am I.' The detective was more blasé about making his own enemies. And now he flirted with the idea of putting this man on the short list for Sparrow's hanging. Was that ludicrous? Would Zappata have the balls to beat up a Girl Scout in a fair fight? In this idle moment of indecision, Riker put a cigarette in his mouth, then slowly fished through his pockets for matches – just to make the man a little crazier than he already was. 'You got one minute of my time.' Did that make the fireman angry? Oh, yes, and so tense his facial muscles were twitching. Some days, Riker really loved the job.

'Your partner got me suspended from the Fire Department,' said Zappata. 'I guess I stepped on her toes last night.'

'Yeah, I heard about you playing detective on the crime scene.'

'That bitch is the one—'

'Nobody heard it from her. She never rats on anybody.'

'Then how—'

'*You* figure it out. And now maybe you can explain the damn lightbulb over the front door.'

'What?'

'Zappata, I got a witness who says that light was out when the firemen got here. Now, I don't figure you guys carry spare bulbs on the truck, so I'm guessing some *jerk* figured the bulb might be loose. So this freaking *idiot* reached up, twisted it. And sure enough, it wasn't burnt out – just loose in the fixture.'

Riker knew he was onto something. There was too much white in the fireman's eyes – fear. 'But this criminally stupid fireman never thought to mention it to the cops. I guess he figured we wouldn't care if the perp was some stranger hiding behind the garbage cans, waiting to surprise that poor woman in the dark. Naw, better we should think Sparrow opened the door for somebody she knew. Then we could waste a few days spinning our wheels.'

There was no one Riker hated more than Zappata. If Sparrow had come down from the rope in time, her coma-blind eyes would not roll aimless in their sockets, and she would not drool.

He had one last salvo to take this man down. 'I'm guessing this moron fireman took his gloves off before he touched the bulb.' Riker turned to the uniformed police officer. 'Waller! Get a CSU tech over here.' He pointed to the light fixture over the door. 'Have him take that lightbulb and dust it for prints.'

Riker turned his back on the subdued Zappata and walked down the street toward his next appointment, on Avenue A, where he planned to kill off a ten-year-old girl for the second time.

The doors opened and the carnage began. Two inexperienced women were roughly pushed aside, and a man fell down on one knee. Shopping in the city was no game for tourists, otherwise known as the halt and the lame. Behind the display counters, men and women flushed with adrenaline, waited on the enemy. Onward marched t' hordes of customers – and one tall blonde in Armani sunglasses. Everything Detective Mallory wore flaunted the idea that she was a cop on the take. The silk-blend T-shirt allowed her skin to breathe in style, and the dark linen blazer was tailor made. Even her designer jeans bore the detailed handwork of a custom fitting. And with dark glasses to cover her green eyes, she bore no resemblance to a hungry child who had once robbed this store on a regular basis, ripping off items from the shopping list of a drag-queen hooker.

Tall Sally had always been fanatically devoted to Macy's and prized their goods above items stolen from any other store. Over time, the sales people had become too familiar with Sal's apprentice shoplifter, ten-year-old Kathy Mallory. Sometimes the clerks had departed from the armor of New York attitude to lean over their counters and wave. This had confused the little thief: for she had only targeted Macy's once a week, and she had never been caught in the act of stealing.

How had they recognized her?

As a little girl, she had not seen the obvious answer in her own intense green eyes and a face that was painfully beautiful – unforgettable. The homeless child had passed by a hundred mirrors in this department store, but failed to notice her own reflection in any of them. It had been a shock to discover that sales clerks could see her.

One day, the child had attempted to solve this old puzzle, deciding that unwashed clothing had made her stand out from the crowd. She had taken more care with her wardrobe, donning freshly stolen jeans before setting out for Herald Square. Her dirty hair had been swept up under a baseball cap, the better to blend with cleaner shoppers. And the little girl had added one more touch to her disguise, a pair of wildly expensive designer sunglasses with real gold frames – which no one in that middle-class throng could possibly afford.

And *then* she had felt truly invisible.

Fifteen years later, Detective Mallory had upgraded to even more expensive sunglasses, and the sales people had also changed. She scanned the unfamiliar faces as she passed the counters, hunting a clerk who was seven feet tall with long platinum-blond hair. Apparently, staid old Macy's had relaxed the hiring policy. Or perhaps Tall Sally had convinced them that a job in their store was the fulfillment of a lifelong dream – and this was true. She found the transvestite working behind a cosmetics counter. Of course. Now Sal could steal all the makeup in the world, and without the assistance of small children. Voice jacked up to a high falsetto, the sales clerk said, 'May I help you, miss?'

Don't you know me, Sal?

No, there was no sign of recognition in the heavily painted gray eyes. Mallory held up her gold shield and ID. 'This is about Sparrow.'

'Put that away.' Tall Sally's voice dropped into a deeper, more masculine register. 'Why're you guys hassling me? I see my parole officer every damn week.'

Mallory lowered her badge. 'Does Macy's know about your rapsheet? . . . No?' What a surprise. Sal had lied on the job application, failing to mention convictions for grand theft and corrupting the morals of minor children. Mallory laid her leather folder on the counter, keeping the badge in plain sight. Sal's eyes were riveted to the detective's gold shield, regarding it as a bomb. 'Sparrow used to work with you. Does that help?'

'It's a big store, honey. What department did she work in? Can't say I recall the name.'

What about me, Sal? Remember running out on me?

Aloud, Mallory said, 'You and Sparrow were booked for prostitution in the same raids. You both gave the same street corner as your employment address. Don't even *try* to jerk me around.'

'Well, back in those days, I knew a lot of whores. You can't expect me to remember every—'

'Does Macy's personnel director know that you're a man?'

'I'm the real deal, Detective.' Sal thrust out a chest of formidable breasts. 'In *all* my parts, if you know what I mean.'

'Sex change?'

Tall Sally nodded.

The parole officer had not mentioned this, and Mallory knew the thief had been incarcerated in an all-male facility. The surgery must have been recent. 'Expensive operation. You didn't get that kind of money working in a prison laundry. Doing your own stealing these days? Or do you still use little kids?'

'I had some money saved.'

In other words, Sal had stolen a *lot* of money. But Mallory had a vivid memory of Sal holding a set of lock picks just beyond the reach of a child and making threats, saying, 'Kid, if you get caught, forget my name, or I'll mess you up real bad.' Ten-year-old Kathy Mallory had snatched Sal's picks, then walked up to a delivery truck and opened the rear doors in record time. The student had surpassed the master.

Remember leaving me behind?

As always, the drag queen had been standing a safe distance away while Kathy had done the robbery alone, a little girl with puny arms struggling to unload VCRs into a grocery cart. At the first sight of a police car, Tall Sally had climbed into a station wagon, obeying all the laws and traffic lights while driving away and abandoning the child.

Two uniformed officers had seen Kathy standing just inside the open doors of the delivery truck – nowhere to hide, no way to run. The small thief had walked to the edge of the truckbed, raised one thin white hand and waved at the policemen. *Big* smile. Grinning, they had waved back, and their car had rolled on by.

All these years later, Tall Sally did not recognize the child all grown up and still holding a grudge.

'So it's just a coincidence,' said Mallory. 'You get a vagina installed about the same time Sparrow gets a new nose.'

'That junkie whore got her nose fixed?' Tall Sally's voice had shifted back to fluttery high notes, for this was *girl* talk. 'So tell me, how's it look?'

And now Mallory could believe that the two prostitutes had no recent history. Tall Sally had always been an inept liar, embroidering

50

details to death and advertising every falsehood – but not this time. There was no exaggerated protest. Sal had never seen Sparrow's new face.

Along Avenue A, half-naked men with jackhammers ripped up the street, choking the air with particles and shaking the pavement in front of the bookshop. Riker had the taste of dust in his mouth as he stood before the display window and perused the tides of worn paperbacks. This morning, he planned to be the first customer.

John Warwick was walking toward him now, thin and wasted, moving slowly, doing his old man's shuffle. He bowed his white head, unwilling to meet the eyes of passing pedestrians. And now he paused at the door to his shop.

'Hey, John. Remember me?'

The bookseller turned his face to the window and spoke to the detective's reflection in the glass. 'Riker. What's it been, fourteen, fifteen years?'

'Sounds right. I came about that old western you tracked down for Lou Markowitz.'

The bookseller drew back, as if he feared that Riker would strike him. 'It's not for sale. You can't have it. It belongs to the girl.'

'She's dead,' Riker lied. 'And you *know* that. Markowitz *told* you—'

'No.' Warwick shook his head. After fifteen years, he still believed that a ten-year-old Kathy had merely been lost. How close to the truth he had come. And he had sussed out his truth aided only by his paranoid distrust of police.

'So you still have the western?' This was impossible, for Riker had found that book in Sparrow's apartment, but evidently Warwick had lost track of the shop's inventory.

'Of *course* I have it. You think I'd give it to anyone but her?'

'It's over, John. The kid's never coming back.' And now he posed a question disguised as frustration. 'When was the last time you heard anyone ask for that book?'

'Every day for the past two weeks.' Warwick winced. 'This woman – a tall devil with blond hair.'

Close, but Riker knew that the man was not describing Mallory. 'Sparrow,' said Warwick. 'That was her name. She wrote it down on a piece of paper – her phone number too. I threw it away.'

'But before this woman came along? Nothing, right? Not a whisper in fifteen years. Doesn't that tell you—'

'The child is alive,' said Warwick. 'You couldn't catch her. No one could.' His thin arms were rising as if to defend himself from a blow. 'And you *can't* have her book.'

Riker wondered how he would phrase questions about Sparrow. He needed a time line for the last days of her life, but he could not interrogate this man in the name of the law. Given Warwick's psychiatric history, that would mean knocking at the door of a very scary closet. 'John? Can we sit down and talk about this? Just for a few minutes. Then I'll go away.'

Warwick pulled out a gray linen handkerchief. He removed his glasses and made a show of cleaning them while casting about for something to say. 'Markowitz put me through a lot of trouble tracking down that novel. He told me to—'

'She's dead. She can't come back for the book.'

'You can't have it!' Warwick shouted, then shrank into himself, hunching his shoulders and furtively looking from side to side, as if he believed those loud words had come from someone else. He continued in a hoarse whisper, 'Because she *might* come back. '

John Warwick was a member of Lou Markowitz's choir. He would never give up his vigil, but the threat this posed to Kathy Mallory was very small. Riker was satisfied that this man had never known her name. In the worst possible case, the bookseller might meet her on the street one day and recognize the remarkable green eyes. Or was he still waiting for a ten-year-old child?

Riker stepped back to reappraise this fragile little person, who had ays teetered on the edge of sanity. The threat of any authority figure terrified John Warwick. Yet he was making a stand against the police, though he trembled to do it. And this was bravery in any man's philosophy.

Please. Don't make me do this the hard way.

The detective sat down on an iron bench in front of the store. Now that he no longer loomed over Warwick, the smaller man relaxed. 'I can't make you talk to me,' said Riker. 'And I can't go away until you do.' He would not risk another cop canvassing this street and stumbling on to a connection between Sparrow and a green-eyed child who loved westerns. He looked down at the sidewalk and whispered, 'Please.'

Shaking his head, Warwick unlocked the door to his shop and shuffled inside. Two minutes later, he was out on the street again, eyes wild and close to tears. 'She stole it! Yesterday that book was on the shelf behind my register, and now it's gone. That woman stole it when my back was turned.'

Playing the public servant, Riker pulled out his notebook to take down a citizen's statement on a theft. 'You said her name was Sparrow? So she was in your store yesterday.'

'And every day for two weeks. Yesterday she was the last customer. It was just a few minutes before I closed the store. So I *know* she's the one who stole it. You write that down.'

Riker glanced at the hours posted in the shop window. Poor Sparrow. She had wanted the book so badly, but there had been no time to read it before she was mutilated and hung.

FOUR

The sunlit room was racked with gleaming copper-bottom pots, more spices than the stores carried and every cooking utensil known to God and Cordon Bleu – and even here, antiques prevailed. Charles Butler lit a flame under an old-fashioned percolator. He was dressed in yesterday's shirt and jeans, and his eyes were sore from working through the night on Mallory's account, though he would never get credit for mending her present, a waterlogged paperback western. Riker had never understood this man's one-sided infatuation with her. Charles was hardly a virgin in the area of abnormal psychology, and he must know what she was.

The detective sat at the kitchen table and opened the restored book to the page with the inscription. Apart from Lou Markowitz's lost signature, there was no sign of damage, and he toyed with the idea of actually giving it to Mallory. 'Good as new. It's magic.'

'The paper was very brittle.' Charles set the table with coffee cups and forks. 'I had to treat it with a matte polymer so the pages wouldn't crumble. Of course, that would've destroyed the value of a rare book. So I did some research first.'

Apparently, this was not a joke. Riker glanced at the stack of volumes on the kitchen table, all reference materials of an avid book collector. Among the tides he found, *The Role of the Western in American Literature.* 'The book is worthless, right?'

'Yes, sorry.' Charles laid the old receipt from Warwick's Used

Books on the table alongside the paperback. 'I can't imagine why Louis paid so much money for it.'

'I told you they were hard to find. It took a while to track this one down.'

'Ah, he hired a book tracer. I use one from time to time. Well, that explains it.' Charles leaned down and pointed to the faded date on the receipt. 'Wasn't that the year Louis took Mallory into foster care?'

Riker felt queer and cold, the sensation of a misstep on a ladder. There were no regrets over stealing the book; he would risk his badge to do it again. No, his great mistake was made in that sentimental moment when he had decided not to destroy it. The second error was bringing the book to the man who loved Mallory. 'Hey, I really appreciate all the time you—'

'It's not like I had something better to do.' Charles set two plates of pie on the table, then turned down the flame on the stovetop. 'I don't think I care for summer vacations. Oh, I almost forgot. I found a list of Jake Swain's work. Did you know he wrote eleven other books?'

'Yeah, I knew that.' Riker wondered how much of the truth he could tell before the whole mess came unraveling.

His host poured coffee into the cups, then sat down on the other side of the table. 'Interesting that Louis would go to so much trouble.' His tone was merely conversational and curious, not suspicious – not yet. 'If he hired a tracer, he must've wanted it very badly.'

Of course, this would be confusing. Charles and the late Louis Markowitz had shared a reading list of more respectable authors. Perhaps he was hoping that this bad novel was some inside joke between Mallory and her foster father.

'No tracer,' said Riker. 'The bookshop owner found it for him.' He sipped his coffee and tasted bile rising in his throat.

'So – how did you know about Swain's other books? They're very obscure. Did Louis mention them?'

'Yeah, Lou read 'em all.' Riker knew he would not be believed though he was telling the truth.

Charles was incredulous. 'Why would he read books – like – *that*?' His gigantic vocabulary had failed him. He could find no better euphemism for *god-awful crap*.

Riker jabbed at the pie with his fork. 'Because it's great literature?'

'No, I don't think that's *quite* it. May I?' Charles reached for the western, then opened it to a page near the end. 'In the last chapter, there's a rather strange gunfight.'

There was no need of the book to refresh his memory. Charles could read as fast as most people turned pages, and he retained everything in eidetic memory. Yet he kept the small conventions of normalcy – always trying to pass for a less gifted man, less of a freak. Riker wondered if this was partly his own fault. Perhaps he should stop referring to the brilliant clients of Butler and Company as Martians. He sometimes forgot that this man hailed from that same far planet.

'Here it is.' Charles looked up from the page. 'First, a gun shoots a red flame like a blowtorch. Then the crowd lets out a cheer. Oh, and the mayor has a few words to say. And *then*, at the other end of Main Street, an aging dance-hall girl faints when she actually *hears* the sound of the bullet entering the opponent's body.' He looked up at his guest. 'Now, given all the action and conversation between firing the shot and hitting the target, I estimate that the bullet took six minutes to travel down the street.' He closed the book, pronouncing it 'Wildly implausible.'

Riker gave him a slow grin. 'You only say that 'cause you never saw Lou on the firing range. A man could wait around all day for one of his bullets to hit a target.' He sipped his coffee, stalling for time, hunting for words that would not sound like lies. 'There were usually two gunfights in every book.' And now he remembered the name of the gunslinger. 'Now I never read this particular book, but I'm guessing that last shoot-out was between Sheriff Peety and the Wichita Kid.' He shook his head slowly in mock sadness. 'So that's how it ends.'

'*You* read them, too?'

'Yeah, maybe half of 'em.' And he had read the books under duress.

Lou Markowitz had wanted a second opinion, for he had never understood why a ten-year-old girl could be so attached to the trashy westerns.

Charles was still skeptical, crediting the detective with better taste in reading material if not suits and ties. And though it would not occur to him to call a friend on a lie, he clearly required more proof.

'In the first book,' said Riker, 'Sheriff Peety watches this little boy grow up in a sleepy burg called Franktown, Kansas. The kid and his mother rode in one day on the Wichita stagecoach.' More of the story was coming back to him now, and his appetite had returned. 'Well, the kid follows the sheriff around like a little shadow. In fact, Peety was the one who started calling him the Wichita Kid. It made the boy sound like a gunslinger. Just a joke, see? But the boy *loved* that name. It really made him strut.'

By the time the Wichita Kid had obtained his first six-shooter, 'a rusty old gun he bought for a dollar,' Riker was done with his pie. 'It was the kid's birthday. He'd just turned fifteen. And that morning, the sheriff wakes up to gunfire. So he comes runnin' out to the street.' The detective looked down at the floor and made Charles see a body there. The stranger in Franktown was an unarmed cowboy lying on his back in the blood and the dust.

'His unblinking eyes stared into the sun.' Riker surprised himself with this hokey line quoted verbatim. 'And guess who's standing over the body?' His hand formed an imaginary gun, and he blew smoke from one finger. 'Looks real bad for the Wichita Kid.'

The situation worsened when the boy stole a horse and rode out of town. In the next chapter, the lawman was saddling a black stallion. 'He's riding out after the kid.' And Riker had finished his coffee. 'Sheriff Peety can hardly see. He's got tears in his eyes. He *loves* the boy. But Wichita killed a man, and he's gotta hang for that. At the end of the story, the sheriff runs the kid off a canyon wall. It's a long drop, hundreds of feet to the bottom of that canyon. But Peety's still tracking the boy in the book after that one.'

'So it's episodic. A series with the same characters.'

'Yeah, and every story has an ending like that one. I guess that's what gets you hooked.'

Charles nodded, then slid the paperback across the table. The matter was closed.

The detective picked up the novel and quickly hid it in his pocket, as if it were a dirty book instead of a dangerous one.

The Ice Queen cometh.

Whiteshield Ronald Deluthe watched the pretty woman crossing the squad room. He recognized money when it walked in the door, shod in a brand of running shoes that no civil servant could afford. No one had to tell him what Mallory spent at her tailor's or the hair salons. And he wondered if she was on the take.

What green eyes you have. How cold they are.

She was blind to him, looking right through him, and yet he resented her less than the others. As a merely average man with an amateur dye job of bright yellow hair, Deluthe knew he was beneath her notice and contempt. It had nothing to do with his rank.

He turned back to his work, typing a meticulously detailed explanation for the news van beating the fire engines to last night's crime scene. Detective Riker would have nothing to criticize this time.

Mallory paused to read the paper sign taped to the side of his computer monitor. Originally, it had been taped to his back. The joke had gone unnoticed until he had removed his jacket and discovered the sheet of paper stuck to the material – and his new job title, *Resurrector of Dead Whores*. He had gamely put the sign on open display and earned a few smiles from passing detectives.

Mallory was not amused.

She ripped the sheet off the monitor, wadded it into a tight ball, then dropped it on his keyboard. He stared at the small white marble of compacted paper; her crumpling style was more serious than Riker's. He looked up as she moved away from him, calling after her, 'Ma'am?'

Did that sound too needy?

She ignored him, but all the detectives did that. He abandoned his report and followed her down a hallway that opened on to a large room with no distraction of windows. Every wall was lined with cork and cluttered with bloody photographs and the paperwork of current cases. Earlier in the day, a detective had given him a brief tour of the Special Crimes facilities, also known as the men's room and the lunch room, but not this place. Of course not. 'Why bother? Folding chairs were set up in audience formation for briefings he would never be invited to attend.

Near the door, a table held a large-screen television set. Mallory stood beside it, speaking to an older man, Janos.

A *real* detective.

Deluthe knew better than to interrupt. But rather than hover like a schoolboy awaiting permission to take a piss, he wandered the perimeter of cork walls, perusing pinned-up pictures and paperwork. None of it pertained to the hanging hooker. Obviously, it was not an important case, and his report was only one more piece of busywork for the son-in-law of the deputy commissioner, a little something to keep him out of the way.

Mallory fed a videotape into the mouth of a VCR. Deluthe was drawn to the screen and its images of fire engines and the crowd that had turned out for last night's hanging. Now he understood why the news director had refused to copy film and outtakes from the fire. The videotapes had already been collected by Mallory.

Detective Janos flicked the remote control and froze the picture. 'That one?' He pointed to a figure standing well back in the gathering, a man dressed in a T-shirt and jeans. 'Yeah, he might be the old lady's man in the tree.'

Deluthe winced at this reminder of Miss Emelda and all that he had missed in his first interview with her. But he had learned a lot from Sergeant Riker, the only detective who had bothered to teach him anything. Perhaps the useless trek to the television station had been a training exercise and not a total waste of time. He cleared his throat before speaking to Mallory. He would rather die than let her hear his voice crack. 'I thought *I* was supposed to talk to the news people. Sergeant Riker told me—'

'I got there first.' Mallory said this with no inflection, yet he drew the inference that he had been somehow remiss.

She undoubtedly knew everything that he knew and then some. Comparing his notes with hers would only be asking for more humiliation. 'I'm almost finished with my report.' His *useless* report. 'What do I do now?'

'I know what you can do.' Mallory smiled.

A sucker grin? Yes, and Deluthe braced himself, wondering if she would tell him to get lost or worse.

She pulled out her notebook. 'Never mind if this takes a few days. You just stay on it.' The detective wrote down the address of a warehouse and the item she wanted, then ripped off the page and handed it to him. As an afterthought, she said, 'That murder could be fifteen or twenty years old.'

And this vague time frame was supposed to help him locate an evidence carton for a homicide with no name or case number? He could search for years and never find a box with a hangman's rope. In effect, Mallory had just told him to get lost. And now she glared at him, perhaps wondering why he was still here.

He marched down the hallway, then crossed the squad room, saying a silent goodbye to the walls and wondering if he would ever see this place again. A few minutes later, the young man slid behind the wheel of his car and discovered that he was out of gas.

My name is Fool.

Deluthe was surrounded by cops with motorcycles and cars. Any of these men could siphon out a pint of fuel, enough for him to reach a gas station. But rather than admit to one more stupid mistake, he abandoned his vehicle and walked toward the subway, hoping it would drop him close to the warehouse. And there he might spend the rest of his temporary assignment, wandering long corridors of dusty shelves stacked with ancient evidence cartons.

Count on it, Fool.

When he reached the subway track, the last car was running away into the tunnel. He sat down on a wooden bench assigned to screw-up cops who missed their trains. The public-address system came alive with an electronic squeal that hurt his ears. An inhuman voice was telling Ronald Deluthe that, wherever he was going, he could not get there, not from here, not today. There was a fire on the tracks, and no more trains were coming his way.

New York was not a town of second chances.

On the other side of the grimy storefront window, an old man sat hunched over a desk as high as a pulpit, the better to catch shoplifters among the aisles of used books, though he had no customers this afternoon. The plaque on the edge of the desk said, 'John Warwick, proprietor'.

Charles Butler entered the shop, announced by a buzzer. Near the door, a table and two chairs were cooled by the steady breeze of a fan. This told him that Mr Warwick was more than a merchant. Only a man who loved his trade would sacrifice valuable floor space to carve out this niche for weary readers.

The bookseller looked up from his work, peering through thick lenses that enlarged his pale gray eyes. And now Charles could see that the man was not elderly, but closer to his own age of forty. He had been duped by Warwick's premature white hair and slumping shoulders that mimicked a hump. The old-fashioned spectacles had also added to the illusion of extreme age. And, although the room was warm, the sleeves of his frayed white shirt were long and buttoned at the cuffs.

'Mr Warwick?'

This was said in a civil voice, but the bookseller seemed confused. Then he took it as a command to come down from his perch, and he was quick enough to rise from his chair, but slow to descend the shor* flight of steps to the floor. Moving in the cautious manner of one with brittle bones, he shuffled across the room to stand before Charles, then lowered his head and stared at his shoes.

Awaiting orders?

'Uh, could we sit?' Charles gestured toward the readers' table.

Obediently, Warwick eased into a chair, as if he did not trust it to hold his leaf-light body. And now he waited for further instructions. His head was still bowed in resignation, accepting another man's authority over him.

Charles recognized the behavioral cues of a patient or a prisoner, someone who had remained too long in an institution. He quickly ruled out prison. Given Warwick's eccentric masquerade as a senior citizen, the most likely scenario was long-term care in an asylum. The symptoms of institutionalization were so pronounced, the damage of prolonged confinement had likely begun when this man was quite young, perhaps in childhood. He wondered if the cuffs of the shirt hid scars of a razor across the frail wrists. How to proceed with such a delicate soul? Well, gently and with references of course. 'I got your name from a friend of mine. Perhaps you know him. Sergeant Riker?'

Warwick looked up for a moment, then lowered his face to stare at the tabletop, keeping custody of the eyes. Charles pulled out his business card and slid it across the table. The bookseller picked it up with grave suspicion in his myopic eyes. 'This doesn't say what you do.'

A valid point. A long string of academic degrees followed several PhDs behind Charles Butler's name, but the card did not mention his profession, and this had been Mallory's idea, to prod him into word-of-mouth advertising by way of explanation. 'I'm in human resources. I evaluate people with unusual gifts, and then I place them with projects in the private sector or gov—'

'You're a *psychiatrist*.' Warwick spat out this last word as if it had a bad taste.

'No, I'm not.' Charles looked down at the card. 'A few of those degrees *are* in psychology, but I've never been a practicing—'

'And now you're going to tell me that Riker didn't lie to me. Am I right – *Doctor*?' Warwick spoke to the tabletop when he whispered, 'I'm crazy not to believe him. Right again?'

'I've never known Riker to lie.' Charles softened his voice, not wanting the man to acquiesce because of some imagined threat. 'I'm sure he wouldn't—'

'More tricks.' Warwick conquered his ingrained posture of compliance and sat up straight. His eyes darted from one bookshelf to another, then locked with those of his inquisitor. As the little man drew a deep breath, he seemed to be inhaling energy. His voice was stronger now. 'You go back and tell Riker—' One tremulous finger rose from a closed fist, and he pointed it like a weapon. 'You tell him – she's *alive!*'

'Who do you—'

'I'm not senile, if that's what you're thinking. First Markowitz, then—'

'*Louis* Markowitz?'

'You think I'd forget that name? There's nothing wrong with my memory. You tell that to Riker.'

'I didn't come here to examine you.' When Charles smiled, as he did now, he knew it made him look like an escaped fool who had dodged his keeper. Such a silly face. Even the most paranoid of lunatics could not perceive him as a threat.

Warwick relaxed by slow degrees. 'It's been a long time, but I remember everything. She was a rare one. Most runaways are teenagers. The little ones like her, they usually go where they're kicked – juvenile facilities, foster homes. You know how she survived the hunt? She was smarter than them. *So* smart.'

'Them? The police?'

'Markowitz and Riker. They staked out my store. What fools.' Warwick pushed the thick spectacles up the bridge of his nose. 'As if they could ever catch her.'

'Who? What was her—'

'The little girl who loved westerns,' he snapped, as if his interrogator should know this.

Charles called up an old photograph from an archive of eidetic memory. It was the picture that Louis Markowitz had carried in his wallet. Perfect recall included a tear in the protective plastic sleeve. 'This child's hair – was it long and wavy? Was it blond?'

'And matted and dirty.' Warwick nodded. 'Her face was dirty, too.' Eyes focused on some middle ground, he was also looking at a memory. 'Her jeans were always rolled up in fat cuffs. Clothes never fit her – except for the running shoes. They were always spanking white. I think she stole a new pair every week. Markowitz said she was robbing New York City blind. But she never stole from me. She'd take a book off the shelf and put back the last one she borrowed.' He smiled now, but not with happiness, more like defiance. 'You see? I don't forget anything.'

'How long did this stakeout last?'

'Off and on? Two months – and they couldn't catch her.'

Charles recalled a different series of events: Louis had been enroute to his wife's birthday party when he had just *happened* upon a strange child robbing a car. Rather than spend the night filling out paperwork, he had taken Kathy home to the party, and his wife had mistaken the baby felon for a present. What a lovely story – told so many times. Riker was not even mentioned in that version. And nothing had ever been said about stalking, *hunting down* a little girl over a period of months.

'And what was your part in this, Mr Warwick? You just loaned her the books?'

'No, no.' The man was exasperated, perhaps still believing that this was a psychiatric interview, a test of trick questions. 'The girl *took* the books, like she had a right to them. She'd take one, then bring it back. That's how Markowitz figured out that she came from a small town.'

'Pardon?'

'Markowitz said, in her part of the world, my little store was probably the size of a public library. He said to me, "The kid brings the books back because her mother raised her right." Then that bastard confiscated her westerns, all but the last one.'

'The book you traced for him?'

Warwick nodded. 'I had to track down all the buyers at the estate sale where I got the others. He paid me, then put the book on the shelf – so she would find it. But she never did. I never saw her again. The last time Markowitz came in, he told me the little girl was dead. He scribbled a few words in the book, then left it behind.'

'So you know what he wrote on the—'

'It was a love letter to a dead child. The words weren't meant for you.' Warwick sighed, then looked down at his hands. 'He wanted me to believe she was dead, but it was just a trick. He was crying that day. I – almost believed him.'

'Interesting pattern,' said Charles. 'The little girl and her books. She must have come in here quite a few times before you reported her to the police.'

'I never did that. I *never* betrayed her.' The bookseller said this with great pride, as if he had defeated yet another trap of the inquisition.

No, that was wrong.

Charles decided that the man's pride stemmed from honoring some unspoken pact with a child, for he was certain there had been no conversation between the bookseller and young Kathy Mallory. 'I bet you couldn't get within three feet of her.' He was working with Louis Markowitz's description of the feral child raised as his own. 'Edgy as a cat, wasn't she?'

Every detail dropped into its proper slot as Charles arrived at an uncomfortable conclusion: Warwick had not wanted the little girl to be caught and locked away in some institution – like the one that had imprisoned him and probably drugged him every day so he would not pose problems for the staff. Warwick had not seen the comforts of adoption or foster care in Kathy Mallory's future. No, this ex-mental patient had seen a kindred malady in a small child, something abnormal and dark. One sick mind had reached out to a—

Charles shook his head in a futile attempt to empty out this idea. Seeking some better reason that he could believe in, he leaned toward the bookseller. 'Her clothes, her hair – you had to know she was homeless. But you never reported her. Why *not*?'

He saw the question in Warwick's eyes, *Would you buy a lie?* And it was all Charles could do to keep from shouting, *Hell, yes!*

John Warwick reacted as if mere thoughts were screams. He ducked his head under some imagined blow. His bony shoulders were rising, and his chin disappeared into his shirt collar, a frightened turtle in retreat.

With deep apology in his voice, Charles leaned forward to lure the man back out with an easier question. 'What sort of books did she like?'

The man's neck slowly attenuated, eyes still wary, searching the room for hidden enemies. 'Only westerns.' Warwick almost smiled. 'And only one writer.' The agitation had abated, and he seemed merely tired as he leaned back in his chair. 'All of Jake Swain's work went out of print long ago – and for good reason. It was terrible writing. But she read those westerns over and over, the same eleven novels.'

'Any idea why?'

'Who knows?' The bookseller shook his head. 'The child was so small and skinny, so vulnerable – always alone. I suppose she read them for comfort. She always knew what would happen in her books.' Warwick turned his face to the window on the street. 'She never knew what might happen out there.'

FIVE

Sergeant Riker crossed the squad room of Special Crimes Unit, a haphazard arrangement of fifteen desks littered with deli bags, pizza boxes and men with guns. On the far side of the room, a wide glass panel gave him a look inside Lieutenant Coffey's private office, where Mallory stood before the desk, her eyes cast down in the manner of a penitent schoolgirl.

What's wrong with this picture?

The senior detective strolled into the meeting and assumed his usual position, slumped down in the nearest chair with a cigarette dangling at one side of his mouth. After a heavy lunch, Riker was not inclined to waste energy on actual words, and so his eyes merely opened a little wider to say, *Okay, I'm here. What?*

'I understand you sent that kid——' Lieutenant Coffey paused to glare at his sergeant's cigarette, as if that ever worked. 'The guy from Loman's squad – what's his name?'

'Duck Boy.'

'You sent him down to the warehouse to go through eight million boxes of old evidence. I'm guessing you hoped he'd get lost down there.'

Riker shrugged. That had been the general idea, but not *his* idea, and Mallory was not stepping up to claim the credit. She was busy with her upside-down reading of all the lieutenant's paperwork.

'Well, the kid got lucky.' Jack Coffey lifted an evidence carton from the floor and settled it on the edge of his desk. 'It only took him five minutes to find your hangman's rope.'

Mallory seemed not to care. Behind the cover of the carton, she teased a red folder from the mess on the lieutenant's blotter and opened it. Riker caught the glimpse of a full-color autopsy photograph, then turned back to his commanding officer, feigning interest in the adventures of Duck Boy. 'So how did he do it?'

'Last month, the warehouse roof sprung a leak and damaged a few cartons.' Coffey opened the box flaps and pulled out a bulky object in brown wrapping. 'A clerk remembered repackaging the evidence. The paperwork was wrecked, except for a few of the case numbers. So Duck Boy – Let's find another name for him, okay? So the kid used the numbers to pull a file from the ME's archive.'

The lieutenant unwrapped a coil of rope, then knocked the carton to the floor and reached out to grab the red folder from Mallory's hands. 'And this is a twenty-year-old autopsy report. It washes out any connection to Sparrow. So we're kicking the hooker back to the East Side precinct. Now she's Lieutenant Loman's headache.' He dropped the rope and the folder on his desk. 'I guess we're done here.'

With an attitude of *not so fast*, Mallory swept the rope off the desk and into Riker's lap, then opened the ME's folder and spread the contents across the blotter. She tapped a photograph in the center of her array. 'Take a look at this one.'

Riker and Coffey leaned over for a closer inspection of a corpse bloated with gas and thriving maggots.

'This was another scalping.' With one long red fingernail, Mallory called their attention to the blond hair matted and plastered to the woman's skull. 'It was hacked off with a razor.'

The lieutenant's smile said, *Nice try, but no sale.* 'I'm looking at a woman with a short haircut, and I don't see any hair packed in her mouth.'

'She was a blonde,' said Riker. 'Like Sparrow.'

'Not good enough.' Coffey rooted through the companion

paperwork, then handed a sheaf of stapled pages to Riker. 'Here, read the report.' The woman was found hanging, but that wasn't the cause of death. Dr Norris was chief medical examiner in those days. He said she was strangled first.'

'Wouldn't be the first time that hack got something wrong.' Mallory sifted through the other photographs. 'Markowitz said he was drunk half the time.'

'No.' Riker slapped the desk. 'I remember that old bastard. He was drunk *all* the time.'

Coffey clasped his hands behind his head and leaned back in his chair. 'So, you guys think a pathologist, drunk or sober, could overlook a wad of hair packed in a victim's mouth?'

'Last night, a *pathologist* pronounced Sparrow dead,' said Mallory.

The lieutenant's smile widened. 'That's pretty lame.'

The boss was entirely too cheerful, and this made Riker uneasy. Though he had no faith in premonitions, he did have a clear vision of Jack Coffey digging a deep pit for Mallory, then concealing it with twigs and branches.

And there was no way to warn her.

She picked up the old autopsy report and leaned over the desk to dangle it in front of the lieutenant's face. 'Did you *read* this?' Her unmistakable implication was that fault had somehow shifted on to Coffey. 'No one assisted on this autopsy. And that's odd, because Markowitz said it took two assistants to cover the old drunk's mistakes. Norris *never* worked alone.'

Jack Coffey was unimpressed. 'Your point?'

'He wouldn't want any witnesses if he was suppressing evidence. So he omitted a few things from the—'

'No, I don't think so.' Coffey ripped the report from her hand.

Fun's over.

The lieutenant was not smiling anymore. 'All right, Mallory. Let's talk about another fairy tale. The old file in Cold Cases? Nobody on that squad remembers a search request from you. I ordered you to requisition that file. I can guess why you didn't waste the time.' He looked down at the report to refresh his memory. 'Natalie Homer. Her murder was never one of their cases.'

'They're lying,' said Mallory. 'They lost the file.'

Even Coffey had to admire gall on such a grandiose scale. 'You're telling me they were too embarrassed to admit they lost a file? So they *lied*?'

'That's right,' said Detective Janos. Three heads turned to the open doorway and a man built like a refrigerator with salt-and-pepper hair. 'Natalie Homer *is* a Cold Case file.' Janos's soft voice was at odds with a face that resembled mugbook shots of the most violent offenders. 'They assigned it to an independent.'

'So they lost the paperwork *and* Mallory's request?' Coffey was not yet convinced. 'And they *lied* about it?' His tone of voice implied that a lying cop might be a new concept in this room.

'Take the charitable view.' Janos smiled. 'Cold Cases moved to a new office. They're a little disorganized. If the boys didn't make a copy before they released the folder, they'd never find it again. The copy holds the transfer sheet. Very minimalist filing system. So, today, a hanged hooker is big news – front pages. And they get a request for a connected file – a *lost* file. Yeah, I think they'd lie to you, boss.'

'But *you* found the file?'

'Better than that,' said Janos. 'The name of the catching detective was in the ME's report. So I took a ride over to his last known address. This old guy answers the door – he's got the damn file in his hand. He says to me, "What took you so long?" And here we are.' Janos nodded toward the stairwell door on the other side of the squad room. 'That's Lars Geldorf.'

Riker swiveled his chair around to face the window on the squad room and a lean, white-haired man. 'He's gotta be seventy-five years old.'

Lars Geldorf had grown tired of waiting for a summons, and now he walked toward the lieutenant's office, not hobbling but making good time. No one had told this retired detective that he had grown old. He wore a silk suit in the best tradition of all the young Turks of his day. The swagger agreed with an arrogant smile, and anyone could read his mind: Geldorf was thinking, *I'm going to save your damn hides.*

'He's gonna be trouble,' said Coffey.

Riker agreed. He was reminded of his own father, another cop who had not had the grace to take up knitting after being pensioned off. Geldorf had the same way of walking, as if he owned all the real estate under his feet. The old man strolled into the private office and shook Coffey's hand in silence, trusting that his name and his fame had preceded him. Then he opened his suit jacket, so as not to wrinkle the silk when he sat down.

Just like Dad.

Riker noticed more trouble when the suit jacket opened. Geldorf wore a revolver holstered at the hip. The old man was definitely back in the game.

Lieutenant Coffey dropped his polite smile. 'I understand you've got something for me.'

'It's all in here.' The retired detective held up a zippered pouch with the smell of new leather. 'The Natalie Homer case. I got the details on your perp's MO from the morning paper.' His eyes narrowed with a foxy smile. 'Too bad you couldn't keep the press away from the crime scene.' This was an unmistakable criticism, for he had done an excellent job of keeping his own case details under wraps. Until today, no one had ever heard of the twenty-year-old hanging of Natalie Homer.

Jack Coffey held up the old autopsy folder. 'But your case didn't have the same MO.'

'Oh, yeah,' said Geldorf. 'It *did*. Every detail matches.'

'Natalie Homer's autopsy didn't mention any hair in her mouth.' And the newspapers had made much of that. Coffey opened the red folder and glanced at the first page of the old report. 'The chief medical examiner was—'

'Dr Peter Norris,' said Geldorf. 'A drunk and a third-rate hack. I'm glad he's dead. And you're wrong, son. *I* pulled the hair out of her mouth before the meat wagon showed up.' He leaned back and smiled in self-congratulation. 'In those days, all the worst press leaks came from the medical examiner's office.'

Lieutenant Coffey read aloud from the old autopsy report, ' "Manual strangulation." According to the ME, your victim was strangled *before* she was strung up.'

'Oh, yeah. What a psycho.' Geldorf smiled. 'Or maybe he only wanted it to look that way.' He glanced up at Mallory. 'What's your theory?'

'I like the psycho,' she said.

The old man turned to Riker. 'And what about you? I'll give you a hint. You wouldn't expect the victim to have a coil of rope lying around the house.'

Riker only drummed his fingers on the arm of the chair. He recognized all the signs of this ritual – Learning from the Master of Old Farts. Previously, he had believed that this was his father's invention, a game devised to drive his son insane. He reached over to take the leather pouch from the retired detective. It was a tense moment, for this file was Geldorf's ticket to ride with Special Crimes Unit, and he would not loosen his grip. Mallory caught the old man's eyes and silently conveyed a threat, *Hey, this is going to happen, old man.* And Geldorf's hand slowly opened. Riker grabbed the pouch and unzipped it, then riffled the contents. 'So what happened to the hair you took from her mouth?'

'It's with the rest of the evidence. After the case went cold, I packed it myself.'

Lieutenant Coffey shook his head. 'No hair.'

'So they lost it,' said Geldorf with a casual lift of one shoulder. 'Happens all the time.'

Riker handed the lieutenant a photograph from the pouch. Natalie Homer's mouth was stuffed with a gag of wadded blond hair.

Detective Janos stood behind Geldorf's chair and leaned down to the old man's ear to say, 'Tell them about the candles.'

What the hell?

Twenty-four candles and a jar of dead flies were the only details not mentioned in the morning papers. Why would Janos confide in the old man? Riker glanced through the rest of the crime-scene photos, but found no pictures of votive candles.

'That summer, the East Village had rolling blackouts,' said Geldorf. 'The electricity was off for three hours after sundown, and Natalie had three candles in her apartment.'

Mallory pulled a bag of melted red wax from the carton. The long tapers were fused together.

'Now you see?' said Geldorf. 'This is how they treat evidence. Those candles were brand-new. Check out the wicks. Never been lit. So I figure the perp showed up while it was still light. Early evening works with Norris's call for time of death.'

The candles were the right color, red, but the wrong shape. Riker counted only three candles – not the dozens found in Sparrow's apartment.

Geldorf was awaiting a compliment on his astute reading of three unlit wicks.

'Nice work.' There was no sarcasm in the lieutenant's voice, though the old man had botched the chain of evidence. Jack Coffey was always respectful to the visiting ghosts. 'I need a few minutes alone with my people. Detective Janos will look after you.'

When the office door had closed on Geldorf and his keeper, Coffey shook his head. 'There's still no case connection.' He held up the photograph Riker had given him. 'This perp has to be in his forties by now, and stringing up blondes is a young man's game.' He tossed the picture back to Riker. 'You guys don't have a serial killer. And Sparrow's still alive. You don't even have a corpse yet.'

Riker turned to his partner. Mallory had been raised by the best poker player in the universe. She was the source of all his hopes for keeping Sparrow's case in Special Crimes Unit.

'I say he's picking out another victim right now.' Mallory took the pouch from Riker's hand and held it up as her hole card. 'I can link these two cases.'

'You think so?' Coffey bent down to the carton at his feet and pulled out a plastic bag with a smaller segment of the rope. It was not a good container for water-damaged evidence. Riker could smell mildew when the lieutenant opened the bag. And now he was staring at a classic hangman's noose with a neat row of coils below the loop.

Sparrow's case was lost.

'Try explaining this away.' Coffey reached into a stack of paperwork and pulled out a photograph of the more recent hanging. 'The nooses aren't the same, not even close. Sparrow's has a simple knot.' He held up the rope used on Natalie Homer. 'This one is guaranteed to kill. If your perp knew how to tie a hangman's noose, why didn't he use it on the hooker?'

Mallory kept her silence. She only stared at the noose, the last piece of evidence Coffey had been withholding, waiting for her to show him everything she had. It looked like a clear victory for the boss, yet Riker sensed that the man's graceful-winner smile was premature, that Mallory was not quite played out.

Jack Coffey continued. 'You know why this case bothered your old man? Markowitz didn't know the hanging was just for show. The autopsy report was sealed. He never knew the woman was strangled before she was hung.'

'He *knew!*'

'*Prove* it!'

Mallory pulled a battered notebook from her back pocket and handed it to the lieutenant. 'You're wrong about the hanging.'

Even without the reading glasses that Riker never wore, he recognized Lou Markowitz's handwriting as Jack Coffey flipped through illegible pages of shorthand punctuated by single words.

Coffey looked up at Mallory. 'I can't even read most of the—'

'I can,' she said. 'The tape on Natalie's wrists was so tight it dug

74

into her skin. But no sign of cut-off circulation. And you won't find that in the autopsy report — *another* screwup. Markowitz could read a corpse better than that drunk Norris. He knew the perp bound a dead woman's hands. He *knew* she was dead before she was hanged, and that rope *still* bothered him.'

Lieutenant Coffey closed the notebook. 'You just made my case. It was a garden variety murder dressed up like a psycho hanging.'

'No! The killer always planned to hang Natalie Homer, but something went wrong.'

'That's reaching, Mallory.'

'If the perp didn't plan on a hanging, why would he bring a rope?' She snatched the old notebook from the lieutenant's hand, then stalked out of the office. An outsider would have read her exit as cold anger. Coffey did. In reality, Mallory simply had a flawless sense of timing. And the time was now.

'Makes sense,' said Riker.

'The hell it does. Natalie Homer's dead body was in that apartment from Friday till Sunday night. Lots of time for the perp to come back with his rope. She's forcing these cases to link.'

'Everything she said panned out.' And Riker would have regarded this as a miracle, but what were the odds that God was on Mallory's side? 'And you gotta wonder what else she found in Lou's notes.' He silently complimented his partner on her early departure with the notebook. 'Give us a week. How's it gonna look if another body turns up *after* you bounce Sparrow's case back to Loman's squad?'

'That's crap, Riker. There's no connection here, and you *know* it. All you've got is two women with bad haircuts and lots of rope.' Coffey covered his face with one hand, for it would never do to let the troops see his frustration. 'So here's the deal. You keep Geldorf and his file out of my shop. And he *never* gets a look at Sparrow's evidence.'

'Deal.' The detective tapped out his cigarette on the sole of his shoe, then rose from the chair. He was uncomfortable with this win. It was going too smoothly.

The lieutenant gathered loose papers and photographs into the red folder. 'And keep Geldorf away from the reporters. I don't wanna read any headlines about a trumped-up case connection.' He tossed the ME's file to Riker, then dropped the rope into the cardboard box at his feet. 'And get this crap out of my office.'

Riker leaned down and picked up the evidence carton. 'I've got a place to stash everything – the old man too.' The boss would not want to hear the name Butler and Company, no hint that Mallory's ties to that firm were still binding.

'Good,' said Coffey. 'If you can't make a case in forty-eight hours, you lose the hooker to Loman.' He lowered his head, pretending interest in the papers on his desk blotter. 'I called the hospital. It doesn't look good for the hooker. She's going sour.' He looked up. 'Sorry about that. You and Sparrow go back a long ways, don't you?'

Riker nodded. He understood everything now. His partner had entrusted him with the endgame, the humiliating part, for Jack Coffey had just made it very clear that this was only charity for an aging detective and a dying whore.

Lars Geldorf opened the door, and Mallory followed him into an apartment that stank of stale ashtrays and yesterday's meals. The frayed furnishings and a small-screen television set were character references for an honest cop living within the means of his pension. A large mirror over the mantelpiece reflected light from windows overlooking Hell's Kitchen along Eighth Avenue. There were no signs that a woman had ever lived here. The dust was thick, the window glass was yellowed with the nicotine of a million cigarettes, and the walls were all about Geldorf.

Framed newspaper clippings were grouped with photographs of his younger self posed with politicians and cops who had died before Mallory was born. One citation hung by itself in the most impressive frame. It was hardly evidence of a stellar career, but he obviously took great pride in it.

The retired detective paused to rock on his heels and smile, to allow time for his guest to admire these mementos. Then he led her into the next room, where another large mirror had pride of place. It almost covered a line of cracked plaster, but its real purpose was less functional. The old man stood before the looking glass, a peacock in a silk suit that was decades out of style. His gold pinky ring gleamed as he straightened his tie and smiled, *loving* what he saw. And now he pointed to another cluster of photographs. 'That one in the middle was taken the night we cut Natalie down. I shot it myself.'

Mallory stared at the framed crime-scene photo. The hair had been removed from the victim's mouth. The prone corpse lay on the floor, displayed in an open body bag, and two grinning detectives stood over the dead woman, posed as hunters with a trophy kill. But the real trophy was the third man, only a visitor on this scene, a celebrated cop who stood between the case detectives and a head above them. The two grinning men appeared to be restraining Louis Markowitz, an unwilling subject for a macabre souvenir. His face was slightly blurred by the sad shake of his head.

Below this photograph was a desk buried under papers and flanked by file cabinets. The most modern piece of office equipment was an early-generation fax machine. Cartons were piled on cheap metal storage shelves, and two large bulletin boards were littered with personal notes. The absence of a computer was no surprise to Mallory. This old man still lived in the century of the typewriter.

'I don't see why we can't work out of my place.' Geldorf pulled a large box from a shelf. 'I'm all set up here.'

'Coffey wants tight security,' she lied. 'And a downtown location is better.'

'Tight security.' Geldorf nodded. 'Good idea.'

The box bearing Natalie Homer's name had been half full when he began to load in more papers. Cartons this size did not travel with Cold Case files. A thick folder should have been sufficient for reports and statements. 'You've been working this murder for a while?'

'Oh yeah, I never let go of a case I couldn't close on the job,' said Geldorf. 'After I retired, I just kept collecting stuff, scraps and pieces. When I was ready to do more interviews, I'd check out the Cold Case file and make it official.'

'So you only work your own cases?'

'That's right. You should've seen this room twelve years ago. So many cartons, you couldn't move. You had to go out in the hall to change your mind.' He waited for her to smile at his little joke – and he waited. Then, slowly, he turned around to face the shelves that were bare. 'So, one by one, I'd close another Cold Case file, get rid of another box, another ghost. Now I've only got a few left.' He lowered his head and focused on the task of packing his box. 'When I was on the job, I only got days to work a murder. Now I got years.' His smile was sheepish when he said, 'I shouldn't have told you. Now you know what a lousy detective I was. But I'm gonna make it right. I'll close 'em – every one.' He dropped more papers into his carton, then folded the cardboard flaps. 'I'm all yours now – full time.'

'And I appreciate that.' She had already laid plans to keep him out of her way. The baby-sitting detail would be split between Charles Butler and Lieutenant Loman's whiteshield, also known as Duck Boy.

She donned her sunglasses, then turned around for a sidelong look at the mirror and Geldorf's reflection. She had been wrong about the peacock trait. All the posturing arrogance fell away when he believed that he was unobserved. It must have been a great strain to keep up that façade. The old man in the looking-glass room shrank and sagged, and his eyes were full of worry. He must see every young cop as a potential threat to his dignity.

Good.

Keeping him in line would be no problem.

Geldorf sealed the box flaps with tape. 'So now you'll wanna talk to everybody who saw my crime scene.' He glanced in her direction. 'You're wondering how your perp found out about the hair in Natalie's mouth.'

Mallory turned around to smile at him. *Crafty old man.* 'You knew it wasn't a serial killing.'

'Couldn't be.' His sly grin explained everything: He had simply wanted to come back to the job – to come in from the cold of his old age. 'My prime suspect died nineteen years ago.'

She almost liked him. With only an exchange of nods and knowing glances, mutual admissions of lies were made and vows of silence taken. They were allies now, and neither of them would give the other away.

'At best, what you got is a copycat.' He lifted the heavy box in his arms, and she showed him respect by not offering to help with the load. Geldorf walked behind her, saying, 'When I find out where your perp got his information, maybe I can close out Natalie's case. Oh, yeah, I think we can help each other.'

You can dream, old man.

She had no intention of working Natalie Homer's homicide. The trail was twenty years old and a cold one. She opened the door for Geldorf, then took his proffered keys and locked it.

'The link is in the details.' He struggled with the bulky carton as they walked toward the elevator. 'I had complete control over my crime scene. No leaks to the media. You know how I pulled that off? I told a uniform to take bribes from the reporters. Well, this kid gets twenty bucks a piece from those bastards, then tells 'em he found the woman swingin' from a rope.'

'So they figured it was a suicide.' Mallory approved. It was always wise to tell the truth when you lied. 'And Natalie Homer got lost on page ten.'

'And just one newspaper, a couple of lousy paragraphs.' He set down the box and pushed a button to call for the elevator. 'So now you'll wanna rule out the possible leaks. Lucky I saved my old case notes.'

Yeah, right.

'You can handle those interviews,' said Mallory. 'I got you an

79

assistant to go along as your badge.' Then she would be rid of Geldorf *and* Duck Boy.

'What about the big guy? Butler? Was that his name?' Geldorf pulled out a card given to him an hour ago at the offices of Butler and Company.

'*Doctor* Butler,' said Mallory, though Charles had never used that title. 'He's a consulting psychologist with NYPD.' Fortunately, there was no useful information on the business card to contradict that lie. 'He'll be working closely with you.'

Charles Butler wore a suit and tie, for this was a workday. Many thanks to Riker's intervention, the tedium of a summer hiatus was finally at an end. He passed through the reception area of Queen Anne furniture and Watteau watercolors, then strolled down a short hall, leaving behind centuries of antique decor that separated the other rooms from Mallory's domain of electronics, of plastic and metal and wire. Her private office at the rear of Butler and Company had some charming features. However, the tall arched windows were hidden behind cold steel blinds, and a plain gray rug strove to disguise the hardwood floor as concrete.

Her three computers sat atop workstations perfectly aligned at the center of the room, and all the monitors were lit. Square blue cyclops eyes focused upon the intruder, and Charles recalled his old dream of kicking in the glass and blinding the little bastards.

The free space of three walls was devoted to gray metal shelving units stocked with manuals lined up precisely one inch from the edge and software components keeping company with hardware. Mallory had refused his offer of paintings, preferring not to clutter the giant bulletin board that covered her fourth wall from baseboard to ceiling molding.

Sergeant Riker was still at work pinning photographs and papers to the cork surface. The detective had given Charles a new project, a present, actually *two* gifts: a twenty-year-old murder and a seventy-five-year-old man.

'When will they be back?'

'Half an hour, give or take.' Riker sifted through the contents of a leather pouch and selected more papers. Handwritten notes and typed statements had been arranged on the wall in no particular order.

'All this to pacify Mr Geldorf?'

'Yeah,' said Riker. 'Think it might keep you busy for a while?'

'Absolutely, and thank you.' Charles was wondering how to broach another subject without seeming ungrateful. He decided that oblique angles were best. 'After Louis died, did Mallory keep any of those old westerns?'

'No!' Riker dropped the pouch on the floor, then bent down to retrieve it.

'What a pity.' Charles faced the wall and studied a diagram of the murder victim's apartment. 'I wanted to read the books, maybe figure out what Louis saw in them. I suppose I can track down other copies, but that—'

'No, you can't.' Riker turned his back on Charles to pin up the full-color photograph of a gutted woman on a dissection table. 'You can't get 'em anymore. Just cheap paperbacks. Nothing you'd find on a library shelf.'

'That's what John Warwick said – almost the same words.'

Riker spread one hand flat on the cork and slowly leaned into the wall. He bowed his head, perhaps bracing for the accusations, a litany of deceits, years of lies, his own and Louis's.

If that were true, he would wait forever.

Charles sat down at the edge of Mallory's steel desk. He waited patiently until Riker turned round to face him, and then he smiled for the man. His inadvertently foolish expression had the same relaxing effect on the detective as it had had on John Warwick. 'Perhaps you could just tell me what happened in the next book?'

'Yeah, give me a second.' Riker settled into a metal folding chair and remembered to exhale. He was obviously relieved, perhaps assuming that nothing more had transpired between John Warwick and a disappointed customer. 'It's been a while. You remember the plot of the first book?'

Charles nodded. 'A fifteen-year-old boy shot a man in the street.'

'An *unarmed* man. In the next book, you find out that cowboy had a gun after all, and it was a fair fight.' Riker turned his head for one furtive glance at the office door. Assured that they were alone, he continued, 'The kid took the other guy's six-shooter 'cause it was better than his old rusty one. But the sheriff never saw that second gun. The kid had it stashed in his belt *before* Peety got to the crime scene.'

Subsequently, Charles learned that the lawman had remained unaware of this exculpatory evidence – while the boy was growing into premature manhood as a fugitive.

'Now they're a year older,' said Riker, 'Sheriff Peety and the kid.' And it was miles too late for the boy to clear his name. 'Wichita won another gunfight and killed another man.'

Riker glanced at the door again, knowing that he would never hear Mallory coming up behind him. She was that quiet. He turned back to Charles and his story. 'The kid's name is no joke anymore. He's a bona fide gunslinger, a real outlaw. At the end of the first book, the sheriff runs him right off the rim of a canyon, a three-hundred-foot drop. The kid was still in the saddle at the time. Down he goes, horse and all.'

'But he survived.'

'Yeah, the horse too. When the next book opens, the kid lands in the river, and the fall knocks him out. He gets washed ashore beside his half-dead horse. An Indian girl finds him and drags him back to her village. She's his age, just sixteen. On the last page, the sheriff's chasin' Wichita again, and the girl buys the kid some time. She throws herself under the sheriff's galloping horse.' He splayed his hands to say, *You see how it works?* He tossed the leather pouch to Charles. 'You and Geldorf can finish setting up the wall, okay? Play detective. Knock yourself out.'

Charles's smile was brief, merely polite this time. The detective had made an interesting point, but the aspect of cliffhanger suspense did not explain why anyone would bother to read the novels twice. And young Kathy Mallory had read them again and again. Why?

The bookseller's theory of a child needing comfort from a fictional world would not hold up. Charles glanced at the surrounding shelves of dry technical journals and reference books. Mallory never read fiction. Louis Markowitz had once told him what a fight it had been to instill a sense of make-believe in his foster daughter, and ultimately he had lost that battle. To Louis's sorrow, she had remained a hardened realist throughout her childhood.

And though she had displayed an early penchant for cowboy movies, he had surmised long ago that it was largely for the companionship of Louis that the little girl had indulged the man in Saturday mornings of gunfights and cavalry charges. From what Charles knew of the early warfare between foster father and daughter, young Kathy would rather have died than admit to this need for his company. For all the years that man and child had known one another and loved one another, she had kept Louis at a distance, never addressing him in any form but Hey Cop and Markowitz.

Charles wondered if Kathy Mallory regretted that now. He thought she might.

Lieutenant Coffey and Detective Janos looked up when Duck Boy appeared in the doorway and hovered there in respectful silence, waiting to be noticed.

Coffey motioned him into the room. 'Yeah, kid, what is it?'

'Sir, I finished all my paperwork.' He held a thick sheaf of papers in his hand.

'If that's the report on the warehouse—'

'No, sir. It's something Sergeant Riker requested, but I can't find him. Do you want it? Does *anybody* want it?'

The lieutenant accepted the report, briefly noted Duck Boy's other name on the first page, then dumped it into his out-basket at the edge of the desk. 'Deluthe, you did good work today. But the paperwork goes to Riker and Mallory from now on.' He turned to Janos. 'Did they give you an address?' What his tone implied was clear: *I don't want to know where they are.*

And now his detective was writing in his notebook, saying to Deluthe, 'This is where you can find them.'

The younger man nodded and stared at the basket with his discarded report. 'So you'd rather have *them* not read it?'

Jack Coffey leaned back in his chair and smiled. There was a brain at work here. At least, the boy had the makings of a smart mouth. And the rookie detective had earned a fair hearing. 'Okay, sit down.'

Ronald Deluthe settled into a chair next to Janos.

'You can report to me,' said Coffey. 'But I only want the gist of it, okay?'

'Yes, sir. I spoke to the mobile news crew. The other night, they were in the area following up on a lead. That's why they got to the crime scene ahead of the fire engines. They were just cruising up and down—'

Damn, a speechmaker. 'What was their lead?'

'Well, this guy phoned in a tip an hour before the prostitute was hung. The news show has a public line called *Cashtip*. But that wasn't the first call they taped. The—'

Janos leaned forward. 'The station *taped* these calls? The news director only gave Mallory video. *Bastards*. So they were holding out on us.' He slapped the trainee on the back. 'That was real nice work, kid.'

'Thank you, sir.' Deluthe continued his dry recital of facts. 'They had another tip for a homicide a few blocks from the crime scene, but that one was last week, and it didn't pan out.'

'So let's get past that,' said Coffey.

'Yes, sir. So the same guy calls back to tip them on Sparrow's murder. This time, he didn't give a name or address. He just told them to look for the smoke. Well, they didn't plan to send out their mobile unit. This guy burned them once before. But then, it turned out to be a slow news day, and they decided—' And now Deluthe must have sensed that interest was waning. His voice trailed off as he said, 'Well, I guess that's the gist.'

Janos put one meaty hand on Deluthe's arm. 'Back up, kid. What about the first tip – the murder that *didn't* pan out?'

'That was five or six days ago. The tipster gave them a name and specific location. But when the news van got to Ms Harper's building, the neighbors told them she was in Bermuda. Then the reporters went to the local police station, and a desk sergeant told them the same thing. He said Ms Harper had gone to—'

'Hold it.' Coffey retrieved the report from his basket. 'How did a cop know where she was? Did this woman ever file a complaint?'

'I don't know, sir. I only spoke to the television people.'

Detective Janos was shaking his head. 'You never mentioned this to Mallory or Riker?'

'It was in my report, but I—'

'Yeah, yeah.' Janos moved around behind the desk and scanned the pages, reading over the lieutenant's shoulder. 'The address is there. I'll get a warrant on Harper's apartment. It's worth a look. Maybe Mallory was right about the perp going serial.'

Jack Coffey pretended not to hear that. He smiled at Deluthe. 'Good work. *Damn* good work. So you got the perp's voice on tape?'

'No, sir. I asked the news director for a copy, but he said that would compromise the integrity of his—'

'Janos!'

'Yeah, boss.'

'Go get that tape!'

Charles stared at the old photographs taken after the body was cut down. Among Natalie Homer's few shabby possessions, all that was hopeful were the potholders, each one decked with a red bud, the promise of a rose. He had come to think of this woman, twenty years dead, in a possessive way, for Riker and Mallory showed so little interest in her. And he had developed a bond with Lars Geldorf, the lady's only champion.

'I'm not sure I follow you.' The retired detective paced the length of the cork wall with the attitude of an inspector general.

'It's a homage to an old friend,' said Charles Butler. 'Did you know the first commander of Special Crimes Unit?'

'Lou Markowitz?' said Geldorf. 'Oh, yeah, I met him once. He was on my crime scene – just stopped by to talk to my partner. Great cop. It was a goddamn pleasure to shake his hand.' He turned back to the mess on the wall. 'Sorry, you were saying?'

'Well, Louis's office used to have a cork wall like this one. It took me a while to figure out his logic. You see, it emerged as he shuffled things around every day.' Charles pointed to one cluster of papers held by a single tack. 'The top layers have pertinent information that overrides what's underneath. You can see the progression of the case at a glance. No time wasted on bad leads and insignificant data. And there's relevance in the juxtaposition. Oh, and prioritizing. The least relevant items are on the outer edges.'

'Not bad, Dr Butler. Not bad at all.'

'Call me Charles.' He was entitled to a doctor's credential, in fact several of them, but his background in abnormal psychology only served as an adjunct to client evaluations. Perhaps a practicing psychologist would have predicted Mallory's reaction.

He heard no footsteps behind him, and only turned around because of Riker's comment from the doorway, a soft 'Jesus Christ.' The words were outside of Geldorf's hearing range. The old man kept his eyes on the cork, and Charles kept watch over Mallory. How long had she been standing there in the center of the room? She took no notice of him, and the moment was almost like stealing, for he was free to stare at her, unafraid that his tell-all face would say foolish things.

He had been working close to the wall for hours, and now he stepped back to see it from Mallory's vantage point. A frozen whirlwind of papers and pictures spiraled out from the center pastiche of crime-scene images. It was the jumble of a brain turned inside out, exposing a unique thinking process, trains of thought splashed over the wall in a starburst pattern as Louis Markowitz's mind of paper debris reached out, stretching – awakening.

Without a word, and unnoticed by Geldorf, she left the room. Riker put up one hand in the manner of a traffic cop, warning Charles not to follow her, then disappeared down the hall. A few moments later, the door in the reception area slammed shut.

Lars Geldorf called his attention to the square crime-scene photographs. 'These are the originals. The blow-ups might be easier to read.'

'I thought the size was unusual.' The Polaroids were much smaller than the eight-by-ten pictures once pinned to the cork wall of Louis's office. Charles pointed to a photograph of the corpse hanging from a light fixture. 'What's this dark area on her apron?'

'Grease. And those spots are cockroaches.' Geldorf leaned down to the cardboard carton at his feet and picked up an envelope. 'I had enlargements made.' He pulled out a group of pictures. 'Now these are grainy, but you can see the bugs better.'

'Indeed.' They were gigantic.

'Oh, you like bugs? I got shots of flies and maggots too.' Geldorf opened another envelope, and this one contained twice as many insects, all in very sharp focus. 'A medical examiner took these shots. That old bastard *loved* bugs. A drunk *and* a freak.'

Charles leafed through the images. 'I gather he was an amateur entomologist.' None of the medical examiner's photographs included cockroaches. 'It seems he preferred flies and larvae.'

The fax machine rang, bringing Riker back to Mallory's office in an uncharacteristic hurry. The detective watched a sheet scroll out of the machine, then ripped it off and left the room.

'I'll be right back.' Charles walked down the hall, following the sound of a one-way conversation. He found the detective in the reception area, slumped in a chair behind the antique desk and speaking into a telephone that was circa 1900.

'Oh, the warrant was easy,' said Riker to the caller. 'But the super didn't have keys to Harper's apartment.' One leg was on the rise, then settled back to the floor; Mallory had trained him not to put his feet up on office furniture. 'I'll make the calls for Heller and Slope . . . Yeah, the locksmith just opened the place . . . Right. Mallory's already on the way.'

Riker set the ornate receiver back on its cradle, then looked past Charles to the young man who had just emerged from the office kitchen with a sandwich in hand. 'Kid? You're driving. Go get your car and pull it up front. I'll be down in a minute.'

The recent fax wafted from Riker's hand to the desk. Charles read the words, *Guys, come home. All is forgiven. Love, Special Crimes Unit.* 'Did Jack Coffey send that?'

'Naw, too affectionate for the boss. And he's still pretending Mallory doesn't work here anymore.' Riker looked down at the fax. 'No, I'd say this is Janos's style.'

'There's been another hanging?'

The detective shrugged into the sleeves of his suit jacket. 'Good guess, and keep it to yourself. Yeah, Mallory was right. We got a serial killer.' He paused with one hand on the doorknob. Without turning round, he said, 'Tell me something, Charles. Would you want to live in a world where all of Mallory's lies came true?'

SIX

They were exiles now, locked out of the room. This was Heller's punishment for breaking a commandment of Forensics: Thou shalt not disturb my freaking crime scene.

The detectives' walk-through had turned into a run-through, battling fat black insects on the wing and biting back vomit all the way to a rear window that had not been dusted for prints. Now Mallory sat outside on the steps of the fire escape, keeping her partner company. The air was sweeter here, but muggy and almost too thick to breathe. The sun was hot, the day was dead calm, and cigarette smoke hung about Riker in a stale cloud.

On the other side of the locked window, most of the insects were still trapped in the apartment. Their buzzing penetrated the glass, loud and incessant. A ripe corpse had emptied its bowels postmortem, attracting every blowfly in the neighborhood and adding to the odor of putrid flesh.

Mallory looked down through the metal grate. More civilians had joined the gathering below. There was nothing to see, but New York was a theater town, and the yellow crime-scene tape was the cue to form a sidewalk gallery. Last week, the killer had probably stood on that same patch of pavement. After calling the reporters to his crime scene, he would have stayed to watch them enter this building, then leave, unimpressed with his work. 'I wonder how long the perp waited for the cops to show. Hours? Days?'

'Must've driven him nuts.' Riker took a drag on his cigarette. 'I've got uniforms canvassing the block. We might get lucky.'

No, Mallory doubted that they would turn up any witnesses who recalled a man loitering on the sidewalk. Too much time had passed between the death and the discovery of the corpse.

Riker flicked his cigarette over the rail of the fire escape. 'I wonder if we'll find any more bodies, maybe a few in worse shape.'

'Not likely. Janos said there were only two calls on the *Cashtip* line.' And despite the killer's telephoned confession and a reporter's visit to the local police station, Kennedy Harper's body had been left to rot for six days in the heat of August. 'He must've figured the cops just weren't paying attention.'

'Well, he got that part right,' said Riker. 'And now we know why he burned Sparrow's window shade. Hard to miss a woman hanging in full view of the street. He wanted a guaranteed audience for his second show.'

Heller stood on the other side of the glass, raising the sash. 'Okay, all the windows are open, and the worst of the stink is gone. You two delicate little pansies can come back inside.'

Without being asked, the tenants kept their distance from the stench of the crime scene. They were gathered at the other end of a long hallway, where Ronald Deluthe questioned a man with greasy coveralls. A large cluster of keys dangled from his utility belt.

'You're the building handyman, the super?'

'Good guess, kid.'

Deluthe could translate that to mean *Who else would I be, you moron?* Not a promising beginning for his first interview of the day, but he pressed on. 'So a body is rotting away for maybe a week, but you never smelled *anything?*' He paused a moment to flick a fly off his face. 'Nobody complained?' An army of insects walked up the walls, and some were strolling across the ceiling.

The high-pitched whine of a woman chimed in behind the detective's back. 'Oh, we complained all right! You think this lazy slob would take six minutes to check it out?'

The far door opened and Mallory stepped into the hall in time to catch the handyman demonstrating a New York gesture for love and friendship, his middle finger extended from a closed fist.

'Harper got new locks!' The man edged closer to the whining tenant so he could yell in her face, 'And I got no keys for 'em! You want I should break down her damn door?'

At the other end of the hall, Mallory called out to Deluthe, 'Chase down the locksmith. Find out when he was here.'

'Oh, I can tell you that.' The handyman's keys jangled as he turned to flash a lewd grin at the pretty detective. 'It was two weeks ago. I watched him do the work.' His eyes undressed Mallory layer by layer, removing her blazer, her T-shirt, her bra.

And now *he* was the focus of *her* attention. 'Was Kennedy Harper home that day?'

'Yeah.' His eyes traveled all over her body. 'So?'

The detective's long legs were encased in blue jeans, but in the handyman's eyes, they were naked. He looked up, suddenly startled. She was moving toward him with long strides and swinging a camera from its strap like a weapon.

Ronald Deluthe wondered if she was only pissed off, or had he missed something – again.

Mallory stood toe-to-toe with the man in coveralls. 'You had keys to the other locks.' This was an accusation.

'Sure. I got keys for the whole building.'

That was so obvious. The buckle on the man's utility belt sagged from the weight of his keys, each one tagged with an apartment number. And now Deluthe waited for some caustic comment from the witness, but the handyman kept a respectful silence, for Mallory stood with one hand on her hip, exposing the shoulder holster and a very large gun. Her eyes were even more intimidating. Did she ever blink? She took two quick steps toward the handyman, who had nowhere to go but flat up against the wall.

'Why don't you have the new keys? You were here with the locksmith. Harper was home that day.'

'I *asked* for 'em. She wouldn't give 'em to me.'

Mallory looked down at the cluster of tags and metal hanging in front of the man's crotch. He squirmed when she reached for it.

'You've still got the old ones.' Mallory stared at the key tag for apartment 4B. 'You had access *before* she changed the locks.'

'And she had no problem with that.' He was a model citizen now, eager to help and talking fast. 'Five years and no complaints. Then one day, out of the blue, I'm a suspicious character. She can't trust me with her damn keys. Go figure.' He turned to Deluthe. 'Don't write that down, kid.'

Deluthe folded his notebook into a pocket, then took out his Miranda card to read the prime suspect his rights. 'You have the right to remain—'

'What are you doing?' Mallory took his card away, then handed him the camera. 'We're done with this man. Go outside and take pictures.'

Deluthe nodded. He was growing accustomed to humiliation and busywork. The killer had no way to know that the body had been discovered, not this time. He would not be among the onlookers. This was Mallory's way of telling him, once again, to get lost.

Riker stood near the kitchenette, where the odor was strongest. He stared at the jar of dead flies on the floor, then counted exactly two dozen saucers, each one containing the melted remnants of a red candle. They formed a perfect circle, and at the center lay Kennedy Harper's remains. She had a noose around her neck, and the double knot was the same as Sparrow's, but this woman had not been found hanging. The light fixture had come loose, and the body had crashed to the floor long before the police arrived. A broken bulb and a shattered white globe lay close to a nest of wires pulled down from the hole in the ceiling. The corpse at his feet was bloated with gas, and the face was partially concealed by shards of broken plaster. Only one eye, clotted with white dust, was visible. It had retracted into its socket.

Or the maggots had eaten it.

Riker turned away, wondering if this woman had been as pretty as Sparrow. He hunkered down on the floor in front of the kitchenette sink and picked up her wallet with his gloved hand. Opening it, he stared at the photograph on her driver's license. Yes, she had been very pretty, but Kennedy Harper had borne no resemblance to Sparrow beyond the hacked-off hair of another scalping. He set the wallet on the floor, positioned as he had found it among the spilled contents of a purse. He moved to one side to allow a crime-scene technician room to dust the jar of dead, dry flies. Even before the man shook his head, Riker knew there would be no fingerprints.

The detective looked up to see Heller standing by the door with a uniformed officer and signing a receipt for an armload of garments in clear plastic bags. After ripping the plastic away from one hanger, the criminalist held up a pale green blouse and motioned to Riker. 'You might wanna look at this.' Heller turned the blouse around to display a large faded X on the back. Affixed to this stain was the dry cleaner's We're-so-sorry sticker.

'I've seen this mark before,' said Heller, 'on a shirt I found wadded up under Sparrow's sink. She used hers for a cleaning rag. '

'So it's not a random killing.' Mallory joined them over the body. 'We've got a stalker.'

'Yeah,' said Riker. The X on the blouse worked nicely with her theory on the new locks installed a week before the murder. 'He sees the women on the street. Then he marks their shirts to make it easier to follow them home in a crowd – like tagging animals in the wild.' Unlike Kennedy Harper, Sparrow had not complained about the stalking, the terror. Prostitutes were not given the same service as human beings.

Sparrow, why didn't you come to me?

* * *

93

The East Side lieutenant had put in a personal appearance instead of sending one of his minions to the crime scene, and Mallory saw this as an admission of guilt for the mistakes made on his watch.

'I brought her package.' Lieutenant Loman spoke only to Riker, pretending that Mallory was not in the room. 'The complaints started a few weeks ago. Some pervert was following the girl.'

After accepting the envelope, Riker pulled out four papers encased in plastic, each bearing the same brief message. Loman was tense, almost standing at attention, and Mallory wondered if this was a habit from the days when Riker had held the rank of captain.

'Kennedy found those notes in her pockets.' Loman mopped his bald head and brow with a handkerchief. 'Pretty harmless stuff.'

Riker responded with a noncommittal nod, then scanned the paperwork attached to the evidence bags.

The lieutenant stared at the stained green blouse draped over the detective's arm. 'She brought that into the station house. She said the perp did it on the subway. You should find a T-shirt marked up the same way. And the notes – every time she found one in her pocket, she'd been in a crowd of people – the subway, a store. That's why Kennedy never got a good look at the guy.'

Mallory noted the use of the victim's first name. It was common for homicide detectives to speak of the dead with this familiarity; but Loman's squad had only known Kennedy Harper as a living woman, one civilian complainant out of thousands. She stared at the man in silent accusation.

You turned that woman into a pet, didn't you?

The lieutenant avoided Mallory's eyes while he waited for Riker to say *something* – anything. 'She never saw the perp's face. What could we do?'

'Did you put an extra patrol on this street?'

And now the lieutenant was forced to acknowledge Mallory, for Riker looked up from his reading, and he was also showing interest in her question.

'No,' said Loman. 'It was that damn virus. The uniforms were spread too thin for extra patrols.'

Mallory only shook her head. It would be gross insubordination to call him a liar out loud. Kennedy Harper was dead before the virus had grown to an epidemic in this part of town. And Loman's men had found lots of time to visit with pretty Kennedy Harper. She had even come to the attention of the squad's commander.

Riker selected one piece of paper with dried blood on it and held it up to the lieutenant's eyes.

It was a moment before Loman spoke. 'That was the last note. The perp used a hatpin to nail it into the back of her neck. Kennedy walked into the station house – dripping blood – and the note was still staked to her skin.'

Mallory knew there was only one reason for a victim to go to that extreme: it was the woman's plea for them to take her seriously – because they never had before.

Riker read the bloodied note aloud: ' "I can touch you any time I want." '

'That was the day she snapped,' said Loman. 'Told us she was leaving town. Well, we thought that was a real good idea. One of my men got her some coffee and a first-aid kit. I made her plane reservation for Bermuda.'

How kind of you, how helpful.

'Did you do anything else for her?'

'Yes!' Loman turned to Mallory, and he was on the offensive now. 'The girl was in shock. I got a police escort to take her to the hospital. And then they drove her back home. After that, all she had to do was take a cab to the airport.'

You left her alone.

Mallory edged toward the lieutenant. 'There was no follow-up?'

'No! What the hell for? As far as we knew, she was on the way to Bermuda.'

Chief Medical Examiner Edward Slope had arrived to give this case his personal attention. He knelt on the floor and rolled the corpse to expose a ruined face for the police photographer.

'Well, this is different,' said Heller, and everyone in the room turned to look at the dead woman. Flies crawled among the strands of long blonde hair that trailed from her mouth. The rope's double knot had snagged on her teeth and pried her mouth open, spreading the lips in a death's-head grin. 'Looks like she almost got away.'

Only Mallory was watching Lieutenant Loman's reaction. His face was pale, and his mouth was slack. This veteran of a thousand crime scenes was about to be sick. He was most vulnerable now, and she stepped closer, her shoulder touching his. 'So then, the reporters stopped by with their murder tip . . . and still no follow-up? *Sir?*'

'My men didn't know about that.' Again, he spoke only to Riker. 'The desk sergeant never mentioned any reporters. As far as he was concerned, the lady was in Bermuda. He was going off duty, and it wasn't worth his time to walk up a damn flight of stairs and talk to us. I promise you, his head's gonna roll.'

Ah, too late.

Mallory perused the folder. 'We need more men to work this case.'

'Well, now you guys got two more. Just tell me—'

'Three,' said Riker. 'Make it three. You came up one short the last time you promised her some help.'

'You got it,' said the lieutenant. 'We're finished?'

Riker nodded, giving a man who outranked him permission to leave. Loman turned on his heel and started across the room. Mallory wondered if he would make it to the street before he vomited.

Dr Slope supervised the removal of the body, then remained behind to study a drawing of the apartment floorplan. Heller squatted next to the victim's fallen purse and began to draw another diagram on his sketch pad, noting all the scattered items and their positions.

Mallory knelt beside him and studied the objects around the purse. 'Looks like a struggle.'

'No.' Heller drew black crayon circles around the fallen items. 'It's a nice tight pattern. These things just fell out when she dropped her purse. The way I see it, she was standing here when something made her jump.'

Riker stared at the front door. 'I count three locks and a chain, but no sign of a break-in. This woman was nervous as hell. I don't see her opening the door for a stranger.'

'Maybe we're looking for a cop,' said Mallory.

'I wouldn't rule it out.' Heller pulled on a new pair of gloves. 'But I don't think the door was locked when the perp arrived. This woman was planning a long trip, so she ran some errands after the cops brought her home.' He picked up a packet of fallen traveler's checks. 'A trip to the bank, right?' Next, he pulled a bottle of pills from a small pharmacy bag. 'And she refilled this prescription. But she forgot the receipt for the dry cleaner. So she came back to get it.'

Riker pulled out his cigarettes. 'Is this a guess or—'

'It's a fact,' said Heller. 'The dry cleaner said she dumped out her purse to look for the receipt. But she'd left it at home. I found it on the counter next to the sink. Now remember, she's got a plane to catch. She plans to grab that receipt and run right out again. So she doesn't lock the door this time.' Heller rose to his feet. 'She's standing here, reaching for it, when the perp startles her, and she drops her purse. I say he walked in right behind her.'

Click.

Ronald Deluthe snapped pictures of civilians on the sidewalk. He had quickly divided the crowd into categories. The out-of-towners were the people disguised as the Statue of Liberty. Their spiked crowns of green foam rubber were purchases from a street vendor working the crowd with a carton of souvenirs. The visitors smiled as they posed for the camera, then took their own pictures of the young detective with exotic bright yellow hair. He had become a tourist attraction.

All the blasé faces belonged to the natives who were almost bored by murder. And lots of them fit Miss Emelda's loose description of the hangman. T-shirts and jeans were the uniform of this neighborhood, and five of the men wore baseball caps.

Click, click.

The freelance reporters were easy to spot. They were the ones hustling every cop in uniform. The pros with real media jobs were disgorged from vans with network logos. Their technicians were setting up pole lights and carrying cameras. A brunette with a microphone was headed his way. She ignored the officers standing behind the blue saw horses. The woman only had eyes for Deluthe as she worked her way around the semi-circle of barricades – so she could be close to him.

She was pretty. He took her picture.

Click.

The reporter smiled for him.

Click, click, click, click.

She called out to him – a siren song, 'It's a murder, right?'

'No comment,' he said. This time, the crime scene was under tight control. Even the uniformed officers could not give any helpful information to reporters, however pretty they might be.

Deluthe was out of film and praying that Mallory and Riker would not show up before Officer Waller got back from the store.

He was saved. The uniformed policeman was fast approaching, elbowing his way through the crowd. Perfect timing. There *was* a God. Waller handed over the back-up film, and Deluthe opened the camera to remove the used roll.

A face in the crowd distracted him. The spectator was staring up at a high window while everyone else watched the front door. The young detective looked up at Kennedy Harper's fourth-floor apartment. All he could see was blue sky reflected on glass. He reloaded the camera, but before he could snap a picture, his subject slung a gray canvas bag over one shoulder and backed up into the crowd. The bag looked like one in the trunk of Deluthe's car, where he kept a change of clothes for a baseball game in Central Park.

And now he remembered to shoot the man.

Click.

Shit.

He had only caught the back of the civilian's head turning away from the camera. Deluthe wondered if he should chase the man down. But what pretext could he use? *Excuse me, sir. You looked up instead of down.* That scene might not play half as well as his attempted arrest of the building handyman.

The odd spectator was forgotten when Deluthe spied a familiar face behind the barricades. It was the fireman who had left the prostitute hanging at the last crime scene. Gary Zappata's eyes were fixed on the door to Kennedy Harper's building.

Waiting for what?

Click.

Detective Mallory stepped out on the sidewalk, followed by her partner. Zappata's angry eyes locked on to Sergeant Riker.

Click.

The detectives would not give his opinion any credence, but they had to believe a picture. Zappata clearly wanted Riker dead.

Mallory walked up to Deluthe, giving him no time to explain his theory on the fireman. She was saying, *ordering*, 'Get out your notebook.'

Deluthe complied, and now his pencil hovered over a clean page.

'Get your film developed,' she said. 'And don't take any grief. You tell the techs you want it *now*. Go back to Special Crimes and clear a section of wall in the incident room. Pin up this paperwork.' She handed him a large manila folder. 'You'll find some still shots of news film on my desk. Compare the faces to the ones you shot in this crowd. Meet Riker back here when you're done. He'll give you another list. *Run.*'

No baseball game tonight.

Detective Janos was a human tank, physically and psychologically. Nothing stopped him. However, if Lieutenant Coffey had sent him out in search of the Holy Grail, he would have been back with it long before now. The more difficult errand had been securing a voice recording for the tip line of a local news program.

He was exhausted.

The television people had called him *Babe*, then misused the word *synergy* twice in five minutes, saying nothing intelligible for another twenty minutes of wasted time. Everyone on the news staff had labored under the whacked impression that the Constitution of the United States allowed them, even encouraged them, to conceal evidence of murder.

Yet Janos had not killed any of these people. That was not his way. He had merely loomed over the news director, one hand outstretched, saying, 'Give me the tape.'

Another member of the staff, the anchorwoman, had expounded on freedom of the press, making it clear that she had never read the pertinent passage of First Amendment rights.

And Janos had replied, 'Give me the tape.'

Half an hour had passed by before the network attorney arrived to yell at his clients, 'Give him the tape, you fucking *idiots*!'

More time had been spent convincing an overworked support technician at One Police Plaza that he could not simply leave the tape and go; he needed a copy for his lieutenant. Mere looming had done the trick with the small man in the lab coat.

And now, finally, Janos carried his hard-won trophy down the hall to the incident room. He opened the door and paused on the threshold, taking a moment to admire a crude flat scarecrow nailed to the rear wall. The boys had been busy while he was away.

He looked down at a gray canvas bag near the baseboard. A pair of wadded gym socks had been dropped on the floor, apparently rejected as feet for the image on the wall. Janos agreed with this aesthetic decision – less was more. In the space below a tacked-up baseball cap was a photograph showing the back of a man's head; this was in keeping with Miss Emelda's sighting of a suspicious character in her tree, a man without a face. Beneath this picture, a T-shirt had been spread out and pinned to the cork. Sturdy nails supported a pair of blue jeans to fill out the lower half of the body. Crime-scene gloves were positioned where the effigy's hands would be, and a nail had been driven into one latex palm to hold the strap of a cheap instant camera, yet another detail from Miss Emelda's description.

Interesting.

However, the truly original touch was a halo of fat black flies impaled around the scarecrow's cap. One was a large horse fly speared on a long pin, but still alive, twitching, buzzing—

At the sound of footsteps, Janos turned around to see the yellow-haired youngster from Lieutenant Loman's squad. Judging by the slim build, Janos assumed that the scarecrow's clothing belonged to this detective. And there was more damning evidence: Ronald Deluthe's face was flushed red with sudden guilt – perhaps because he carried a living, squirming fly impaled on a hatpin.

'Deluthe, you're very young to be this jaded.' Janos smiled at the blushing whiteshield, who now realized that this was a compliment and resumed breathing.

This meeting place had been chosen to increase the prostitute's anxiety, but Daisy was too stoned to appreciate the decor of framed photographs and citations that screamed, *This is a cop bar!* Detective Mallory kept fifteen feet of mahogany and five drinking men between herself and the aging whore with electric-red hair.

The skeletal woman perched on the edge of her stool, one eye cocked on the door. Riker was ten minutes late, and the woman would not wait for him much longer. Mallory put on her sunglasses when the hooker glanced in her direction, though it was doubtful she would be recognized; they had both changed so much. Kathy the child had grown into a woman, and Daisy the whore had become a superannuated corpse.

In the old days, this redhead had been a long-haired blonde who had shared heroin with Sparrow. They had done everything together. Mallory had a childhood memory of the two prostitutes vomiting in the same toilet bowl.

Daisy's bright red mouth formed a suggestive smile for a male customer. The man turned to catch the attention of the bartender, another recent redhead, though, unlike Daisy's color, Peg Baily's was a shade found in nature. Also, Baily was softly rounded, glowing with good health, and, in her younger days, she had been a decorated police officer.

The customer arched one eyebrow to ask why a sickly hooker had been allowed to stay so long. Tradition demanded that Daisy be kicked into the street, literally, with the press of a boot on her backside. Peg Baily held up two fingers to let him know that the whore was on the way out in just a few minutes.

Trouble.

This was a new location for the bar. Perhaps it was a coincidence that Baily had moved her business to Riker's neighborhood, but Mallory thought otherwise.

The bartender looked up at the clock on the wall, then turned to the detective. 'Your partner's not gonna show, kid. I'm tossing that hooker out of here right now.'

A whore wasting from AIDS was bad for trade.

Mallory turned to the window – and inspiration. The former Angie Riker was opening the door to a barber shop across the street. Riker's ex-wife was leading a parade of four teenage boys, the brood of her second husband. Mallory wondered if it was pure accident that her partner had set this time for the interview. Or was he still keeping close tabs on Angie?

The bartender rapped the mahogany to get Mallory's attention, saying, 'Time's up, kid.'

'Quick question, Baily? You knew Riker when he was married, didn't you?'

'You *know* I did.' Peg Baily's eyes were suddenly unfriendly,

102

silently asking, *What are you up to?* 'I was his partner. You know that too. What's this—'

'How come you never told him his wife was playing around behind his back?' As a child, Mallory had learned many things by listening in on her foster parents' late-night conversations. 'You knew Angie was a slut. But even after the divorce, you never told Riker. He still doesn't know you held out on—'

'You wouldn't be threatening me, would you?' Baily leaned on the bar. 'I wouldn't like that, kid. And if you say one word to him, I'll mess your face up so bad.'

Mallory smiled, for she was younger, faster, and had no healthy sense of fear. Oh, and she was the one with the gun.

Riker had arrived. He stepped out of the car at the curb and watched Deluthe drive off in search of a parking space.

The two women fell into an uneasy silence. The bar's lighting was low key. Mallory and Baily had no worry of being caught in an act of voyeurism, for Riker was standing in bright sunlight, and the plate glass would act as a mirror. He was slowly turning round, responding to Angie, who hailed him with waving arms. His ex-wife left her children on the curb and crossed the street, dodging traffic and mouthing a happy *Hello!* As the former Mrs Riker drew closer, Mallory realized that Peg Baily's new hair color was the exact same shade of carrot red.

Riker faced the window again, pretending interest in the posted hours of his favorite bar as his ex-wife came up behind him. Angie was still a pretty woman, but he would not look at her. She stood beside him, cheerful and chattering, probably asking how he had been – as if they did not see one another all the time. His own apartment was only a block away from hers. However, it was enough that Riker could be near this woman, and that he could see her face every single day; he never spoke to Angie anymore – he never would again. It was just too hard on him.

The woman put one hand on her ex-husband's sleeve.

Peg Baily's hands curled into fists.

Riker lost his slouch and stood up straight, rigid and stone silent. He stared at the window, seeing nothing, hearing nothing. Angie's shrug said, *No hard feelings.* Then, giving up on him, she crossed back to the other side of the street.

Not wanting to witness any more of this, Peg Baily walked off to fetch a glass of club soda for her ex-partner, who never drank on duty. Mallory continued to watch the man lingering on the sidewalk, staring at his shoes and collecting his sorry wits. She was now convinced that there had been no affair between Riker and Sparrow. He was still in love with his ex. And why would he take up with a whore when Peg Baily was still waiting for her own turn?

He entered the bar and waved to Baily. She started to slide his soda down the bar when he put up one hand to stop her, then ordered cheap bourbon.

More trouble.

He loosened his tie as he sat down beside Daisy, and the hooker promptly ordered a champagne cocktail.

Riker was working on his second shot of bourbon as he listened to the prostitute's slow drawl, so like Sparrow's. Years ago, the hookers had been the best of friends, two small-town southern girls against the city. So far, the interview had turned up nothing useful, and now he stirred up a memory of old times. 'Remember that little blond girl who used to run with Sparrow?'

'Wasn't just Sparrow. That kid used to work a battalion of whores.' Daisy signaled Baily for another champagne cocktail.

'What was her name?'

'Oh, darlin', she had a lotta names. One hooker called her the Flyin' Flea, and Sparrow called her Baby.'

'And you?'

'Hey Kid – that's what I called her. First time I ever saw her was in a crackhouse.' The hooker paused to inhale her drink. 'She came in lookin' for Sparrow. What a dirty little face. And those eyes – tiny green fires, but so *cold*. Nothin' warm and cuddly 'bout *that* little girl. And *mean?* Oh, darlin', you got no idea. Ah, but her face – I saw it when it was clean. God don't make angels that pretty. But I don't mean to say that God made her. I don't blaspheme. My mama raised me better.'

This was going to take a while. Riker had no idea how Daisy made a living on the city streets, where time was money. She hailed from a more temperate climate, where customers and cops could wait around all day for a whore to finish a thought.

'So, like I was saying, I'm in this crackhouse, and I hear a noise in the dark. At first, all I see is her eyes – cold, empty. *Scary* eyes. That little girl had no soul. She comes up to me and hands me a cigarette case – *real* silver. And she gives me this ratty old book with cowboys on the cover. Not *my* taste. Well, she swipes away the needles and trash so she can sit down beside me. Then she kicks out one little foot to make the rats run. And she says, "Read me a story." She don't say please, nothin' like that. Just says, "Read me a story," like that's my job in life.'

'So the kid couldn't read?'

'Oh, yeah, she could,' said Daisy. 'Better'n me. She helped me with the hard words. But that night – that first time – she lays her head down in my lap and waits for her story to begin. So I read till she fell asleep. Then I sat up all night long to keep the rats away from her. I had to, don't you see?'

Riker nodded. 'You were her mother that night.'

'Other nights it was other whores – when she couldn't find Sparrow.'

Riker looked up from his drink. Mallory sat at the other end of the bar. If she lowered the dark glasses, would Daisy recognize her? Not likely, but the long green slants of her eyes had never changed. They might spook a whore who believed in ghosts.

'So you looked after the kid,' said Riker.

'Sometimes,' said Daisy. 'Well, she could never count on Sparrow.

That junkie whore was always gettin' stoned and wakin' up in strange places. Lucky the kid knew how to fend for herself.'

Yeah, what a lucky little girl.

Sometimes Kathy had lived out of garbage cans, finding a cold supper there. 'You remember the day Sparrow got stabbed?'

'Oh, darlin', I'll never forget. I went to the hospital to visit. The kid was there, too. Poor baby, she fell asleep sittin' bolt upright on the edge of Sparrow's bed. Too tired to lie down or even fall down. That's the last time I saw the kid alive.'

'Remember anything else? Did Sparrow say who stabbed her?'

The hooker was wary now.

'Hey,' said Riker, 'I don't need a witness. That stabbing is old history. This is a personal thing, okay?' A twenty-dollar bill slid across the bar. 'Do you know who stabbed her?'

'I'd be guessin'.' The prostitute's hand closed over the money. 'Only *guessin'* – hear me? Sparrow might've mentioned Frankie D. You remember that twisted little bastard?'

Riker nodded. Frankie Delight had been that rare drug dealer who was not strictly cash-and-carry. 'So Sparrow was trading skin for drugs?'

'No, she'd never do that freak for a fix. I don't care how bad she was hurtin'. No, darlin', she was tradin' brand-new VCRs. Still in the cartons. One of Tall Sally's jobs went wrong and—'

'I know that story,' said Riker. And ten-year-old Kathy Mallory would have been on the stealing end of that arrangement.

The great VCR heist.

He remembered the report from Robbery Division. A patrolman's log had mentioned sighting suspicious persons in the vicinity of the crime, among them a little blond girl with green eyes. Lou Markowitz had read him the details, then said, in a tone between awe and pride, 'The kid robbed a damn *truck*.'

Daisy nudged Riker's arm to call him back to the world, asking, 'Whatever happened to Frankie?'

Riker had never been certain until now. 'I heard he left town.' One could say that the dead were way out of town. 'So, Daisy, what's Sparrow been up to? You guys keep in touch?' He doubted that this whore read the papers, and her television set would have been pawned long ago to buy drugs.

'No, we don't talk no more.' She stared at the bottom of her glass. 'Not for a long time. But I did hear a rumor today. Some bitch told me that Sparrow was the hooker who got herself strung up last night. Well, I knew that wasn't true. My Sparrow got clean · kicked them drugs. And she stopped liftin' her skirt for a livin'. That was years ago, darlin'. *Years* ago.'

He gave her another ten dollars. She snatched it from his hand, then climbed down from her bar stool and backed up all the way to the door, eyes trained on Peg Baily. Daisy whirled around and fled, rather than risk an injury by staying a second too long.

Riker ambled toward the end of the bar, where his partner waited, attracting stares from every man in the room. He sat down beside her. 'Well, that was a waste of time. We're not gonna find a stalker with hookers. Sparrow got out of the life years ago.'

Mallory the unbeliever shook her head. She would not seriously consider any good thing said about Sparrow.

Once a whore, always a whore?

'How did it go with the theater group?'

'That was a dead end,' said Mallory. 'Sparrow was a last-minute substitute in the play. None of those people met her before the rehearsal. And that was the day she was hung.'

'Well, somebody got her that job. We might find a tie between Sparrow and Kennedy Harper.'

'No, Riker. This wasn't a Broadway production. She answered an ad posted on a supermarket bulletin board. The director gave her the part because she showed up in costume and knew all the lines.'

Riker tried to imagine Sparrow memorizing Chekhov. He drained his shot glass and laid his money on the bar. 'So what's next? Morgue time?'

'No, Slope's working on a fresher corpse right now.'

'Okay,' said Riker. 'A local cop, Waller, looked over your video-tape. He gave Janos a name and address for the man in the T-shirt and jeans. You know that big church on Avenue B?'

'A priest?'

'You got it.' Riker stared at his empty glass, turning it over in his hands. 'If you want off this case, I can work it alone.'

'No.' She gathered up her car keys, then left an obscene tip on the bar. 'I'll see it through.'

The East Village park was full of music, rock and rap, Hispanic and soul. It poured out of radios and CD players. Some youngsters sported earphones, and Riker had to guess their songs by the cadence of their struts, their bounces and glides.

At the heart of Tompkins Square was a stellar memory of the night his father had thrown him out of the house – an elegant solution to the problem of a teenager's dissident music. Young Riker had waged a showdown in the old band shell, the spot claimed by another boy, whose music had been a self-portrait, cool and dark, a jazz riff played on a clarinet. Riker had shot back a volley of rock 'n' roll, louder and longer. And they had dueled awhile before laying down their instruments.

After a bloody fight, each boy had won his cuts and bruises. And after too many beers, they had ended the night blind drunk, arms wrapped round each other for support, one musically discordant creature in a four-legged stagger walk.

How he had loved those days.

Startled pigeons flew up in the wake of a passing boom box. Riker put out his cigarette and returned to the church, where he discovered that Mallory's plan to torture a priest had somehow gone awry.

The church was no cathedral, but it held all the trappings of stained-glass windows, a giant crucifix and rows of votive candles blazing at the feet of plaster saints.

Mallory had laid out twenty dollars for a disposable camera just to rattle the priest, and the man's laughter was a disappointment. He *liked* the idea of taking part in a photo lineup of murder suspects. 'No, don't smile, Father,' she said. 'So Sparrow belonged to your parish?'

'Now how did you manage to make that sound like a guilty thing?'

Father Rose was having entirely too much fun sparring with her in this novel departure from a priest's workday. She doubted that he would make her short list for a double hanging. She glanced at Riker, who sprawled in the front pew, waiting to play his role of the easygoing policeman, everybody's friend.

Mallory lowered the camera so the priest could see her slow grin. She had a repertoire of smiles, and this one made people nervous. 'A witness can place you at the crime scene last night.'

'Yes, there was quite a crowd – even before the fire engine showed up.' The priest turned to the side. 'Want a profile?' He froze in position, waiting for the flash. 'Your witness is an old woman. Am I right? *Very* thick glasses? She was sitting in the window across the street, watching the whole show, and—'

'A *show*? Is that how you saw it, Father?' She shot him again. 'Why were you at the crime scene? Forget something?'

'So I *am* a suspect.' He seemed almost flattered.

'You were out of uniform last night.'

'I leave the collar home when I work at the neighborhood clinic. I donate my time three nights a week. Mostly bandaging cuts, dispensing aspirins – that kind of thing.'

She looked up from the camera so he would have no trouble reading distrust in her eyes. 'I want names. Who can vouch for your time – say an hour before the fire?'

'The nurse who runs the clinic. We were leaving together when we heard the fire engines. Is this—'

'When did you talk to Sparrow last?'

'Sunday, but I didn't—'

'Did she mention any enemies? Somebody out to get her?'

The priest shook his head.

'No? You don't know or you won't say? Want to lawyer up, Father? You have the right to an attorney during—'

'That's *enough*, Mallory.' Riker rose from the pew, acting the part of an annoyed superior. 'Go check out his story.'

She walked down the altar steps, passing her partner as he climbed upward in dead silence. Riker was already departing from the script. There was nothing amiable in his face as he squared off in front of the priest. Mallory stayed to watch.

'I know you tried to get access to that crime scene,' said Riker. 'My witness is no old lady. He's a big hairy fireman.'

'Yes, he must be the one who told me Sparrow was dead. Well, she's Catholic. She was entitled to last rites.'

'The fireman said you knew her name before the cops identified her. You *knew* that was her apartment. So you've got what – two hundred people in your parish?'

Father Rose wore a slightly pained expression. He understood that this was a test. 'I recognized her face when—'

'So you had a good view of the *show*, right? Front row – close to the window. Notice anything unusual?'

'The hair jammed in her mouth?' The priest was rallying, almost smug. 'No, too obvious. That made headlines, didn't it?' He folded his arms. 'You must mean the candles. I don't recall any mention of them in the newspaper.' Father Rose waved to a nearby alcove that housed a plaster saint and a few small flames burning among tiers of candles. 'Like those. Yes, I saw them in the water.' His smile was wider now. 'But Sparrow's were red. *Mine* are white.'

So Father Rose had failed to notice a thousand dead flies spread on the water. At least one crime-scene detail was secure.

The priest was smiling, triumphant.

'Having fun, Father?' Riker moved closer, forcing the other man to back step. 'Sparrow is a friend of mine, and I'm not enjoying this much. So do me a favor and stop *grinning* at me.'

Father Rose's head snapped back, as if the detective had sucker-punched him — and he had. Riker backed off a few paces to reward the priest's more somber attitude. 'Maybe we have a religious connection. How would you explain all those candles?'

'Well, they weren't for ambience.' And lest Riker take this for humor, the priest hurried the rest of his words. 'All the lights were on in Sparrow's apartment before the firemen broke the—'

'Why do *you* light candles?'

'Ritual.' The man was not so sure of himself anymore. 'Burnt offerings. A light in the darkness. Hope?' This last word waned to a whisper as he watched the detective descend the stairs.

Riker's back was turned to the priest when he asked, 'Did you know Sparrow was a prostitute?'

Mallory watched the priest's stunned reaction. He opened and closed his mouth like an air-drowned fish. And she knew he could tell them nothing more, not even if he violated every secret of the confessional. Sparrow had never confided in him. The two detectives walked down the wide center aisle, then paused at the sound of running footsteps.

The priest called out, 'Wait!' He hurried from statue to statue, lighting all the wicks. 'Just another minute. *Please.*' He lit every candle on the altar as well. 'I'm sorry.' The priest walked toward Riker. '*So* sorry. Sparrow is a special person to me.' His face showed deep contrition. 'She has a good heart — better than most. She's better than she knows.'

Riker nodded and cracked a smile, raising his opinion of this man who could admire a whore.

'And I was wrong about the ambience,' said the priest. 'Maybe that *is* your angle. Candles make for great theatre — even when all the electricity is turned on. Look around you.'

Candles flickered beneath the crucifix. The man on the cross writhed in an illusion of lights. And all along the wall, flames beneath the other figures created animation, action — actors.

'Thank you, Father.' And Mallory meant that. His idea was worth consideration, but from a different angle. What if religious candles had the same significance as a jar of dead flies?

SEVEN

Autopsy – *Autopsia* – seeing with one's eyes.

When Mallory was a child, she had learned her essential Latin from Chief Medical Examiner Edward Slope.

A refrigerator and sinks gave the doctor's dissection room the character of a large kitchen. Long tables were laid with tools for slicing and dicing meat. A small metal platform the size of a butcher block held intestines in a shallow tray, and another body part lay in the bed of a hanging scale. Dr Slope called out the weight, then switched off his recorder. 'Hello, Kathy.'

'Mallory,' she said, correcting him as she always did. She approached the steel table and looked down at the gutted remains of a woman her own age. A wide red cavity ran from the breast bone to a mound of blond pubic hair, and the smell of chlorine mingled with the reek of meat gone bad.

Hoc es corpus. This is the body.

Today she had missed these words that began every autopsy, but now she watched the process in reverse. A few organs had been set aside. The parts that would be buried with Kennedy Harper were being returned to her hollowed-out corpse. Mallory leaned down for a closer examination of small holes in the cadaver's flesh. 'What's this? It looks like a shotgun splatter.'

'That's from the maggots exiting the dried-out skin.' He picked up his magnifying glass and held it on the area above the collar bone. 'You see? The rims of the holes are turned out.' One bloody, gloved hand pointed to ravaged skin at the cadaver's throat. 'Now this is more interesting. The rope did lots of damage here, but the killer wasn't responsible for it.' He watched her face and waited for the student to ask the master, *Why not?*

If she encouraged him in this old game, it would take forever to glean a few simple facts. The doctor was determined to continue her education, and he was too fond of long lessons. So she waited him out, arms folded, blinking only once before he gave in.

'The damage was self-inflicted.' He turned his eyes down to the work of coiling the large intestine. 'This woman was very cool under pressure.'

That sounded like another contradiction, but she recognized an old logic trap. *No, I'm not going to ask.*

As Dr Slope finished stitching skin to close the gaping wound, he shifted his tactics, offering Mallory a bizarre piece of candy. 'You'll *never* attend another autopsy like this one.' And with this hook, he led her over to the steel counter by the refrigerator, where he wadded his bloody surgeon's gown and tossed it into a barrel with his gloves.

'I've seen a lot of hanging victims, mostly suicides, but nothing like this.' He sorted through a group of photographs. 'Normally, I find a ligature mark at the back of the neck where the knot is.' He selected a picture of the victim's face, taken when the rope was still caught between her teeth. 'But this woman was facing the knot. Now I never expect a classic hangman's noose. It's usually a slip knot.'

'I *know*.' She kept her sarcasm to one syllable, a subtle reminder that she had been present when the noose was removed. 'This one was a double knot. Heller already—'

'And it didn't close off the carotid artery. So Miss Harper didn't black out or succumb to euphoria.'

'Transient cerebral hypoxia,' said Mallory.

'You *do* pay attention.' Dr Slope graced her with a half smile as he unfolded a diagram of the crime scene. 'Heller assisted on this part. We choreographed the last minutes of her life like a ballet.' The doctor pointed to the roughly sketched countertop by the kitchen sink. 'This is where Heller's forensic team found footprints and partials. Note the distance to the ceiling light.' His finger moved across the paper to a drawn circle. 'That's where she was left hanging, playing dead.' He looked up at Mallory. 'Miss Harper was still alive when the killer left the scene. First, she kicked off her sandals. We found them under the body. When she raised her leg, she could just barely reach the counter with one toe. So she pushed off to make her body swing away and back again.'

The doctor laid out photographs of the Formica surface covered with Heller's black dust. One close-up showed a partial footprint layered over the mark of a toe. 'Here you've got more of the foot,' said Slope. 'Her body swings in a wider arc each time she pushes off Finally, she lands both feet on the countertop. Now her weight is supported at two points – feet on the counter, neck in the noose. See here?' He pointed to a shot of two full footprints on the Formica beside the sink. 'Both soles are flat. Now she has the leverage to rotate her body until she's facing the knot. That gives her an inch of air between her throat and the noose. She worked her chin under the rope. That's when it snagged on the upper teeth. I can't tell you how long she hung there.'

Patiently waiting for the cavalry to come and rescue her – just like Sparrow.

'She couldn't dislodge the rope or the hair in her mouth,' said Slope. 'She could've screamed – but no intelligible sounds.'

The neighbors didn't come. The cops didn't come.

Dr Slope pushed the photographs aside. 'I can tell you she died six days ago, but the cause of death wasn't asphyxiation. It was heart failure.' He picked up a pharmacy bottle bagged and tagged as crime-scene evidence. 'I called the prescribing cardiologist. Miss Harper had a congenital heart defect – inoperable. All her life, she's been living with a time bomb in her chest.'

'Good practice for a hanging,' said Mallory.

'It does explain a lot, doesn't it? Twisting on the end of a rope, but no panic. And she nearly escaped.'

Mallory thought of the day this woman had walked into a police station with a bloody note staked to her neck. The hanging scenario worked well with that kind of poise. But now she had two victims who were accomplished at playing dead while their hearts were beating a million times a minute. What were the odds against *that*? She turned to the medical examiner and smiled.

You wouldn't hold out on me, would you?

The doctor would never volunteer what he could not swear to in court and back up with evidence, but if he thought this was the end of the autopsy, he was dead wrong. She glanced back at the dissected woman on the other side of the room. There was cutting and there was cutting. 'So I've got a perp who can't tell the living from the dead. That's *it*? That's *all* you can tell me? The hangman's just another screwup who can't find a pulse?'

Dr Slope hesitated for a moment. He had always fancied himself a great poker player, born with a face of stone that gave up nothing in his hand. Yet Louis Markowitz had beaten him in every bluff, and everything that cop knew about poker and Slope he had passed along to his foster child. Even if she could not read the doctor's face, she knew what he was thinking: she was an ungrateful brat, and he was going to put her in her place.

The man's voice was testy, but still in the lecture mode. 'You assume he believed his victim was dead. Well, *I don't*. After he strung her up, she was getting oxygen, but not enough to keep her conscious for long. So I know the killer left the scene immediately. Otherwise, there wouldn't have been time enough or strength enough for Kennedy's aerial ballet. He didn't stay to *watch* her die.'

Just like Sparrow – a pattern.

A few minutes with this medical examiner was worth ten hours with any psychiatrist, for most witch doctors were light years removed from the carnage of murder. She turned her back on Slope and crossed the room to the steel table and the body of Kennedy Harper all sewn up with crude stitches – a Frankenstein scar. Mallory was striving for the sound of boredom when she asked, 'What else can you tell me? Anything *useful*?'

The doctor's poker discipline was shot to hell. His face was now an easy read, waffling between surprise and indignation. He marched up to the table and confronted her across the body, firing off another contradiction. 'I'd say your man's not the violent type. That may seem a bit odd—'

'Odd?'

'All right, *Kathy* – it's *insane*. But he didn't go off on either of the women. He didn't beat them or—'

'He cut off their damn hair.'

'But no cuts to the flesh, no fractures from a fist. And the other one, Sparrow – she didn't have a single defensive bruise. I've seen every unspeakable act a man can commit on a woman's body.' The doctor looked down at the corpse laid out on the table, the woman he so admired. 'But I don't see that kind of violence here – no loss of control, no rage.'

This did not square with a note staked to the neck of a living woman, and she was about to tell him that when he held up one hand to forestall any more arguments.

'I'm out of my depth,' he said. 'This man didn't *care* if the women lived or died. He's a walking paradox – a serial killer who's not all that interested in killing.'

The murder of Kennedy Harper had taken over an entire wall of the Special Crimes incident room. Mallory posted the autopsy pictures next to Heller's crime-scene diagrams. Sparrow also had a wall to herself. The throwaway whore had become a priority case.

Rows of metal folding chairs were filling up with detectives. Four men gathered around the audio equipment and listened to the *Cashtip* recording of the killer's voice, playing again and again, unwilling to believe that it did not offer more. The volume was turned up each time they heard the ambient sound.

Pssst.

One man timed it by the second hand on his watch. Mallory used a natural clock, a quirk of the brain that told her this sound occurred every twenty seconds. It reminded her of Helen Markowitz's spray starch on ironing day.

She walked to the hangman's wall and stared at a photograph of the back of a man's head. The image, crowned with a baseball cap and encircled with dead flies, was as worthless as the lame description of T-shirt and jeans played out in the clothing pinned to the cork.

Pssst.

Janos stood beside her. 'So what do you think of our scarecrow?'

'Is that what we're calling him now?'

'Yeah.' He turned to look around the room. 'Hey, what happened to your partner?'

'He'll be back.' She had kept track of all the passing minutes since Riker had slipped out of the room. After the ambush in front of Peg Baily's bar, he would not miss an opportunity for a drink today. Each up-close encounter with his ex-wife was a prelude to a binge. Her internal timepiece had moved well past his three-minute walk to a nearby watering hole.

Pssst.

Riker would down his bourbon in no time. Mallory allowed extra minutes for his return trip. He would not walk back here with the same urgent speed. She factored in another minute so he could trade insults with the desk sergeant before climbing the stairs and ambling down the hall to the incident room.

Mallory turned her face to the door, and her partner appeared.

Pssst.

She saw nothing amiss. Riker prided himself on never stumbling in the daylight hours. There were no new spills on his suit, nothing more recent than his interview with Daisy, and that splash of bourbon had dried long ago. He sat on the chair next to hers and peeled the wrapper from a roll of mints. 'Did I miss anything?'

'No. We're still waiting to hear from Tech Support.'

Pssst.

The detectives around the tape player walked away from the machine, allowing the recording to play out at full volume, and still the suspect's voice was subdued.

' *a woman has been murdered in the East Village—*'

It was an empty monotone, lacking the bravado of a man on a quest for fame, and one more motive died.

'*—name is Kennedy Harper—*'

The mechanical tone almost qualified as a speech impediment, or that was the excuse offered by technicians at One Police Plaza. They had not yet fixed the suspect's home state.

'*—You can find the body at—*'

This man, so adept at theatrical staging, was so bland in his recital of bare facts – a death, a name, an address.

Pssst.

Mallory was fleshing out the portrait of a killer whose emotions were dead, not the type for a thrill kill. He was a tidy man, well organized. A man with a plan? She stared at the scarecrow on the back wall. *What the hell do you want?*

'We got it!' Janos hovered in front of a computer monitor and read the pertinent details as he scrolled down the screen, 'The scarecrow is from the Midwest. They're still trying to nail down the state. The techs say he wasn't calling from a cell phone or a payphone. And the ambient sound might be from an early-model humidifier or an automatic plant mister.'

Jack Coffey entered the room and shut off the tape player. 'Listen up!' All conversation stopped and every pair of eyes turned his way. 'Riker's witness, Miss Emelda, is worth her weight in gold. Our perp was the old lady's man in the tree – the guy with a Polaroid camera.'

He held up two plastic bags, each containing a small box with a Polaroid logo. 'These film cartons were left at both crime scenes, and they weren't left by accident.' He held one higher than the other. 'And the box we found today has a twenty-year-old expiration date.' He tossed the bags on the table. 'Kennedy Harper died six days ago that's official. Six days and twenty years ago, another hanging victim was found.'

The lieutenant turned to face Mallory. 'It was an anniversary kill. And *now* we have a solid connection to the Cold Case file.' He pointed to Janos. 'You're the primary on Kennedy's case. And, Desoto, you got Sparrow.'

Mallory watched Riker's face go gray. His eyes were all the way open now, and his head was shaking from side to side, silently saying, *This can't be.* How could he lose Sparrow's case to another detective? He was rising from his chair when she caught his sleeve and pulled him down.

'If we can't get Sparrow back, we'll work her case on the side.'

Was he hearing her? Yes, he was nodding.

Jack Coffey had finished handing out assignments to the others, and now he stood before Mallory and Riker. 'You guys are working the Cold Case file. We got a copycat, and I wanna know where he got his information.' The lieutenant paused, correctly reading Mallory's expression of ennui. 'You're not baby-sitting Geldorf. *Use* that old man. Just keep him the hell out of Special Crimes.'

Lars Geldorf was hoarse from explaining and explaining, then shouting in exasperation. His opponent was a small, wiry woman with dark Spanish eyes, a deeply suspicious nature and a mission to clean Manhattan. She pulled a mop from her rolling cart of cleaning supplies and said, once more, 'I'm gonna do Mallory's office now.' Nothing would stop the intrepid Mrs Ortega, certainly not this old man – gun or no gun.

The retired detective informed her that this room could *not* be cleaned until his case was wrapped. He distrusted all civilians, and she should understand that it was nothing personal. Charles intervened, suggesting that, since it was so late in the day, Mrs Ortega could skip this room. The cleaning woman countered with 'Mallory's orders, not yours.' And eventually, the matter was settled.

Mrs Ortega ruled.

But Geldorf was adamant that Charles remain in the room until 'that – that *woman*' was done. Then, with great dignity, he left the office with his relief watcher, a young detective with unnatural bright yellow hair.

After the door slammed behind them, Mrs Ortega plugged in her vacuum, then shook her head, saying, 'Damn, that baby cop's got one bad bleach job.'

Charles nodded. 'It's interesting, though. Perhaps he's making some kind of statement.'

'Yeah, like – look at me, my head glows in the dark.'

'Exactly what I was thinking.' Charles turned his attention to the cork wall. Where should the giant cockroaches go? Well, the only place for them was underneath the maggots. Where else?

The carpet was spotless when Riker strolled in. He nodded his hello to Charles, then flashed a big smile for the cleaning woman. 'Hey, how've you been?' He was genuinely happy to see her, though she used him for verbal sniper practice each time they met.

She glared at a spot on Riker's suit, singling it out from all the other stains, then stopped her work to clean him with a bottle of solvent and a cloth, as if he were any other object in her path. 'Next time you drink crummy bourbon for lunch, mop it up.'

Charles's nose was larger, but Mrs Ortega's was truly gifted. However, she was not an olfactory savant. She had not identified the alcohol by scent, nor discerned that it was stale, not fresh, and neither had she found the bouquet a bit wanting – a lesser brand. This was only a parlor trick. Cheap bourbon was Riker's habitual choice, and the spill might reek, but it was dry, suggesting a drink earlier in the day. After erasing the evidence of his on-duty imbibing, she went back to dusting the shelves and muttered, 'My tax dollars at work.'

'Mallory's on the way,' Riker said to her back. 'You got fifteen minutes.' The detective also knew *her* soft spots, and now Mrs Ortega's duster doubled its speed. She would not want Mallory to walk in while there was still a dust mote at large.

'You never finished the story,' said Charles. 'What happened to that Indian girl after she—'

The man shook his head to say, *Not now*, then quickly glanced at the cleaning woman. When Mrs Ortega had packed up her cart and gone home, Riker was still uneasy as he continued the unfinished tale. 'The Wichita Kid got away. When the next book opens, you find out the Indian girl is dead.' He sagged back against the wall, and his face turned toward the open door.

Keeping an eye out for Mallory?

Yes, and he was also telegraphing the terrible importance of the books, which had nothing to do with plots and everything to do with a recent murder and a child who loved westerns.

'Sheriff Peety's horse crushed the girl's skull,' said Riker. 'So he broke off the chase and carried the body back to her village. Wichita never found out that the girl died to save him. He just went on loving her for the rest of the book.' The detective was about to say more when something caught his eye, a folded newspaper on the desk. His left shoe began to tap in a steady rhythm, though he was not given to nervous mannerisms.

The newspaper belonged to Charles. He had finished the detailed account of a hanged prostitute and noted the similarities to Natalie Homer's murder. However, the most startling lines described the crime-scene floor awash in water from a fire hose. Given the time of night and the degree of dampness in a paperback western called *Homecoming*, he now knew how the book had gotten wet. It was possible that the detective had innocently dropped it in the water, but the man's uncharacteristic anxiety suggested that the truth was even more out of character than Riker telling lies and drinking on duty. Though Charles suspected the book had been stolen, all he would say to his friend was 'Tell me how the story ends.'

Riker's eyes were on the door, and there was some strain in his voice when he said, 'Sheriff Peety hears about another gunfight with the Wichita Kid — another man killed. He picks up the trail outside of El Paso, Texas. At the end of the book, the sheriff's riding into an ambush — forty-to-one odds. He knows what's comin'. He *knows* he can't win. But he keeps on riding.'

The apartment had a formal dining room, but Charles preferred the casual warmth of the kitchen, where a Bach concerto played at the low volume of background music. He turned down the gas flame under a bubbling pan of red sauce for Sergeant Riker's favorite meal. His dinner guests had not waited on ceremony. Riker and Mallory sat at the table demolishing salads of olives and purple onions, red lettuce and fettuccine, as if they had not eaten in days and days.

Charles poured out a sample of cabernet sauvignon, then set the bottle on the table. 'You're going to love this.' It was an old vintage, deep red and fine. He swirled the glass, and the bouquet summoned up the warm sun of France, country air and the scent of rich earth among the ripe grapes. He tasted it. Potent magic, a rare wine to stimulate the intellect and turn a stammering fool into a poet. He owned first editions of Blake that had cost him less, but this was truly a work of art that one could swallow.

And Riker did. He slopped it into a glass and slugged it back in one long, thirsty gulp, neatly bypassing every taste bud.

After a time, Charles closed his mouth and opened his eyes again. 'Anyway,' he said, turning back to the stove, 'it was the best I could get on short notice.'

'It's wonderful,' said Riker. Food had greatly improved the man's mood, perhaps with a little help from the wine.

'I'm glad you're taking an interest in Lars Geldorf's case.' Charles

123

opened the oven and released the aroma of warm garlic bread. 'He thought you were only humoring him.' After setting the bread basket on the table, he watched them empty it by half before he could ladle spaghetti and meatballs into their bowls, and it was a race to pour the sauce before they picked up their forks. Now he worked between the movements of silverware to add the grated cheese. 'Riker, what do you call that detective, the one with the yellow hair? He was here and gone so fast.'

'The son-in-law of the deputy commissioner. That's the kid's full name.'

'Ronald Deluthe,' said Mallory.

'Alias Duck Boy.' Riker inhaled his spaghetti, then smiled at his host. 'So, Charles, how was *your* day? Did the old guy give you any trouble?'

'Not at all.' He sat down at the table and salvaged what he could of the bread and the wine. 'I like his stories.' He turned to Mallory. 'Did you know that your father visited Natalie Homer's crime scene?'

'I know.' Mallory opened a small notebook to a page of Louis Markowitz's handwriting, then pushed it toward him. 'Take a look.'

Charles recognized a few of the lines she had transcribed last night on her computer. He found it easy to break the simple shorthand code. 'So Louis was in the room for only a few minutes.'

Riker nodded. 'That was after Geldorf removed the hair from the woman's mouth. Lou didn't know about that.'

Charles read on for a few more lines. 'He thought Natalie Homer was gagged with tape – not hair – but he doesn't say why.' And now he turned the pages faster, easily deciphering chains of sentence fragments. Apparently it was typical of Louis Markowitz to write down only the last words in a long passage of thoughts. 'Lipstick.' He turned to Mallory. 'Maybe he saw a piece of tape with her lipstick on it? Of course that word is miles from the part about the gag.'

'Cryptic bastard.' Riker reached for a slice of garlic bread and dipped it into his spaghetti sauce. 'He wrote in code so the lawyers couldn't subpoena his personal notes. What about Geldorf's stuff? Have you seen all the photos – the reports?'

'Not yet. Lars is bringing in another carton tomorrow.'

Mallory's fork hung in midair. 'He was holding out on us?'

'I wouldn't put it that way,' said Charles. 'He has a few things that didn't qualify as evidence. Said he didn't want to confuse the larger picture with minutiae.' Or, in Geldorf's words, the *small shit*. 'He has a few more photographs and notes.'

'A *carton* of 'em,' said Riker.

Charles looked from one detective to the other, then realized that the short answer should have been, yes, Geldorf had been holding out on them. 'Well, he probably didn't think you'd care. But when he found out you were planning to work on the case—'

'Never mind.' Mallory pushed her bowl aside. 'What've you got so far? Anything unusual?'

'A few discrepancies – one major problem.'

Riker helped himself to a second bowl of spaghetti. 'Did you point that out to Geldorf?'

'No, I thought it might be rude. '

'Good,' said Riker. 'Whatever you come up with, bring it to us, not him. Geldorf's not a cop anymore. He's just visiting.'

Mallory rested one hand on Charles's arm, and it had the effect of a warm current of electricity. She so rarely touched anyone. 'What's the problem?' she asked.

Well, there was a flock of butterflies crashing about inside his chest cavity. That was a problem. And he was wondering how long this contact with her would last if he sat very, very still, if he never moved the arm beneath her hand, not by so much as a hair.

Mallory leaned toward him – so close. 'Charles, are you breathing?'

'What?'

She lifted her hand from his arm, realizing that he was not choking on his supper, and the man with total recall forgot the threads to their conversation. Heat was rising in his face, the prelude to a blush. Riker gave him the kindest of smiles, the one that said, *You poor bastard.*

'The problem?' said Mallory, impatient with him now.

Oh, the lock on Natalie Homer's door. 'Sorry.' Damned sorry. 'According to the landlady's statement, the odor in the hall was overwhelming, and she was desperate to get into Natalie's apartment. The old woman had the key, but it wouldn't open the door. You see, the lock had been changed or another one added – that part's not clear.'

The detectives exchanged long glances.

'Natalie had security issues.' Charles paused again as both of them turned to stare at him. 'She was being stalked. Perhaps this is something you already know? I don't want to—'

'Go on,' said Riker. 'You're not boring us.'

'Well, the landlady made one more try at opening the door – right before she called the police. Now the first officer on the scene made a very detailed report – but no mention of kicking down a door or breaking a lock. He just entered the apartment. So, obviously, some third party opened that door before—'

'And Geldorf didn't catch this?' Riker refilled his wine glass. 'Naw, I don't see him missing a thing like that. There should be paperwork for repairs on a busted lock. It travels with the Cold Case file.'

'No,' said Charles. 'I read every word of that file. Between the landlady's call and the police response, there was a four-hour interval. I gather a bad smell wasn't a high priority. So, during those four hours, somebody opened the door with a key.'

'The perp must've had Natalie's key,' said Riker. 'He'd be the one who locked up after the murder. So he forgot something and went back to—'

'No,' said Mallory. 'He wouldn't risk it – not that day.'

'I agree,' said Charles. 'Between the heat and the insects, that body was badly decomposed. The stench was incredible – that's in the officer's report. The killer would've realized the police were on the way. Also, this was a Sunday evening. Most of the tenants would've been at home. More risk of—'

'Okay,' said Riker. 'Let's say the intruder wasn't the killer.'

'But someone with his own key,' said Charles. 'Maybe a lover. If he saw the crime scene — it was horrific — that might've left him unhinged. Now he's not the man who murdered Natalie Homer—'

'So he's the one who did the copycat hangings.' Mallory turned to Riker. 'It fits with the anniversary kill, a woman with Natalie's long blond hair. Then Sparrow—'

'Poor Sparrow.' Riker poured the last drops of wine into his glass. 'Nothing personal, the freak just needed another blonde.'

On toward midnight, Mallory circled the block once more, then cut the car's engine and turned off her headlights as she coasted silently to the curb. Her eyes were fixed on a third-floor window dimly lit by the screen of Riker's television set. She knew what he was doing up there. He was chain-smoking cigarettes and sipping bourbon — medicine for missing his ex-wife. Every glass in the apartment might be dirty, yet she knew he would not be drinking from the mouth of a bottle.

Riker's rules — only winos did that.

Mallory covertly kept him company for a while, sitting in the dark of her car, keeping watch on his window. It was the kind of thing one partner did for another — as if she could fly that high when his gun went off.

A year had passed since the last time his ex-wife had inspired a day-long binge. Mallory had helped him stagger up all those stairs, then rolled him on to an unmade bed, where he had slept in his clothes, but not his shoes. And she had also removed his gun that night and taken the bullets away.

He was a sorry alcoholic; that would never change. And Mallory was also constant.

The light in the window went out.

'Night, Riker.

She started up her car and headed home.

He would not kill himself in the dark; it would be too difficult for a blind and trembling drunk to thread his finger into the trigger. And she could not foresee him dying in the bathroom by the glow of his plastic Jesus night-light.

EIGHT

The rear office was flooded with morning light. Charles thought the room temperature had chilled by a few degrees since he had last looked in, but little else had changed. Mallory was still averting her eyes from the paper storm on her cork wall, an anathema to someone who straightened paintings in other people's houses. She sat at a metal workstation, but no longer communed with her network of computers. The three machines hummed amongst themselves while she leafed through Louis Markowitz's old notebook. The only human sound was the tap of Lars Geldorf's pacing shoes.

Impatient to begin the day, the retired detective removed his suit jacket and loosened his tie, but this clue was lost on her. Occasionally, she looked up from her reading to watch his travels about the room – *her* room – as he inspected metal shelves stocked with electronics. Geldorf wore a brave pretender's smile and nodded in a knowing way, though he had no idea what her machines could do. They were new, and he was old.

She rose from her chair and approached the cork wall to stand before a haphazard arrangement of crime-scene photographs. Charles observed tension in her face, a small war going on at the core of her as she struggled with the urge to place every bit of paper at perfect right angles to the next.

Lars Geldorf hurried across the room to join her. And now Charles understood what the last fifteen minutes of silence had been about. Mallory was teaching the old man to follow her lead. There should

129

never be any doubt about the hierarchy in this room, and Geldorf should not call her *honey* one more time. Charles decided that she must like the old man, for this was the mildest and most drawn-out show of contempt in her repertoire.

She lifted the edge of a grainy photograph to expose a small square one pinned beneath it. Then she looked under the other eight-by-ten formats in this group, each one covering a picture from an instant camera. 'All you've got are Polaroids and blow-ups.'

'Yeah,' said Geldorf. 'So?'

'Where are the originals?'

'That's all of 'em, kid.'

'Mallory,' she corrected him.

'Suppose I call you Kathy?'

'Don't.' And that was a threat. 'So there was no police photographer on the scene?'

'Yeah, we had one, a civilian. But he didn't last three minutes.' Geldorf waved one hand to include all the images of a hanged woman, two days dead in the heat of August, an incubator of maggots. 'The photographer got sick and dropped his camera. We couldn't get it to work after that. So we borrowed one from a neighbor.'

Mallory stared at a shot of the hanging rope draped over a light fixture. 'What's that brown smear on the ceiling?'

'Bugs on their way to a meal,' said Geldorf. 'Cockroaches *love* their grease. And here.' One bony finger pointed to another photograph depicting a large brown glob on the kitchen floor. 'Roaches swarming over a frying pan.' He squinted. 'You see those little logs on the floor? Those are sausages and more bugs. The ceiling light was coming loose and cracking the plaster. Must've been a nest of 'em up there. I had more blow-ups made.'

Geldorf edged a few steps down the wall, where the medical examiner's materials were grouped together. He perused the pictures of flies hanging with their spawn. 'Charles? What did you do with my best cockroaches?'

'They're pinned up under the maggot pictures. Seemed like the only logical place for them.'

'What?' Mallory stared at him, clearly wondering where logic entered into this.

Geldorf answered for him. 'Flies are the only useful bugs at a crime scene. Roaches can't tell you nothin'.'

'Right,' said Charles. 'So I pinned them up under the more useful—' There was not much point in finishing his thought, for Mallory had tuned him out. She was staring at her nails. Perhaps she had found a flaw in her manicure that would take precedence over an insect monologue.

She looked up. 'Done? Good. Let's get the roaches up front.'

When Charles had removed the covering pictures of flies and their larvae, Mallory appraised the giant cockroaches pouring out of the ceiling and making their way down the rope to the corpse. The photo that caught her attention was a shot of the victim's apron and a rectangular stain spotted with brown insects.

Geldorf stepped close to the wall. 'Looks like she dropped her frying pan in the scuffle and splattered the grease. There was a utility blackout at dusk, so—'

'No.' Mallory looked down at the baseboard where the actual skillet leaned against the wall. She tapped the picture of the apron stain. 'That's *not* a grease spatter.'

Charles knew she was paraphrasing a line in Louis Markowitz's old notebook, the words, *No splash – a smear*. Louis had found that observation worthy of an underscore but it was never explained until now. The two long edges of the rectangle were fairly well defined. This was not a splatter pattern.

Mallory turned to the retired detective. 'Natalie was cooking a meal, maybe expecting company. You interviewed her friends?'

'She didn't have any,' said Geldorf. 'When she was married, her husband wouldn't let her get a job. Never gave her any money. She hardly ever left the apartment. After the divorce, I guess she forgot how to make new friends.' He stared at the close-up of the sausages on the floor. 'It was probably a meal for one.'

Charles noted Mallory's skepticism, then counted up the sausages. During a summer of utility blackouts that made refrigeration unreliable, Natalie Homer would not have purchased more food than she could eat at one sitting, and such a slender woman could not eat so many sausages – not by herself. Who was the dinner guest? He inclined his head toward the smaller man. 'Natalie was also alienated from her family, right?'

'Yeah,' said Geldorf. 'A year after she got married, her sister stopped talking to her. But that wasn't in the statements. How'd you know?'

'It fits a pattern of spousal abuse. Forced dependence, isolation.' Charles turned to Mallory. 'Her husband may have knocked her around a bit during the marriage.'

'Right again,' said Geldorf. 'That's what Natalie told me.'

Mallory's voice was all suspicion now. 'You *talked* to her?'

'Yeah, of course I did. Twice, sometimes three times a week.'

'I think I mentioned the stalking last night.' Charles walked toward the center of the wall and a cluster of papers. 'These are samples of her complaints.' He unpinned the paperwork and handed her five stalker reports.

'The trouble started right after her divorce.' Geldorf leaned down to pick up an envelope propped against the baseboard. 'This is the rest of 'em.'

'And after she died?' Mallory stared at the thick envelope. 'All those complaints – no leads on the stalker?'

'She never saw the guy's face,' said Geldorf. 'The first time she came in, we thought she was just paranoid. I mean, sure, men were gonna follow her around.'

'Because she was pretty,' said Mallory, though not one image on the wall could have told her that. In death, Natalie was grotesque.

'She was beautiful.' Geldorf bent down to the carton he had brought

132

in that morning. He pulled out a brown paper bag and removed a packet of photographs. 'I didn't think these belonged with the evidence.' He held up one smiling portrait of a young woman with blond hair falling past her shoulders. Natalie's eyes were large and blue.

Mallory folded the envelope of complaints under one arm, then carried the pictures to a clear section of wall and pinned them up with machinelike precision, each border exactly the same distance from the next. 'A pro took these shots.'

Charles agreed. The lighting was perfect, and the subject's pose was not candid, but artful.

'The photographer was another dead end,' said Geldorf. 'That woman was older than I am now.'

Mallory had yet to open the envelope of complaints. She merely hefted its weight in one hand. 'Natalie spent a lot of time in your station house. A *lot* of time. When you figured out that she wasn't paranoid – what then?'

'We went after the ex-husband and told him to stay away from her. He was a cool one. Never owned up to nothin'.'

'And after the murder?'

'We hauled him in for questioning. But he had an alibi for the time of death. He was in Atlantic City all weekend. That's where he was gettin' married to the next Mrs Homer. Jane was her name. They never left the hotel room all weekend. That's what the staff said. But how much would it cost to buy an alibi from a maid and a bellboy? And the statement from the second wife, Jane – that was worthless. Two days married, and that bastard had her cowed.'

Mallory was not listening anymore. She had discovered one of the stalker's notes in a clear plastic evidence bag. She took it down from the wall and stared at a brief message penciled on thin airmail paper. The letters were painstakingly drawn in varying sizes and scripts.

'All seven of 'em say the same thing,' said Geldorf. 'We figured they were traced from magazines. No newsprint smudges on the paper. Natalie found 'em under her door at night when she got home from work. Be careful,' said Geldorf, as she pulled them out of the bag. 'That paper's really fragile, and you don't wanna smudge the pencil.'

Charles expected Mallory to be annoyed with this lecture on the handling of evidence, but she only stared at the paper, transfixed by the words, *I touched you today.*

Geldorf never noticed her reaction. Hands in his pockets, rocking on his heels, he stared at the photographs of the murder scene. 'That kid photographer who dropped his camera – he wasn't the only one who got sick that night. There was this young cop – the uniform who found the body – I can't remember if it was Parris or Loman.'

Mallory looked up from her reading. He had her undivided attention now.

Geldorf continued, 'We couldn't get him back inside the apartment again. An hour later, he's at the stationhouse, still batting off flies and stomping his feet to shake roaches out of his pantlegs. Well, there weren't any bugs on him – not one – not then, but he could still *feel* them. Oh, and the stink. You can't take a picture of that. But you know what I remember best? I could hear it outside in the hall when I was walkin' toward that apartment. When I opened the door – it was *so* loud, so many of 'em. Scared the hell out of me.' He closed his eyes. 'I can hear it now. The roar of flies – *thousands* of flies.'

Sergeant Riker entered the office, arms laden with the bags of a delicatessen breakfast. 'Did I miss anything?'

Riker lured Geldorf down the hall to the office kitchen with promises of coffee and food. After settling the deli bags on the table, he fumbled with the wrappings, hunting for a bacon-and-egg on white toast dripping with heart-attack grease. He spread the packages on a red-checked tablecloth, the only bit of charm to survive the ruthless takeover of Mallory's machine decor.

After writing down the delicatessen's phone number, he handed it to Geldorf. 'Lose this and you'll starve.' While he and Mallory covertly worked on Sparrow's case, Geldorf would have to fend for himself.

Charles would be no help in foraging for food around the office; on principle, the man ignored all kitchen appliances with control panels more complex than the dashboard of his Mercedes.

'Deluthe should've made the deli run. What good is a slave if he doesn't do errands?'

Geldorf grinned. 'Mallory's got him chasing down personnel files for all the cops from my crime scene.'

'Well, that should keep him occupied.' A whiteshield in training pants would have to stand in line all day long at One Police Plaza. But Duck Boy's report would reinforce the fiction that they were working on Natalie Homer's murder. He handed a paper coffee cup to the retired detective. 'I hear you've been working cold cases for six years. You missed the job, huh?'

'Yeah, I like to keep—' Geldorf was facing the kitchen door when he stiffened slightly, then sat up very straight. This was Riker's clue that Mallory was standing behind his own chair. Obviously, she had been training the help again. Every time she entered a room, Duck Boy had this same conditioned response.

She laid a stack of paperwork beside his coffee cup. Riker leafed through the familiar forms of citizen complaints. Natalie Homer had been a frequent visitor to her local police station. This was a replay of Lieutenant Loman's squad making a stationhouse pet of Kennedy Harper.

'There's a big gap in the dates for these complaints,' she said.

Geldorf nodded. 'The pervert gave her a breather. Two weeks later, he was stalking her again, and he was escalating. That's when he started leaving those notes under her door. And phone calls – no conversation, and no heavy breathing either. I think he only wanted to hear her voice.'

Riker fished through his pockets for matches and cigarettes. 'Was the ex-husband in town during those two weeks?'

'Oh, yeah. The guy never missed a day of work at the post office. But I knew he was guilty.'

135

After emptying the cigarettes from his crumpled pack, Riker hunted for one that was not broken. 'So you never developed other suspects.'

'What for? Erik Homer did it,' said Geldorf. 'If only the bastard hadn't up and died on me. He had a heart attack a year after the murder.'

Mallory laid down another sheet of paper. 'This is the ex-husband's statement. There's just one line about Natalie's son. How old was the boy when his mother died?'

'Oh, six or seven. The kid's father had sole custody. After the divorce, she never saw her son again.'

Mallory's eyes locked with Riker's. He nodded, holding the same thought: Natalie's son would be twenty-six years old today, a prime age group for serial killers. He lit a cigarette, then exhaled and watched the smoke spiral up to the ceiling. 'You know where that kid is now?'

Geldorf shook his head. 'After his father died, the stepmother told me she gave the boy to Natalie's sister – a cop hater. Zero cooperation.'

'So she's holding a grudge.' Riker looked back at the kitchen counter, seeking something to pass for an ashtray. 'All this time and no leads on her sister's murder. I can't blame her.'

'Me either,' said Geldorf. 'But Natalie's sister didn't have the boy. That's all she'd say. I figure she fobbed him off on another relative. A few months after I checked out the Cold Case file, I asked her to tell the kid that I never gave up on his mom. Then I left her alone.'

Riker stole a glance at Mallory. Was she also wondering if Lars Geldorf had triggered a murder spree?

The old man grinned at each of them in turn. 'I know what you guys are thinking. You figure the boy's grown up and gone psycho, right? You think he's your perp for that hooker hanging?' He shook his head. 'How would he get the details? Only the killer could've told that little boy about the hair packed in his mother's mouth. I don't see his dad sharing that with him.'

Mallory pulled up a chair at the table. 'So you never talked to the boy.'

'No, there was no point in it.' Geldorf rose from his chair. 'I'll be back in a minute.'

When the bathroom door had closed at the other end of the hall, Mallory handed Riker a twenty-year-old statement signed by a rookie patrolman. 'Is that Lieutenant Loman's first name? Harvey?'

Before Riker could respond, *Jesus Christ, yes it is*, Charles Butler entered the kitchen, saying, 'I can tell you why Natalie had those photographs taken. It was an actress portfolio.' He handed Riker a photocopy of a newspaper column. 'I found that on microfiche at the library. It's the only mention on the death of Natalie Homer.'

And the press had not wasted much type on the lying headline, *Suicide*. Riker skipped over the first dry lines and read the short story of Natalie Homer's life and death. '"She served cocktails at a local bar from six o'clock till closing time."' And every Wednesday afternoon she sat in the cheap seats of off-Broadway theaters, watching matinées in the dark and learning another trade. She was too poor to pay for acting lessons, so said her landlady. The rest of Natalie's days were spent dogging miles of pavement, making the rounds of theatrical agencies that never found her any work. Every day she reminded them that she was still alive and still determined to make it in New York City. ' "That girl worked so hard," said the landlady. "She was tired *all* the time. You *say* that when you write about her. You say something *nice*." ' According to police sources, the young actress was found at the end of the day ' "at the end of a rope" .'

Mallory waited for Detective Janos at the address he had given her along with his promise that she would find it interesting, but he had said nothing about the actress connection, not within earshot of Lieutenant Coffey.

The lot next to the narrow building was a dusty construction site. The only structure was a portable restroom the size of an upended coffin, and a troupe of children formed a wriggling column at the door. The day-camp supervisor, a very tired woman, called out her thanks to the men in hard hats. Her young campers were making a toilet stop while roaming the neighborhood on a nature walk, though the flora of this East Village street was limited to scrawny city trees dying of heat and urine showers. And the wildlife only amounted to one dead squirrel in the gutter and a pigeon strolling down the sidewalk. The bird was followed closely by a homicide detective carrying a rolled newspaper. The children were impressed by the man's large size and his brutal face. They laughed, pointing fingers like guns, and then used one another for human shields.

'Hey, Mallory.' Detective Janos joined her at the door of the narrow shop which now served as a makeshift theater for art films. 'You were right. Everybody wants to be in show business. Kennedy Harper worked second shift. That left her days free for auditions.'

'So she had an agent?'

'No, she didn't need one. There's open auditions all over town.' He handed her a page torn from an old copy of *Backstage*. 'Heller found a sheet like this in her trash – ripped to shreds. I'm guessing the auditions didn't go well.' He handed her his rolled newspaper. 'This is a recent edition.'

The pages were turned back to columns of dates and locations for open casting calls. 'There's at least five auditions a day.'

'Not if you scratch the out-of-town locations and the song-and-dance gigs. More like one or two. I just came from an audition. Must've been a hundred actors standing in line on Spring Street. I figure that's how he found Sparrow and Kennedy. He just walked down the line and picked out the blonde he liked best.'

'So now we're three for three,' said Mallory. Natalie Homer, Kennedy Harper and Sparrow had all been aspiring actresses.

'Yeah, and I think you're right about consolidating the cases, but Coffey's never gonna buy that. The boss figures our chances are better if we work the fresh hangings. And he'd go nuts if he knew I was here.'

Janos's implication was clear: there would be no more covert meetings. He turned to the grimy window of the Hole in the Wall Theater. 'An actor in Sparrow's play tipped us off to this place. They're running a videotape of her dress rehearsal.'

A handmade poster taped to the window had retitled Chekhov's play *The Three Sisters* as *The Hanging Hooker*. Alongside the poster was the attendant publicity. Front-page stories of New York tabloids had also given star billing to the comatose prostitute.

You're famous, Sparrow. You made it.

And now, if only the whore would finish this dragged-out affair of her dying.

After Janos had walked back to his car, she paid the three-dollar admission at the door, then passed through a curtain to enter a dark room that stank of smoke and sweat. There were chairs for twenty, but only two other patrons watched the television monitor. One of the men rose from his chair, muttering, 'Rip off.' He was obviously disappointed that *The Hanging Hooker* was actually a classical play – no nudity and nothing lewd. The second man followed him out of the room, equally offended, leaving the detective to watch the video alone.

Only the keenest observer would have noticed the change in Mallory as her young face took on the conviction of a stubborn child. She sat very still, eyes fixed on the screen, a window she watched with great expectation – waiting for Sparrow. She had been waiting for years.

An elderly crone appeared on stage in company with a young actress, a beautiful girl so far removed from the drooling, eye-rolling dementia of the coma patient. The voice that filtered through Mallory's shock was familiar and not.

'*Nothing ever happens the way we want it to—*'

Sparrow was dressed in the clothes she had worn to her hanging. The southern accent had been erased, and a gifted surgeon had made her too young for the part of Olga. Years had passed since Mallory had last checked up on Sparrow, and now she saw another change in this woman, something surgery could not provide. The whore was lit from within – fresh fire. Even Sparrow's eyes had made a comeback, clear and bright, seeing the world for the first time – all over again, an encore of youth. This was what she had looked like on the night they first met.

And how old was I, Sparrow? Eight? Nine?

It was winter then, a sudden storm, and a feverish young Kathy Mallory had crawled into the last remaining telephone booth in New York City, the only one with a door that she could close against the stinging snow. She had fed money into the coin slots, a daily habit and the only constant of a childhood on the streets.

More than a thousand miles away and years away, a dying woman had written a telephone number on the little girl's palm. All but the last four digits had been smudged off her hand before that terrible day had ended. Kathy continued to obey long after her mother had died. Though she had forgotten the reason for these telephone calls, she continued making up numbers to replace the three that were missing. Whenever she heard a feminine voice on the line, the child would become inexplicably hopeful and say the ritual words, *It's Kathy. I'm lost.*

None of the startled women on the receiving end of these calls had known who she was, thus giving themselves away as impostors. That night, one of them had cried into the telephone, 'Won't you tell me who you are? How can I—'

Click. And another connection was severed, another woman left in tears, and hope died. The child had become an addict of hope, and the best part of this game was that she could get it back again every day, any time she wanted it.

The fever had given way to violent chills. Her small hands were shaking as she tried her last coins, her last call, saying, 'It's Kathy. I'm lost.'

Out of a thousand women, only Sparrow had responded, 'Where are you, baby? I'll come get you.' This had been said with the lilt of the Southland – so like a dead mother's voice.

Anticipation had kept Kathy from giving into sleep and death while she waited for the Southerner to come and find her. The little girl's eyes had begun to close when she saw a shadow on the other side of the fogged glass. It was coming for her, moving quickly, flying through the storm. The door opened, and a woman's arms reached into the telephone booth to gather up the shivering child, warming Kathy with fake fur and perfumed body heat.

While the delirium lasted, the little girl believed that her dead mother had come to carry her home, and all that was lost had been restored. The night of the snowstorm, pressed up against the warm breast of a whore, was the happiest time that Kathy Mallory had ever known.

'—our life is not over yet,' said the actress on the screen.

The summer heat was stifling in the small theater, yet the young detective remained in her seat after the play was done. Head bowed, she sat in absolute darkness, awaiting the video's next run – so she could continue to nurse her deep hatred of Sparrow.

Riker had already made a case for combining the investigations, and he had lost. Mallory should have handled this, but she had failed to show, and this worried him. Coming late to any appointment was outside the pathology of a punctuality freak.

She was still wearing dark glasses when she entered Jack Coffey's private office and pulled up a chair without waiting for an invitation to sit down. Riker smiled in the belief that she had picked up this bad habit from him.

Lieutenant Coffey leaned back in his chair, only glancing at his wristwatch to remind Mallory that she was late. 'Riker tells me the scarecrow has a type – stage-struck blondes.'

'Hmm. His victims were stand-ins for Natalie Homer.' Mallory seemed almost bored as she leaned toward the stack of newspapers at the edge of the desk. 'Her case is the key to the scarecrow's hangings.'

The lieutenant was not rising to this bait, but it was early in the game, only round one by Riker's reckoning. The boss kept his silence, expecting Mallory to elaborate. She picked up a newspaper, cast it aside after a minute, and opened another. After folding back a page, she glanced at Coffey, her eyebrows arching to ask him why he kept her waiting.

'The scarecrow is a copycat, and a bad one,' said the lieutenant. 'He was nowhere near Natalie Homer's crime scene.'

Did that sound defensive? Riker thought so.

'And I say he was there.' Mallory lowered her sunglasses to scan a column of newsprint that interested her more.

'Too many things don't fit,' said Coffey, 'all those candles, the wrong noose. I know this perp never saw that crime scene.'

'I would've thought just the opposite,' said a friendly voice, and Coffey spun his chair around to stare at the tall man whose head barely cleared the top of the door frame. Misunderstanding the look of surprise, Charles Butler glanced at his watch, saying, 'Oh, sorry. I'm too early?'

The lieutenant would be wondering why a civilian had been invited to the briefing. Riker gave up on the idea of damage control and braced himself for a shouting match. It was predictable that Coffey would do all the yelling. Mallory would sit back and let the man knock himself out. And perhaps then she would drop the bomb of Lieutenant Loman's presence on Natalie Homer's crime scene.

There were no free chairs, and Charles Butler was always self-conscious about inadvertently dwarfing people and their furniture. He leaned against the glass wall, believing this would make him smaller and more polite. 'The inconsistencies make sense to me.'

The lieutenant was forcing a smile. 'So you're siding with Mallory?'

What a damn surprise.

'Yes,' said Charles. 'The scarecrow is working from a twenty-year-old memory – bound to be errors. At least, he has a fair idea of how many flies were at the original crime scene. I understand he brings them in a jar.'

Coffey turned an accusing eye on Mallory, but before he could nail her to the wall for this breach of case details, she said, 'He's our consulting psychologist. I know how much you hate the department shrink.'

The lieutenant nodded, for this was true. The consultant on call for Special Crimes was an incompetent hack and an irritant to the entire squad. A year ago, he had offered the job to Charles Butler only to discover that the city of New York could not afford a man with more than one PhD. 'It's just too bad we don't have the budget for him.'

Riker had the distinct impression that the lieutenant was overacting.

'Not a problem.' Mallory was still working through the stack of newspapers. 'He can't earn any more money this quarter.'

'Right,' said Charles. 'It's a tax thing. I'm at your disposal, free of charge.'

The lieutenant was rightly distrustful of something for nothing, but he had not yet worked out the potential for treachery.

Mallory folded the last newspaper from the pile on the desk. 'There's nothing in here on Kennedy Harper. And the reporters botched the story on Sparrow's hanging. They're still calling it a hooker's sex game. Sounds almost accidental. Charles thinks this will send the scarecrow into a homicidal rage. The next kill could be any day now.'

Riker could see that this opinion was a big surprise to her new consulting psychologist.

'If you believe the papers,' she said, 'the only women at risk are hookers. It's time to go public.'

'All right,' said Coffey, 'we'll give the actresses a sporting chance to stay alive.' He turned to face his generous gift from Mallory – Charles Butler. 'Let's say you're right about the scarecrow being pissed off. Why doesn't he call the media and set them straight?'

'It's just my impression, but I think he wants the police to work it out.'

'And he's stalking the next victim right now,' said Mallory. 'We need the public tip lines up and running.'

Coffey shook his head. 'We don't have to panic every blonde in the city – only women who fit the profile. And we're not gonna mention the Cold Case file to the press.' He turned to Charles Butler. 'Any more ideas about the scarecrow?'

'I assume his tie to Natalie Homer is very strong. He's restaged her murder twice.'

'Well, that's one theory.' Coffey turned to his detectives. 'I put Gary Zappata on the short list.'

Mallory abandoned her role as the Laid-back Kid. Her fist came down on the arm of her chair. 'What *possible*—'

'Hold it.' The lieutenant put up one hand to silence her. 'Did you know his father was a detective? Yeah, Zappata wanted to be one, too.' Coffey turned to Charles. 'When this guy was a cop, he was real close to getting fired. That's when our desk sergeant sold him on the idea of applying to the fire department. Sergeant Bell told the kid it was easy to make the fire marshal's squad. Then he could carry a gun and play detective.'

Riker nodded. This friendly gesture fitted so well with Bell's philosophy: Always stay on good terms with a psycho cop.

'The other night,' said Coffey, 'our boy turns up on the scene of a murder and runs the damn show.'

Mallory's red fingernails drummed the arm of her chair. 'So Zappata is hanging women – as a *career* move.'

'Hear me out.' This was not a request. Coffey was ordering her to keep her mouth shut. 'I can place him on two crime scenes. His face is in the crowd shots outside of Kennedy Harper's place.'

'So he's got a police scanner in his car,' said Riker. 'You know three people who don't?'

The lieutenant ignored this remark and spoke to his new consultant. 'This man was voted most likely to come back here with a shotgun and blow away his ex-coworkers. Does that help you?' Coffey shuffled the papers on his desk until he found the report he wanted. 'Zappata started his shift the minute Sparrow's 911 call came in. The firehouse was two blocks from the scene. I'm surprised their Dalmatian didn't suss out the smoke a lot faster.'

'You figure he hung her, then ran two blocks to the firehouse to set up an alibi?'

'Yeah, Mallory.' Coffey paused a beat, perhaps to remind her that sarcasm was insubordination. 'The sloppy noose and a slow death bought him some time. But he *did* want her to die.' He turned back to Charles. 'According to a report filed by Zappata's own crew, he physically restrained another fireman when the guy tried to cut Sparrow down.'

Riker faced his partner. 'It's got some merit.' And this, of course, was code for, *Play nice, or he won't consolidate the cases.* And when was she planning to bring up Lieutenant Loman's connection? That would get the boss's attention *real* fast. He caught her eye and mouthed the name.

Mallory shook her head, then turned to Coffey. 'How would Zappata get details of a twenty-year-old murder?'

'I think his old man told him,' said Coffey. 'Look at all the details that don't match up. He knew there were candles, but not how many. He knew there was a noose, but not what kind. This fits with third-hand information. Twenty years ago, Zappata's father might've had connections to one of the crime-scene cops. We're checking that now.'

'There wasn't any fire at Kennedy Harper's apartment. If Zappata was—'

'Maybe he was practicing, Mallory. Or maybe he knew that woman. Suppose he killed Sparrow to draw us off the—'

'No,' said Mallory. 'You *want* it to be Zappata. I don't like that creep either, but there's a problem with your theory. Sparrow could've taken him down with a dull kitchen knife.' She spoke with something close to pride in an old enemy. 'Even without a weapon, that whore would've done a lot of damage. She was that good.'

Riker could attest to that. Sparrow would have been damned hard to intimidate. Once, the hooker had survived a stabbing that should have been fatal. Fifteen years later, she was still proving impossible to kill. Against the best medical advice of her doctor, she had lived through another night.

Jack Coffey was smiling at Mallory — always a bad sign. 'So why didn't Sparrow bone the perp like a fish? No answer? I'll tell you why. He rushed her in the dark. The lightbulb over her door was unscrewed.'

Riker stared at his shoes. He knew what was coming. He had forgotten to tell her—

'One more thing,' said Coffey. 'And you can thank your partner for this. He called CSU back to the scene to dust that bulb, and they found Zappata's prints.'

Riker glanced at Mallory. To the extent that she was capable of pity, that would best describe her smile and the slow shake of her head. 'That's good,' she said. 'You found a fireman's prints — at the scene of a fire.'

Damn fine shot. Elegant, simple. All that remained was to have her name engraved on the winner's cup. But Riker could see that Jack Coffey was not about to concede. The boss was smiling when he said, 'All right, here's my best deal. We keep the motive open — the suspect list too. But you and Riker stay on the Cold Case file.' He splayed his hands to say, *See? I'm a fair man.*

The actress hangings, old and new, would remain with their assigned primaries and their separate lines of investigation. Riker knew that was not going to change. But Mallory had poisoned the lieutenant. All day long, it would worry Jack Coffey that she might be right, that the next kill would happen on his watch.

While Mommy drank paper-cup tea with another mother, the child had been drawn away from her and toward the sound of flies round the other side of a garbage drum. He was quite impressed by the sight of them, a living, swarming blanket over something small yet wonderfully stinky at the center of a piece of wax paper. The grass of Tompkins Square tickled his bare knees as he knelt before the frenzy of insects and wondered what they were attacking. Might their prey still be alive and twitching? Hopeful, he prodded the fetid meat, using a common stick of the sort that is issued to all boys at their birth. He found the underlying flesh to be squishy but definitely dead, impervious to pokes. Somewhat disappointed, he continued to watch the writhing mass of legs and wings and fat black bodies. The loud buzzing was really evil, quite delightful.

The boy's interest waned and he wandered to a nearby bench and a man clad in jeans and a baseball cap. This figure was as rigid as any beast in a long parade of dead hamsters, songbirds and goldfish. He was as lifeless as the flesh beneath the flies, though not one winged thing dared approach him. The child solved this mystery as he drew closer to the bench and caught a whiff of insecticide on the man's clothes. An open gray bag on the ground held a canister of the stuff Mommy used when she chased down lone bugs flying through the rooms of their apartment. The bag also contained a large glass jar half filled with dead dry flies and a few that were still alive.

A collector.

Well, now the world made sense again as the boy connected the man to the foul-smelling meat and the swarm. An excellent solution – no need to chase the flies down.

The man took no notice of the little boy, and this was odd behavior to a child who knew himself to be the center of the universe. The man never blinked, never moved. The boy's eyes rounded as he watched intently for some sign of life. At the end of his attention span, perhaps half a minute, he pronounced his subject dead as a dead hamster. But just to be sure, and only in the spirit of scientific enquiry, he poked the dead man's leg with his stick.

The corpse turned its head, and the child screamed.

Fast mother steps came up behind him, fleshy arms wound round his small body, lifted him and bore him away. As the boy bounced with his mother's running gait, he looked over her soft shoulder to see the dead man don a pair of yellow rubber gloves. Now the man approached the mass of buzzing flies with his insecticide can and rained down clouds of aerosol poison on the swarm.

The young actress had won a seat on the subway by beating another straphanger to a crack between two passengers on the plastic bench. She carved a wider niche with her squirming backside and settled in for the long ride home to the East Village.

After inspecting her suit jacket for battle scars, she removed one long blond hair from the lapel. The pale blue linen matched her eyes, and it was the most expensive outfit she had ever owned. Perversely, she regarded the suit as her lucky charm, though it had failed her in one audition after another.

In dire need of distraction from the sweaty press of flesh, she balanced a new packet of postcards on her knee and penned her weekly lies to the Abandoned Stellas. She borrowed a phrase from the rack of advertisements posted above the car's windows, *New York is a summer festival.*

A canvas bag hit her in the side of the head.

'Hey!' she yelled, just like a real New Yorker. 'Watch it!' She looked up to see the crotch of a man's faded blue jeans a few inches from her face. He reeked of insecticide. She lowered her eyes to the postcard and wrote the words, *I love this town.*

She wanted to go back home to Ohio.

Last year, as the family's first college graduate, she had qualified for the traditional entry-level job of all theater majors – serving fast food to the public. And this had come as a bitter surprise to the Abandoned Stellas, two generations of tired truck-stop waitresses, impregnated and deserted before the age of seventeen.

Grandma, the original Stella, had cashed a savings bond to send the aspiring actress to New York City, a place with *no* roadside diners, and more money had followed every month. The second Stella, also known as Mom, still waited on tables and sent all the tips to her daughter, the only Stella ever to leave Ohio.

The train's air-conditioner was not working, and Stella Small resented everyone around her for using up precious oxygen. She singled out the woman seated next to her for The Glare, a practiced stare that said, *Die.* The other woman, beyond intimidation, happily chomped a meaty sandwich that was still alive and moving of its own accord. Rings of onion and dollops of mayonnaise slithered from the greasy slices of bread and added a new odor to the stink of sweat and bug spray. Stella slipped the finished postcard into her purse and began to spin a new lie, this one for her agent. How would she explain losing a role to an idiot with no acting experience?

The train was one stop away from Astor Place and home. The smelly sandwich eater got up, leaving a residue of tomato slices on the plastic seat. This prevented other passengers from sitting down, but Stella could not stand up against the press of new passengers, nor could she edge away from the scratching man seated next to her. Had she already contracted body lice? The flesh of her upper arm felt crawly, itchy. Her hand moved to her sleeve to scratch it, then touched something alive and twitching.

Oh, shit!

A fat black fly. And now a rain of flies fell down on her head in the numbers of a biblical plague. Incredibly, most of them were dead. Others still twitched, only sick and sluggish, crawling slowly across her lap – down her legs.

Up her skirt! *No!*

She jumped up from the bench, wildly slapping her hair and her clothes. Insects dropped to the floor around her shoes and crawled in all directions. Stella screamed and set off a chain reaction of squeals from other riders. People were trampling one another to get to the other end of the car. Dry fly carcasses crunched underfoot as she jumped up and down, trying to shake loose the bugs that were still alive and crawling up her pantyhose. Other riders joined the hysteria dance, feet stomping, hands waving, fingers flicking. One passenger accidentally dislodged a note taped to Stella's back; it drifted to the

Carol O'Connell

floor as the train lurched to a stop, and all the doors opened. The small piece of paper and its message ran away stuck to the bottom of another woman's shoe.

NINE

Charles Butler stood at the center of the Special Crimes incident room, only glancing at the flanking walls, each one devoted to a hanged woman. Now the rear wall – that was fascinating. The halo of dead flies around the scarecrow's baseball cap was definite proof of creativity. He turned to the detective beside him. 'Seriously? Ronald Deluthe did this?'

'Yeah.' Riker diddled the controls of a small cassette player. 'I may wind up liking that kid.'

Pssst.

'Then why not stop treating him like a half-bright child?'

'Okay, I'll buy him a beer. That's the highest honor I'm allowed to confer on a lame trainee.' Riker raised the volume of the cassette to play a few words spoken in an empty monotone. This was the voice of the scarecrow alone in a gray landscape, a monotonous plain with no rise of emotion, no depth of despair. The only relief in this flatline existence was the ambient sound.

Pssst.

Charles stared at the other walls papered with handwritten notes and typed reports, fax sheets and photographs. He could perceive no order in this work of many hands and minds. 'Can we take the paperwork back to—'

'No,' said Riker. 'We can't remove anything from this room. Can't copy it either. Coffey's orders. So just read *everything*.'

And now that Charles understood his role as a human Xerox

machine, he walked along the south wall, committing the paperwork of Kennedy Harper's murder to eidetic memory. Obviously all the autopsy information had been pinned up by Mallory. It was a small oasis of perfect alignment on an otherwise sloppy wall where neighboring papers hung straight only by accident.

The detective walked alongside him, working the volume of the cassette player as they crossed over to the opposite wall. 'Listen to this one more time.'

Pssst.

'Regular intervals,' said Riker. 'We know it's automated. Our techs think it might be a plant mister in a florist shop or a commercial greenhouse.'

'I'd rule out a workplace,' said Charles. 'If the scarecrow was worried about being interrupted, you'd hear that in his voice. But it's level, isn't it? Utterly flat.' He listened to another sentence fragment, then – *Pssst.* 'There – a breath pause. The rhythm of his speech works around the ambient sound. It's like punctuation. I'd say he's been living with that noise for a very long time. It might come from a machine related to health issues.' While Charles was speaking to Riker, in another compartment of his mind, he was absorbing the text of Edward Slope's autopsy report on a living woman. 'Doesn't this coma patient have a last name?'

'Sparrow,' said Riker. 'That's it.'

Mallory was in the room, but Charles could not say just when she had arrived. Cats made more racket with soft padding paws. He sometimes wondered if this was her idea of fun, watching startled people jump – as Riker did when he noticed her strolling along the wall behind them. She showed little interest in the photo array of Sparrow's nude body. Only one picture at the edge of the group attracted her, a close-up of a vicious wound on the victim's side. The scar was an old one, a gross knot of flesh grown over a hole. Mallory closed her eyes, a small but telling gesture, and he read much into it. She had more in common with Sparrow than a paperback western retrieved from a crime scene.

Mallory looked up to catch Charles staring at her. 'What?'

Pssst.

'There's something I'm curious about.' He stepped back to the group of photographs taken at the hospital. Edward Slope's signature appeared on the last page of notes in Mallory's rigid handwriting. He pointed to the picture of Sparrow's scar framed by the gloved hands of the medical examiner. 'Evidently, Edward spent some time exploring this wound, but you didn't mention it in any of your notes.'

'It's old history,' she said. 'Nothing to do with this case.'

'So you know how it happened.'

Pssst.

Riker was suddenly leaving them with uncommon speed, moving to the other side of the room, and that was the only warning that Charles had trodden on some personal landmine.

'It's an old knife wound. *Very* old. A waste of time.' She ripped the photograph from the wall. 'It shouldn't even be here.'

'But you told Coffey this woman was good with a knife.'

'None better.' She crumpled the photograph in one hand, and Charles could see the bright work going on behind her intelligent eyes.

Because he was handicapped with a face that could not run a bluff in a poker game, most people wrongly assumed that he could not tell when he was being lied to. Mallory never made that mistake. He guessed that she was simply wondering what half-truth might be most misleading.

'It wasn't a fight,' she said. 'Sparrow never saw the knife coming.'

'So she had a blind side?'

'No!' She wadded the photograph into a ball, then rolled it between her palms, making it smaller and smaller. 'Yes.' And now her voice was smaller too. 'You could say she was blindsided by a joke.' The little ball of paper disappeared into her closed fist. 'Sparrow was laughing when he did it to her.' And while Charles was watching this little magic show, her other hand flashed toward him, and he was lightly stabbed in the chest by one red fingernail.

'And now you can *forget* the scar,' she said to him, *ordered* him. 'We're clear on that?'

Oh, yes, the threat was very clear. Mallory crossed the room with long strides. She could not leave him fast enough. Charles wished she had slammed the door on her way out; that would have told him that she was merely angry, that he had simply annoyed her. But that was not the case; he had damaged her somehow. There would be no more mention of Sparrow's scar, not ever, for he sensed that it was also Mallory's scar. However, the photograph was locked in his memory. He could not let go of it, and now it began to grow, attracting other bits of paper, a fifteen-year-old receipt from Warwick's Used Books, an inscription to a child on the title page of a western. When had Mallory witnessed that piece of violence?

If one truly wanted to maim a human being for life, it was best to start when the victim was very young – ten years old?

Now that the field was clear of explosives, Riker was strolling back to him, folding a cell phone and saying, 'Okay, Charles, you got your wish. I gave Duck Boy a real job. He's taking the old man on a field trip – an interview with the cop who found Natalie Homer's body. Are you happy now?'

Hardly.

At the top of the page, Ronald Deluthe had identified the interview subject as the first police officer to enter Natalie Homer's crime scene. During a testy silence, he wrote down a careful description of Alan Parris's apartment, noting worn upholstery, cracked plaster and all the dust and grime of a man who had hit bottom before the age of forty-two.

Parris's personnel file had listed only the dry statistics of a short career with NYPD, but the garbage pail overflowing with beer cans indicated a serious drinking problem. The sink in the galley kitchen was piled high with dirty dishes and one cracked teacup with a delicate design, perhaps something the man's ex-wife had left behind when the marriage ended twenty years ago – only a few months before Natalie Homer's death.

Alan Parris's T-shirt was stained; his boxer shorts were torn; and dirty toenails showed through the holes in his black socks. The man was so underwhelmed by the interview style of Lars Geldorf that he appeared to be nodding off.

No, Alan Parris was drunk.

'You're *lying!*' Geldorf paced the floor and raised his voice to rouse the man from lethargy. 'I *know* one of you bastards leaked the details. It was you or your partner. Now give it up!' The old man leaned down, bringing his face within inches of Parris's. 'Don't piss me off, son. You won't like me when I get mad.'

All the incredulity that Parris could muster was a small puff of air escaping from pursed lips, a lame guffaw. He kept his silence, showing remarkable patience with the retired detective and his ludicrous threats.

Lars Geldorf's promised anger was unleashed, and Deluthe took faithful shorthand, recording every obscenity. The old man finally succeeded in triggering Parris's temper. And now the four-letter words were flying both ways as Deluthe's pencil sped across the page of his notebook, not resting until Geldorf stomped out of the apartment.

This was Deluthe's cue to pull out his list of prepared questions. The script Geldorf had outlined for him was reminiscent of days in uniform and visits to elementary schools in the role of Officer Friendly. 'Just a few more questions, sir.' He gave Parris a lame smile, and the man rolled his eyes just as the schoolchildren had done. Another tough audience.

Screw Geldorf.

Deluthe dropped his smile, then folded the paper and slipped it back into his pocket. 'What about neighbors? Do you remember anyone in the hall near the crime scene? Maybe there was a—'

'It was a long time ago, kid.' Parris leaned down and moved a newspaper to one side, exposing a beer can crushed and discarded after some previous binge. He upended it over his open mouth to catch the last drops of flat warm liquid.

Though the ex-cop showed no sign of anxiety, soon he would be eager to get to a liquor store and replenish his supply of booze.

'Take your time,' said Deluthe. 'I've got all damn day for this.' *Now* he had the man's attention. 'I saw the photographs of the crime scene. If it was me, I couldn't have forgotten anything about that night.'

'You got that right, kid. But I never talked about the murder. The leak didn't come from me.' Parris stared at the front door left ajar, then raised his voice, correctly sensing that Geldorf hovered on the other side. 'And you can tell that old bastard – it wasn't me he posted outside in the hall. It was my *partner*! Maybe somebody got by *him*.' His voice dropped to a mumble. 'But I couldn't say for sure. Harvey never talked about that night, either – not even with me. We worked together for years, and we *never* talked about it.'

'If your partner was posted at the door, then you were inside the apartment the whole time.'

'No – only a few seconds. I'm the one who found the body. God, the smell. It was enough to knock a man down. When I went home that night, it was still in my clothes, my hair. I can smell it now. I can still feel the cockroaches crawling up my legs. And the flies – a million of 'em. *Jesus*.'

'So you closed the door and waited for the detectives and Crime Scene Unit?'

'Naw. The way that woman was hanging, I couldn't see the tape on her wrists. Me and Harvey figured it for a suicide. Like I said, I was only in there a few seconds. Suicides don't rate a visit from CSU. The dispatcher only sent detectives.'

Deluthe flipped back to notes of yesterday. 'Wasn't there someone else on that scene?'

'The photographer? Yeah, he came with the dicks – just a kid. Younger than me, and I was only twenty-two. He got sick and dropped his camera – broke the damn thing. So I borrowed another one from a neighbor. Then the dicks sent me out to buy more film. I think I made two runs to the store that night.'

'Did your partner mention any civilians around the crime scene while you were gone? Harvey—' Deluthe checked his notes, as if his own lieutenant's name might be easy to forget. On Riker's orders, no one would be apprised of the case connection to a command officer. He put his finger to a blank page. 'Loman, right? Harvey Loman? Was he outside the door the whole time?'

'Yeah. Well, no. When I got back from the store, he was down the hall settling a beef with some old lady.' Parris paused for a moment, then covered his eyes with one hand. 'Awe, what the hell.'

Deluthe's pencil hovered over his notebook. 'What?'

'There were two kids right outside the door – real young, a boy and a girl. Harvey – he never saw them. Well, the door was open 'cause of the smell, and those kids got an eyeful before I chased them away. That always bothered me. Probably gave them nightmares. I felt bad about it, sure, but I had no—'

'So your partner lost control of the crime scene. He screwed up. And you didn't want him to get in trouble, right?'

Parris's head lolled on his chest, as if he could no longer support the weight. 'Geldorf, bad as he is now – he was worse in those days. He would've nailed Harvey's hide to the wall for letting those kids get past him. That old prick still thinks he's God. I hate detectives. No offense, kid.'

'Did the kids see the hair in the victim's mouth?'

'Yeah, they saw everything. The body hadn't been cut down yet. The dicks were still shooting pictures.'

Neither of them had heard the door open, but now Lars Geldorf was standing on the threshold. The old man was smiling, and Deluthe could guess why. The retired detective was relieved that another cop had lost control of the crime-scene details. And now no one could ever say that this major screwup was *his* fault.

* * *

157

Pssst.

Charles Butler studied the stalker's notes to Kennedy Harper. By comparison, the old ones left for Natalie Homer were almost poetry. He turned to Riker. 'Did you tell Deluthe to ask if Natalie's door was locked when the police arrived?'

'No, Deluthe can't ask about that, and I'm hoping Alan Parris won't volunteer anything.' Riker turned off his cassette player. 'We have the old statement from Natalie's landlady, and she says that door was locked.'

'I'm sure it was when she called the police. But when they arrived—'

The detective put one hand on Charles's shoulder. 'If the door wasn't locked when the first cop showed up, then eight million New Yorkers had access to the crime scene. That makes it hard to narrow it down to a boyfriend with his own key. The district attorney won't like that if the case goes to trial. You see the problem?'

Charles nodded absently. He was still preoccupied by the difference in the notes. 'The man who killed Natalie Homer loved her obsessively. He crushed her windpipe with his bare hands – an act of passion. I rather doubt that he made a habit of it. Emotionally, the scarecrow is his polar opposite.' He tapped the autopsy report on Kennedy Harper. 'And the date – an anniversary murder suggests long-term planning. The man who did this was only obsessed with the act itself. A hanged woman, a few dozen candles, a jar of flies – all props. The scarecrow decorates his stage and goes away. It's that cold. Oh, and he's quite insane.'

'Suppose we bypass a jury trial?'

'Wise decision.'

'What are the odds of getting the scarecrow to confess?'

'Nothing easier. All you have to do is catch him. He'll tell you everything he knows. In fact, he's doing that right now, but no one is listening.' Charles unpinned the plastic bag containing a bloodstained note. It was disconcerting to see that the scarecrow's rigid printing so closely resembled Mallory's.

'You analyze handwriting?' asked Riker.

'No, sorry, I don't do voodoo.' Charles turned the bag over and showed Riker the deep grooves on the back of the paper. 'If his pen had pressed down any harder, he would've torn the paper. I suppose you could read frustration or anger into that.'

'He staked that note to a woman's neck with a hatpin – a live woman. Yeah, I'd say he was angry.'

'Oh, the rage is limited to his penmanship. It wasn't directed at Kennedy Harper. I don't think he expected her to feel any pain from the hatpin. She was an object – a bulletin board. But I think he definitely has issues with *your* people. He had to know she'd head for the nearest police station. This note was meant for *you*.' Charles crossed over to Sparrow's wall and stood before the photographs of the coma victim. 'A recent razor slash on Sparrow's arm – I'm guessing that's an escalation because the police clearly were *not* getting his message. Incidentally, why didn't she report that assault?'

'Because she had a whore's rapsheet. Sparrow didn't think the cops would care. And she was right about that.'

Riker handed a cup of coffee to Charles, who must be uncomfortable at the small table built for people of normal size. But the man had wanted privacy, and there was no more secure room than the one that housed the lockup cage. 'We can finish this up at your place if you like.'

'No, I'm fine, really.' The man sipped from his cup and pretended to find the brew passable. 'Just one more question.'

'Shoot.' The detective turned a chair around and straddled it, bracing his arms on the wooden back. 'Anything you want.'

'I gather Louis took an interest in Kathy some time before the night he brought her home. When exactly was that?'

Riker's blood pressure soared, but he had to smile. Brilliant, Charles. A police station was the perfect location for stressful questions. But this time the truth was harmless. 'This is just between us?'

'Of course.'

'Late one night, a social worker turns up in the squad room. Now Lou owes the woman a favor, so she begs him to find this kid – a very special kid. I guess Kathy was nine, almost ten. She used subway tunnels to get around town, but she didn't always ride the trains. Earlier this same night, the kid played a game of chicken with an engineer in the tunnel. She stood on the track till the train was almost on top of her. At the last possible second, she jumped out of the way.' Riker's own private theory was that the child had wanted to die that night.

'She almost gave this poor bastard a heart attack. So now the engineer's afraid she'll electrocute herself on the third rail. He calls out the Transit cops, and they block off the tunnel. Six of those clowns couldn't catch one little girl. She *laughed* at them. So now the social worker arrives. This woman walks into the tunnel and rounds up the kid in two minutes flat. You know how she did that? Kathy walked right up to her, this tall blonde—'

'Like your friend Sparrow.'

'Yeah, and the kid was real happy to go anywhere with this woman. Kathy even held the social worker's hand while they were filling out paperwork at Juvie Hall. So the kid's in custody. She's been cleaned up and fed, all settled in for the night. But now the social worker goes home and leaves her alone in that place. Well, no tall blonde – no Kathy. The kid left five minutes later, and the guards never figured out how she got away. She was their only escapee – ever.'

'Sounds like she picked up bad habits from the Wichita Kid.'

Riker froze. How long had the door been open? How *long*?

Jack Coffey stood on the threshold, saying to him, 'You've got a visitor.'

And then, as if Charles Butler knew how dangerous the westerns were, he said, 'I'm so sorry.'

When Riker returned to his desk in the squad room, an old friend was waiting for him. There was nothing in Heller's expression to say that he had good news or bad, for he was the king of deadpan. He held up a business card. 'You know this guy, right?'

Riker took the card and read the name aloud, 'Warwick's Used Books'. His stomach knotted as he eased into the chair behind the desk, and his mouth was suddenly dry. 'Yeah, I interviewed him.'

Heller slowly swiveled his chair, turning away to look out the window. 'John Warwick came in while I was here, and Janos palmed him off on me. So this little guy's all excited. He waves a newspaper in my face. Then he goes into a ramble about some paperback book. He doesn't *ask* – he *tells* me I found it in Sparrow's apartment. Says he *knows* I found it – and he wants it back. Seems the hooker stole it from his store an *hour* before she was hung.' He turned back to face the desk and the sorry-looking detective. 'Warwick says you'll vouch for that 'cause you took his statement.'

'Yeah, I did.' Riker tapped the side of his head, a gesture to say that the bookseller was not quite sane. 'The paperback probably went into the fire, but I didn't tell that to Warwick.'

'*I* told him,' said Heller. 'And you're right – he *is* nuts. The little guy broke down and cried. I guess that book was pretty important to him – and Sparrow.'

'I guess.' Riker was recalling his suit jacket all buttoned up – very fancy for a sweltering crime scene. And Heller, a man who could do a postmortem on a dead fly, would have noticed the damp spot on the breast of that jacket – and every other detail of that night in Sparrow's apartment.

Heller looked down at an open notebook in his hand. 'Warwick says the title is *Homecoming*, by Jake Swain.' He looked up. 'But I figure you already knew that.'

This man had run cops off the force for stealing trinkets from crime scenes. If Heller developed a case for tampering with evidence, he would prosecute in a New York heartbeat, no exceptions for friendships that spanned twenty years. They stared at one another, and the silence went on for too long.

'After Warwick left,' said Heller, 'I went back to the lab and sifted through ashes and fragments. Some of the magazines were intact, but no sign of a paperback. Now that's strange – even with the age of the book, the brittle paper. You'd think the core would've survived, a good chunk of pressed pages. There are tests I could run. You want me to keep on looking?'

Riker slowly shook his head, and this must have passed for a confession.

Heller nodded, then ripped the sheet from his notebook and dropped it into a wastebasket. 'Well, I guess that's the end of it.' With no goodbye, he rose from his chair and crossed the squad room to the stairwell door.

Riker knew he would keep his badge for lack of physical evidence to hang him – but this man was no longer his friend. And *that* was what Heller had dropped by to tell him.

Café Regio on MacDougal Street was filled with the metropolitan babble of foreign languages. Charles Butler looked around the large single dining area crammed with people, paintings and eclectic furnishings. He spied an acquaintance at a corner table.

Anthony Herman was a child's idea of a pixie, not quite five feet tall, with a small bulbous nose and pancake ears sticking out at right angles. His light brown hair was swept back to display a pronounced widow's peak, a sure sign of witchcraft, though his true profession would seem rather boring to most. The little man nervously adjusted a red bow tie while doing his best to hide behind a menu, though it was long past the dinner hour.

When Charles sat down at the table, the antiquarian book dealer handed him a package wrapped in brown paper and said, 'That's the whole set. Don't open it here.'

A very generous check crossed the table and found its way into Herman's pocket. The little man looked around, as if the other late-night diners might be watching this exchange and making notes or taking blackmail photographs. His toes just barely reached the floor to tap it, and his fingers rapped the table. 'If you ever tell anyone I was tracing those—'

'I know,' said Charles. 'You'll hunt me down and kill me. Your reputation is safe.' He set the package of books on the table. 'How did you find them so fast?'

'There's a collector,' said Herman. 'Well, hardly that – not at all discriminating, but the man's a repository of every western ever written. I had to go to Colorado. That's why the bill is so high. The books didn't cost a dime. I won them shooting pool with a rancher who thinks that crap is high art.'

While Charles was grappling with the odd idea of Anthony Herman as a pool hustler, the man added, 'The rancher also has first editions from the penny-dreadful era. If you want them, *you* go shoot pool with the old bastard. '

'I don't suppose you read any of these novels?' Charles watched Herman's eyes grow a tad fearful. 'You *did* read them, didn't you?'

'I might've *glanced* at one on the plane.' The little man's mouth dipped down at the corners, silently intoning, *What a question*, making it clear that he was hardly the type to read this sort of trash, and his client should know better.

Charles opened the package, despite the book detective's sudden violent shaking of the head, begging that he not do this in public. After leafing through a chapter of the first volume, he smiled at Herman, another great speed reader, for this was a talent that went along with the trade of manuscript comparisons. 'Light stuff, isn't it? Lots of white space. How long was the plane trip? Three or four hours?'

'All *right*.' Herman bowed his head. 'I read them. All twelve.'

'I'm sure you had other reading material with—'

'It's your fault, Charles. I just had to know why you wanted them so badly. Then I got caught up in the whole thing.'

'They're not very good, are they?'

'No. The writing is awful, the plots are thin. Very bad – *very* – all of them.'

'But you read the entire series.'

'Don't do this to me.'

'So what did you think of the resolution to the ambush?'

'Oh, that was the best.' Herman's sarcasm was surprisingly light, and his face had gone suddenly sly. 'No, wait. The best one starts in *The Cabin at the Edge of the World*. In the previous book, the Wichita Kid was bitten by a mad wolf. The animal was frothing at the mouth, the whole nine yards.'

'But there was no rabies vaccine in Wichita's century.'

'I know that,' said Herman, no dilettante in the field of history. 'Rabies was a death sentence in that period.'

'So he's cured with a folk remedy,' said Charles. 'Something like that?'

The little man's smile was coy. 'No, that's not it.'

'Well, I know he's alive in the last book, so he can't possibly die of—' Charles leaned back in his chair and smiled, for he had just exposed himself as another victim of Jake Swain. 'Touché.'

And now – a turnabout.

He spread the books over the table for all to see, then studied the lurid covers of smoke and guns and rearing horses, much to the discomfort of Anthony Herman. 'I know someone who thought the world of these novels. She read them over and over. Now that you've had a chance to evaluate the lot of them – any helpful insight?'

'Well, no.' Herman seemed honestly mystified. 'The only reason for reading any of them is to find out what happens next. I assure you there's no reason to read them more than once.'

'There has to be more to it than that.' Charles gathered the westerns into a stack, then looked up at the book detective. 'So what's it all about?'

'Ultimately,' said Herman, 'it's about the redemption of the Wichita Kid.'

* * *

Riker had finished his first drink by the time he came to the end of the written interview. The detail was fanatical, right down to Alan Parris's dirty toenails. 'And all this conversation – this is word for word?'

'I take shorthand.' Deluthe sipped his beer, then tried to make his voice sound casual when he asked, 'So what're my chances for getting a permanent assignment to Special Crimes Unit?'

'Today? Slim and none. You got no experience, kid.' Only a handful of detectives were ever promoted to first grade, and ten of them were in Special Crimes Unit. 'We don't take whiteshields. And you're what – twenty-five, twenty-six? Most of the guys are in their thirties and forties. We only got one cop your age.'

'And *coincidentally* Mallory is the daughter of the former commander of—'

'You're out of line, Deluthe. She grew up in Special Crimes Unit. When she was still in grammar school, she logged more time on the job than you've got.'

'He's right.' Their bartender had been introduced to Deluthe as Riker's former partner from younger days. Peg Baily leaned into the conversation to replace Riker's empty glass with a fresh bourbon and water. 'That kid was our only technical support. In those days, we had crappy secondhand computers. Didn't work half the time. The kid got the whole system up and running when she was thirteen years old.' Peg set down a beer for Deluthe. 'But you're wondering how Mallory got the rank of detective first-grade. She chased down the perp who murdered her old man. Highest-priority case in New York City. That's getting ahead the hard way.'

Peg Baily wandered down the bar to fill another glass, and Riker completed the trainee's education, giving equal weight to every word, 'Nobody ever questioned Mallory's right to a place in Special Crimes.' As he leaned toward the younger man, his face relaxed into a smile. 'Now, as the son-in-law of a deputy commissioner, you've got a lot more to overcome.'

'Suppose I divorce my wife?'

'It's a start.' Riker pulled a wad of papers from the pocket of his suit jacket and slapped it on the bar. 'This is your background check on the cops at Natalie's crime scene. We already had this information. Mallory pulled it off the computer. Took her two minutes.'

'So that assignment was just busywork.'

Riker ignored this statement of fact and spread the sheets flat on the bar. 'This is only worthless because you took a computer spit-out, something a clerk gave you over the counter. Now a look at the original files – that might've turned up some dirt. But you can still learn a lot from the official fairy tale. I'll teach you how to read the disappearing ink.' He put the first sheet aside, saying, 'There were five cops on the scene, three dicks, two uniforms. Four of them left the precinct in a group. That's a stand-out fact.'

'I *saw* that,' said Deluthe, defensive now. 'But it had nothing to do with the murder. That was six years later.'

'But all in the same four-week period. That tells you Internal Affairs was all over that copshop.'

'There are no charges on their records, nothing to say—'

'Deluthe, I *told* you this was a fairy tale. Now do you want your bedtime story, or do we call it a night?'

'Sorry.'

'Just drink – quietly.' Riker's finger moved across the lines of text. 'So, one of the uniforms, Alan Parris, was fired for insubordination. Now that's bogus. You'd have to shoot a sergeant to get fired on a charge like that.' Riker turned to the next page and the next man. 'The week before that, his partner, *your* boss Harvey Loman – he gets reassigned to another precinct. That tells you Loman rolled over on his partner to cut a deal with Internal Affairs.'

He moved on to another sheet. 'Here we got one detective who resigned to take a job in the private sector. The real story? They forced him out. Not enough proof to hang him. This guy's next job was cleaning out toilets. He drank himself to death years ago.'

Now the final sheet. 'And here we have one more dead detective, a suicide. So, dead or alive, four out of five men leave the department at the same time. The man who shot himself was probably looking at jail time. That means he was the last one to give it up, but there was nobody left to rat on. If he hadn't died, he would've been the sacrifice, the cop who went to prison.'

Of course, Riker was cheating. The nest of shakedown artists in that stationhouse had been the worst-kept secret in NYPD. 'Your interview with Alan Parris only looks good on paper. The two witnesses – the little kids in the hall? Parris gave you a lot of convincing details, but nothing to help you find them. That story could be smoke. So Parris goes on the short list.'

'But the FBI profiles for serial killers—'

'And that's another fairy tale,' said Riker.

The remainder of Stella Small's night was a self-imposed blur. She was using rum concoctions to drown the image of a subway full of dead and dying flies and stampeding passengers. Another hour had ended in yet another crowd. On the next bar stool was a tourist in a T-shirt emblazoned with the city motto, 'I love New York'.

New York sucks.

The young actress's sinuses were clogged with cigarette smoke, and she fancied that she could still smell the insecticide from the subway fiasco. Her head was swimming in rum, and the world swirled around her. Perhaps it had been a mistake to order drinks decorated with paper parasols. But she was not up for the humiliation of tears in a room full of out-of-towners, and the booze, so much tastier than Valium, kept her eyes dry.

One of the customers slammed into her back as he moved toward the men's room. Stella turned to yell at him, but he was lost among a gathering of drinkers.

Damn tourist.

Another patron took advantage of her distraction to cop a feel of one breast. Stunned for a moment, she spun her stool around too late. The man who had sat beside her was gone, lost in the crowd. Stella laid her head down on the bar and knocked it twice against the wood.

I will not cry, I will not cry.

And she did not. She gathered up her house keys and left the bar. Half a block down the street, she noticed a man who was definitely on a mission, marching in the perfect parade-time of a soldier. No – more like a toy soldier, so mechanical, all springs and levers. Mimicry was her art, and she employed it now, stiffening her limbs to follow the marching man.

When he arrived at the broad avenue, he turned left, then stopped, and so did Stella. By the better light of a street lamp, she could see the gray gym bag in his hand. This was the bastard who had cupped her breast in the bar.

The mechanical man turned sharply on his heel, suddenly changing his direction. Stella saw the spinning red light before she reached the avenue where two police officers were padding down a teenager pressed to the hood of their car. She turned to look for the wind-up man and found him escaping, marching off in double time, afraid that she would report him as a deviant. Well, that was a small victory, but one to savor.

A few minutes later, she was fitting her key into the door lock, though she had no memory of having climbed the stairs to her apartment. Her blue linen blazer was neatly folded over one arm. Miraculously, the material was unmarked despite the subway panic, the rain of flies and the assault of the mechanical pervert. It had come through the day-long odyssey stain-free and hardly wrinkled – certain proof that the suit was magical.

Stella opened her front door and walked into a muggy wall of heat at least ten degrees higher than the outside air. Her one-room apartment had the decor of student housing with mismatched furniture dragged off the street one step ahead of the garbage truck. And all the houseplants had succumbed to neglect, even the artificial varieties. Never once dusted, her plastic ivy had taken on the gray color of authentic death.

She stepped out of her skirt, then clipped it on to a hanger with her blazer. When her lucky suit was in the closet and out of danger, she switched on the air-conditioner and stood in the cool breeze as she stripped off her blouse. Before she could toss it on the couch, which was also her bed, she noticed the black ink stain on the white material, a large *X* made with a thick marking pen.

Weary beyond belief, the actress whispered somewhat insincerely, 'I *love* this town.' What was she doing here? She stared at the family photograph on the wall, and the Abandoned Stellas smiled back at her. Gram and Mom were so hopeful for her prospects far from the roadside diner and the randy, fertile truck drivers, the fathers of them all.

Stella held up the blouse, shaking her head in deep denial, as if this might make the big black *X* fade away. She sank down on the couch, then cradled her head in both hands and cried, finally releasing the day in tears.

Had a fellow thespian done this to her during the morning cattle call? The blouse had been fully exposed when the actors were herded into the waiting area. She had put on the blazer just before walking onstage to deliver her lines to a casting director.

No, most likely the vandal had been in that crowded subway car. Was he the same freak who had unleashed the downpour of dead and near-dead insects? Maybe he had been one of the local barflies in the last crowd. Yes, the tourist who had slammed into her back to distract her while he mutilated her only good white blouse.

'Creep.' Her other suspect was the pervert who had cupped her breast. 'Creep number two.'

She wadded up the shirt and dumped it in a wastebasket lined with a plastic bag. And now, since it was trash night, she picked up all the stray bits of debris around her one-room apartment. She held her nose before braving the door of the refrigerator, knowing the smell of rancid milk would make her vomit. And there were other horrors growing on the wire shelves, unidentified critters with coats of furry fungus, abandoned bits of fruit which had crawled off to die in the back of the box. But she never attempted the door to the freezer, for there an arctic winter had settled in to seal half a package of peas in a block of ice, preserving it for future generations.

All the rest was swept into the trash bag, a major job and an important step in making a fresh start. There was another audition tomorrow, and her lucky blue suit had come through the day unscathed.

A good omen.

The *X* on the discarded blouse was now covered with rotted garbage, solidified milk, bottle caps, candy wrappers and deli containers. Stella never saw the folded note in the garment's small breast pocket; it was lost in the clutter of her life. And so she never read the words, *I can touch you any time I want.*

TEN

The early morning temperature was eighty-two degrees, and the East Villagers were already showing some wear as they moved down First Avenue in the rush-hour traffic of wheels and feet.

The tour guide stood at the front of the bus beside the driver. Microphone in hand, she pointed out the more colorful examples of New Yorkers in the wild. However, most of the Finnish tourists were fixated upon one specimen; though this man was clad in the common uniform of T-shirt and jeans, he stood out from all the rest. His torso and head appeared to be made of one rigid piece of wood, and his hands swung by his sides to the beat of a metronome – tick, tick, tick. He carried a gray canvas bag, but its weight never hampered the synchronous movement of both arms, and every step was of equal length and speed, never slowing to avoid other people on the sidewalk, never deviating from a straight line.

For the past hour of gridlock, the bus passengers had been bored out of their minds. Their translator had taken sick this morning, and the American tour guide had not yet grasped that they neither spoke nor understood English, except for the word *tourist* and a few helpful obscenities. Now they crowded together on one side of the vehicle, their sense of expectation heightened as they watched the strange man moving down the sidewalk.

Something was about to happen.

The traffic was beginning to move again, and the bus kept pace with the wooden man, following him as he turned a corner and marched

171

down a side street. Most of the other pedestrians moved out of his way, but two smaller people collided with him. Their bodies yielded to the impact – his did not. Crossing Avenue B in advance of the bus, the man kicked a dog, but not in anger. The spaniel was simply in the way of his foot. The animal's owner yelled at him, and he passed this woman by, blind to her raised fist and every living thing in his path.

He pivoted neatly to march in front of the bus, and the driver slammed on the brakes. The riders smiled in unison. Finally, something of interest – a near-death experience.

The Finns moved to the windows on the other side of the bus, and every pair of eyes followed the man's progress to the opposite sidewalk, where he took a baseball cap from his gray bag and pulled it low to shield his face. Then he reached into his pocket for the giant I-Love-New-York button and pinned it to his T-shirt. He moved through a crowd of people, pushing them out of his way without raising a hand, walking into their bodies, never seeing or hearing them, and they fell off to the side with angry shouts and obscene gestures.

The Finnish tourists heard a loud bang, and some of them ducked, for they had seen entirely too many movies about New York and its heavily armed residents.

The man stopped, and so did the bus. It knelt down on one blown-out tire as the driver muttered a word for defecation and frustration. The tour guide cautioned her disembarking passengers not to wander off before the replacement bus arrived. Even if the Finns had understood what she was saying, her warning would have been unnecessary, for they had no intention of going anywhere.

They formed an audience on the sidewalk, and, behind the safety of their sunglasses, they watched the wooden man. He stood near the door of an apartment house. A fence of bars protected a tiny courtyard and a bed of daisies gamely growing in the heat. The man moved closer to the iron gate. He opened his canvas bag and pulled out a camera, then stared at his wristwatch.

The Finns understood that he was also waiting for something

to happen. They waited with him, watching him between the bodies of pedestrians marching toward the subway. Except for the large souvenir button on his T-shirt, many of the commuters were dressed in the same casual clothes, but the wooden man could not quite blend in with real life.

He glanced at his watch again, and the tourists nodded to one another. It would not be long now.

The man turned his entire body to face the door in the courtyard fence, and twenty pairs of Finnish eyes were looking over his shoulder.

Beyond the iron bars, a red door flew open. A slender blonde crossed the small courtyard with a fast click of white high heels. Her blouse was also white, and the pale blue skirt matched the garment slung over her arm. The young woman opened the iron gate and hurried to the curb, one hand raking through her long hair, combing it on the run. She lifted a waving arm to fish a cab from the stream of traffic.

The Finns stared at this attractive woman, wondering if they should recognize her from television or the cinema. They wanted her to be an actress, for they had not seen one celebrity in the past two days.

After donning sunglasses, the man moved toward the pretty blonde as a tight group of pedestrians passed between them. The sun glinted off a piece of metal when the man lurched forward through the press of bodies and collided with the young woman.

She yelled, 'Damn tourist!' And the twenty Finns were startled, but took no offense.

The man pointed his camera at her. Some reflex made the woman toss her hair and pose for him with a smile. A cab stopped, the blonde stepped in and rode off, never noticing what the wooden man had done to her.

The show was over. The man moved on. And the Finnish tourists looked the other way. In the best tradition of New York City, they had elected not to get involved.

* * *

173

The cab was trapped in midtown traffic, and Stella Small's anxiety was climbing with every dime on the meter. She banged on the bulletproof glass that separated her from the driver. Of course, he would not turn around. What was the point? He spoke no English, and Stella knew that when she yelled, 'There won't be any ransom! I'm dead broke!'

The turbanned cabby nodded to assure her that they would be moving soon. He was very polite, more proof that he was not a native New Yorker.

She looked down at her watch for the third time in as many minutes, and she was still late.

'Okay, you win!' She waved money so the man could see it in his rearview mirror. After paying him, she stepped out of the cab two blocks from the hotel. Her pale blue blazer was carefully folded over one arm to protect it from soot and the droppings of low-flying pigeons.

She was swept up in the crowd of pedestrians and moving along the sidewalk at a fast clip. Two women walking toward her were actually slowing down, completely misunderstanding the concept of rush hour. And now they were breaking the prime law of survival in New York City, going beyond dangerous eye contact to overt staring. Stella wondered if they had recognized her from a recent walk-on part in a television soap opera.

Dream on, babe.

An old man stopped to gawk at her, and Stella smiled for him.

Yes, it's me, the famous actress with no speaking roles.

She was attracting hard looks from everyone she passed. A middle-aged couple stopped to point at her, their mouths working in silence, obviously starstruck. The daytime soaps must be more popular than she had supposed.

Don't you people have regular jobs?

The actress pushed through the hotel door and walked into an icy wall of machine-made air. Near the entrance, a bored young man never even glanced her way. He plucked a sheet of paper from his stack and waved it in her general direction. A woman near the closed doors to the ballroom was calling out the names that began with *R*. Stella Small sighed – saved by her rank in the alphabet.

She donned her suit jacket and joined the other actresses in an area roped off for the cattle call. None of these women paid any attention to her. Each pair of heavily made-up eyes was glued to a line of script on the hand-out sheet. Stella looked down at her own sheet. One line, *six* words. How much study did that require?

She stood near the wall behind a potted fern, away from the press of other bodies, determined that no one would wrinkle her lucky suit or stain it. When her name was called, she entered the ballroom beyond the great doors and stood before a long dais decked with bottles and glassware, paperwork and food trays. On the other side of the linen tablecloth, the casting director and producer were seated in the company of assistants. Before Stella could even say her line, these men and women were all agog, eyes popping. She flashed them with her best smile. They were dazzled, riveted, stunned – though still awaiting her first word.

The actress felt a slick of something wet on her hand and looked down at a long thick line of blood seeping through the sleeve of her blazer. Inside the casing of linen, more blood was rolling down the skin of her arm and dripping off the tips of her fingers.

'I hate it when this happens.' Line delivered, though it was the wrong line, Stella Small closed her eyes in a dead faint, and the back of her head met the hardwood floor.

Green curtains formed three walls of the emergency-room cubicle, a thin layer of privacy for the young couple. Stella Small's legs swung from the edge of the metal examination table, and the physician's smile was shy as he treated her wounded arm.

The doctor's head snapped to one side, suddenly distracted by a shadow looming close to the flimsy curtain. Though the silhouette was all wrong, Stella instantly recognized this scene from the movie *Psycho*. One shadow hand was on the rise, reaching higher, higher, and then –

the green curtain was violently ripped to one side. And now the startled young doctor was staring at a stout woman with a pyramid of dark hair and a long black dress that flowed like a nun's habit.

Stella had always suspected that her agent could smell fresh blood from great distances. Martha Sutton was a formidable woman, a drama queen extraordinaire and scarier than *real* nuns.

'Nice entrance.'

'Oh, Stella, *Stella*.' The woman's gleaming eyes appraised the lacerated arm and the bright red stains on her client's clothing. 'You look *marvelous*!' In agent speak, this meant *publicity worthy*.

The young doctor turned back to his chore of irrigating a long thin wound. 'I think we can get away without stitches.' He applied a few small bandages shaped like butterflies. 'It's a clean cut – very shallow. But I don't see how a camera could've done this. Even if a piece of broken metal was—'

'I'm telling you,' said Stella, 'this tourist bumped into me with his damn camera. I was standing outside my building, hailing a cab—'

'All right, have it your way.' The doctor walked away from the examination table, saying, 'But it looks like you've been slashed with a razor.'

Martha Sutton's eyes turned gleeful and sly. She whispered to her client, 'Great line. We'll keep it in the act.'

'But it was a *camera*.' Stella was more insistent now.

The agent pointed toward the far wall, where a man was standing behind a glass door. 'See that guy? He's a reporter. Now how bad do you want a career, baby doll?'

'Oh.' And by this, Stella meant, *I've got religion – I've seen the light*. Aloud, she said, 'I've been slashed with a razor.'

'That's my girl,' said Sutton. 'And play up the idiot who carried you across that hotel lobby. He's one of my clients. Lucky he didn't have the brains to stop your bleeding. That trail of blood on the carpet was priceless. Now remember to spell your name for the reporter. He's another idiot.' The agent turned to leave, then stopped with an afterthought. 'I made you an appointment for another audition. Something different – a police station. I just got off the phone with a cop in SoHo. He only wants blond actresses with dry cleaning problems. Do you by any chance have a blouse with a big X drawn on the back?'

Stella nodded. 'Some bastard got me with a black pen.'

'Wonderful. The cops are looking for a serial vandal. Pray for a slow news day. Maybe we'll get your face on TV. And take that blouse with you. It'll make a great prop.'

'But I don't have it anymore,' said Stella. 'I threw it away.'

'No, honey, don't tell me that. Look me in the eye and tell me you *saved* that blouse.'

Well, how hard could it be to mark up another one?

'Okay, I saved it.'

'That's my girl.'

Two hours later and home again, fresh from the shower and clean of blood, Stella Small opened a can of beer in hopes that it might dull the throb in her wounded arm. She spotted a pair of sneakers only partially hidden by her cast-off clothes. No, bad idea. Her agent had given her too much Valium, and tying shoelaces might be too hard. She reached under a chair for a pair of sandals.

Stella flopped down on the couch in a cloud of dust and consulted a copy of *Backstage*, the only newspaper she ever read. The turned-back page with the schedule of auditions listed nothing for today. Yet she could not lose the nagging idea that she was supposed to be somewhere this afternoon.

She picked up her TV remote and flicked through the channels until she found a children's program.

Good. Cartoons were easy.

The television screen went black, and no button on the remote control could bring it back to life. This was a bad omen, but Stella was not completely shattered – not yet. She had a fascination for how long a disaster streak could go on and how awful it could become before playing itself out. The young actress was also determined that no life experience would ever go to waste if she could only stay alive in this town.

A bug was moving up her leg. Mid-scream, she stopped and smiled. It was only a spider. She flicked it off her skin and watched it crawl across the floor. It was a big one, but the Abandoned Stellas had always said that a spider in the house was good luck. However, it *was* a big one. She rolled up her newspaper and smashed the creature flat.

The Abandoned Stellas had said a lot of things.

She reached down to the floor and picked up the bloodstained suit jacket. While going through the pockets, preparing to throw it away, she found a note in her agent's handwriting.

Oh, right – the cattle call. She read the address of the SoHo police station and the time when she was expected along with a few hundred other actresses. The stationhouse was within easy walking distance, and there was at least an hour to kill.

The telephone rang, and Stella cringed. She let her answering machine take the call. The young woman from Ohio was much too fragile to deal with New Yorkers right now.

She paid more attention to the machine when the words *police department* filtered through her Valium fog. Stella grabbed up the phone. 'Hi! Is this about the actress interviews in SoHo? . . . No? Midtown? I thought— Oh, right. Sorry. I didn't know . . . Yes, I'll be there.'

And now she recalled her agent dragging her out of an emergency room, though she had been told to wait there until a police officer arrived. She had left the hospital in the company of a tabloid reporter who had taken precedence over the law.

How much trouble was she in?

The timing would be close. With a little luck and a functional subway, she could make the appointments at both police stations, but only if the SoHo interviews went by alphabetical order. Martha Sutton's note reminded her that she needed a vandalized blouse for a prop.

After rummaging through the closet and the drawers, every article of clothing was strewn about the small apartment, and all the effort of last night's cleaning binge had been undone. This was so disheartening. Just looking at the mess made her weary. She turned to the smiling portrait of the Abandoned Stellas, but they had no homilies to cover a life spinning out of control.

In the pile of clothes at her feet, she found an old thrift-shop garment that would do nicely. Then she went off to make another mess of the kitchenette, emptying the catch-all drawers in search of a pen to make a large X on the back of the blouse.

The ground floor of the SoHo police station was packed with actresses, all sizes and every color of hair, though Special Crimes Unit had specifically requested blondes. Jack Coffey stood near the street door and stared at the double-parked news vans. Reporters were roaming the sidewalk in gangs.

He turned to Detective Wang. 'Exactly what did you say to the talent agencies?'

'Just what you told me. I said we were investigating vandalism on the subway.'

Detective Desoto folded his cell phone and turned to the lieutenant. 'One of the agents tipped the reporters. She told them we were hunting a sex maniac with a thing for blondes.' He looked toward the open door and its view of reporters milling on the street. 'But none of those bastards made a connection to Special Crimes Unit.'

Lieutenant Coffey silently thanked the city accountants for being too cheap to paint the name of his unit on the door at the top of the stairs. 'Okay, take the actresses up to the squad room, ten at a time. And pass the word – nobody mentions Special Crimes. I don't want anybody handing out cards to these women – I don't care how pretty they are. Now weed out the brunettes.'

Coffey watched the actresses being herded toward the staircase, where Desoto pulled out the women with dark hair. The first group of blondes climbed the stairs behind Detective Wang. They were all so young, so unprepared for what was going to happen to them.

A few minutes later, when Lieutenant Coffey entered the squad room, the actresses were lined up in a tight row, all but standing at attention. Detective Janos played the part of their drill sergeant, pacing back and forth in front of them, inspecting his troops. 'If you're jerking us around to get your names in the paper, you'll be charged with obstruction of justice. That means time in lockup.'

Though the man had a gentle voice, he also had a thug's face and the gravitational mass of a small planet. The blond heads turned in unison, following his movements back and forth.

'Our lockup isn't very clean. Fleas, lots of fleas.'

Two dishwater blondes were edging toward the stairwell door while the other women were still debating flight.

'Oh, and lice are a problem, too.' Janos sighed. 'So you'll be stripped and deloused in a gang shower.'

After the mass exodus of actresses, all that remained was one intrepid blonde in the fairest range, and the large detective engaged her in a staring contest. She burst into tears, then ran toward the door, where another ten women were waiting in line. And Janos hollered, 'Next!'

ELEVEN

Charles stood apart from the others as they argued in Mallory's private office at Butler and Company.

Chief Medical Examiner Edward Slope said, 'No, Riker, I'm not going back to that hospital, not for at least ten years.' And now that the subject of the dying coma patient was closed, he turned back to his study of Natalie Homer's *new and improved* autopsy photographs blown up to many times the original size.

Mallory's magic had created sharp definition from grainy enlargements, using her computer to refine light and shadow, replacing ambiguity with certainty and exposing details never seen in the originals. Although it appeared to be the camera's eye of truth, Charles suspected that she had cheated the pieces, the pixels that made the pictures, and the result was only the best guess of artificial intelligence.

'Okay,' said Riker, somewhat testy. 'Can you give me a second opinion on this?' He handed the pathologist an X-ray of Natalie's head, something Mallory had not retouched.

The doctor held up the film to the light of the windows. 'You're right. It looks like my predecessor missed everything but the cause of death. It's a skull fracture. I can't tell if it rendered her unconscious, but it certainly stunned her. The fracture agrees with a blunt object. I could swear to that much.'

Next, Riker handed him an enlarged photograph of Natalie's right hand. 'This is the burn shot.'

Dr Slope shook his head. 'Can't help you on this one. No way to tell if the flesh was burned before the insects got at it.'

Riker consulted a transcription of Louis Markowitz's notes and pointed to a line of type. 'Right *here*. Lou says the hand was burned.' And another argument had begun.

'That's because of the roaches,' said Charles, stepping into the conversation in the role of a peacemaker. 'Louis saw them clustered on her hand. That would indicate the presence of grease. If it was hot from the frying pan—'

'Speculation,' said Edward Slope. 'I only testify to facts.' He glanced at his watch. 'Unless there's something else—'

'About Sparrow,' said Riker. 'Maybe you could just talk to her doctor on the—'

'Not a shot in hell,' said Dr Slope. 'Now Charles could take on that lightweight intern. He knows all the jargon.'

'Sparrow's dying,' said Riker. 'I need a *medical* opinion.'

'If it's coma related, then Charles is your man.' Edward Slope walked toward the door, saying, 'I promise you, nobody on that hospital staff knows more about the human brain.'

The door closed, and a defeated Riker slumped into a chair behind the desk. 'Sparrow's doctor hates cops. He won't even talk to me. Can you help?'

'Well, Edward exaggerates,' said Charles. 'I only published one paper on the comatose brain. However, I could probably negotiate a conversation with her doctor.'

'Sounds good. Thanks. But Mallory doesn't need to know, okay?'

Riker closed his eyes and put his feet up on her desk, a sign that she was not expected back for the duration of a catnap. And Charles was left to wonder why Riker would keep the hospital visit a secret. Surely his own partner had an equal interest in this crime victim. It was an interesting problem, and the solution lay in the certain knowledge that Mallory would not forgive any act of concern for an enemy.

Both men jumped at the sound of a crash in the next room.

'Kids.' Riker's feet hit the floor. 'You can't turn your back on 'em for a second.'

When they entered the office kitchen, they found Ronald Deluthe dressed in a replica of Natalie Homer's apron, ruffles and all. He was holding an unplugged electric skillet. There were spills on every surface and puddles of water on the floor. Wet enlargements of crime-scene photos were spread across the tabletop.

'This is my fault,' said Riker. 'I told him to work out a fly-on-the-wall scenario.'

Charles looked down at a splash of water near the stove. 'So that's supposed to be grease from Natalie's sausages?'

'Yes, sir. Watch.' Deluthe filled the frying pan with more water, then treated them to a demonstration of backswings and overhand strikes. Most of the liquid spilled behind him, and the remainder sloshed forward toward an imagined assailant, splattering an innocent refrigerator. His right hand was wet, and the rest of him remained dry. 'It never spills on the apron. So she wasn't using the frying pan for a defensive weapon. I figure the killer was holding it.'

'That makes sense,' said Riker. 'Slope confirmed the skull fracture. Maybe the perp used the pan on her head. Good job, kid.'

'Now clean up the mess.' Mallory had materialized in the doorway. Her eyes roved over the wet floor and the rivulets streaming down every wall. She turned to Deluthe in stone silence. He scrambled to grab a sponge from the sink, then knelt on the tiles and began to wipe the puddles.

'You're wrong about the frying pan,' said Charles. 'Natalie *did* use it as a weapon. But the mistake is understandable.' He pointed to the electric skillet with its built-in computer panel for timing meals. 'That's aluminum, and the handle never gets hot.'

'What?' Deluthe slowly rose from his crouch on the floor.

Charles excused himself for a few moments, then returned to the kitchen, holding the frying pan found at the crime scene. 'This is Natalie's — solid iron. The handle would've been very hot. She'd need a potholder.' He pointed to one of the pictures on the table. 'See the hooks on this wall? Here by her stove – one hook for each potholder, and they're all in place. But the sausages weren't done yet. See? The front burner is still glowing. She was interrupted.'

'Right,' said Deluthe. 'She died.'

'But first – something less dramatic,' said Charles, 'like a knock on the door. Natalie had time to hang her potholder on a hook before she opened that door to her murderer. She wouldn't leave sausages unattended for long, so you know the fight began immediately.' He took the sponge from Deluthe and wiped spots off a crime-scene photo. 'Judging by the number of sausages, I'd say you used too much water for your experiment.' He glanced at a photo of Natalie's apron. In Mallory's enhancement, the longest borders of the grease stain were more sharply defined. Louis Markowitz's notebook entry had been correct. This was not a splash or a splatter. It was a smear.

After separating one photo from the rest, Charles pointed to a mass of roaches on Natalie's right hand. 'Let's assume she burned her hand. She also had a bad fall, and it knocked her out or stunned her. Natalie never got to swing the skillet. But she *intended* to use it as a weapon. Oh, and the killer never touched it at all.'

Deluthe folded his arms. 'How could you know if—'

'Because your apron is dry, and the rest of the kitchen isn't.' Charles ran the frying pan under the tap, then returned it to the stove's front burner. 'Natalie's facing her killer. No time to pull down a potholder – she grabs the skillet—' He grasped the handle and raised the pan quickly, spilling a bit of the water on his hand and arm. More liquid hit the floor behind him on the backswing. 'The hot iron and grease burn her hand. Natalie lets go of the handle before she can swing the skillet forward.'

Charles released the pan, and it clattered to the floor beside him. 'The killer advances. She backs off.' He edged away from an invisible man. 'She has grease on her shoes and loses traction. Her legs fly out from under her, and she falls facedown.'

Deluthe was in denial. 'How do you know she fell? Or how she landed?'

'Logic,' said Charles. 'If all the facts only fit one scenario, that's the way it happened. May I?' He held out one hand to take the proffered apron, then spread it on the floor. 'Natalie's down. She's not moving. Probably hit her head on the corner of the stove. I know her skull fracture wasn't made by an iron skillet. That would've caved in her skull.' He straightened up and turned to Deluthe. 'You'll notice that my grease puddle is smaller than yours. It's covered by the breast of the apron.' He tapped the photo of the garment. 'The edges of the grease stain wouldn't be this straight if she struggled. So she was stunned or unconscious when he dragged her across the floor.' Charles reached down and pulled the apron toward him. When he picked it up, the wet spot was the size and shape of the stain on Natalie Homer's apron.

'And that's what the fly on the wall saw.' Charles's tone was almost apologetic when he said to Deluthe, 'I'm sure you could've worked this out. But you've never cooked anything, have you?'

The floor had been recently mopped, and it bore the same chlorine odor as the city morgue. Riker could hear Charles Butler speaking to the young intern in the hallway outside the hospital room.

The rolling of Sparrow's eyes was involuntary; Riker knew that, but this guise of dementia might be a window on her mind – what was left of it. He resisted the temptation to close her eyelids, a service performed for the dead.

The detective sat beside the bed, making confetti out of the hospital's request to give the patient a more complete identity. He knew her full name, but he would never surrender it. Sparrow would not have wanted that. She had told him so one rainy night when he had given her coffee and shelter in his car. The prostitute had been sickly and bone thin all that winter. He had believed that she was only days away from dying, and that was before she had mentioned the plans for her gravestone.

He remembered laughing when their macabre conversation had

turned to braggadocio. *Sparrow* – that was all she had wanted on her monument – no dates, no message, only the one name engraved in bold letters like a Las Vegas marquee, a token of fame. It fit her character so well, this gross presumption that cemetery visitors would know who she was . . . who she had been.

Done with his hallway consultation, Charles Butler entered the room and closed the door softly, as if Sparrow were not beyond being disturbed. 'Well, you were right about her doctor. He hates policemen, but he's giving her the best of care. One might say he's on a mission to keep her alive.' He nodded toward the pole beside the bed. It supported a plastic bag of liquid that flowed into the patient's arm. 'That's an antibiotic to fight infection. And a collapsed lung explains the tube down her throat. Apparently this woman had a very hard life. For one thing, her doctor suspects a history of chronic respiratory ailments.'

Riker nodded. 'She got sick every winter.'

'And then there's the long-term damage of malnutrition and drugs. Given her history as a prostitute, the doctor thinks venereal disease might account for a dysfunctional kidney. So it isn't just the coma – it's a gang of complications.' He rested one hand on the detective's shoulder. 'I'm so sorry.'

Riker stared at the woman on the hospital bed – his friend until she died. 'Could she be in there? I mean – with a brain going on all cylinders?'

'It's possible.' Charles stared at a machine by the bed, watching the dip and spike of lines running across its screen. 'Her present condition is best described as a dream state. In all likelihood, she'll be dreaming when she dies. No pain, no fear. Does this help you?'

'Yeah, it does. Thanks.' Riker listened to her mechanical breathing and stared at the tubes running in and out of her body.

'We should be leaving soon,' said Charles. 'I promised Mallory I'd get you to Brooklyn on time.'

'Yeah – soon.' The box of tissues on the nightstand was empty.

Riker set the paperback novel on the bed, then searched all his pockets for a handkerchief.

'I might have something to cheer you up,' said Charles. 'A lead on William Heart, the photographer who dropped his camera at Natalie's crime scene. I called a gallery that—' He picked up the western and idly leafed through the pages. 'Did you finish this yet?'

'Never started it.' Riker wiped away Sparrow's drool.

'I don't blame you. The writing is terrible.' Charles stared at the woman on the bed. 'I imagine Mallory was a child when she met Sparrow — maybe ten? Younger than that?'

Riker froze in the act of dabbing Sparrow's lips. He wanted a drink so badly. He was damned if he lied or told the truth, and even his continuing silence said too much.

Charles looked down at the book in his hand. 'I managed to find a complete set of these westerns. I read them all last night.'

The handkerchief dropped to the floor. Riker closed his eyes and hoped that his voice conveyed only weariness when he said, 'Bet that took all of four minutes.'

'Longer, I read them twice. And I still don't understand why Kathy read them so many times.'

These days, it was rare to hear Mallory's first name said aloud. He knew Charles was speaking of Kathy the child he had never known. She had been all grown up when Lou Markowitz had introduced this man to his pretty daughter, the cop. On the day they met, Mallory had arrived at the SoHo café for a ritual breakfast with her foster father. Charles, normally a graceful man, had risen too quickly, knocking over his chair in a rush to play the gentleman. In another departure from grace, he had stared at her remarkable green eyes throughout the meal and smiled a foolish apology each time she looked his way. His every gesture, the food spilled in his lap and an overturned juice glass had said to her, *I love you madly*.

'No accounting for her taste in reading,' said Charles. He was still turning the pages of the last western. 'Even at the age of ten, she would've been brighter than most adults.'

Only the bookseller could have revealed the little girl's obsession with westerns. Riker would never have believed that John Warwick, paranoia incarnate, would open up to a stranger. But how had Charles sussed out Kathy's childhood relationship to Sparrow?

'The paper seems to be holding up well.' Charles fanned the pages of the book, testing his handiwork. 'Have you made a decision yet? Do you plan to give this to Mallory? Or will you destroy it?'

The detective settled into a chair beside the bed. His smile was one of resignation, and he was only half joking when he said, 'You're a dangerous man, Charles.'

'Oh, I already burned my copies. Don't let that worry you. They went into the fireplace last night. I suppose Louis did something similar while Kathy was still very young. He wouldn't want evidence to tie his child to a little thief who loved westerns. I gather her early days were more – more *colorful* than I thought. So Louis destroyed all her books? All but the last one?'

Riker only nodded. The less said, the less this man would have to work with. 'I can't tell you any more about the westerns.'

'Especially the last one,' said Charles. 'Yes, I imagine you're giving me deniability of a crime. Something like that?'

Riker took a moment to digest these words. Was there anyone left who did *not* know that he had robbed a crime scene? That was the problem with spontaneous criminal acts, no planning, no time to cover tracks. And here he was still holding stolen goods. Any half-bright petty thief would have made a better job of it.

'I guess I'll never know what she saw in them.' Charles looked down at the cover illustration of Sheriff Peety on a rearing stallion, two six-guns blazing fire, and the ricochet of sunlight from a golden badge. 'Do you think she believed in heroes?'

Riker shrugged. Lou Markowitz had once held the darker idea that Kathy had identified with all the cattle rustlers and the stagecoach robbers.

A nurse entered the room to bathe the patient, and the two men took their leave. As they strolled down the corridor, Charles told the story of *The Cabin at the Edge of the World*, a book that Riker had never read. As they neared the parking lot, the Wichita Kid had been bitten by a mad wolf frothing at the mouth a century before the rabies vaccine was invented. When they reached the other end of the Brooklyn Bridge, the outlaw lay unconscious in a burning cabin surrounded by a mob of angry farmers with torches and pitchforks. A preacher was denouncing a witch, an old woman also trapped in the fire, and blaming her for the drought that was killing the crops.

'No, don't tell me,' said Riker. 'This con man, the preacher, he actually brings on the rain. That puts out the cabin fire and ends the drought. So now the farmers are real happy, and they decide not to kill the old lady. And then the preacher does another miracle and cures Wichita's rabies.'

'Not even close,' said Charles. 'When the next book opens, the Wichita Kid is still surrounded by flames. There's no way out.'

Riker knew a better escape yarn, a true one, but there was no one he could share it with now that Sparrow was dying. He had missed her company over these past two years, and now he was grieving for her, though she was not altogether gone.

The Mercedes was approaching the Brooklyn Bridge when Charles asked, 'How did Louis trace Kathy to Warwick's Used Books?'

Riker stared out the window at the water. *Shoot me — shoot me now.* 'We just got lucky one night.'

He had a demoralizing old memory of running out of breath as he watched the child's shoes skimming along the sidewalk, outdistancing him with no effort at all. She had laughed as she dusted off Lou Markowitz, a man with fifty pounds of excess weight. Poor Lou had been wheezing when he caught up to Riker, who was hugging a lamppost, convinced that his heart had stopped.

'Then we spotted the kid in Warwick's window.' He recalled the baby thief leaning one small hand on a bookshelf as she nonchalantly perused her westerns. Though she had just run two cops into the ground – nearly killed them – only Kathy's eyes seemed weary, just like any other child at the end of a busy day.

'So we go inside the store, and Lou tells the owner no more customers for a while. Then we go to collect the kid, but she's gone, and the back room was locked up from the inside. It drove us nuts. You've seen that place. There was no way she could've made it out the door without being seen.' Then they had noticed the fear in the bookseller's eyes. Lou had gathered his hound-dog jowls into a dazzling smile to win over the merchant with personal charm – or so he had believed at the time.

The mystery of Kathy's escape had not been solved that night or the next. 'Lou spent a week of off-duty hours staking out the store and reading all of Kathy's westerns.' He had also developed a rapport with the fragile bookseller. 'Finally, Warwick tells him how Kathy got away that night. For maybe three seconds, our backs were turned from the rear wall while we talked to the owner. That's when she climbed up the bookshelves – quick as a monkey, quiet as smoke – all the way to the top, where there was just enough room to squeeze between the shelf and the ceiling.'

'Then the bookseller must have watched her do it.'

'Yeah, and he never gave her up, even though just the sight of a cop scared the shit out of him. The whole time Lou was talking to this frightened little man, Kathy was up there listening to him, laughing at him.' The detective shrugged. 'So we were outmatched by a ten-year-old girl. Not our best night.'

That was when Lou Markowitz had begun to realize who and what he was dealing with – no ordinary child, but a full-blown person. And he had amended the résumé of a street thief to include the grand title of Escape Artist. Kathy had earned Lou's respect. She had also cut out his heart, but that was another night, and the child had almost won that time, almost destroyed the man.

Though it would have been some comfort to him, Riker could

never share the story of Kathy's best escape act. And now his mind reached back across the bridge, across the water to the sleeper in her coma dreams to tell her that she was not dying alone.

Sparrow, the secrets are poisoning me.

Mallory watched Charles's Mercedes drive off as her partner slid into the front seat of her tan sedan.

'It's that one.' She nodded toward the building directly across the street. Natalie Homer's sister lived in an area of Brooklyn prized for views of Prospect Park. Apparently Susan Qualen was doing well in the world. 'It's better if we catch her outside.' Then the cop hater would have no door to slam in their faces. 'The neighbors say she runs in the park – same time every day.'

'Must be a health fanatic.' Riker wiped the sweat from his brow. 'She's gonna kill herself in this heat.'

The front door opened and a trim woman in shorts and a T-shirt appeared at the top of a short flight of stairs. Natalie's sister was tall and blond with a familial face. Before the woman could descend to the sidewalk, the two detectives were out of the car and moving toward her, each holding up a leather folder with identification and a gold shield.

'Miss Qualen? I'm Detective Mallory, and this is—'

The woman's face turned angry and hard. 'Go away!'

Riker stood at the bottom of the stairs. 'Ma'am? We'd rather do this at your convenience, but you—'

'I read about your last hanging in the papers,' said Susan Qualen. 'You bastards couldn't cover up that one. Not so easy this time, was it?'

'Ma'am,' said Riker. 'We don't work that way. Sometimes we have to withhold details so we can—'

'I've heard that one before. Twenty years ago, the cops told the reporters my sister was a suicide.'

'The cops didn't tell you much, did they?' Mallory moved up the staircase, advancing on the woman slowly. 'They told you it was murder, and you knew about the rope.' But no cop would have revealed the details of the hacked-off hair jammed in Natalie Homer's mouth.

Mallory was one step away – touching distance. *Nervous, Susan?* 'So how did you make the connection between your sister and a hanged hooker?'

'I read the story in the damn papers.'

Mallory shook her head. 'No, you're lying. The link had to be more than rope. All those details in the paper – why did you connect them with—'

'I'm done with you.' Susan Qualen started down the staircase.

'Hold it.' Mallory blocked her way. 'Where did you get the—'

'My lawyer says I don't have to talk to you.'

'No,' said Mallory. 'That's what people say when they *haven't* talked to a lawyer. Your sister's murder is still an open case, and you *will* talk to us.'

Riker climbed a step closer to the woman. His voice was more reasonable and friendly. 'We turned up some inconsistencies in Natalie's murder. We think her son might be able to straighten it out. So where's the kid now?'

'I don't know where he is,' said Susan Qualen.

'I read a follow-up interview with the boy's stepmother,' said Mallory. 'She claims you took the boy after his father died.'

And Riker added, 'That would've been a year after Natalie's murder.' His tone of voice said, *Hey, just trying to be helpful.*

'But we had a problem with that.' The threat in Mallory's voice was impossible to miss.

'You see,' said Riker, dialing back the tension, 'the little boy never went to school after his mother died. When summer vacation was over—'

'So the family moved out of the school district.'

'No, Miss Qualen,' said Mallory. 'The stepmother still lives at the same address.' Mallory edged closer. 'She told a cop named Geldorf that *you* had the boy. Why would she lie? And when that same cop called you, why didn't you set him straight?'

There was confusion in Qualen's eyes. Civilians were amateurs at deception, unable to remember the details of lies told in the distant past, and they were all so easily rattled. Riker smiled at the woman, as if they were old friends discussing weather and books they had read. 'It would help if you could tell us what happened to Natalie's son.'

'And where he is now.' Mallory made the short step from accusation to attack. 'Talk to me! What did you do with him?'

Susan Qualen lost her hard-case composure and made a mad sprint down the staircase, slamming into both detectives in her haste to get away. Mallory hit the sidewalk at a dead run, and Riker lunged to catch her arm, yelling, 'Whoa! First, let's interview the stepmother. Then we can nail Qualen for obstruction. We'll toss her in the lockup cage for a while. It'll be scary but legal.'

Mallory watched the woman's hands flailing as she ran down the sidewalk, escaping. Passersby must believe that they had drawn guns on her. Even now, the distance could be so easily closed, and when Mallory caught up to Susan Qualen, the woman would be vulnerable, breathless and frightened.

'Trust me,' said Riker. 'It'll be more fun my way.'

Not likely.

William Heart cringed at the noise. The recluse was not good with human interaction and did what he could to avoid it. Worst was the knock at the door, the sound of a trap closing. He stood very still, hardly breathing, but his visitors would not go away, and now he heard the voice of the landlord saying, 'I know he's in there. Takes him all damn day to open the door. Bang *harder*.'

However, the stranger was more polite, only lightly rapping, as he said, 'Thank you,' to the dwindling footsteps of the landlord. And now the visitor spoke to the locked and bolted door. 'Hello? Mr Heart? Your gallery gave me your address.'

The cultured voice was reassuring and carried the lure of a potential sale. William opened the door to see a fairy-tale bag of metaphors. This tall man had the body, the clothes and patrician air of a prince, but eyes like a frog and the beak of Captain Hook. The broad shoulders were threatening, magically enlarging in every passing second.

When William stepped back a pace, his visitor took this for an invitation. The man walked past him and paused by the couch, a threadbare affair of lumpy cushions and barely contained stuffing. It was the only piece of furniture that might accommodate his large frame. The chairs were made of flimsy wooden sticks.

'May I?'

William nodded, and the frog prince sat down.

'My name is Charles Butler.' The man's grin was so foolish, William smiled against his will as Mr Butler handed over a business card. 'Your gallery dealer tells me you do crime-scene photography.'

'No, that was a long time ago. I don't do it anymore.'

Butler was staring at a radio on the coffee table, and William wondered if he recognized it as a police scanner. He cleared his throat. 'I mean – I don't work for the police anymore. I do car wrecks, that kind of thing.'

'Yes, I know. Your work is almost tabloid genre, wouldn't you say? High contrast, hard light, black shadow. And some cruelty in every image.'

The photographer vacillated between flight and a faint. Charles Butler was obviously an art collector and well heeled, but several of the degrees on his business card related to psychology. William distrusted head shrinkers.

'I'd like to see your earlier work,' said Butler. 'The crime-scene photos. I'm particularly interested in Natalie Homer. Perhaps the name's not familiar. It was twenty years ago. The newspapers called it a suicide by hanging.'

'I didn't keep—' William shook his head and began again. 'I couldn't do the job. My camera was broken.' Even as these words trailed off, he realized that he was not believed. Charles Butler's face expressed every thought and doubt. William could actually see himself being measured and evaluated in the other man's eyes. He even saw a hint of pity there.

'It's not a picture most people would want in their heads.' This was a true thing. Only a specific type of ghoul sought that kind of image, and Butler did not seem to fit that category.

'So you did take at least one shot.' The man was not posing a question but stating fact.

William clenched his sweating hands, then looked down at the leather checkbook which had suddenly appeared on the coffee table beside an old-fashioned fountain pen. And now he relaxed again, for this was merely a money transaction, a simple purchase.

'That's one photograph I'd be very interested in.' Butler opened the checkbook. '*Very* interested.' He glanced up at William and broadened his smile, killing all trace of alarm and increasing the comfort level in the room – then delivered his bomb. 'You knew Natalie, didn't you?'

William could not have spoken had he wanted to.

Mr Butler continued, 'It's a reasonable assumption. Your landlord tells me you've lived here all your life. I understand you inherited the lease from your mother. And this building is only a block from where Natalie died. Must've been difficult to photograph the body of someone you knew.'

'I didn't – know her.' William wrapped himself in his own arms to quell the panic. He could see that, once again, he was not believed. In that tone of voice reserved for the confessional, he said, 'She only lived in this neighborhood for a little while. I never spoke to her.' Losing control of his nerves and his mouth, he continued in a chattering stammer, 'But I used to see her on the street sometimes. She was so pretty. She didn't belong here. Anybody could see that. God, she was beautiful.'

He had never lusted after her as the other watchers did, for her smile had reminded him of the painted madonnas and statuettes that had adorned this apartment while his mother was alive. Pretty Natalie in her long summer dresses.

William studied Charles Butler's tell-all face, checking for signs that he had given away too much. 'It wasn't just me that watched her, you know. She turned heads everywhere she went. All those men, they just *had* to look.'

'And after she died, you took her photograph,' said the visiting mind reader. 'Nausea doesn't come on in an instant. I'm guessing you had time to get off one shot before you vomited. You're such a fine photographer. It would've been a natural reflex action – taking that picture.'

So he knew about the vomiting too.

'All right. I'll give it to you.' William was actually relieved, though this certainly meant that Butler was a ghoul, the kind of customer who paid the rent, but a twisted type he had never wanted to confront outside of an art gallery. So this was really all the freak wanted, a grisly crime-scene souvenir.

Upon entering the bedroom, William locked and bolted the door behind him. When he emerged again, a print of the old photograph was in his hand.

After the man had departed with his purchase, William noticed that the amount entered on the check was more generous than the quoted price. He looked around at the evidence of his poverty, and he was frightened anew, for he suspected Charles Butler of being a compassionate man and not a freak after all.

William Heart returned to his bedroom. Again, he carefully locked the door and drew the bolt, though his landlord had no keys to this apartment. He lay down on the bed and stared at the opposite wall. Every night, before switching off the lamp, this was what he saw, a wall of a hundred pictures, all the same – the same face, the rope, the massing insects. This photograph was the best work he had ever done. The flies had been so thick and fast that the camera could only capture them as a black cloud surrounding the Madonna of the Maggots and Roaches.

TWELVE

Erik Homer's second wife, now his widow, lived in a large apartment on East Ninety-first Street. 'It's rent control,' she said. 'Two-eighty a month. Can you beat that? This used to be such a crummy area. But look at it now.'

Detective Riker guessed that this woman's view of her neighborhood was limited to what she could see from the nearby window. He nursed a cup of strong coffee and longed for a cigarette, a little smoke to kill the stench of a sickroom.

Jane Homer was a mountain of sallow flesh, and he could roughly guess when she had become housebound, unable to fit her girth through a standard doorway. Her hair was a long tangle of mouse brown. Only the ends had the brassy highlights of a bleach blonde. Vanity had died years ago.

On the bureau, there were dozens of photographs of her younger self posed with her late husband. Jane had once been as slender as the first Mrs Homer. There were no portraits of her stepson.

A visiting nurse bustled about in the next room, chattering at Mallory while cleaning up the debris of a meal.

Mrs Homer's handicap worked in Riker's favor. Like most shut-ins, she was eager to gossip, and now she was saying, 'I saw the TV coverage the other night. Natalie's hanging was never on TV.'

Riker smiled. 'Yeah, the murders are a lot alike, aren't they?'

The woman nodded absently, and this gave him hope. He waited until he heard the door close behind the departing health-care worker. 'Did your husband ever talk about the murder?'

'Oh, yes. Erik and Natalie's sister – what was her name? Susan something. No matter. They talked on the telephone for hours. Erik made the funeral arrangements – paid for it, too. He didn't have to do that, you know.'

Riker thought otherwise. Taking possession of his ex-wife's body fit the pathology of a control freak. Even in death, Natalie never escaped Erik Homer. 'What about the little boy? How did you get along with your stepson? I mean – after his mother died.'

There was a touch of surprise in her eyes, or maybe guilt. 'Junior was no trouble.'

'No trouble? I'll bet.' Mallory had quietly entered the room. She held a silver picture frame in her hands as she glared at the woman on the bed, saying, accusing, 'You palmed him off on a relative after your husband died.'

'Yeah,' said Riker. 'That was in your last statement to the police. You said you gave the boy away.'

'Well, Erik's life insurance wasn't exactly a fortune.' Jane Homer's eyes were fixed on the picture frame in Mallory's hand. It was something she prized or something she feared. 'And I had all these medical problems that year. My thyroid gland and all. Junior loved his grandparents.' The woman stared at Riker, then Mallory, perhaps realizing that she had made some mistake. She filled their silence with a rush of words. 'I couldn't take care of him. You can see that, can't you?'

Mallory stepped closer to the bed. 'You told a detective the boy went to Natalie's sister in Brooklyn.'

'That's *right*,' said Mrs Homer, trying to appease Mallory with a feeble smile. 'I remember now. My father-in-law had Alzheimer's. Well, his wife probably couldn't cope with that and a little boy too. So, after a while, Junior went to live with Natalie's sister. *That's* what I meant.'

Mallory reached out across the body of Jane Homer to hand the silver frame to Riker. He turned it over to see a picture with the familiar backdrop of the Bronx Zoo. There were light creases through the image of a man and a woman, as if someone had crumpled it into a ball before it was framed. Had Jane Homer rescued this picture from a wastebasket? Yes, that was exactly what had happened. This one flattered her more than the others. The girl in the photograph was not yet wearing a wedding band, and she had been happy that day. A third person had been cut from the photograph. All that remained of the unwanted figure were the fingers of a small child caught up in the much larger hand of his smiling father.

'Was the boy having problems?' asked Riker.

Mallory leaned down very close to the other woman's face. 'How did Junior adjust to his mother's death?'

'Natalie died in August,' said Riker. 'And we know your husband didn't send Junior to school in September.'

'Tell me what you did with that little boy,' said Mallory.

Jane Homer's eyes widened with the realization that she was caught in the middle of a police crossfire. 'His grandparents—'

'No!' Riker scraped the legs of his chair across the floor, edging closer to the bed. 'No, Jane, I don't think so.'

Mallory leaned close to the woman's ear. 'I know how Erik Homer treated his first wife. He never gave her any money – never let her out of the house. Is that—'

'Erik did the shopping. I didn't need to go out. I didn't—'

'Your first police interview was right after your marriage,' said Riker. 'The cops thought you were afraid of your husband.'

'When did the beatings start?' Mallory raised her voice. 'On your honeymoon? Was that the first time he knocked you around?'

'You have lots of photographs.' Riker nodded toward the cluster of frames on her bureau. 'I see you and your husband, but not the little boy. You never lived with Junior, did you?' He caught the sudden fear in the woman's eyes. 'What did you do to Natalie's son? Is he *alive*?'

Jane Homer shook her head from side to side.

'Is that a no?' Mallory asked. 'The boy's dead?'

199

The woman trembled, and her bosom heaved with sobs. Speech was impossible. Her mouth formed the words *I don't know*.

Mallory moved closer. 'How could you *not* know?'

Riker leaned toward her. 'Did you think your husband went off on the kid, maybe killed his own son?'

The woman's head moved from side to side, splitting her halting words between the two detectives, anxious to please them both. 'The night they found Natalie – Erik got back – very late. I asked him where the boy was. Erik – hit me – *hard*.' One hand drifted to her mouth. 'He broke my tooth – then he – got rid of Junior's things – toys, clothes. And the pictures – he tore them to pieces.'

Jane Homer stared at the photograph that Riker held, the image of her husband and her smiling self in better days. In a small act of defiance, she grabbed the silver frame from Riker and held it to her breast, covering it with both hands, protecting the happy times. Huge tears rolled down her face, and they could do no more with her – or to her.

Outside the SoHo police station, young actresses were ganging on the sidewalk, posing for the cameras of reporters and tourists. Uniformed officers grinned with their good luck – they had gone to cop heaven. They worked the crowd, tipping hats to brunettes and sending them on their way, then filling out forms for all the blondes, taking down names and telephone numbers, as women filed past them and through the front door to interviews with Special Crimes detectives.

Mallory's car pulled to the curb. She left the motor running after Riker opened the passenger door. He had one foot on the pavement. 'You're not coming in?'

'No, I'm going over to Natalie's apartment building.' Then she added, with no enthusiasm at all, 'Come if you like.'

'Naw, I did a drive-by. Too much renovation. The new owner probably rearranged half the walls.' He kept her a while longer with one foot on the floor mat of her car, acting as if a sidewalk choked with pretty women was an everyday thing with him. 'I'm sticking a couple of uniforms on Susan Qualen. You're gonna miss all the fun when they drag her in.' After a few seconds of dead silence, Riker realized that she was not even tempted. He stepped out on to the sidewalk, closed the door and waved her off, then disappeared into a blond sea of actresses.

Mallory drove across town and through the East Village, heading for the twenty-year-old crime scene and blaming Jack Coffey for another fatal mistake. He had pulled men off their independent lines of investigation to work on the actress interviews, as if they could find the next victim that way.

Another woman was going to die.

She turned the wheel on First Avenue and rolled along the side street toward Avenue A. Once, this area had provided cheap housing for the poorest of the poor. Now, none of the former residents could afford to live here.

Mallory parked her car in front of the building where Natalie Homer had lived and died. Only the architectural bones would match Lars Geldorf's old photograph. Peeling gray paint had been sandblasted to expose the red brick. The windows were modern, and the wrought-iron rails of Juliet balconies had been restored. According to Geldorf's personal notes, the previous owner had died, and all the old tenants had departed before the renovation.

Riker was right. This was a waste of precious time.

And a woman was going to die.

Yet she left her car and walked up the stairs to ring the bell for the landlord's apartment. The front door was opened by a softly rounded woman with a warm smile for a stranger. The new owner was obviously not a native New Yorker, but a transplant from some smaller, less paranoid town.

'Mrs White?' The detective held up her badge and ID.

The woman's smile collapsed. 'It's about Natalie, isn't it? I wondered when you'd come.'

* * *

The civilian police aide for the midtown precinct was a short thin woman with brown hair and a dim view of blondes. Eve Forelli held up her favorite tabloid with the headline: ACTRESS STABBED IN BROAD DAYLIGHT. She glared at the tall, pretty woman seated on the other side of her desk. 'You look better in person.'

And this, of course, was sarcasm, for the grainy newsprint photograph only showed the back of the actress's head; the face was pressed to the bosom of another actor, a man holding the unconscious, bleeding victim in his arms while he postured and smiled for the camera.

The blonde's blue eyes opened wide. 'How could it be in the paper? It just happened this morning.'

Forelli pointed to the line below the newspaper's banner. 'It's the late edition.' She could see that the younger woman was not following this. 'It's a *second* edition.' And it had been free, a promotional gimmick for a failing newspaper. 'Now I need the correct spelling for your last name. The hospital only used one *L*. It doesn't look right.' She handed the newspaper to the blonde. 'And this story didn't even mention your name.'

The startled actress tore her eyes away from the clock on the wall to scan the article. 'Oh, damn, you're right.'

'The *spelling*, Miss Small?'

'Just the way it sounds. Call me Stella.' The woman flashed a smile. 'Look – is this going to take much longer? I've been waiting for over an hour. I'm already late for another appointment in SoHo.'

Eve Forelli only glared at the woman. This – *blonde* had left the hospital before giving a statement to the police. One of the little princes from Special Crimes Unit downtown had reamed out a desk sergeant and demanded the missing paperwork on the reported stabbing. Her supervisor, in turn, had crawled up Forelli's own scrawny tail. Further down the food chain, the frazzled police aide had screamed at the hospital staff. And, finally, the errant actress had been identified. And now Forelli prepared to marry an illegible attending physician's report to the crime victim's account. 'So you were stabbed by—'

'Oh, Jesus, no!' said the actress. 'I don't want any trouble with the cops. Look, I'm sorry, Officer, but this—'

'I'm not a cop.' Forelli pointed to the name tag pinned to her blouse, clearly identifying her as a civilian aide. 'You see a badge here? No, you don't. I just do the damn paperwork.'

'Sorry.' Stella Small touched her bandaged arm. 'A camera did this. No big deal.'

Eve Forelli's face was deadpan. 'A guy *stabbed* you – with his *camera*.' Of course. And this added credence to her pet theory that the roots of blond hair attacked brain cells.

'No.' The actress waved the newspaper. 'The reporter got it wrong. I wasn't stabbed – I was *slashed*.'

'With a camera.'

'But it was an accident.' The blonde slumped down in the chair. Her blue eyes rolled back, and then she sighed a clear sign of guilty defeat. 'Okay, *this* is what happened. My agent thought getting slashed with a razor was better than a guy just bumping into me on a crowded sidewalk.'

'Yeah, that would've been *my* choice.'

'I didn't know the doctor was going to file a police report.'

'Ah, doctors.' Forelli sighed. 'They fill out these reports for every shooting, stabbing and slashing. Who knows why? It's a mystery.'

'You're not going to get me in trouble, are you?'

'Naw, what the hell.' Forelli was overworked, very tired and feeling giddy. Inside the appropriate box of her form, she typed the words, *Professional bimbo collides with camera. Damn every tall blonde ever born.*

Her supervisor would not like this entry, assuming the lazy bastard ever bothered to read it – fat chance. All her best lines were lost on that illiterate fool. And now she would have to phone in the details to a detective from Special Crimes, another brain trust who had problems with the written word.

'But no more false police reports, okay? You can go to jail for that.' Forelli was not certain that this was true, but it did have a frightening effect on the blonde.

After the actress had departed, the police aide opened a window and leaned outside to smoke a cigarette. She looked down to see Stella Small standing on the sidewalk below, looking left and right, lost in yet another blond conundrum – which way to go?

Forelli, for lack of any better spectacle, watched as the young woman removed a wadded-up blouse from her purse, then tossed it into a trash basket near the curb.

Before the clerk had finished her smoke, an older woman came along. This one, with ragged clothes and matted hair, fished the blouse out of the wire basket and briefly inspected it. Though the material was stained with a large *X* on the back, the homeless woman stripped off her shirt – right in front of a *police* station – no *bra* – and put the trashcan find on her back.

Mallory listened politely as Mrs Alice White gave her a walking tour of the residence, rambling on about the problems of renovation. 'The place was a rabbit warren, all broken up in small spaces. Now there's only a few apartments left at the top of the house.' The rest of the floors had been restored to the former proportions and appointments of a family home.

'Where did the murder happen?'

'If I recall the old floorplan—' Alice White pulled open two massive wooden doors and stepped into a formal dining room. 'It was probably in here.'

Another doorway gave Mallory a view of the adjoining sit-down kitchen. *Always go to the kitchen.* This was a lesson handed down from Louis Markowitz. Interview subjects were less guarded in that more casual room, for only friends and family gathered there.

Mrs White's voice was jittery and halting. Police had that nervous effect on civilians, but Mallory suspected another reason.

Planning to hold out on me, Alice?

The woman paused by a large oak table surrounded by eight carved chairs. 'Yes, I'm sure of it now. This was where Natalie's apartment used to be. And it was no bigger than this room.'

Though the new owner had been a child when the victim had died, it was obvious that they had known one another. Whenever the conversation turned back to murder, the hanged woman was always Natalie to Mrs White.

Mallory was done with the pleasantries, the getting-to-know-you courtship. She decided upon a style of bludgeoning that would leave only psychic bruises and fingerprints. She raised her face to stare at the chandelier above the table, perhaps the same spot where Natalie Homer had hung for two days in August. 'You can almost see it, can't you?'

Gentle Alice White was *forced* to see it now; the woman's gaze was riveted to the ceiling fixture, and her mind's eye showed her a dead body twisting on a rope, rotting in the summer heat. And from now on, she would find Natalie hanging there each time she passed through her dining room.

The detective slowly turned on the freshly wounded civilian.

Can you hear the flies, Alice?

As if this thought had been spoken aloud, the startled woman's hand drifted up to cover her open mouth.

'Mrs White? Could I trouble you for a cup of coffee?' Caffeine was the best truth drug.

'What? Oh, of course. I've got a fresh pot on the stove.' Alice White could hardly wait to leave this room, this ghost, for the safety of the next room, and the detective followed her.

Mallory sat down at the kitchen table and unfolded a packet of papers, spreading them on a flower-print cloth. 'I understand you bought this building five years ago.'

'No, that's wrong.' Mrs White poured coffee into a carafe. 'I didn't buy it.' Next, she opened a cupboard of fine china cups and dishes, and this was a bad sign; she was putting out her Sunday best for company.

'I like coffee mugs, myself,' said Mallory.

'Oh, so do I.' The woman smiled as she pulled two ceramic mugs from hooks on the wall, then set them on the table.

'Maybe it's a clerical error.' Mallory held up a photocopy of the ownership transfer. 'This says you purchased the building from the estate of Anna Sorenson.'

Alice White, carafe in hand, hovered over the paper and read the pertinent line. 'No, that's definitely a mistake.' She poured their coffee, then sat down across the table. 'I didn't buy the house. Anna Sorenson was my grandmother. She willed it to me.'

'And you visited your grandmother – when you were a little girl.' Ten seconds crawled by, yet Mallory did nothing to prompt the woman. She sipped her coffee and waited out the silence.

'Yes.' Alice White said this as a confession. 'I was here that summer.'

Their eyes met.

'The summer Natalie died.' Her hands wormed around a sugar bowl and she pushed it toward Mallory. 'The coffee's too strong, isn't it? Norwegians make it like soup.' She reached for a carton of cream. 'Would you like some—'

'No, it's fine.'

And now it begins, Alice.

'So, the last time you saw Natalie Homer—'

'I was twelve.' Mrs White made a small production of pouring the cream carton into a pitcher, buying time to hunt for the right words. 'She was so pretty – like a movie star. That's what my grandmother said. Natalie gave me her old lipsticks and a pair of high heels.'

'So you spent some time with her. Did she talk about herself?'

'No – not much.' Alice White was so rattled, she stirred her coffee, though she had added neither cream nor sugar. 'I know her people were from the old country, but not Natalie. My grandmother said her Norwegian wasn't good.' The woman forced a bright smile. 'I don't speak a word myself. My parents only used it when they didn't want me to know what they were saying. So when Natalie spoke Norwegian to Gram, I knew I was missing all the good stuff.'

Mallory shuffled her papers, then handed the woman another document. 'This is a copy of Natalie's marriage certificate. Her maiden name was an odd one, Qualen. That's Norwegian?'

'Never heard of it.' Alice White stared at the certificate. 'Maybe it's a corruption. A lot of foreign names were changed at Ellis Island. I bet the original spelling was *Kv* instead of *Qu*. But that still wouldn't make it a common name.'

'Good,' said Mallory. 'That'll make it easier to trace her family. It would help if I knew what state they live in. The only next-of-kin we have is a sister in Brooklyn. And she hates cops.'

'So did my grandmother. She said they were all thieves. They were always ticketing the building for fake violations. Then Gram would give them some cash and—' She gave Mallory a weak sorry smile, suddenly remembering that her guest was also police. 'But that was a long time ago. I've never had any problems like—'

'Can you remember anything that would tie Natalie to relatives out of state?'

'I think she came from Racine, Wisconsin. My parents live there, and Gram asked Natalie if she knew them.'

Mallory reached for a folded newspaper at the edge of the table. It was days old. She opened it to the front-page picture of Sparrow being loaded into an ambulance. 'Can we talk about this now?'

Alice White's eyes were begging, *Please don't.*

'You knew the police would come.' Mallory pushed the newspaper across the table. 'This hanging was a lot like Natalie's – the hair cut off and packed in her mouth. When you read the paper, you recognized the details. That's why you were expecting me. I know you saw Natalie's body. We have a statement from the police officer who saw you in the hall with another kid, a little boy. How old was he?'

'Six or seven.' Alice White was mistaking Mallory's guesswork for absolute certainty. She showed no surprise, only the resignation of a true believer in police omniscience.

'The two of you saw everything,' said Mallory, 'before Officer Parris chased you away.'

The woman nodded. 'Officer Sticky Fingers. That's what Gram called him. Or maybe that was the other one.' She looked up. 'Sorry – the cops in uniforms—'

'They all look alike. I know. So you saw everything, the hair, and the—'

'I can still see it.'

'Who was the little boy? Your brother?'

'No, I never knew his name. Gram found him wandering in the hall. She took him inside and went through all the stuff in his little suitcase. I remember she found a phone number, but there was nobody home when she called.'

'Why didn't she turn him over to the cops?'

'She'd never—' Mrs White shrugged. 'Like I said, Gram hated the police. She'd never trust them with a child, not that one. You see, there was something wrong with the boy. He couldn't talk, or he wouldn't. Well, my grandmother figured somebody must be expecting him for a visit – because of the little suitcase. When she opened it up, everything was still neatly packed. He smelled bad – I think he'd messed in his pants. Gram gave him a bath and changed his clothes. Then she went from door to door, all over the building, the whole neighborhood.'

'So you were alone with the boy when the cops showed up.'

'Yes. My grandmother was the one who called the police, but it took them forever to get here. This awful smell was coming from next door. Gram was just frantic. She had a key to Natalie's place, but it didn't work. A few hours after Gram left, I heard the cops out in the hall. One of them yelled, "Oh, God, no!"'

'And you were curious.'

'You bet. More police showed up, men in suits. One of the men in uniform was guarding the apartment and shooing people away. I waited

208

till he walked down the hall to talk to a neighbor. Then I went to Natalie's door. It was wide open.'

'And the boy was with you.'

'I was holding his hand. Gram told me not to leave him alone. Well, I saw the body hanging there – but it didn't look like Natalie. Her eyes and that beautiful long hair – it was just—' Alice White took a deep breath. 'And the roaches – they were crawling down the rope to get at her. The men just left her hanging there while they took their pictures. Then another policeman chased us off.'

'What happened to the little boy?'

'That night, a man came to take him away.'

'Did you recognize him?'

'No, I was in bed. I only heard the voices in the other room. I think Gram knew him. Or maybe she tried that telephone number again, the one she found in the suitcase. Yes, she must've talked to him on the phone. He didn't have to say who he was when he came to the door.'

'Did you tell your grandmother what you and the boy—'

'God, no. Gram would've been so angry. She told me to take care of that boy – not give him nightmares for the rest of his life.'

Charles Butler was no stranger to Brooklyn. He frequently made the trek to this outer borough for a poker game with friends. However, like any good New Yorker, he only knew his habitual routes. Before Riker had allowed his driver's license to lapse, every other road had been a mystery, even this broad avenue along Prospect Park.

He waited in his car as the detective crossed the street and joined two uniformed policemen standing by a squad car. They were too far away for Charles to hear any conversation, and so he eavesdropped on their body language.

One of the officers shrugged to say, *Sorry*. Riker's hands rose in exasperation, and he must have uttered at least one obscenity, for now the officer's hands went to his hips to say, *Hey, it's not our fault*. Behind dark glasses, the slouching detective stared at one man and then the other, giving them no clue to his thoughts. Suddenly both officers were talking with upturned hands, offering new forms of *Sorry*, probably accompanied by a mollifying *sir*. In an economy of motion, Riker waved one hand to say, *Awe, the hell with it*, then turned his back, dismissing them both. He was one very unhappy man when he slid into the front seat of the Mercedes.

'Not good news, I take it.' Charles started the engine.

'Natalie's sister left town in a big hurry.' Riker nodded toward the men in uniform. 'And those two clowns just stood there and watched her drive away – with a *suitcase*.' His head lolled back on the soft leather upholstery. 'They keep changing the rules on me, Charles. Apparently, if you can say the word *lawyer* three times without interruption, the cops have to let you go. My fault. I used the word *detain* instead of *arrest*.'

'Bad luck. Sorry.' The Mercedes pulled away from the curb.

'Yeah. And I was really looking forward to scaring the shit out of that woman.' Riker fell into a black silence until the great arches of the Brooklyn Bridge loomed up on the road before them.

Charles sensed there was more to the detective's dark mood than a lost witness. How else to account for this sadness? When the car stopped in traffic, he turned to the man beside him. 'Is there anything I can do to help?'

'Yeah, there is.' The detective stirred, then sat up a bit straighter. 'I've been thinking about the Wichita Kid and that wolf bite.'

This was highly unlikely, but now Charles understood that the real problem was none of his business. 'You want to know how—'

'Naw, here's my best guess. I figure there's a one-in-a-million chance the Wichita Kid could survive rabies without a vaccine.'

'That's actually true, but I don't think Jake Swain was aware of it when he wrote the book.' As they crossed the bridge, Charles launched into the story of Sheriff Peety's travels from town to town, hunting an outlaw infected with rabies. 'So he's chatting up all the local doctors along the way when he meets one who's heard the story of the rabid wolf that bit—'

'Hold it,' said Riker. 'Don't tell me. The sheriff finds out that the wolf never had rabies in the first place. Am I right?'

'Right you are. He discovers that someone else was bitten by that same wolf and survived. The animal actually had distemper. Looks the same as rabies, lots of frothing at the mouth, but it's not transmissible to humans. However, the wound wasn't cleaned properly, so Wichita suffered a massive infection — fevers, hallucinations — but no symptoms of hydrophobia.'

The detective politely raised one eyebrow, though he seemed to have lost interest. After a few moments of silence, Charles said, 'You've had news from the hospital. Your friend—'

'Yeah.' Riker turned his face to the passenger window and its view of the open sky over the water. 'Her one good kidney is failing.'

And even Jake Swain could not have written an escape for Sparrow. However, pressed by deep concern for a friend, Charles now came up with the next best thing — an emergency epiphany. 'There was an eye-witness to Natalie Homer's murder. Does that cheer you up?' The car came to a standstill in heavy traffic halfway across the bridge. Riker turned around to face him with a look of surprise, successfully distracted from pain.

Charles changed gears as the traffic moved forward again. 'My theory works nicely with the problem of the locked door.'

The detective turned back to face the passenger window, his way of saying, *Oh, that again.*

'Bear with me. Previously, I assumed that someone used a key to open Natalie's door before the police arrived. But my witness wouldn't need a key — not if he opened the door from the *inside.*'

'And here's the flaw,' said Riker. 'That would mean your witness was in the apartment for two days — watching a woman's body rot.'

'Yes. Now back up a bit. The night she died, Natalie was cooking a meal for two. She had no friends, and she was on bad terms with

211

her sister. So the dinner guest was her son.'

'Interesting,' said Riker, which was his polite way of saying that it was not at all interesting. 'So, before Erik Homer goes on his honeymoon, he leaves the kid with his ex-wife? No, Charles. This guy was a control freak. After the divorce, he *never* let Natalie see that kid, not *once*. This can't work.'

'Why not? Erik Homer was getting married again. He had a new woman to control. And this baby-sitting arrangement would be for *his* convenience. *That's* what makes it work. And no one ever interviewed the boy. We don't know where Junior was for two days in August or anytime after that.' Charles could see that Riker was not buying any of this. 'Only a small child would have stayed in that room with the body. The boy wouldn't want to leave his mother. Dead or alive, she was his whole world.'

'Let's see if I understand this.' Riker's voice was strained in an effort to quell the sound of condescension. 'It was a studio apartment. No place to hide a kid, even a small one. But Junior managed to—'

'Riker, all over the world, mothers tell their children to wash up for dinner. It's a universal thing. The boy was in the bathroom the whole time that man was killing his mother.'

'It was August,' said the detective. 'No air-conditioner in Natalie's place. Rolling blackouts. The lights were off half the time. The stove burner was left on. *More* heat when—'

'Yes, and after two days, the little boy's survival instinct overcame trauma, and he left the apartment. This explains the unlocked door. Also, it very neatly explains your contrary reports of the boy's whereabouts. The father sent him away. Erik Homer didn't want the killer to find out that his son was a witness.'

Charles and Riker were still at odds when they entered the back office of Butler and Company.

Mallory never acknowledged them. She was deep in conversation with her machines, speaking to them with keyboard commands. They responded with screens of data and papers pouring from the mouths of three printers. She sat with her back to the discordant men and the mess on her cork wall. Her vision was thus narrowed to a sterile field that hummed with perfect harmony.

Charles rounded the computer workstation and saw the cold machine lights reflected in her eyes. He looked down at the thick cable that fed her electronics through a dedicated line of electricity, and he played with the idea of *accidentally* kicking the plug from its socket and disconnecting her that way.

Riker rapped on the top of the monitor, and when this failed to get her attention, he said, 'Charles thinks he's got an eyewitness to the murder of Natalie Homer.'

'Hmm. Natalie's son.' Mallory never lifted her eyes from the glowing screen. 'He's the one who unlocked the door to the crime scene. But I don't know what name Junior's using these days, so we'll just stick with the scarecrow.' She smiled at her computer, as if it had just said something to amuse her. 'And now we've got a game.'

THIRTEEN

Charles said a silent goodbye to Louis Markowitz. His old friend's personality was being erased from the cork wall by layers of lopsided pictures and papers.

Mallory walked along the cork wall, ripping down reports and sending tacks flying through the air. Photographs of fat black flies hit the floor where they mingled with enlarged cockroaches and smiling portraits from Natalie Homer's actress portfolio. Given that Mallory was a pathologically tidy creature, Charles thought this might qualify as a loss of control, a display of temper, though she never raised her voice when she said, 'So Natalie's sister got away.'

'Yeah,' said Riker. 'I put the dogs on her. We might get lucky before she ditches the car for a plane or a bus. Maybe Susan's more afraid of her nephew than us.'

'She should be,' said Charles. 'If Natalie's son is the scarecrow—'

'He is.' The soft plof of papers and pings of pushpins followed Mallory to the end of the wall, where she tacked up the print bought from William Heart. 'It all fits.' She pointed to the open bathroom door in the background of this photograph. 'Charles is right. The boy was probably in there while his mother was being murdered. Two days later, he was found wandering in the hall with a suitcase and all the symptoms of shock. And that was *before* the first cop opened the crime scene.'

'Okay,' said Riker. 'Say the scarecrow is Natalie's kid all grown up and not too shy about cold-blooded murder. If he knew who killed his mother, he'd just off the bastard.'

'No,' she said. 'The boy was hiding, watching through a keyhole or a crack in the door. Maybe he never saw the killer's face.'

'Or even the actual murder,' said Charles. 'The scarecrow doesn't imitate his mother's death by strangulation – only the postmortem hanging.' And now he noticed the dead quiet in the offices of Butler and Company. 'So where's Lars Geldorf?'

'I had Deluthe take him home. The old man is out of the loop. We're consolidating all the hangings. From now on, he doesn't get past the front door.' She turned her eyes on Charles. 'You've got a problem with that?'

'Well, he has so much invested in Natalie's murder.' And now, judging by the hand gravitating to her hip, Charles realized that the correct response would have been, *Oh, hell no.* But he rather liked the old man, and so he persisted. 'Lars could still contribute to the—'

'Wrong.' She turned her back on him. 'All Geldorf ever had was a stalker pattern and an ex-husband, every cop's favorite suspect. He spent all his time trying to break Erik Homer's alibi.' A more linear personality was taking shape on the cork wall as Mallory finished pinning up a straight line of text and pictures. One red fingernail tapped the statement of Susan Qualen. 'Natalie's sister hated her brother-in-law. Every other word on this paper is *bastard.* But later the same night, she was talking to Erik Homer for hours, and they weren't discussing funeral arrangements.'

Charles nodded. 'You think they conspired to hide the boy.'

'Right,' said Mallory. 'They didn't want the killer to know there was an eyewitness. That's why no one could find Junior. He was shipped off to relatives out of state.'

A computer beeped to call for Mallory's attention, and she sat down at a workstation to watch the text scrolling down her screen. 'An hour ago, I found rapsheets for Rolf and Lisa Qualen, a husband and wife in Wisconsin. They were arrested for kidnapping a little boy, but the age doesn't match Natalie's son.' Mallory scrolled down the single-spaced text. 'One hell of a lot of material.' She watched bundles of paper pouring into all the printer beds. 'I've got a time problem here.'

Laden with Mallory's printouts, Charles had retreated to the comfort of his own private office, a soft leather chair and a wooden desk from a less technical age. When he had finished speed-reading the last of the court documents, a trial transcript and attendant reports from social workers and police, he looked up at his audience. The weary detectives were pressed deep into a plush sofa. They were raiding delicatessen bags and awaiting his synopsis on the arrest and trial of Rolf and Lisa Qualen.

'Mr and Mrs Qualen had a son named John, who drowned shortly before his eighth birthday, and that was a year before Natalie Homer's murder. Two days *after* Natalie's body was found, the Qualens abandoned their house in Racine, Wisconsin, and resettled in a small town a hundred miles away. That's where they enrolled their dead son, John, in grammar school.'

'Freaking amateurs,' said Riker.

'Hmm.' Mallory finished her bagel. 'Bad match for Natalie's son. The dead boy's birth certificate was off by two years.'

'The school principal noticed that, too,' said Charles. 'He was told that the boy's scholastic records were lost in a fire. Eventually, he located those records in Racine – along with a death certificate for the real John Qualen.'

'So that's when the cops were called in?' This was Riker's polite way of moving the story along, for it was not his habit to state the obvious. And now he glanced at his watch in yet another attempt at being subtle.

'Yes,' said Charles. 'The police suspected kidnapping, but the Qualens wouldn't cooperate with the investigation and neither would the little boy.'

'Junior was scared,' said Mallory.

'That was the case detective's opinion,' said Charles. 'The police had no idea where the boy came from. He didn't match any reports on missing children. So they put him in foster care, and the Qualens went to trial. The kidnap charge was never proved, but they were found guilty of falsifying records, and that got them a stiff fine. The foster-care records were sealed, and the boy disappeared into the bureaucracy.'

Riker pulled out his notebook and pen. 'What've you got in the way of case numbers?'

'For the boy? There's nothing attached to the court documents. Sorry.' He held up a sheaf of papers. 'This is a brief filed by the Qualens' attorney. They tried to adopt the boy, but they weren't even successful in getting visitation rights.'

'That's why I can't find him,' said Mallory. 'Social Services saw the Qualens as a threat. So they changed Junior's name again and gave him a new case number. We don't even know what age they settled on.'

'With what we got so far,' said Riker, 'we'll never get a court order to open sealed juvenile records. And he's probably out there right now stringing up another woman.'

'Then we'll know soon enough,' said Mallory. 'He escalated with Sparrow. This time, he'll put on a bigger show.'

Riker's kitchen was wrecked, drawers pulled out, cupboards rifled, and a slice of pizza was glued upside down to the linoleum where he had dropped it the previous night – or perhaps the night before. And he had not yet found the playground tape. Years ago, he had put it away for fear of breaking it after running it so many times.

He glanced back at the living room. Charles Butler sat down on the sofa, and a dusty cloud rose up around him. At the man's feet, cardboard take-out containers and months of newspapers were loosely piled, as if set apart for recycling, a practice Riker had only heard about, and all the ashtrays were overflowing with stale butts. However, Charles was so polite, so well bred that no one would have guessed he was not accustomed to squalor.

At last the detective found the videotape and fed it into the VCR in the living room. He handed his guest the last clean glass (Riker's own version of good breeding) filled with bourbon and a splash of water, then made his own drink a bit stronger and settled into a leather armchair.

'A friend of mine confiscated the tape from a pedophile. The freak was cruising Central Park for victims.' He turned to Charles and noted the sudden rigid set to the man's jaw. 'Relax. He never got near the kid. He could only catch her on film.' Riker hit the play button on his remote control. 'This is what really got Lou's attention. The film was a few years old when we saw it for the first time.' In the absence of children of his own, the pedophile's video was Riker's substitute for home movies.

The screen brightened to a clear summer day, and the show began with the close-up shot of a small blond girl in a dirty T-shirt that fitted her like a tent. Riker pressed the pause button. 'Kathy's probably eight years old on this tape, but you can see she's been out on the street too long.'

He pressed the play button, but the little girl remained frozen on the grass at the edge of a playground. She tilted her head to one side, not yet committed to going or staying. The homeless child must have known that she belonged here with kids her own age. Perhaps she recognized a normalcy that had been ripped away from her. So here she was – looking to fill a need.

Doing the best you can.

Kathy came to play.

Charles Butler leaned toward the screen, spellbound by the beautiful little girl, a miniature Mallory. All around her the world was aswirl with action and sound, small feet running in packs and tiny screams of outrage and joy.

The solitary child hesitated another moment. Then, light stepping, cautious as a cat, she padded toward a row of swings, gray boards dangling from long metal chains. She took her seat among the rest, looking right and left with grave suspicion, and she began to swing in a small tentative arc. Now Kathy leaned far back to steepen the pitch and made a soft giggling sound at the wonder of flight. On the upswing, she soared above a line of cruel spikes atop an iron fence. An illusion of the camera made these spears seem close enough to impale her.

Fearing nothing from the hard ground below, she leaned farther back to make the swing fly higher. Reckless and grinning, she soared up and over the heads of wild-eyed women, mothers and nannies, their waving hands and their screams of *Come down!*

Riker turned to Charles. The man's mouth was working in a silent prayer, *Don't fall.*

Toes pointed toward the sun, she rushed up to the sky, laughing – laughing.

All the joy died when Kathy looked into the camera lens. Her eyes were suddenly adult and cold. Her hands let go of the chains, and she took flight; literally airborne, she flew out of the camera frame, and the screen went black.

Though Riker had watched this film a hundred times, his hand tensed around the bourbon glass. For him, the child was still flying and always would be – a tossed coin that could never land.

Charles slept soundly on his office couch, still wearing yesterday's clothes. Only Mallory was awake to watch the sun come up. She had returned to the offices of Butler and Company with a stack of morning newspapers, and now she sat in an armchair, sipping coffee and hunting for a police press release. It had not made any of the front pages. The scarecrow's crimes were old and stale, last week's news.

The dog days of August marked the close of tourist-hunting season in Central Park, the scene of another daylight stabbing, but today's headline victim was a man decapitated by a flying manhole cover described as the blown cork of a broken water main. The next runner-up was a woman killed by a stone gargoyle that had fallen from a crumbling building façade on Broadway. All the signs of a town out of control were here in black and white, decay and corruption from the sewers to the skyline.

And then there was Riker.

Yesterday, his sallow skin had been stippled with the small wounds of a shaving razor. His hands always trembled the morning after a binge. Booze poisoning was running its course and killing him slowly. With most cops on the decline, integrity was the first thing to go. Riker had clung to his long after everything else had been lost. He had always commanded great respect, even while crawling out of a bar on his hands and knees.

Why would he risk his job to rob Sparrow's crime scene?

It was a common form of larceny for cops and firemen, stealing cash and baubles from the dead. But she had believed that all the manhole covers would blow up and the town would fall down before Riker would steal *anything*. And she still believed that, for now she suspected him of a worse crime — holding out on his partner, secreting evidence and working it on the side.

Mallory turned another page in search of the official press release, a warning to every blond actress in New York City. She found the story at the bottom of page three. Lieutenant Coffey had come through on his promise to give the next victim a sporting chance, but the scarecrow had also warned his prey; he had all but pushed the women into the arms of the police. Why?

She blamed her lack of sleep for seeking logic in a madman's plan.

The young actress had grown up wearing the discards of the Abandoned Stellas, twice- and thrice-handed-down clothes bought from secondhand stores. Only the fabulous blue suit had never been worn by anyone else, and now it was ruined New York style, with blood, and she had lost her armor. Every passerby could see the genes of a third-generation bastard, the highway debris of traveling men.

This morning, Stella Small stood in front of an uptown cash machine and stared at her bank card. She never balanced her checkbook, for that sucked the last bit of charm out of life, and it also frightened her. She could roughly guess her account balance, enough for underwear, but she was hoping for more. A brochure was clutched in her other hand, and she paused to pray over it, *God bless junk mail.* Designer suits were featured on the second page of sale items. The fashion outlet store was only one block away, and she had an hour to spare before the next open audition. Stella had gambled a subway token on her belief in synchronicity, and now she fed her bank card into the magic slot.

Her eyes were scrunched shut. *Please, please, please.*

Stella's white blouse and skirt had been washed and ironed twice, yet she could detect the smell of a thrift shop in the material. It was the odor of failure. Her head was bowed and her shoulders slumped in a loser's posture. But that was about to change.

When she had finished her ritual prayer words over the cash machine, it disgorged all the manna she needed to replace the ruined audition suit. Her first thought was that this was her rent money, that the Abandoned Stellas had made an early deposit to her checking account. Her second thought was that there *was* a god of cash machines, and he loved theater folk.

She ran to the end of the block and joined a herd of shoppers gathered outside the department store, all awaiting the early-bird sale. Stella had her battle plan ready. The doors opened, and the chase was on. She sped past older women in support hose, descended the stairs to the basement level, then charged toward the back wall where the suits were hanging. If the clothes fit, if the producer liked what he saw – her entire life would change. Her future might be literally hanging on the rack before her eyes, and she was rushing toward it.

And then she stopped.

Damn – another New York moment.

A lumpy woman with brown hair and gray roots pulled the only blue suit from the group of size eights. Stella watched, dumbfounded, as the middle-aged shopper popped a button trying to close the blazer over her bulging stomach. Oh, and now the evil bitch had left a smudge of makeup on one sleeve.

Stella was distracted by the sight of her own face in a mirror on the nearby wall. Without intending to, she had slipped under the skin of the aging brunette, imitating the scowl, the narrowed mean little eyes and the absence of a soul.

The older woman gave up the attempt to shoehorn her body into the suit jacket, and she stormed away with heavy footfalls. Stella retrieved the fallen button and collected her prize from the floor where it had been dropped, but not, *Thank you, God*, trodden upon. She checked the label. It belonged to a designer she had actually heard of. The price had been slashed in half, another divine act, or, as the Abandoned Stellas would say, *Jesus saves.*

She glanced at her watch. It was late, but she would make the audition *if* she hurried, *if* the line at the cashier was not too long, *if* the trains were not late. She was still chaining her conditions of success when she ran into the fitting room, where she stripped, tried on the suit and pronounced it a perfect fit.

Stella slung her old skirt over one arm as she walked toward the cashier's counter. Miraculously, there was no one in line. This afforded her the luxury of a few minutes of preening before a three-sided looking glass, admiring herself from every angle. The makeup stain was invisible as long as she kept her right hand by her side. And there was more than enough time to sew on a button during the subway ride. For a whole year, she had carried a small traveler's sewing kit in every purse she owned, just waiting for a day like today, when her life might hang upon a button.

She was knocked into the mirror by a hard slam to her back. Stella sucked in her breath, then braced both hands on the glass. In one of the three reflecting panels, she saw a man standing behind her, breaking the rules, for all New York collisions were hit-and-run affairs. Everyone else in the crowd was in motion, hustling from rack to rack, flinging clothes and hangers. Only this man was absolutely still, and he only had eyes for Stella.

CHAR SCHOOL

the light, crowded as it in motion, in chair, from back to rack, lingering
clothes and blazers. Ott, this man was completely still and he was
had eyes to Stella.

FOURTEEN

The man in the department store mirror was obviously another fan of
daytime soap operas. Stella smiled at his reflection.

Yes, it's me.

He did not acknowledge her smile, nor did he make eye contact like
any normal person. The man stared at her as if she were an object all of
one piece and without eyes of her own to see him. She stiffened her
body, imitating his posture, then focused on her own reflection and
watched her eyes go cold and colder. Her mouth became a simple line,
committed to no expression. And now she had his likeness inside and
out. There was no one home inside of her anymore – just a little
graveyard dust.

The man did not seem to appreciate or even notice her artful
portrayal of him. Beneath the brim of a baseball cap, his face was
unchanged, frozen, one inanimate object facing another – herself.
Pushing the likeness just a bit further, Stella's eyes had gone entirely
dead, and she became—

The audition!

She was going to be late.

Stella broke off this eerie connection to glance at her watch. When
she looked up again, she saw the reflection of his baseball cap just
visible above the heads of female shoppers as he moved backward,
blending into the crowd, a player doing his walk-on in reverse.

Mesmerized, Stella did not move until he was out of sight. Again,
she looked at her watch. More time had passed than she would have

believed possible. Other customers were moving toward the cash registers. She ran full-out to beat a slow-moving elderly woman to the checkout counter. Hunched over, neck-and-neck with the stooped, white-haired shopper, Stella unconsciously mirrored the sudden alarm in her opponent's eyes. The old woman put on some speed toward the end, then gave up the foot race to youth; panting and wheezing, support hose bagging at the ankles, the loser stood in line behind the grinning actress.

When it was Stella's turn to be waited on, her mouth dipped down on one side, copying the face before her, and she also assumed the overly efficient air of the sales clerk. 'I'm in a big hurry. Just cut the tags. I'll wear it.' Stella pushed her old skirt across the counter. 'And bag this, okay?'

'Suit yourself.' The clerk's voice was the monotone of a telephone company recording. 'No returns on sales.'

Stella held out one pale blue sleeve so the other woman could snip off the price tags. 'You be careful with those scissors, all right?'

The clerk's voice betrayed a sudden annoyance. 'Like I said, lady – no returns.' Not quite so efficient anymore, the woman allowed Stella's arm to hang in the air. Taking her own maddening time to put the blond actress in her place, the clerk picked up the old skirt 'twixt thumb and forefinger, then held it at the distance of a bad smell before dropping it into a bag. Finally, she reached for her scissors and *slowly* cut the tag strings from Stella's sleeve. The cashier glanced at the mirror behind the line of customers, saying, 'You know this jacket is damaged, right? Stained?'

Oh, the makeup smudge.

'No problem. I can get that out.'

'Yeah, *sure* you can.' The clerk watched the blonde walk away with a black *X* scrawled on the back of the new suit. Then she turned a merciless eye on the next customer in line, an elderly woman slowly approaching the counter. '*Move* it, lady!'

* * *

Lieutenant Coffey watched the last actress leave the squad room in company with two detectives, the number of men it took to escort a pretty woman downstairs. The deputy commissioner's son-in-law passed them at the stairwell door, and now he walked toward the private office.

So Mallory and Riker had managed to lose Deluthe again.

While the lieutenant checked his list of blondes for the second day of interviews, the younger man stood at a respectful distance and waited to be acknowledged. Coffey liked the deference to rank, but he had his doubts that this youngster was going to make it as a detective.

'I thought you were watching Lars Geldorf.'

'He's staying home today. I'm looking for Sergeant Riker.'

'He'll be here in half an hour.' Coffey held up a tabloid with the headline: ACTRESS STABBED IN BROAD DAYLIGHT. 'Okay, kid, make yourself useful.' He pointed to the handwritten notes and a telephone number scrawled across the top of the front page. 'This Midtown precinct never called back with a name on the actress. Find out who she is, then check the interview list. If we haven't talked to her, get her down here today.'

'Yes, sir.' Paper in hand, Deluthe swooped down on the nearest vacant desk and picked up the phone.

Jack Coffey had only a few minutes to settle in behind his desk before the rookie rapped on the frame of his open office door. The lieutenant waved him inside. 'What've you got, kid?'

'The actress is Stella Small. I talked to a police aide, Eve Forelli. She says it was just a publicity stunt.'

The lieutenant nodded toward the tabloid in the younger man's hand. 'Did you *read* that article?'

'No, sir. I thought you wanted—'

'*Read* it. You'll find the first mention of blood in the opening paragraph. It's a puddle on a hotel carpet.' He leaned over the desk and ripped the paper from Deluthe's hand, then pointed to the photograph of an unconscious woman. 'Oh, and the dark stain on her sleeve?'

That's blood too.' He slammed the newspaper down on his desk blotter, yet his voice remained calm. 'In my experience, very few actresses ever mutilate themselves for a mention in the tabloids.' And now he stopped, for it was not his job to train the rookie from Lieutenant Loman's squad. 'At least you got her name. That's something.' He consulted his list of blond interview subjects and found Stella Small among them. 'Her agent set up an interview, but Small was a no-show. Apparently this woman doesn't watch the news or read the papers. *Find* her.'

'The police aide already took her statement,' said Deluthe. 'The actress told her she had a street altercation with a tourist. You see, the guy hit this woman with his camera, and she needed a few stitches. That's it. So then her agent shows up at the hospital and gets the idea to make the wound a little more newsworthy. That's when it turned into a stabbing.'

'A police aide did the interview? A *civilian*? Well, that's just great.' He tossed the newspaper to the rookie. 'Get a copy of that statement from Midtown, and get that actress down here.'

'But it's just—'

'Busywork? Most of my damn day is busywork. I'm one goddamn busy man. Now can you handle this or not?' What he had really wanted to ask Deluthe was why the man dyed his hair. And of all the colors in the world, why choose glow-in-the-dark yellow?

Detective Janos stood at the front of the squad room and addressed the rest of the men. 'We got a thirty-second spot on the morning news and a full minute on radio. We might get lucky with the tip lines.' He held up the newspaper page that listed the dates and locations of open casting calls. 'And there's two auditions today. We got twenty minutes to make the one on—'

'Hey!' Detective Desoto, who sorted the tip-line calls, yelled, 'Listen up! A woman with an *X* on her back just passed the corner of Sixtieth and Lex. I got a guy calling from a payphone. He says she was

227

headed for the subway. She's got blond hair, and she's wearing a light blue suit.'

'A suit,' said Riker. 'I'll bet she's on her way to the midtown audition.'

'It's on the West Side.' Janos was heading for the door, issuing orders on the run. 'Get a unit over there. She'll make the crossover over at Forty-second Street.'

'Maybe not.' Arthur Wang grabbed his gun from a desk drawer. 'If she sees that X on her back, she might pack it in. I know my wife would—'

'Subway!' yelled Janos.

Every man but Deluthe was up and running. Sergeant Riker stopped to tap his shoulder, saying, 'You're with us, kid.'

And they were off. Lieutenant Coffey's busywork errand was forgotten as Deluthe fell in with the gang of running detectives heading downstairs for the cars. One by one, the unmarked vehicles raced their engines. Mobile turret lights were slapped on to the roofs as they sped down Houston, zooming toward the West Side Highway.

Heading uptown.

What a ride!

The police cars were strung out in a wedge, forcing cabs to dodge and weave, and terrifying the amateur drivers. Five sirens screamed, and bullhorns shouted, *'Outta the way! Move it! Move it!'* Every cross-town light was magically green until the convoy pulled to the curb in front of Forty-second Street Station.

The men left their cars at a dead run, hustling down the subway stairs in close formation, flying through the long tunnel, leather slapping cement, adrenaline rushing, hearts on fire, finally emerging in the shuttle bay.

Full stop.

Something's wrong.

There were too many people milling around at this time of the morning.

Three detectives climbed up on a bank of concrete and scanned the heads of waiting straphangers, looking for the blonde with an *X* on her back. Six men circled around to the other side of the track to search the rest of the crowd, then returned, heads shaking.

The woman was not here.

The surrounding passengers had the makings of a mob, feet stamping, voices rising, tempers close to exploding in the hot muggy air around the shuttle bay. Most had wandered away from the track, but hopefuls still stood on the edge, eyes fixed on the dark tunnel with a New Yorker's certain knowledge that watchers, not switchmen, made the trains come.

The crowd was still growing, not conversing but growling, voices rumbling in one sentiment, *Death to all transit workers – kill them all*. Here and there, a passenger went off like a firecracker, screaming obscenities. It could only be a matter of minutes before the first punch was thrown. This vast space would become a bloodbath from wall to wall.

Near the police booth, a band of musicians were unpacking instruments and plugging in amplifiers. This was the city's emergency response to impending violence among disgruntled subway riders.

Janos folded his cell phone. 'We got uniforms at the exits. No sign of her yet.'

Detective Desoto had disappeared into the mob, and now he was running back to them. 'The good news? A suicide. A jumper got himself smeared across the tracks. All these people are from the rush-hour crowd. That's how long they've been waiting.'

'And now the bad news,' said Riker.

'They just finished cleaning up all the blood and guts. The shuttles are on the way. We're gonna lose the whole crowd in five minutes flat.'

Deluthe understood this worst-case scenario. What were the odds that any of these stressed-out citizens would miss a ride out of hell to talk to a cop? 'Can't we just stop the trains?'

Desoto gave him a look that asked, *What hick town are you from?*

229

'Maybe you didn't hear me, kid. The last guy who stopped the trains is *dead.*'

'We got five minutes,' said Riker. 'Deluthe, you work the passengers near the track. Hit on the women. Men are useless. They only see breasts, not backs. The rest of you guys are with me.'

The detectives moved in tandem, walking toward the small band of musicians. Their body language changed as they drew closer to the light Latin tempo intended to soothe ugly tempers with the soft strings of a guitar and a bass – and a drummer with nothing to do.

While Deluthe was taking statements of 'I didn't see nobody' and 'I don't know *nothin*'', Riker was taking a guitar away from one of the teenage musicians.

Deluthe watched the action through breaks in the crowd near the track. The senior detective's hand flew up and down the neck of the electric guitar, playing riffs of rock 'n' roll, and he was good – *damn* good. The younger passengers were drifting toward the music, fingers snapping, heads bobbing to the beat – reborn.

The musicians were playing backup as Riker was gliding and sliding, strings zinging, the crowd cheering. He ripped out notes in a one-handed frenzy as he rolled the other hand toward the band to jump up the tempo. The bassman's fingers moved faster and faster. The drummer went insane with his sticks, smashing cymbals and beating on skins.

Janos pulled a woman from the crowd, and now they were gyrating, twirling and writhing. Other detectives grabbed strange females, danced them ragged and discarded them quickly. All the people were in motion; the place was rocking, cooking, jumping. The beat vibrated across the concrete and came up through the soles of Ronald Deluthe's shoes.

The crowd formed a ring around Riker, hands clapping, whistling high and shrill. Janos swung a new partner around, then lifted her high off the floor and let her go – airborne. She squealed with delight when he caught her. Riker ripped out another riff, and the crowd went wild.

A shower of coins chimed into an open guitar case, and the band went demonic, pushing the tempo, faster, harder, louder. The trains came; the people stayed – stoned on music. The detectives changed partners and fired questions, never losing the beat.

Two hands shot up with high signs.

Finale.

Riker made a cutthroat gesture to the band, and the music died suddenly, as if a door had closed upon it.

And the world stopped moving.

The musical detective wiped the sweat from his eyes and took a deep bow to thunderous hand clapping. He turned to Janos, hollering to be heard above the racket, 'What've you got?'

'A woman spotted the *X*. Our blonde didn't cross over. She stayed on the downtown Lexington line, and she was crying.'

'She's going home,' yelled Desoto. 'Yesterday another woman saw a blonde with an *X* on her shirt. Now here's where it gets a little weird. She was fighting off a gang of dead flies in the station at Astor Place, and that's where she got off the train.'

Deluthe moved against the flow of boarding passengers and fought his way out of the mob in time to see the squad of detectives flying into the pedestrian tunnel. When he emerged from the subway at street level, the other men were piling into their vehicles. The caravan drove off, sirens squealing, red lights spinning. And the young policeman was left standing alone on the sidewalk, breathless, as if he had also danced to the music of Sergeant Riker's band.

FIFTEEN

The blinking light on the answering machine was pulsating to the beat of a human heart – Stella's. The message could only be from the police. They would want to know why she had blown off her appointment at the SoHo station, and she had also missed the morning try-out for a play. Her agent had given her one last chance to redeem herself, a late evening audition, and it was not the standard cattle call. This time, she would be one of four actresses up for the part.

And Stella had nothing to wear.

The contents of her closet and drawers were strewn about the apartment in piles of thrift-shop clothes and hand-me-downs. When she wore these garments, they changed her into something lesser, lower. And now, in her mind, she had already failed the last-chance audition. Before day's end, she would have no career, no agent and no point in living. Stella sat on the edge of the sofa bed, then fell back and stared at the ceiling, eyes wide, unblinking, playing dead – just getting used to the idea.

The brand-new suit jacket lay on the floor, marred with another *X*. She had discovered the stain on the subway after removing the jacket to sew on a button. And now her eyes were raw and red from crying. The rent money was gone, and she could not ask for more. The egos of the Abandoned Stellas had been worn away so long ago; they would never understand the fragility of hers and the great importance of a magic mantle of pale blue linen.

She could not go home to Mom and Gram, though she pined for

them. Tomorrow, she would send another postcard, another lie: *Fame and fortune can only be hours away*. Then she would find a job as a waitress and never tell them that their worst fear had come true.

Another thought overshadowed failure and the loss of home – the stalker. She could not go to the police for help, not after spinning a lie to get her name in the papers. That woman, Forelli, would have informed them by now. She imagined the police department as a colony of telepathic spiders, all busy weaving traps to catch her. Adding to her crimes against them, she had missed the SoHo interview for vandalized blondes. And now that she had a suit jacket with a legitimate *X*, she was no better off. The cops would never believe it was the real thing.

Stella rose from her bed and straightened her spine. She was an *actress*. She would *make* them believe her. All it would take was attitude and the right persona, but which one? Turning to the mirror on the wall, she asked, 'Who am I today?'

Nobody, said the mirror. *You're just a little girl from Ohio*.

Stella nodded, then picked up the ruined suit jacket and traced the nasty black *X* with one finger. Every nice thing was ruined in this town, Bitch City.

Heavy footsteps were coming down the hall. They stopped outside her apartment. The police? She held her breath and played the statue, eyes fixed on a white envelope sliding under her door. It must be a summons. Oh, she was in so much trouble. The footsteps trailed off toward the stairs. Overwhelmed by dread, her feet weighed a hundred pounds, each one, as she approached the envelope on the floor. It was another few minutes before she gave herself up for dead and opened it.

Impossible.

It was a gift certificate from a Fifth Avenue department store where she could not afford to breathe the air. So much money. This would replace her ruined suit with something from the designer section – and shoes, new shoes.

Fifth Avenue was singing to her, *Get your tail down to the store, babe*.

On her way out the door, she considered the source of this bounty,

233

quickly ruling out her Sunday school God, Who would not have survived for six minutes in New York City. Her savior could only be an apologetic vandal, a disturbed soap-opera fan who had gone too far and wanted to make amends.

Blessed are the mental cases.

Halfway down the stairs she stopped. There was no air-conditioning in the common areas of the building, yet she felt an icy sensation in her chest. In movie lore, scary cold spots marked the presence of haunts in abandoned houses. And women?

He knows where I live.

Sergeant Bell sat behind the front desk facing the door of the police station. He was waiting for Lieutenant Coffey's order to send up the suspect. In peripheral vision, he kept watch over the fireman. Gary Zappata was working the cops in uniform, slapping backs and politicking, though he had never had a single friend in this precinct.

The detectives walked in the front door – three of them, if Sergeant Bell counted the whiteshield from the East Side squad. Riker had a few words with Deluthe, who then raced up the staircase to Special Crimes Unit, his feet hitting every third step like a galloping puppy.

Riker and Mallory were in no hurry as they crossed the wide floor, walking in tandem. They ignored the rookie fireman swaggering toward them.

Zappata squared off, legs apart, hands on his hips, then yelled, 'I know what you did to me, Riker! You cheap shit! You snitch!'

The desk sergeant silently begged, *Please, Riker, don't do anything stupid.* It was worth a lawsuit if the detective slugged this man. And perhaps that was what Zappata was hoping for, since he was out of a job with the fire department and could never come back to NYPD.

The fireman strutted toward the partners. 'You ratted me out.' He glared at Riker, then puffed out his chest. 'You drunken asshole.' Zappata turned his smug face to Mallory, saying, 'Well, if it ain't the Ladies' Auxiliary. Stay out of my way, *bitch*.' He glanced over his shoulder and smiled at the battery of men and women in uniform, as if expecting applause for this very big mistake.

Mallory never flinched, but Riker's hands balled into fists. Sergeant Bell thought of calling the lieutenant down to end this before it—

The desk sergeant looked up to see Jack Coffey standing at the top of the stairs, hands in his pockets, quietly watching.

The short fireman moved to block Riker's path.

Another big mistake.

'You couldn't face me like a man,' said Zappata. 'You back-stabbing piece of crap.'

The two detectives closed their distance with the fireman.

Any second now.

The phones stopped ringing. The only noise came from a civilian clerk, fingers typing, lightly skimming the keys.

—tap, tap, tap, tap—

The fireman was playing to his audience of uniforms, and he was so cocky, rocking on his heels, smiling too wide for a man so off balance. The dead silence from the uniforms gave him no clue that Riker was about to pound him into the ground.

It was not a sucker punch, though Zappata never saw it coming, not from the Ladies' Auxiliary. One moment he was standing up – Mallory's fist shot out fast and sure as a hammerfall, and then he was lying on the floor, having a quiet nosebleed.

She stood over Zappata's prone body, braced like a prizefighter awaiting the payback that would surely follow when this man found his feet again. With one quick glance at Riker, she warned him away. Sergeant Bell smiled, and there were nods of approval all around the room. Markowitz's daughter would not look to her partner or anyone else to finish off Zappata. By Mallory's stance, he could even guess which knee she planned to smash into the fireman's testicles.

The man at her feet was conscious, but he would not or could not move. He lay on his back, staring at the ceiling with an idiot gape of wide eyes and slack mouth.

The clerk stopped typing. The uniforms were stealing glances at Mallory, the bomb at the center of the room. A telephone rang to jangle nerve endings, and then another phone went off. Papers shuffled, typing and conversation resumed. Officers walked to and fro, some stepping over Zappata's body on the way to the door – life went on.

Once the squad room door was closed and Jack Coffey was facing Mallory, she missed her opportunity to say, *I told you so*, but the sentiment was clear when she turned her back on him and walked down the hall toward the incident room.

Sergeant Bell opened the stairwell door and leaned in, asking, 'Hey, Lieutenant? You still wanna question Zappata?'

'No, just roll him out on the sidewalk.' Coffey planned to follow the lead of ten uniforms and the desk sergeant, to say that he had been looking elsewhere when the fireman *tripped*. A blue wall of cops was securely closed around Mallory. Not that Coffey worried about consequences. What were the odds that Zappata would file a police brutality suit against a *girl*? Mallory was going to get away with this. The lieutenant watched her disappear through the door at the end of the hall.

'Maybe you noticed.' Riker slumped down in a chair. 'Your favorite suspect has a glass jaw.' He pulled out a cigarette. 'Now Sparrow was a big girl, and real good in a street fight – better than Mallory. There's no way that twerp could've taken her down.'

'Even with a razor in his hand?'

'You think he'd know what to do with it? I don't. We're looking for somebody a lot scarier than Zappata.'

Riker stood before the back wall of the incident room and cleared a space for a photograph from Natalie Homer's actress portfolio. The hangings had finally been merged into one case. He pinned the woman's smiling face to the cork alongside the effigy made of clothes. Now they hung together, Natalie and the scarecrow, mother and child.

Detective Janos pinned a note near the newspaper account of a stabbed actress. 'I talked to Stella Small's agent and the doctor who treated her razor cut. They both say the assault happened on a crowded street. Now that works with what you got from Lieutenant Loman. All the hassling went on in crowded places.'

'That pattern won't hold up for Sparrow, not the week before the hanging.' Riker walked over to the next wall and pulled a statement down, then handed it to Janos. 'That's the interview with the director of the play. Sparrow told him she was between day jobs, and she spent four days learning the lines of the play before she auditioned. Well, that just impressed the shit out of him. That's why he gave her the part. And there were no open auditions the week before she died, so she wasn't commuting on the subway at rush hour.'

'Okay,' said Janos, 'but you know this whole town is one wall-to-wall crowd.'

When the big man had left the room, Riker turned back to the wall and the job of merging the paperwork of all the cases. Janos was right. New York City was one big swarming—

'Crowds of hookers,' said Mallory.

He jumped in his skin. She was standing right behind him.

'If you see one hooker,' she said, 'you see eight or nine.'

Riker shook his head. 'No, Daisy said Sparrow was out of the life. Maybe the scarecrow marked her while she was—'

'Sparrow was still working the streets.'

'And how do you know that, Mallory? Were you stalking her again?' Only someone who knew her well would see the sign of damage in her face, her frozen stance. And now Riker added his words to the list of things he wished he had never said.

Years ago, Sparrow had told him about being covertly followed and catching the young cop in the act from time to time. Mallory had the bizarre idea that she could shadow people unnoticed, that she could walk down any street, enter any room, without attracting stares. At Riker's last meeting with Sparrow, the prostitute had turned to her own

237

gaunt reflection in a store window, then covered her eyes with a bone-thin hand and said, 'I know why Kathy's following me. The kid thinks I'm dying – and she wants to watch.' Two years had passed since then, and he should have known that Mallory had not stalked Sparrow recently, for she had not recognized the crime-scene address or the surgically altered face. He had wounded her for no good reason.

Her voice was mechanical when she said, 'I found the plastic surgeon. He does a lot of work on battered women. Sparrow's new face wasn't free, but he gave her an installment plan. That's where all her money went. She was still turning tricks to pay for the operations and chemical peels. So Daisy lied to you. What a surprise, huh?'

'But you don't *know*—'

'Yes, I *do*. Those payments weren't cheap, and hooking was the only trade Sparrow ever had. That and one pathetic acting gig. She never had a pimp, so she always hung with other whores, lots of them. Safety in numbers – in the *crowd*. Then you've got the summer conventions, the boat shows, car shows. Lots of men – hooker heaven – crowds.'

'All right,' said Riker. 'I'll find her hangout whores.' Even in a coma, Sparrow still had the magic to string him along, and the price of being blindsided was very high. 'I'll chase down Tall Sally and talk to Daisy again.' If one of them could point him to a likely street corner, he would do a raid. He would wait until it was too late for arraignments and bail. Most prostitutes were junkies who would shop their own mothers before they would spend eighteen hours in lockup.

Deluthe pulled the new reports from the wall on Riker's instructions to copy updated material for Charles Butler. He was careful to keep his distance from Mallory, and she had almost forgotten he was in the incident room, until she found another mistake – his.

She stared at the front page of a newspaper pinned to the wall. The actress in the photo was a blond stabbing victim. Deluthe's initials appeared on a brief companion note in longhand, a few lines for the actress's name, her address and the words *publicity stunt*. But that would not square with the dripping blood reported in the article. 'Where's the follow-up interview for Stella Small?'

Deluthe looked up from the Xerox machine. 'I never got to talk to her. But I left a message on her answering machine.'

Mallory searched the wall for other paperwork. 'Where's the statement from the midtown precinct?'

'A police aide was supposed to fax it from the—'

'This article mentions an ambulance. Where's the attending physician's report?' She turned to look at him. It was obvious that he had no answers. Still, she would not follow her first inclination, which involved a bit of violence. Mallory *never* lost control of her temper. The incident with the fireman did not count, not in *her* scheme of denial. She had not struck Zappata in anger. That blow had been the simple expedient of getting Riker through the day without a suspension. Yes, *Riker* was the one with the bad temper, or so she decided, founded on absolutely no proof of this defect in his character. And *she*, of course, had reined in her own temper, safely gauging her punch to harm no more than the fireman's ego. She had hardly tapped him. Though Mallory had created this version of events only moments ago, she found no flaws in it.

The whiteshield detective stood beside her, nonchalantly gazing at the photograph of a recently assaulted blond actress, who lived in the East Village. Could this woman have more *precisely* fit the profile of the next murder victim?

Deluthe had his excuses ready now. 'I was going to call the actress again. But I had to put it off. Sergeant Riker—'

'That was a mistake.' Mallory's words all carried the same weight, and she kept her eyes on the board when she spoke to him. 'Don't phone her. Go to her apartment. Get a statement.'

Still he lingered, and then she said, '*Now*, Deluthe. *Before* she dies.'

Mallory followed in the wake of the running rookie, though at a slower pace. Her feet were dragging, and she was feeling other effects of lost sleep. She pulled out a cell phone and placed a call to the police station with jurisdiction on the actress's assault.

Ten minutes after making contact with a midtown sergeant, she was sitting in the squad room. Her head rested on the back of her chair, and her eyes closed as she waited for the man to locate paperwork on Stella Small's stabbing. Finally, he returned to the phone, saying, 'Sorry, Detective. I found the statement, but it won't help. Our police aide, Forelli – she's been doing creative writing on the job again.'

One hand tightened around the phone, but Mallory's voice was calm when she said, 'Read it to me.'

'All right. "Professional bimbo collides with camera. Damn every tall blonde ever born." You see the problem?'

Mallory's face was devoid of expression as she studied her right hand. The pain had ebbed away since decking Zappata. She flexed her fingers, then curled them tight, and her fist crashed down on the desk, bringing on fresh hurt and restored focus. And then, so that clarity would last a while longer, she smashed her fist into the wood a second time – crazy naked pain.

SIXTEEN

A fence of iron bars protected a tiny courtyard and the red door to Stella Small's apartment building. Mallory stood outside the gate and pushed the intercom buttons. When none of the residents responded, she pulled a small velvet wallet from the back pocket of her jeans, then unfolded it and perused her collection of lock picks. At the age of ten, she had stolen this set from her mentor Tall Sally, then lost it for a time – the rest of her childhood. The velvet wallet had turned up in the safety deposit box of the late Louis Markowitz. Sentimental man, he had not been able to throw away baby's first toys.

Before she had made her selection of tools to work the fence lock, Ronald Deluthe came through the red door and crossed the small courtyard to open the gate. 'There was nobody home,' he said, 'so I left my card under her door.'

'How do you know she's not home?'

'I'm telling you,' he said, 'there's nobody in there. I checked.'

Mallory pocketed the velvet wallet, though she did not believe that he would recognize burglar tools. 'You *checked*. And how did you do that?'

'Well, I banged on the door. No answer. I couldn't hear anybody moving around inside. It didn't sound like—'

'What does a hanging woman sound like, Deluthe?'

'Right.' He walked back to the red door and unlocked it.

'Where did you get that key?'

'The management company down the street.' Deluthe held the door open for her, then slipped past her to lead the way up the stairs to the second floor. 'They wouldn't give me a key to her apartment — not without a warrant.' He stopped at the door to 2B. 'This is it. You're sure it's legal to go in there?'

'*Yes*, if we believe she's *dying*.' Mallory did not appreciate having to repeat a lesson that he should have learned at the police academy. Deluthe had obviously not excelled in academics. So far, in *every* way, the son-in-law of the deputy commissioner was a mediocre candidate for the NYPD Detective Bureau.

He motioned for her to move away from the door. 'I'll take care of it.'

Yeah, right.

Mallory stood to one side, arms folded.

Apparently, Deluthe had learned nothing on the subject of locked doors either. Putting all his might behind his right foot, he kicked the door dead center, and, of course, the locks held. There was not even a dent on the heavy metal surface. Mallory decided that some lessons should be learned the hard way, and so she waited patiently as he made a second attempt to break his foot, then asked, 'Are you done?'

It was gratifying to see him limp as he backed away from the door. She pulled out the velvet wallet, selected two pieces of metal and worked close to the door, blocking Deluthe's view. First she opened the top lock, the one reputed to be pick-proof.

He edged around to one side of her, trying to see. 'What are you doing?'

'I'm using a bobby pin,' said Mallory, who owned no hair pins. 'I always carry one for emergencies.' And now she was done.

Like most New Yorkers, Stella Small had not bothered with the other two locks. The knob turned easily, and the door opened on to a room of cheap furniture and cheaper clothes strewn about amid the general clutter of dirty dishes and an unmade bed. A couch cushion lay on the floor, half covering a copy of *Backstage*.

'Looks like she's been robbed,' said Deluthe.

Mallory shook her head. She recognized Riker's modus operandi in this mess. 'Stella was only looking for something to wear.' In Riker's case, he would have been hunting for the wardrobe item with the fewest stains and cigarette burns.

'No corpse hanging from the ceiling.' Deluthe looked up at the light fixture and smiled. 'I *told* you she wasn't home.' A pale blue garment lay in a heap on the floor – in plain sight, yet he did not find this at all interesting.

'That woman you guys were chasing,' said Mallory. 'What was she wearing?'

'A light blue suit,' said Deluthe. And *now* he noticed the material on the floor. Sheepish, he picked up the blue blazer and unfolded it to display an *X* on the back.

'Stella Small is the next victim,' Mallory said, believing that this needed to be spelled out for him. She took the suit jacket from his hands and checked the label of a very respectable designer. The lines were good and so was the material. She walked among the piles of clothing and hangers on the floor. With an eye for what was out of date, she could tell that most or all of the wardrobe was secondhand. Yet there was an innate sense of style in a few good pieces of vintage clothing. The ruined blue suit was the best of the lot. Though Mallory's blazers were all tailor made, she pronounced this one excellent. A cash receipt in the pocket bore out her suspicion of a discount house, a liquidator of unsold designer stock.

A pile of unopened letters lay on a table near the door. The loose stack was labeled with a yellow Post-it that bore the words *hate mail* – all bills and none of them paid. Mallory opened the table drawer and hunted among the contents till she found a checkbook. All the actress had listed in the register were check recipients – no amounts, no running balance, and none of the checkbook entries were for credit card companies. So the woman was flat broke and would not be doing any more shopping today.

Mallory turned to the window on the street. It cost money just to walk out the door in this town. The impoverished actress would probably be home soon. 'Deluthe, stay here and wait for Stella. I don't care if it takes all day – all night. You got that?'

Given his choice of interview rooms, Riker had selected the lockup, the smallest space in Special Crimes Unit. The walls were brownish yellow, and it had taken years of cigarette smoke and the projectile vomit of junkies to produce this special patina. Half the room was taken up by a flimsy coop of chain-link steel and wood. The door of this cage stood open, as an invitation and a threat to the tallest platinum blonde in New York City.

The transsexual sat on a metal folding chair and knocked knees on the underside of the table. 'Where have you been, man? I've got a date tonight.'

Riker closed the door behind him – slowly – and glanced at his watch. 'This shouldn't take long, Sal. Tell you what. If you're in a rush, we can do it tomorrow. Suppose I have a police car pick you up at the store on your lunch hour?'

'Oh, yeah. Now that's a favor and a half. No thanks.' Tall Sally was staring at the clock on the wall and fidgeting with brassiere straps and flyaway strands of hair. 'I already talked to that other cop. The blonde with the Armani sunglasses.' And now, the ex-prostitute, ex-male, ex-thief forgot the ladylike façade. '*Armani*. Tell me that bitch ain't on the take.'

'I know what you told that detective.' Riker dropped an old folder on the table. 'And I know you lied.' He sat down and put his feet up on the table in the posture of a man who had all the time in the world. 'Let's talk about Sparrow. Or, if you like, we can talk about old times.' Riker turned the folder around so that Sal could read the name of the subject in capital letters, FRANKIE DELIGHT. 'It's been fifteen years, but his murder is still an open case, and I can put you on the scene.'

Score.

The transsexual was backing up while sitting in a chair, all four metal legs scraping the floor. 'I had *nothing* to do with it! Frankie was seriously crazy. Must've been a hundred whores lined up to kill that little bastard.'

'You're probably wondering how I know you were with him the night he died.' Now that Tall Sally had decamped from the male gender and joined the ladies, Riker was the only man alive who knew that Frankie Delight was the corpse found in the ashes of a fire. 'There's no statute of limitations, Sal. Murder never goes away.'

'If Sparrow says I'm the one that knifed him, she's a liar.'

Frankie Delight, known to the medical examiner as John Doe, had indeed been killed with a knife. Sal was reaffirming a long-held belief that criminals as a class were stupid to the bone.

'Now that's another problem,' said Riker. 'Sparrow got stabbed the same night Frankie died.' He opened the folder and scanned the four sheets of paperwork necessary to requisition an electric pencil-sharpener. 'Here's a statement from the ambulance driver. He was heading for the scene when he saw a seven-foot-tall blonde hightailing it down the street.' That was actually true. However, fifteen years ago, Riker had been the only one to hear that statement, and he had never written it down. 'So, Sal, can you—'

'If it wasn't for me, that junkie whore would've bled to death.' Sal's hand waved in the air in a girlie affectation. 'Or the rats would've got her. I saved her damn life.'

This did not work with what Riker knew about the ex-convict's character; Tall Sally did not have one.

'I know you used a ten-year-old girl to heist VCRs off a delivery truck.' He opened the folder again, feigning interest in another piece of paper. This one was blank. 'I got two cops who can place you on that scene. When their patrol car showed up, you left that poor kid behind.'

'What makes you think that I—'

'You answer *my* questions, Sal. That's how it works. I know that little kid gave the VCRs to Sparrow. Then you caught Sparrow fencing them for heroin. You stabbed her and killed the drug dealer. I've got motive, opportunity – everything I need to close this case.'

'Frankie was dead when I got there. You know my rapsheet. Any knives, *any* weapons? No!' Hysteria was rising in Tall Sally's voice. '*Frankie* stabbed Sparrow. And I carried that bleeding whore on my back for three blocks.'

'You moved her body away from a crime scene – so you could go back and get your goods without wading through ten cops.'

'No, that was the kid's idea. The brat drags me to this empty building on Avenue B. Used to be a crackhouse before the cops raided it. And there's the whore laid out on the sidewalk. So I'm carrying this half-dead whore, and the kid runs up ahead, looking for a phone that wasn't broke. She used *my* damn change to call 911! Then I laid Sparrow down—'

'And you went back to the crackhouse to get your VCRs. So that's when you saw Frankie's body? Is that your story, Sal?'

'Damn kid didn't mention that – a dead man lying next to my VCRs. So much blood. I swear, every drop in his body bled out. Still had the knife in his leg.' Sal pointed one finger at Riker, saying, 'And that was Sparrow's knife. Big ol' *S* on the hilt.'

'Too bad we never recovered the murder weapon.' That was a lie. Riker had personally disposed of that knife long ago. 'Maybe the kid can back you up. Got a name for her?'

'No, just street names. I called her the Flying Flea. Damn, that girl could run. Anyways, she's dead now. Sparrow said the kid got cooked in a fire.'

Riker was finally convinced that this ex-con would never connect the name Kathy to a cop with the same green eyes. 'The evidence makes you look bad, Sal. We can get you a lawyer, or we can make this old business go away. You run into Sparrow now and then, right? If you lie to me, I'll have your parole revoked.'

They played a waiting game, and finally Tall Sally leaned forward, saying, 'That other cop, the tall blonde? She said the whore got her nose fixed. Now if I did see Sparrow – it would've been before that.'

'You can do better, Sal. I need to know how Sparrow was spending her time the week before she died.'

'Man, I can't give you what I don't have. Three months ago, I was leaving town for the weekend, so I'm sittin' in traffic at the Lincoln Tunnel, and there's Sparrow, working the cars with all the other busted-up whores. Damn queen of the commuter blowjob.'

'You're lying. There haven't been any hookers around that tunnel for over a year.'

'You don't drive much, do you, Riker?'

Why would Sal spin him a lie that was so easy to break? The detective heard voices on the other side of the door, and one of them was Ronald Deluthe's.

'Okay, you can go.' He actually felt a breeze when Tall Sally sprinted from the room. Deluthe smashed himself against the door frame when the giant blonde sped by him. And Riker could not help but notice that Sal's hair color looked more natural than the cop's.

'Okay, kid, what've you got for me?'

'All the stuff you wanted me to copy for Mr Butler.' Deluthe set a pile of paperwork on the table, then took the chair that Sal had vacated. His back was turned to the door when Mallory appeared on the threshold.

Riker patted the paperback in his pocket. He had been hoping to find a private moment to give her the old western, but this was not the time. She was wearing dark glasses, her idea of hiding. Tall Sally would not be back, but there were more interviews to come, other whores who would remember Sparrow's golden shadow, a child with strange green eyes. Mallory must feel trapped.

No, there was something else on her mind. Her attention was focused on the young cop seated at the table. Soundlessly, she moved into the room and stood behind Deluthe's chair. She bent down to his ear and said softly, 'I told you to stay at Stella Small's apartment – her *unlocked* apartment.'

247

She might as well have shot him.

Deluthe's hand went to his chest as he lifted his head and stammered to the ceiling, 'I got a uniform to stand guard in front of her door.'

Mallory sat down at the table, the picture of calm, shaking her head slowly from side to side. 'No, you don't get to issue orders to the uniforms. That's not your job, and you don't have the rank.'

'And it pisses off their sergeants,' Riker added.

Mallory lowered her glasses so Deluthe could see that she was three seconds away from doing some real damage. 'That uniform was pulled off guard duty to settle a domestic dispute in another building. Nobody bothered to tell his sergeant that waiting for Stella Small was a matter of life and death.'

Deluthe could not look away from her. He was waiting for the explosion of temper, but Mallory was only stringing out his imagination, his anticipation of what she *might* do.

'I'll go back.' Deluthe was rising from his chair.

'No you won't.'

He froze in an awkward stance, half sitting, half standing, awaiting permission to wet his pants.

She never raised her voice. 'I patched things up with the cop's sergeant. He gave me a guard for the door and another man to canvas the neighbors in her building. That was also your job.'

'You didn't tell me that you wanted—'

'I shouldn't have to tell you every damn thing, Deluthe. Sit *down*.'

He sank to the chair.

'The uniforms will do the job,' she said. 'You stay the hell out of it. Just sit on your hands.'

Riker kept silent until she left the room, and then he turned to the problem of rebuilding the shattered whiteshield. 'How long were you with Loman's squad? Four months?'

The younger man nodded.

'Did they teach you *anything*?'

'Yes, sir.' There was a curious lack of sarcasm in Deluthe's voice when he said, 'I know which guys take cream and sugar, and who likes their coffee black. I know who wants mayo on their sandwiches and who wants butter. And I never get their deli orders wrong.'

'Yeah,' said Detective Janos. 'The tunnel's crawling with whores.'

Hookers had reinvaded old territories while the mayor was concentrating on a new psychosis, exterminating all winged insects that might be carrying the East Village virus. This summer, insecticides had killed two elderly people with severe emphysema, and the insects, who had killed no one, were being executed *en masse*. But the hookers had escaped the city-wide extermination of bugs and old people, or so said Janos as he lumbered down the sidewalk with Riker.

'You gotta see it for yourself.' Janos's large hands were rising, thick fingers fluttering, delicately plucking words from the air. 'All those whores at the mouth of the tunnel. Well, the whole tableau is just *gorgeously* phallic.'

This from a man with the face and physique of a bonecrushing hitman. Riker turned around and waited for Deluthe to catch up. 'Hey, kid. You wanna go down to the Lincoln Tunnel and roust some whores?'

'Yes, sir.' Deluthe was grinning.

'You can't wear gloves. That's the giveaway that we're gonna chase 'em down. So think about it, kid. We're talkin' body lice and head lice, crabs and herpes – every disease in the world is down there.'

Janos smiled. 'It's God's little waiting room for dying whores.'

'Should be fun,' said Riker. 'Still wanna go?'

'Yes, *sir*.'

Lieutenant Coffey watched the television set in the incident room. Stella Small was now the subject of a fifteen-minute news segment. The police were requesting public assistance in the hunt for a potential crime victim. 'Prime-time news. This is too good to be true.'

'Oh, they were happy to do it,' said Detective Wang. 'It's ratings week. This'll send advertising revenues through the roof. They *loved* the part about the serial hangman.'

The reporter on screen interviewed a bartender in Stella Small's neighborhood. The tavern's customers leaned into the shot and waved to the audience. The camera panned to the window, then out the door and into the street, turning left and right. The reporter asked, 'Where is she now? Have you seen her?' His voice had the tenor of a game-show host inviting the home viewers to play.

A banner ran across the bottom of the screen with telephone numbers for the police tip line as the picture changed to a group of small children in costumes. Coffey wondered how a local news station had obtained this video of a kindergarten play in Ohio. A child-size Stella Small wobbled onstage, precariously balanced atop a pair of grown-up's high heels. The little girl promptly fell off her shoes and landed on her little backside, endearing her to two homicide cops and eight million New Yorkers. Tiny snow-white socks waved in the air while the child cried, 'Mommy!'

'Oh, no.' Coffey knew where the film had come from. 'It was that damn agent. She turned the reporters loose on Stella's family.'

Ronald Deluthe parked the car some distance from the mouth of the tunnel, where a battalion of women were working the lanes of congested traffic. Slow-stepping in high heels, the whores flashed bosoms pearled with sweat. Cars crawled through the street market of skirts hiked up to buttocks, twin moons in every shade of skin, spangles and cheap wigs in copper and gold – red, *red* mouths.

Some of the women were diving into cars, heads down and disappearing from view, then emerging with cash.

'Hookers never file complaints,' said Riker, turning to the young cop behind the wheel. 'And they never identify suspects. You know why? When the perps get out on bail, they beat the crap out of the women – or they kill them. Dead witness? Case dismissed. That's our criminal justice system. So we need to convince the ladies they'll never make a court appearance. But leave that to me, kid. I've got more experience lying to women.'

He loosened his tie and buttoned his suit jacket so the gun and holster would not show. 'Give me fifteen minutes. I'll pick out some likely whores. Then we'll try to bag two or three.'

Riker stepped out on the pavement and raised the hood of Deluthe's car, disguising it as a disabled vehicle. Then he wandered toward the women, weaving slightly and snapping his fingers, but not in time to the blaring music from a slow moving car, for he was playing the role of a harmless drunk out of tempo with the rest of the world, so as not to trigger the hookers' cop radar.

Twenty minutes later, he had picked out three junkies, older prostitutes in Sparrow's age bracket. They would be climbing the walls inside of an hour in custody, and a dope-sick whore was a talkative whore. One looked familiar, but if he had ever arrested her, she did not remember him either. He had asked no questions about Sparrow, for these women were streetwise, but he had managed to pick out regulars who had worked this part of town when Sparrow was last seen whoring.

The detective looked at his watch. Where was Deluthe? More than the allotted time had passed, and one of his best whores was getting away.

A red sedan crawled by, and a pair of high-heeled sandals clacked alongside the moving vehicle as a woman leaned down to smile at the driver, singing to him, 'Hey, sweet thing.' The prostitute rolled on to the hood of the car and rode it into the mouth of the tunnel, shouting into the windshield, negotiating her price with the driver.

Riker turned around to see the rookie cop make a hasty exit from his car. Now Deluthe remembered to slow his steps as he approached the women. What was he carrying? Riker squinted, and then his hand went to his own jacket pocket.

Empty.

The paperback western must have fallen out in the car.

Deluthe was trying not to stare at all the undressed skin, and this attracted immediate attention. Alerted now, the women lifted their heads, all but sniffing the wind for the smell of a cop. Some edged away, and some stayed to watch from a distance, wary and tense, ready to fly. And Riker knew he would be lucky to catch a single whore.

Could it get any worse? Oh, yeah.

There was only one stiff breeze in the entire month of August and it had to be tonight. Deluthe's suit jacket was blown open. Three of the hookers could see the gun in his brand-new shoulder holster. And now they were melting away in the heat.

The whore-store was closing.

All the brunettes edged away, but one blonde sang out to other blondes as she strolled toward Ronald Deluthe.

Go figure.

Riker had seen hookers gang together by race, but never by hair color. Two more blondes were drifting toward the young detective. And now the dark-haired whores had forgotten their fear and proceeded to steal all the trade, picking off commuters, climbing in and out of cars, raking in cash by tens and fives.

Deluthe was deep in peroxide heaven and mounds of pale skin escaping from halter tops. The women stroked his hair, his chest and thighs. They smiled at him with broken teeth and gold teeth, with a 'Hey, baby' and 'Hi, sugarman.' One whore tapped the book in his hand, saying, 'So – you know how this story ends?'

Riker's jaw went slack as he watched Deluthe open the paperback western. The young cop then read aloud to a group of very attentive, nearly naked book fiends.

SEVENTEEN

Lieutenant Coffey closed the door of his office, wanting more privacy for this delicate telephone call to Ohio. He spoke gently to Stella Small the elder, while Stella Small the younger cried on an extension phone. The mother soon faded out of the conversation, but the grandmother remained on the line until weeping made talking impossible.

He set down the telephone and turned to the small television set in the corner of his office. The live coverage from Ohio had resumed as the two Stellas returned to the reporter in their living room. Beyond the couch where the women were seated, Coffey had a picture-window view of their trailer court. A circus of media were camped outside.

The reporter was asking the mother and grandmother about their telephone interview with Special Crimes Unit in New York. 'Do the police believe they'll find Stella before she dies?'

No mercy.

The lieutenant looked up at the glass partition and counted up the whores passing by his office, ten of them. Leading this parade was Ronald Deluthe. Riker was the last one through the stairwell door. All the detectives in the squad room were smiling, heads swiveling to follow the women, and Jack Coffey had no trouble reading their minds: *More blondes. God is good.*

The lieutenant opened his office door and called out to Riker. 'Charles Butler is here. He said you sent for him.'

* * *

Charles sat in a narrow darkened room rather like a theater audience. Rows of comfortable chairs were raised in tiers, and there was not a bad seat in the house. The stage was a large bright space on the other side of a one-way glass, where Ronald Deluthe was holding the door open for a group of blondes in various stages of undress. The women took chairs around a long table. He could see them all talking at once but heard nothing of their conversation.

Riker entered the room and flopped down in a front-row seat, his tired face illuminated by the light from the window.

'Hard day?'

'Surreal.' The detective rolled his eyes. 'I'm trolling for hookers with the baby cop, and the ladies are crawlin' all over him. Now you might think they want Deluthe's sweet young body.'

'No,' said Charles. 'That would be too easy.'

Riker sighed. 'They wanna discuss *literature* with him.' He held up the old western as he stared at the larger room beyond the glass. 'What you're lookin' at out there – that's the Kathy Mallory Hooker Book Salon. Those women can name all the characters from Kathy's westerns. They used to read to her when she was a kid, but only for an hour at a time. Some of them knew the beginning of a story, and some knew the middle or the end.'

'But none of them ever read an entire book.'

'Right. So this is what they used to do between tricks – they'd marry up the plots of the whole series. Other hookers joined up from word of mouth. And then they started running ads in the *Village Voice*. It took them years to find each other. And tonight they see Deluthe come along with a book by their favorite author, and it's one they've never seen before.'

'The last western,' said Charles. 'They wanted the story.'

'Yeah. Well, Deluthe tells 'em he's only gotten a few pages into it. So he opens the book and starts reading to a gang of whores. Now the traffic *really* slows down. Nobody's ever seen anything like *that* in New York City. Then the kid stops reading, and he says, "Hey, I know somebody who's read the whole book." So now the hookers think it's a *great* idea to go to a police station. It gets better. They invite some more blondes with street-corner addresses. I had to send out squad cars to pick 'em all up.'

'And how can I help you?'

'I've read maybe half those books, but that was fifteen years ago. You're the only one who's read 'em all. We're gonna trade plots for information. At least half of these women know Sparrow on sight. I need a time line for the week before the hanging.'

'And you're hoping one of them got a look at the scarecrow.' Charles turned to the glass and watched Deluthe set up room dividers to create two small cubicles and the illusion of privacy.

Following Riker's lead, he rose from his seat, and the detective put one hand on his arm, saying, 'Just one more thing, Charles. Listen carefully. None of those whores know Mallory's right name. Sparrow was the only one who ever called her Kathy. But you're gonna hear stories about a little girl with blond hair and green eyes. That kid is officially *dead*. If she doesn't stay dead, she's facing charges of murder and arson.'

On that warning note, a startled Charles Butler was quickly ushered out of the room. Riker locked the door behind them, then opened his hand to display three keys. 'That's all of 'em.' For added security, he inserted a toothpick into the lock and broke it off at the lip of the metal. 'We don't want any eavesdroppers.'

The detective strolled into the interview room, saying, 'Ladies, you came to the right place.' He clapped one hand on Charles's shoulder. 'We know how *all* the stories end.'

And this earned them a round of applause.

If Riker had intended to shelter her from the hooker reunion of Sparrow's friends, he should have posted a guard. Locked doors had always intrigued her, though this one did not pose much of a challenge. Mallory teased the toothpick out with her fingernails, then made short work of picking the lock. Upon entering the darkened room, she removed her sunglasses and sat down in the front row of chairs facing the one-way glass. And now she waited for the performance to begin.

Something was wrong.

Mallory leaned closer to the glass. She recognized most of these prostitutes from the story hours of her childhood, even women who had been badly altered by scars and broken teeth. It was surprising how many had survived, though this was but a fraction of their original number. The common denominator for these women was not Sparrow, but herself.

What was Riker playing at?

Deluthe stood at the head of the table of whores, writing furiously in his notebook, probably taking orders for a deli run. Riker would not want him in the room when this interview started.

Mallory turned on the sound system. It was another shock to hear Charles Butler's voice. When he stood up, she could see his head above the gray partition of the far cubicle. Riker was introducing him to a prostitute. Would Charles have enough sense to wash up after shaking hands with Greta? His new friend, the whore, was missing half an ear, old damage from long ago.

Deluthe was on his way out the door to fetch the orders from the delicatessen, and now the interrogation would begin. Mallory raised the volume on the intercom. The sound system was intended to eavesdrop on one voice at a time, not six conversations. She closed her eyes to all distractions, then sifted through the babble, seeking out one man's voice and then the other's.

How did Charles know the plots of her westerns?

She listened a while longer, concentrating on a single voice. Charles had finished telling Greta how *Far Trails* had ended, and now he was asking her questions about Sparrow's movements.

Mallory shifted her attention to Riker's cubicle, where he was seated with another whore. A few minutes into this conversation, she knew he was trying to solve the wrong murder.

* * *

'Markowitz didn't know Sparrow was tight with the kid, he just wanted a pair of eyes on the street,' said Belle. 'You know, like if she saw the kid—'

'A little blond girl,' said Riker, attempting to speed up the interview, for he already knew this part of the story. He had been the one who had approached Sparrow for information, but Lou Markowitz had put up the money.

'Uh, huh. The cops were really hot to find that girl. Offered Sparrow cash – not chump change either. And then, up front, she got a get-out-of-jail-for-free card, and it was signed by Markowitz himself.'

Riker gave up the idea of moving this woman along any faster. Whatever drug she was doing, it was not laced with speed.

'So Sparrow started out the day as a hooker,' said Belle. 'Then she turned into a snitch that afternoon. And that same night, she was warehousing stolen goods for a ten-year-old thief. So you can see how her career just wasn't going real well.'

'Warehousing goods?' Riker feigned skepticism. He was hoping this was the shipment of VCRs. 'It's not like the kid was ever more than a small-time thief.'

'Hey, who's telling this story? Well, I'm walking down the street with Sparrow. She's already decided to blow off Markowitz. And along comes the kid wheeling a grocery cart full of VCRs. Brand-new, still in the cartons. I ask her if she wants me to read her a story, and she says no. Well, that was a first. The kid looks to Sparrow and says she needs a place to stash her stuff.'

And now Riker listened to another version of the great truck robbery. In this one, Kathy took all the credit for the theft.

'So now the kid wants to change the goods into cash. Tall Sally's the only fence Sparrow knows, but the kid won't deal with Sal. Never would say why. So they got another buyer for the VCRs.'

'Would that buyer be Frankie Delight?'

Belle shrugged off the question. 'Who the hell knows? I sure

257

don't. Now what happens at the end of *Shadowland*?'

Riker knew this book well. It was his personal favorite, and he did not even care about the glaring flaw of long-range shooting in the dark of a moonless night. 'It ends with an ambush. Forty rustlers are up on the cliffs, guns aimed, waiting for Sheriff Peety to come through the canyon. And he's got a bad feeling about this trail, like he knows what's coming, but he's got no choice. He has to follow the Wichita Kid.'

'"Cause that's his job.' Belle recited words from the first page of almost every book. 'His life is the law.'

'Right. But all he's got is two six-shooters and no extra bullets. It's a cloudy night, no stars, not one, and that's the worst of it for him. He believes he's never gonna see their lights again. And he's lost without 'em – no markers in the sky to help him find his way. So he reins in his horse and sits awhile. He wonders what his life is all about. He's lost his faith, he's lost his way. Can't even see the badge on his chest – it's so damn dark. The book ends when the sheriff digs in his spurs. He rides into the canyon at a gallop, *knowing* it's a trap – a fight he can't win. The rustlers open fire. He looks up and sees the bright lights of guns firing from every ridge – like *stars*.'

'That's beautiful,' said Belle, rising from her chair.

Riker nodded to the next woman in line. 'Your turn.'

The second prostitute's name was Karina, and she had a few questions of her own. 'Did I hear right? You talkin' about Frankie Delight? Whatever happened to him? Not that I care about that squirrelly little bastard. Just curious is all.'

'Last time I saw him,' said Riker, 'he was toast – dead on a slab in the morgue.'

Mallory's eyes snapped open. How could Riker know about the murder of Frankie Delight? The drug dealer's body had been destroyed in the fire. No one could have put a name on that charred corpse.

Crazy Frankie.

She closed her eyes again and called up the jittery image of a drug dealer in a deserted building on Avenue B, a skinny white boy in dreadlocks, ripped jeans and gold chains.

The jewelry? Was that how Riker had identified the body?

She could see the deserted building again, deep in shadow, half the interior walls knocked down and rats everywhere – only one way out. She could pinpoint the moment when Sparrow had realized that Frankie planned to rob her, to take the VCRs without paying. No knives had come out, not yet, but whore and dealer circled round and round.

Unconsciously, Detective Mallory's hand made the shape of a pistol as Kathy the child drew her pellet gun on the drug dealer. It was happening all over again. Frankie Delight was in her sights when he dropped to one knee, holding his sides because he was laughing so hard it hurt. Pointing to her plastic gun, he giggled out the words, 'Oh, you're gonna make a big hole with that sucker.' He turned to Sparrow, saying, 'Hey, bitch. Your needles make bigger holes.' Not done with humiliating a child, he turned back to Kathy as he rose to his feet, still in good humor. 'You could really mess up a big-assed cockroach with that thing. You shoot that bug in the leg, and he'll never walk again.'

And Sparrow was laughing, too – when he jammed his knife into her side, then twisted it to rip her up some more.

Oh, the look of surprise in the whore's eyes.

How Frankie had laughed at the comical sight of Sparrow sliding down the wall, leaving a smear of blood in her slow descent. His laughter had drowned out the screams of a child.

Riker lit Karina's cigarette. 'So you're the one who set up the meeting.'

'Yeah, Sparrow wanted to unload some VCRs. A little kid ripped 'em off. Can you beat that? Well, I knew this half-assed drug dealer, the only one who'd deal for goods. Everybody else was cash or nothin'.'

'Sparrow wanted to swap the VCRs for drugs?'

'Yeah, but what she really needed was cash. Her rent was way past due. So she figured to get drugs for the VCRs, then change the drugs into money on the street – selling to the johns.' Karina exhaled a cloud of smoke. With all the authority of a jailhouse lawyer, she said, 'That's twice removed from the truck robbery.'

Riker smiled. It was the first instance ever of laundering illegal proceeds with drug money – very creative.

May smiled at Charles, showing him all her broken teeth and one gold cap. 'What happened after that ambush in *Shadowland*?'

'It's still going on when the next book opens,' said Charles. 'The gunslinger was clear of the canyon before the rustlers opened fire on the man who was chasing him.'

'Sheriff Peety.'

'Right. Well, it looks like there's no way out for the sheriff. He's almost out of bullets. But then the Wichita Kid turns his horse around and comes riding back into the canyon to save him.'

'I *knew* he would,' said May. 'But there were forty rustlers up on the ridge. How did Wichita shoot all of them?'

'Oh, he didn't shoot any of them. He shot the sheriff.'

May's head tilted to one side to say, *What?* And now she leaned far forward, her expression clearly implying, *You're nuts.* And aloud she said, with great conviction, 'Wichita would *never* do that.'

'I swear that's what happened.' Charles was perplexed by the sudden hostility. It was only a story. 'He shot the sheriff. Mind you, it was only a shoulder wound, but it knocked Sheriff Peety right out of the saddle. Actually, it was quite a clever ruse. You see, when the rustlers thought the old man was dead, they stopped shooting at him.' Not that there had been much danger of them hitting their target in darkness described as absolute. 'The rustlers even cheered the Wichita Kid for making this really great shot from a galloping horse.' In fact, it was an impossible shot, but logic was not the author's forte.

'I *love* that boy.' The prostitute clapped her hands together.

'My turn,' said Charles. 'Now the last time you saw Sparrow was how long ago?'

'Four months, maybe longer.'

Charles looked up at the woman behind May's chair. 'Madam, you're next.'

Mallory found it difficult to concentrate on conversations in the next room. A cascade of pictures were dropping into her mind, and she could not block them out. Through the eyes of a child, she watched Sparrow writhing on the floor, losing a river of blood from the knife wound in her side and crying, 'Jesus! Jesus!'

Kathy knew Jesus, too. He was the King of Pain, crowned with thorns and stabbed with nails. And she had sometimes called on Him in this same way, with no expectation of help – just another ritual like the story hour.

Riker recognized the woman now, but not by her face, not even by her name. The prostitute's neck scarf dropped to give him a glimpse of a familiar scar, a souvenir from the man who had slit her throat rather than pay for her services. He would tread carefully with this one. She was the hooker who had tied Sparrow to the little girl who died in the fire, and all for three seconds of fame on the evening news.

The whore gave no sign of remembering the detective. All cops and customers must look alike to this aging parody of a dead actress. Marilyn's red mouth was drawn well outside the lines of her thin lips, but her voice was breathy and sexy, so close to the real thing.

'Sure I remember,' said Marilyn. 'It was maybe fourteen, fifteen years ago. I brought Sparrow's stuff to the hospital. That was the day after she got stabbed.'

'Her *stuff*. You brought her *heroin*?'

'Oh, just a taste, a snort. Not enough to mess her up. I had a personal interest in Sparrow's health. She owed me money. God, she was strung out. What I gave her didn't help much.'

Riker leaned over to light the woman's cigarette. 'Did the little girl ever visit her?'

'Uh huh. When I came in, she was sittin' on the edge of the bed. Sparrow was feeding her off the hospital tray. The kid was eating an apple one minute, and then she was dead asleep. Her eyes closed, and the apple just rolled out of her little hand. Ain't it funny – the things that stay with you for years?'

'What else happened that day?'

'Sparrow shook the kid till she woke up. Reminded her she had something to do – and fast. I never found out what that was about. So the kid climbs down from the bed. So tired. Poor baby. She was weavin' on her way out the door. And that was the last time I ever saw that child alive.'

Mallory leaned forward, straining to catch the details of her hospital visit. That was the day Sparrow had sent her back to the deserted crackhouse – the day of the fire. This was a memory she did not want to relive, but images broke into her conscious mind against her will – the rats were eating the dead man, and she could hear the sucking sound that Sparrow's knife made when it was pulled from the body.

'No, babe,' said Crystal. 'Sparrow ain't worked the tunnel in a while. Last time I saw that whore, she was planning to get her nose fixed. Later, I heard she was working uptown hotels. I'm telling you, that must've been one hell of a nose job. I wouldn't last six seconds in one of those hotels before they threw my ass out the door. So what's the rest of the story?'

'First, tell me something,' said Charles. 'Why do you care about these books?'

Crystal gave this some careful thought, then smiled with her broken mouth. 'It's like you're always waiting for the other shoe to fall. You know that saying? You do? Good. Well, babe, I've been waiting for fifteen years. Now give me the rest of my damn story.'

'All right. Remember the first cowboy Wichita ever killed?'

Exasperated, she said, 'Of course I do. All the girls know that story. That was the only one we got paid for.'

'Pardon?'

'That first story – the kid paid for it. Well, she paid for the first hour. She'd give a whore something she stole, something real fine. I gotta say, the girl had good taste. Then, after that first time, all her stories were free. All she had to do was say, "Read me a story," and some whore would take her home.'

'And you all read to her – because you had to know how the books ended?'

'Now you got it. But it was never the same book twice in a row. You'd wind up an hour into a completely different story – and no end. Or maybe you'd get the end, but you wouldn't know how it started.'

'Well, in *Homecoming*, you discover that the first dead cowboy was a murderer. He was part of a gang that killed Wichita's father and stole his cattle.'

'So that's how the kid's mother wound up as a dancehall girl. I always wondered about that. She was the only church-going slut in Franktown.'

'Right,' said Charles. 'It was either work in a saloon or starve, and she had a child to support. Well, in this book, Wichita's almost done. He's tracked down the last gang member, a man hiding out in Franktown. And he kills him in a gunfight.'

'Does the sheriff arrest the Kid?'

'No.'

'So the Kid just left town, right? He got away again?'

'Well, not in this one.' Now Charles realized that this woman was unaware that *Homecoming* was the end of the series.

'You don't mean Wichita gave himself up?' She read a worse fate in Charles's giveaway face. 'No,' she said. 'Don't tell me he *died*? Don't you *dare* tell me that!' She shouted, 'How can the Kid be *dead*?'

All around the room, conversations stopped abruptly as ten hookers went into mourning for the Wichita Kid.

* * *

263

Mallory sat in darkness, eyes closed, slowly moving her head from side to side. She could not remember a book called *Homecoming*.

Riker waited out the silence. Finally, the whores rallied, for they had other unresolved issues.

'So tell me what happened to the horse,' said Minnie. 'Ol' Blaze rolled off a cliff at the end of one book. At least tell me the *horse* didn't die.'

'Well,' said Riker, 'I know it looked like old Blaze was goin' sour, but the horse came back in the next book. Now this Indian girl—'

'Gray Bird? The one who loved the Wichita Kid? He talks about her in most of the stories.'

'That's the one, yeah. She nursed the horse back to health with magic and herbs. The girl died, but the horse was good as new.'

'Ain't that romantic?'

'Yeah.'

Mallory left the building and walked past her car, heading for the next block and her office at Butler and Company. It was trash collection night, and the street was rimmed with garbage and a rancid stink. As she passed each metal can, something slithered away in the dark. Eyes shut tight, she pressed her hands over her ears, trying to kill the sound of rats' feet scrabbling across a rotted wood floor, racing one another to the fallen, bleeding Sparrow. She could not lose the smell of kerosene, smoke and burning skin.

Stopping by a payphone, she fed coins into the slot. Mallory dialed three random numbers and then the four she knew by heart, though she had not performed this ritual since childhood. The phone was ringing, and she felt the same excited anticipation. But why? Was it comfort she expected at the other end of the line?

A woman answered, 'Hello?' One more stranger out of a thousand calls from the street said, 'Hello? Is anyone there?'

Mallory had not forgotten the ritual. She knew what came next, the words, *It's Kathy, I'm lost*, but she could not say them anymore.

'Hello?' The stranger's voice was climbing into the high notes of alarm.

Oh, lady, can you hear the rats on the telephone line?

Charles abandoned his previous theories. The child had neither believed in heroes, nor had she relied on fictional people for friends. Far from it. She had once ruled a stable of prostitutes bound to her by stories. It was an ancient lure dating back to the cave, the need to know what happens next.

Brilliant child.

He pulled another chair into his cubicle for Gloria and Maxine. The women were not related, but resembled one another and even dressed in twin red halter tops and shorts. They were younger than the rest. Their makeup was low key, and they were not battered where it showed. The two prostitutes had insisted on being interviewed together.

'We do everything together.' Gloria's smile was very friendly. '*Everything*, hon.'

On request, Charles was about to finish a story begun in *The Cabin at the Edge of the World*.

'And don't tell us that preacher made it rain,' said Gloria.

'Oh, no, nothing like that. When Wichita comes out of the fever, the cabin is still in flames. Now if you recall the cliffhanger in the previous book—'

'Like we'd forget that,' said Gloria. 'The farmers think the old woman's a witch and she caused the drought. They move burning bushes in front of all the windows and the doors. Every wall is on fire, and Wichita's dying. That's what the old woman thinks. So she gets down on her knees and screams to God for mercy.'

'Right,' said Charles, recalling the final sentence, '"A scream that shivered the stars in the firmament." Well, in the next book, Wichita wakes up and soaks the old woman with a bucket of water. He slings her over one shoulder, then leaves by the front door. Walks right through a wall of fire.' And now he thrilled the prostitutes with another quotation from the page, ' ". . . stripped to the waist, his long golden hair flying in the wind and burning with sparks, his skin steaming with the burnt sweat of his fever." It's an imposing sight on the heels of a very loud prayer from the old woman. Now the fake preacher gets religion. He falls down on bended knee and declares the outlaw is an angel. Well, as you can imagine, that gives a few of the farmers pause. Then the Wichita Kid draws his six-gun, and the rest of them have second thoughts about this business of witch burning.'

The prostitutes were enthralled. 'The Kid walked through fire.'

'Yes,' said Charles. 'But then, toward the end of the book, he guns down another man.'

'Oh, he always does that,' said Gloria. Apparently, this credential of a serial killer was a character flaw she could live with. 'So the Wichita Kid walked through fire.'

'Now,' said Charles, 'I believe you mentioned running into Sparrow recently.'

'Last week,' said Gloria. 'Maxine and me, we were cruising for johns at the computer convention in Columbus Circle. Sparrow was there. Wasn't she, Maxine?'

'She was.' Maxine resumed chewing her gum.

'She was workin' the crowd, same as us,' said Gloria. 'But nothin' obvious – no flash. She didn't look like a whore no more. She looked real nice, didn't she, Maxine?'

'Very nice.'

'Excuse me,' said Charles. 'Did you ladies notice anything odd that day? Something out of the—'

'You mean Sparrow's new nose job? Or the guy who slashed her arm with a razor?'

Deluthe sat at a squad-room desk, very close to Maxine, as the woman concentrated on the computer monitor. They were attempting to create their own monster with photographic slices of other people's faces, eyes and noses, ears and mouths, assisted by FBI software.

A few desks away, a sketch artist was working with Gloria and using an old-fashioned pencil. 'Can you describe him a little better?'

'Yeah, he was a cold one,' said Gloria.

'Well, that doesn't—' The exasperated sketch artist saw Riker's hand signal to keep his mouth shut, and the man fell silent.

'The color of his hair,' said Riker. 'Was it light or dark?'

'Blond,' said Gloria, raising her voice to be heard across the room. 'His hair was blond, wasn't it, Maxine?'

'No,' her friend called back. 'It was brown, average old brown.'

'Maxine, you're nuts. He was blond, I tell ya. But real natural.' The prostitute glanced at Ronald Deluthe's head. 'Not a bleach job.'

Hoping to strike a compromise, Riker said, 'Maybe it was blond hair that went dark when he grew up.'

'Yeah,' said Maxine. 'That's it. His hair looked like Gloria's roots.' She turned to Deluthe. 'Make it brown.'

The sketch artist's version was gray charcoal pencil. 'No, this isn't working,' said Gloria. 'Start over. Make it a profile picture – like a mug shot, 'cause that's all I saw of him. Maxine saw his whole face.' She called out to her friend. 'Didn't you, Maxine?'

'I did.'

Gloria went on with her story of the encounter for Riker's benefit. 'Well, I was gonna say hi to her when this stiff-lookin' jerk comes up behind her. So I just stand there. Didn't wanna say nothin' to queer it for Sparrow. But the john, he don't say nothin', either. Sparrow hasn't even noticed him yet. Then this freak pulls a box cutter out of his gym bag.'

Gloria looked up at Charles, who wore the expensive clothes of a man unfamiliar with box cutters. 'It's a big metal grip with a razor.' She turned back to Riker. 'He cut her arm. I couldn't believe it. All them people around, and he cut her right there. Cold as you please. Then he walks away, real calm, like he does this kind of thing every day. He stuck the box cutter back in his bag before Sparrow even knew she'd been slashed. She didn't know till I told her. I said something like – Hey, you're bleedin'. Isn't that what I said, Maxine?'

'That's close.' Maxine was no longer listening to her friend. She was staring at Deluthe's monitor. The computer-generated image was taking shape faster than Gloria's drawing. Deluthe had picked up on the other woman's cue of a cold stare. A pair of vacant eyes slipped into place on the screen.

'It's better,' said Maxine, 'but it still needs work.'

Charles crossed the room with a photograph retrieved from the cork wall of Butler and Company. He handed Maxine a wedding portrait of Erik Homer, the scarecrow's father.

'The eyes aren't the same.' She turned to Deluthe. 'The mouth is, but don't make him smile like that.'

Riker handed Gloria a roast beef on rye. 'Do you remember anything about the bag he was carrying?'

'Nothin' special. Right, Maxine? His bag wasn't special.'

Maxine shook her head. 'It looks just like my gym bag. Got it on sale at Kmart. Paid almost nothin' for it.'

Riker moved to Maxine's chair and handed her the container of soup she had ordered from the deli. 'What did the bag look like?'

'It was gray with one stripe.'

Deluthe stopped work. 'A *red* stripe?'

'Yeah, just like mine.'

The young cop stared at the image on his screen, then crossed the room to look at the sketch artist's pad. 'I've seen this guy. He was in the crowd outside the last crime scene. I remember his bag. I've got one just like it. But his had a red stripe. That was the only difference.'

'Kmart?' asked Maxine. 'Nylon, right?'

'No, L.L. Bean.' Deluthe turned to Riker. 'My bag is canvas, and so was his.'

Riker turned to Charles. 'Keep the ladies company.' He grabbed Deluthe by the arm and propelled him down the hall to the incident room. They walked to the wall where exterior crime-scene photos were pinned up alongside autopsy pictures of Kennedy Harper.

'Which one?' Riker pointed to the pictures of the crowd gathered outside Kennedy Harper's building. 'Which face?'

The younger cop turned to point at the rear wall and the photograph between the scarecrow's T-shirt and the baseball cap. It was the picture of a man whose face was turned away from the camera. 'He's that one . . . Sorry.'

A breeze swept papers and cigarette packs down the narrow SoHo street, and a car alarm went off with a high-pitched incessant squeal. An irate tenant on an upper floor leaned far out his window and hurled a dark missile to the pavement, but the bronze baby shoe fell short of the offending vehicle and narrowly missed the two walking men.

Riker glanced up at the civilian and yelled, 'Lousy shot!' In a lower voice, he said to Charles Butler, 'But it could've been worse. It's scary how many of these people have guns.'

Another man emerged from a building just up ahead. He held a baseball bat. When he spotted Riker and Charles, he thought better of leaving the shadows of his doorway. As the two men came abreast of him, the bat disappeared behind the man's back.

'Now *that* guy means business,' said Riker, when they were well past the car with the screaming alarm. 'He'll get the job done.'

They turned the corner at the sound of breaking glass and the bangs of wood on metal – followed by blessed silence.

They were heading toward Charles's building on the next block. Mallory would be at work in the back office at Butler and Company, and there might not be another opportunity to speak privately with Riker. 'When you said the little girl was dead – well, obviously, you didn't mean Kathy had actually died. So presumably—'

'I've seen her death certificate. It was backed up by sworn statements from two fire marshals. And neither one of those guys owed any favors to me or Lou.'

'You're not going to explain that, are you?' Charles's tone was fatalistic. 'Not a hint, not a clue.'

'Nope.'

'And that business of murder and arson charges—'

'Not a chance.'

EIGHTEEN

Mallory stood in the office kitchen and poured another cup of coffee. Her eyes were closing. When had she slept last?

Old pictures were breaking into her thoughts again, wreaking havoc with her concentration. The rats were coming for the whore. Greedy vermin. Not content with the blood and meat of Frankie Delight, they wanted Sparrow too.

Mallory turned on the faucet, then leaned over the sink and splashed her face with cold water. She sat down at the kitchen table. Her coffee cooled in the cup. Her eyes closed, and down came the curtain between waking and sleeping dreams. Though she had never had the smoker's habit, one hand went up to her mouth as she lit a cigarette that was not there. She was ten years old again. Sparrow was bleeding, saying, 'Don't cry, baby.'

But Kathy could not stop crying. The frantic child shook Sparrow to keep her from drifting into sleep and death. 'I'll get help!'

'Don't leave me,' said Sparrow. 'Not yet.' The prostitute nodded toward the shadows where the rats were fighting over the corpse of Frankie Delight. 'Keep 'em off me – till it's over.'

'You *can't* die.'

Sparrow gently touched the child's face. 'Baby, I'm always telling you stories. *Read me a story* – that's all I hear from you. Suppose you tell me one. But mind you, don't make it a *long* story.' Sparrow's eyes were closing as she smiled at her own little joke.

'You need a doctor!' Kathy shook Sparrow until the blue eyes opened. The child put her hands over the open wound, trying to keep the prostitute's blood from leaking out.

'Don't leave me for the rats,' said Sparrow. 'Tell me, how did that book end? *The Longest Road*, yeah, that one. The Wichita Kid decided he was goin' home. Did he ever say why?'

'It ends when he's on the trail.' Kathy emptied Sparrow's purse on the floor, straining to see by the daylight streaming in from the street door. 'Wichita stops his horse in front of the sign for Franktown.' The room was growing darker; the day was ending; Sparrow was dying. The child found a handkerchief. 'He just stares at that sign for a while.' She used the square of white linen to cover the stab wound. The cloth was soaked with blood the moment she pressed it to Sparrow's side. 'Then there's these lines near the end. But I don't—' Though the little girl knew all the books by heart, her panic was overwhelming her. Sparrow could not *die*.

'What lines, baby?'

Kathy bit her lip until it bled into her mouth. She needed this pain to concentrate, and now the passage came into her mind, clear as the spoken word, and she recited, '"It was more than the call of home. He was riding toward his redemption."'

'You know what that means, baby?'

'No.' And she did not care. Kathy unclipped a long strap from Sparrow's purse and used it to hold the red handkerchief in place. 'I'm going for help. I'll come right back.'

'No, baby. *Stay* with me.' Sparrow's next word was hardly more than a whisper, a sigh. 'Redemption.' Her voice was stronger when she said, 'How can I put that so a little thief can understand?'

The rats were coming. The child stamped one foot and screamed at them, 'You stay away! She's not dead! She's *not*!'

'That's right, baby. You tell 'em.' Sparrow's voice was failing. 'Redemption – that's when you buy back all your bad karma – so you can steal heaven.'

What was karma?

The prostitute closed her eyes again, and this time Kathy could not wake her. The child's head snapped toward the shadows and the sound of a rat's feet. She waved her arms, but the creatures had no fear of her anymore. The lure of blood was strong. And now another rat appeared at the edge of the failing light from the street door.

'Stay away!' Kathy pulled out her pellet gun and fired on the rat, missing her mark. She was crying, vision blurring, yelling, 'She's not dead! *Not yet!*'

The child reached down to the debris from the prostitute's purse and found something hard, a missile to throw. It was a silver lighter she had stolen for Sparrow. She held it tight, then picked up one of the cigarettes that had spilled on the floor alongside a can of hairspray. Kathy hunkered down beside the purse, smiling – inspired.

Once, Sparrow had nearly set her hair on fire, smoking a cigarette while waving the hairspray can.

Kathy lit the cigarette, puffing and coughing until it burned. She stared at the glowing ember and waited, fighting down the panic until the rat was close to her feet. She pointed the aerosol can at the animal, then pressed down on the nozzle, wetting the rat through and through. It squealed with the pain of hairspray in its eyes. The child dropped the cigarette on its fur and stood back as the animal burst into flames and screamed.

Another rat came out of the shadows, drawn by the smell of live cooking meat. Hunched over, Kathy crept forward to meet the creature. Holding the cigarette lighter low to the ground, she pressed the nozzle of the hairspray, aiming it at the tiny flame, and the chemical spray became a blowtorch. The second rat was burning, running in circles, streaking fire round and round. It was crying in a human way and drawing cannibals from the corpse of Frankie Delight.

Kathy was numb, too stunned to care what the rats were doing to one another. Working by slow inches, the child struggled with her burden, dragging Sparrow out of the dark building and into the waning daylight where more rats awaited them, scrabbling out from between the garbage cans on the sidewalk.

In the kitchen of Butler and Company, Mallory lurched to one side. Chair and woman crashed to the floor. Her face was pressed to the tiles, and she lay there for a few seconds of absolute stillness, quietly seeking her true place in time and space. Then she rose to her feet and gripped the edge of the counter for support. Her hands were shaking when she splashed more water on her face. If she could not stay awake, Stella Small would die.

'It'll never work.' Riker turned his back on Mallory's computers. 'There's gotta be ten million people in Wisconsin.'

'Closer to four and a half.' Charles could quote the atlas statistic to the last individual, but that would be showboating. 'And we're only looking at one small county where the boy went into foster care.'

Riker shook his head. 'We're running out of *time*. Stella Small could be hanging by her neck right now – still alive.'

Mallory looked up from her monitor. 'What do you want me to do, Riker? Go door to door with those worthless cartoons?' She nodded toward the cork wall where he had pinned up the hooker sketches.

Indeed, Charles thought the images were more of a guide to what the man did *not* look like. He was not thin or fat, not African or Asian descent, and his hair was neither long nor short.

Mallory turned back to her computer monitor. She was also showing signs of strain. 'I'm checking every newspaper with a database. If anything jumps out—'

'It'll take forever,' said Riker.

'And thank you for your support,' said Mallory.

Charles watched the screen over her shoulder, scanning text as fast as she could scroll down the columns of newspaper archives, and in another compartment of his brain, he addressed Riker's concerns. 'You have two possibilities. Some recent event triggered these hangings, or the scarecrow started acting out antisocial behavior with early juvenile offenses.'

'Then we're still screwed,' said Riker. 'The criminal records of juveniles are sealed.'

'But not newspaper archives. The county is mostly small towns. Any sort of stand-out behavior would be worth a mention in a local newspaper.' Charles could see that Riker was unconvinced. The man was looking at his watch, a reminder that Stella Small was running out of time, and now he left the room. A moment later, the door to the reception area slammed shut.

Mallory handed a cell phone to Charles. 'I've got a Wisconsin detective on the line. She works in Juvenile. Can you give her a profile for the scarecrow?'

The small phone all but disappeared into Charles's larger hand as he described a tortured child to the caller, explaining that the boy had lost everything, his parents, his home. He was sent away to live with strangers, and they were also taken from him. Then police custody, foster care, more changes and strangers to deal with. 'Too many traumas in quick succession. I'd look for a history of petty criminal acts and small-scale violence. Sociopathic behavior could've started as early as nine or ten years old. Or even—'

Charles watched Mallory's eyes close. Her fingers ceased to tap; her hands were suspended over the keyboard. And he wished he was dead. He had just created a general profile for her as well.

He quickly added one qualification never mentioned in Kathy Mallory's own childhood history and said to the caller, 'You might find incidents of torturing and killing small animals.'

Stella Small listened to the public-address system. A small fire had broken out on an upper floor, and all customers were urged to make an orderly evacuation of the store.

What fabulous timing. The new suit was paid for, and she was wearing it. However, she had not yet replaced her snagged pantyhose with the new ones, and a saleswoman was barring her way to the changing room. Stella shrugged. There was time enough to go home and change hosiery before the evening audition in Tribeca. She joined a stream of shoppers moving toward the escalator with great resolve despite the protests of store employees who tried in vain to turn the herd toward the fire doors and a stairwell.

There was one motionless stand-out among the onward-marching shoppers and the arm-waving clerks. A man was waiting near the bottom of the escalator. Though he wore dark glasses, Stella recognized him from her last shopping expedition. This was the soap-opera fan who had stood behind her in the mirror of the discount store. Yes, it was the same baseball cap and stiff posture. She was sure of it now. He was the vandal, the stalker, the giver of gift certificates. And the gray bag, she had seen that before too, but where? She stared at him, wondering, *How crazy are you?*

He climbed up the steps of the down escalator, unhampered by all the people who blocked his way. He passed through the press of bodies, crushing them into the sides of the escalator as he closed the distance to Stella while the mechanical steps sought to take them both down. He came abreast of her and slapped a note on the lapel of her new suit jacket. The man never looked into her eyes. He might as well have taped his message to a kiosk instead of a living woman. She ripped the note off her jacket and read the words, *I can touch you any time I want.*

Charles sprawled on the leather couch, one of few office furnishings that was not an antique, but custom-made to fit his longer-than-average legs. He was nearly done with the last batch of fax transmissions. Occasionally, he interrupted his reading to glance at the portable television set. Mallory had given it to him so he could keep track of local news bulletins. And now he was startled to see a familiar face on the screen. 'Mallory!' he yelled, to be heard in her office across the hall. 'Riker's on TV!'

No response. Well, she was busy.

Charles turned back to the screen to watch Detective Sergeant Riker being introduced to the viewers. Poor man. He looked so pale beside the healthy orange glow of the anchorman's stage makeup. He held up a photograph of a fugitive witness, Natalie Homer's sister.

Stella fought against the tide of the crowd spilling off the escalator. She saw another exit sign and ran toward it, only glancing back once to see the baseball cap bobbing above the heads of the shoppers. Everyone was being turned away from the bank of elevators. Store employees barred the doors, shouting that the elevators had been disabled. Others directed people to the fire doors where a line of people filed through to a stairwell.

First Stella caught a whiff of insecticide, and then a hand grazed her face. She turned to see the stalking man walking away from her, moving toward the line for the stairwell. He turned around to look in Stella's general direction, never making eye contact, perhaps perceiving her as a store manikin. Was he waiting for her to join him in the line?

You think I'm crazy, too?

She turned around full circle, searching every wall for another red-lettered sign to show her a way out. The escalator was barred by three women with folded arms. Drunk with power, they turned shoppers back to the stairwell, shouting, 'That's the fire exit!' And they were so unimpressed with Stella's note from a madman. 'Lady, look around. You see any cops? No.' And once again, she was directed to the stairwell, the only *approved* exit, where her personal stalker stepped out of line to wait for her by the fire door. This was so unfair. She had obeyed all the rules regarding New York wildlife. She had never tried to pet the lunatics grazing on the city sidewalks, never fed them or looked them in the eye.

Now Stella saw another sign and ran toward it. After closing the restroom door behind her, she depressed the lock button on the brass knob, for it was unlikely that a lunatic would be put off by the 'Ladies Only' sign of sanctuary. All the stall doors were open, and there were no sounds but her own footsteps as she walked toward the line of sinks to lay her packages down on the long marble countertop. Stella never considered the possibility of burning alive in a blazing building. She had lived in this town too long to take any fire drill as seriously as the more immediate threat of a deranged stalker – or shopping – and she planned to wait it out until the store refilled with customers and clerks, a simple matter of killing time.

After stripping off her ruined pantyhose, she fumbled with the cellophane wrapper of the new pair. A clock on the wall gave her hours to make the late audition. She stared at the mirror, in love with the new suit. Her lipstick had been bitten off, but there was time for a complete overhaul of makeup, and she rifled her purse for cosmetics. Oh, wait. She should use the toilet before the fire drill ended. Stella gathered up her purse and packages from force of habit. No New Yorker would leave a possession unguarded.

She was sitting on the toilet when she heard the door open. Heavy steps, a man. He would have to be a store employee. Who else would have a key to the lock? The door closed again, and she sat very still, holding her breath and holding her water. After what seemed like forever, Stella knelt down on the floor and looked toward the stalls left and right.

No one there. And yet, after leaving the stall, she could not lose the feeling of being watched. And what was that sound? A fly? More than one?

'This woman is wanted by the police.' The newscaster held up the photograph of Susan Qualen. Though the woman was in her forties, Charles thought the family likeness was striking. The picture of Natalie's sister was joined by a portrait of Stella Small.

'If you've seen either of these women today,' said the voice behind the photographs, 'call the number on your screen. And now a few words from Detective Sergeant Riker.'

Riker leaned into the microphone. 'Miss Qualen has information on the whereabouts of the missing actress. We have to find Stella tonight. She's in a lot of trouble, and she needs your help.'

'As we speak,' said the anchorman, 'our broadcast is also being shown on our sister station in Wisconsin.' He turned to his guest. 'So you believe Susan Qualen is hiding in the vicinity of Racine?'

'Yeah, she could be enroute right now,' said Riker. 'But I'm hoping she's still in the tristate area.'

'If this woman has important information, why is she evading the police, Detective Riker?'

'Because she doesn't care if Stella Small lives or dies.'

Very impressive, Riker.

No one could have put the case more eloquently.

He knew how to jack up the speed of the human heart from a startled flutter to BAM, BAM, BAM! And how to slow it down. Or paralyze it.

Though he neither liked his work, nor disliked it.

Almost ready.

The man sat on the toilet seat, tailor fashion, so his feet would not show in the openings between the stall doors and the floor. He slowly unzipped the gray canvas bag on his lap and reached for the camera, ignoring the large glass jar beside it, for he had no interest in terror on a small scale.

The jar contained a black soup of flies. Some of the insects were still alive and moving slowly, drunk on insecticide. They animated the bodies of the dead, all in a panic, crushing and crawling over dry corpses, breaking wings and ripping off legs in a frightening struggle to reach the top of the jar, one inch of air – and life.

And then they struggled in the dark, for the man had closed the gym bag. With equal indifference, he aimed the camera lens at the opening between the stall door and its frame. He watched the blond actress through his viewfinder. The young woman stood by the sink, too wired to put her lipstick on straight. She picked up a tissue and made short, nervous dabs at her mouth. Turning her head to one side, she sniffed the air now scented with the insect spray that clung to his clothing. She batted at an imagined fly, created by the power of suggestion and the low buzz from the jar in his bag.

The ready light on the camera had been amber and now it was green. As if the woman had heard the change of colors, she dropped her lipstick, then jumped at the sound of the metal tube hitting the tiles and rolling across the floor.

She gathered up her shoes, her purse and packages, then left the ladies' room, running barefoot.

Charles rose from the couch and stretched, then walked across the hall to the back office. Deluthe was nowhere in sight, and Mallory was facing a computer monitor, her hands resting on the keyboard and lightly tapping the keys.

'Mallory?' Charles bent down to retrieve another stack of paper from a printer bin. He had already scanned a thousand sheets of newspaper archives to no avail. 'I haven't found anything yet.' During the scarecrow's boyhood years, the children of Green County, Wisconsin, had been remarkably well behaved. 'Perhaps this is a waste of time.'

She only tapped the keys, giving no sign that she was even aware of him. He approached her with some caution, not wanting to break her concentration. If she ignored him to some purpose—

Oh, God, what's this?

Her eyes were closed in sleep, yet her fingers continued to type. Her repetitive movements produced only gibberish on the computer monitor, yet Charles could not rid himself of the illusion that the machines were now operating Mallory. He lifted her into his arms and held her tightly, regarding her sleeping face with enormous concern. He carried her back to his own office, where the machines could not get at her, and there he laid her down on the soft leather couch. Covering her hands with his own, he forced her fingers to stop typing across the air.

The store was empty and eerie. The customers and clerks should have returned by now, for there was no sign of a fire, no sirens and not a trace of smoke. Stella walked the vacant aisles alone – and not. Every manikin drew her startled eye. And now she was one of them, neither moving nor breathing. She could only stare at the gray canvas bag on the floor in front of the escalator.

Where was he now? Was he watching her? Her eyes searched the vast space with a thousand hiding places. She ran toward the bank of elevators and found a crude out-of-service sign posted above the dark call buttons. She tried the nearby stairwell door, but the knob would not turn. Another sign, this one merely an arrow, directed her away from the stairs and toward a freight elevator. It stood open, waiting for her. She stepped inside and pushed the button for the ground floor.

Stella was slipping her new shoes over naked feet when she looked up to see the man holding the doors to prevent them from closing. He appeared not to see her as he stepped inside and set his gray canvas bag on the floor. She could get around him if she acted right now – if she was fast. She willed her legs to carry her away.

The moment was missed, the elevator closed.

Stella watched the lighted numbers overhead. They were going down. The canvas bag on the floor was open, and she was staring at the razor tip of a box cutter. They descended in silence – except for the buzzing sound from his bag, low and ugly, insectile. The shrill high noise of her screaming was purely imagined.

When Mallory opened her eyes, her head was pillowed in Charles Butler's lap. What time was it? She had no idea. Her internal clock had failed her.

Unaware that she was awake, Charles absently stroked her hair, and she listened to the soft shuffle of paper, then watched the white pages sail by on their way to the pile on the rug below. She should rise now – time was precious.

The hand lightly moving over her hair was intoxicating. The human touch was rare since she had lost the Markowitzes, first Helen, then Louis. During the years that followed his wife's death, the old man had made a point of kissing his foster child twice at each encounter – a sorry effort to make up for her loss of a mother – and he had rarely missed an opportunity to capture her in a bear hug – hugging for two. And then he died.

She was always losing people.

Mallory closed her eyes and listened to footsteps in the hall. Now Riker's voice called out, 'It's me. How's it going?'

'One possibility,' said Charles, 'though not what I had in mind. Here, take a look at this article.'

'Foster Care Fraud,' said Riker. 'Catchy headline.'

'That foster child ran away when he was twelve years old, but the police were never notified.'

'And these people kept collecting his support checks?'

'Right,' said Charles. 'The boy was put in their care the same year Natalie's son was taken from the Qualens.'

Another hand, Riker's, rested on Mallory's shoulder a moment, then gently brushed the hair from her face. 'I've never seen her sleep,' he said. 'I always figured she just hung from the ceiling like a little bat. Damn, I hate to wake the kid up.'

'Then don't,' said Charles.

'But I got her a present – Susan Qualen. The woman turned herself in. Janos is walking her over here now – in handcuffs.'

'Why here?' asked Charles.

'More privacy.'

Stella pressed her back to the wall of the elevator and watched the man open a metal panel with one of a gang of keys hanging from his belt loop. A janitor? 'So you work here?'

No answer. He was not aware of her on any level, and this was hopeful. It could all be one ghastly coincidence. This man worked here; he *belonged* here. Of course, he would give her a gift certificate from this store. He probably got an employee discount. And now he was merely rounding up a stray shopper and escorting her to safety.

Stella acted the part of a woman who could believe all of this, but she could not sustain the role for long.

When he closed the metal panel, the light for the ground floor was no longer glowing. They were on their way to the basement level. Her heart beat faster and adrenaline gorged every muscle for flight. When the doors opened, her legs ran away with her, flinging Stella headlong down a wide aisle of cardboard cartons. There were no hurried footsteps behind her. He had no worries that she would get away. Why should he? It would be so easy to follow her by the clack of high heels. *Idiot.*

She slipped off her shoes and ran in barefoot silence down a corridor of boxes, running from the light, swallowed by the dark.

All the television stations ran hourly updates on the plight of Stella Small, showing photographs of her early years and reading excerpts from letters to her mother and grandmother, known to locals as the Abandoned Stellas. The written words of the youngest Stella were upbeat and hopeful, full of the dream: she was going to be somebody, and fame could only be minutes or hours away.

'What was that?' Riker turned off the volume, and now he could more clearly hear a knock on the door in the reception area. 'That's gotta be her.'

He answered the door and greeted Detective Janos with a smile. Natalie Homer's sister needed no introduction. Riker's face was grim when he turned to the woman in handcuffs, only inclining his head a bare inch to say, 'Miss Qualen.'

Stella shrank into a small space behind a carton, playing the mouse, shaking and listening to the footsteps coming closer, stopping now. A nearby box was being moved. Eyes shut tight, her thoughts went out to the Abandoned Stellas. How sorry she was to let them down, yet she knew they would cope well with her dying, for that was their strength of purpose. They were younger than she was now when they had committed themselves to their own slow deaths at the roadside diner.

But wait. This was New York City — different rules: no cowards allowed.

An inspired Stella sat in the dark and prepared herself for something finer than slaughter by box cutter. Adjusting her chin to a determined angle, she created the role of a lifetime, imagining her own heart engorging and growing into the part, pounding harder, louder — *stronger*.

Can you hear it, you son of a bitch?

The box was moved aside. A hand reached out for her, and the greatest thing that ever came out of Ohio jumped to her feet. She raked his chest with five long fingernails that left red streaks on his T-shirt. He stopped, as if his batteries had suddenly run down, stunned that an *object* would fight back. And then she clawed his face.

Stella had drawn first blood, and now she ran for the light at the end of the box corridor, screaming, 'I'm gonna *live*, you *bastard*!'

Janos leaned against the door to the back office, making it clear to the prisoner that she was not going anywhere. Mallory and Riker closed in on Susan Qualen. The woman backed into a computer station and slipped. Her handcuffs bound her wrists behind her, and she could not break the fall. She awkwardly managed a squat, then rose to a stand and revolved slowly, looking from face to face. 'Why am I under arrest?' She jangled the chain of her manacles. 'I haven't done *anything.*'

'You got that part right,' said Riker. 'You wouldn't help us. You ran away.'

The words were spoken in a monotone, but the woman behaved as if he had screamed at her. She bowed her head and stared at the floor. As a reward for this attitude of contrition, Janos removed the handcuffs, then stepped back.

Mallory kicked a chair toward the suspect. It fell over, and Riker commanded, 'Pick it up!'

Susan Qualen did as she was told.

'Sit down!' said Janos.

'That day you came around—' Qualen's voice faltered and cracked. 'I couldn't help you. I didn't—'

'You have to sign this.' Riker held a small card that listed her rights under the constitution. 'We'll get you a lawyer if you want one. Do you understand your rights?'

'I don't need a damn lawyer. I didn't do—'

'Then *sign* it!' Riker was not play-acting. He was angry when he grabbed a clipboard from the desk, then attached the card and a pen. She accepted the board, fingers slowly closing around its edges, and quickly signed her name. Mallory tore the clipboard from the woman's hands and threw it across the room. Qualen jumped as it skittered across the floor for the last few feet before hitting the wall.

'And now,' said Riker, 'tell us that twisted freak didn't look up his Aunt Susan the minute he got to town.'

'It's *your* fault!' Qualen faced each of them in turn. 'You *lie* to people. You don't—'

'All those details in the papers,' said Mallory. 'You *knew* there was a link between the last hanging and—'

'And my sister? The police only told me Natalie was murdered. I read about her hanging in the newspapers – the fake suicide, a damn cover-up!' Susan Qualen's voice was in the high, wavering pitch of hysteria. 'Nobody wanted to solve Natalie's murder.'

'Your nephew gave you all the details,' said Mallory. '*That's* how you knew. When you saw the story in the papers, it was Natalie's murder all over again.'

'*Stop it!* Junior didn't tell me anything!' She was in tears. 'That little boy could barely speak. He was almost catatonic.'

'So you sent him away. You conspired to hide the only witness who could've helped the police find your sister's killer.'

'Oh, that's rich.' Susan Qualen was not frightened anymore. She was angry. 'Who do you call when a damn *cop* kills your sister – the cops?' She wore a grim smile and took some satisfaction in their stunned faces.

Running toward the light at the end of the corridor, Stella turned a corner of boxes and saw a small office walled in glass. The door was ajar, and she pushed it wide open. At the point of slamming it behind her, she regained her sanity, then closed the door quietly and turned a knob to lock it. The desk offered the only cover in a room made of glass, and she crouched behind it, taking the telephone with her. She dialed 911, but the call would not go through. And now she listened to an automated recording that instructed her to dial another digit for an outside line.

He was coming.

She could hear him walking at a mechanical clip. Stella held her breath as the man tried the knob, and then she heard metal on metal – a key in the lock.

Oh, you stupid fool. He's a damn janitor. He has all the keys.

Stella closed her eyes and covered her ears, blocking it out, wishing it away, this thing at the door. The lock came undone. The door opened, and that insect smell was in the room with her. She opened her eyes. Very slowly, deep in shock, she lifted her face. He was standing beside the desk, looking down at her, yet not really seeing her. And he said nothing; one did not converse with objects. She saw the sign behind him, the shield of the alarm company pasted to the glass wall encircled by metallic tape. If she could break the glass, that would trigger the burglar alarm and bring a watchman.

Susan Qualen was all but spitting the next words at them. 'If I'd given him up, how long would that little boy have stayed alive? The only witness to a cop killing his mother. I lived in that neighborhood for years. Drug dealers bought the police for a song. And you guys always cover for your own.' She put up one hand, sensing Riker's intention to interrupt. 'Don't start with me. I did the right thing, and you *know* it!'

'He ran away from the foster parents,' said Mallory, 'a pair of chiselling—'

'And he went back to my cousins. They took him to Nebraska. When he grew up, he had a lot of questions about his mother. They told him everything they knew. Then he came back.'

'Back home,' said Mallory. 'To you.'

'He only spent a few hours with me. That was a long time ago.'

'You didn't want to see him again.' Riker folded his arms. 'He scared you, didn't he?'

'No! He wasn't some whacked psycho. He was as normal as I am.'

Janos pulled out his notebook. 'Where's your nephew now?'

'I don't know.'

'What does he call himself these days?'

'Junior, I guess. That's what he always called himself.'

'I want a straight answer.' Janos moved closer. 'Did you hear the question? What name is he—'

'I don't know!'

'Right,' said Mallory. 'You don't know anything helpful. I keep forgetting that. So why did you run?'

Susan Qualen sank into the chair, trembling, not with fear but excess emotions, none of them good ones. Hate predominated overall.

'Okay,' said Riker. 'Here's an easier question. Why did you come back?'

Stella had no clue to the source of sudden strength in her arms. She picked up the heavy wooden desk chair and sent it hurtling through the glass wall, fracturing it into a hundred pieces. The man turned to a panel of buttons beside the door and cut off the alarm while it was merely a squeak and before the glass shower had ended. One long shard lingered in the frame, then toppled and shattered across the office floor. The broken pieces crunched under his shoes as he walked toward her, one hand rising, reaching out.

'No,' she said. 'No!' she yelled.

And now she realized that she was invisible to him. He walked past her and took a card from a rack on the wall, then fed it into the slot below the time clock. Because this was such a normal act for any employee beginning his shift, it unhinged Stella's mind. The night watchman was never coming to her rescue. *He* was the watchman.

'I came back to beg you not to kill Natalie's son.' Susan Qualen doubled over, as if they had kicked her. 'Killing is what you do best, isn't it?' She was nearly spent. Anger was all that sustained her. 'You gun-happy bastards kill people all the time. *You* made Junior what he is. A goddamn cop killed his mother. So I figure you owe him a life. You can't just put him down like a sick animal.'

Riker could see that Janos was losing the heart for this. The man's voice was too soft when he said, 'Tell us where your nephew lives. If we have some control over the capture—'

'I don't *know!*' She shook her head. 'That's the truth. I told you – I only saw him for a few hours. That was three years ago, and *he* asked all the questions.'

Mallory gripped the woman's arm. 'What did your relatives tell you? What was he doing for a living when he—'

'He was a *cop!*' Susan Qualen's face was wet with tears. 'Can you believe it?' Her words came out in a stutter of sobs. 'A cop . . . like you . . . so don't . . . don't kill him.'

Stella backed up to the wall, cutting her bare feet on broken glass and never feeling the pain. Her mouth was dry, and her eyes were on the box cutter in his hand. Involuntary responses came first, cold chemicals flooding her veins. Her palms were clammy, and her heart banged in a full-blown panic attack. There was nowhere to go but into the corner. She pressed up against the plaster, eyes wide, staring at the razor. Her sweaty hands spread out on the corner walls, and she climbed them, finding traction with the sticky flesh of palms and soles. Her feet were inches off the floor, toes curling over the baseboard – a human fly.

'Please don't.' She was stripped down to the naked personality of the little girl from Ohio. 'Please,' she said. 'Please,' she whispered.

Jack Coffey looked up to see two visitors in his office. New Yorkers had come to know these women as the Abandoned Stellas of Ohio. They stood before his desk in sturdy, serviceable shoes and their best dresses. They had brought him their frightened eyes and wavering smiles, brave then not, and all the baggage of hope. First, they destroyed him, they broke his heart, and then they said hello and 'Did you find our Stella?'

Another bag of delicatessen food sat on the floor at Ronald Deluthe's feet. He was operating a laptop computer and scanning all the transcriptions of tip-line calls. The sightings of Stella Small spanned four states. Charles Butler sat beside him on the leather couch, rolling one hand to tell the younger man to scroll faster. 'Stop. Highlight that one too.'

Mallory stood over them, saying, 'What? Let me see.'

'Here,' said Charles. 'Multiple sightings in department stores. Look at this last one. Stella was shopping rather late this evening.'

Deluthe shook his head. 'This can't be right. The discount store I can see, but where would she get the money to shop on Fifth Avenue?'

'Hmm. Bergdorf's had a moonlight sale,' said Mallory. 'So did Lord and Taylor.' She leaned over to look at another highlighted entry. 'That designer outlet store checks out. That's where she bought a suit this morning, and the bastard ruined it.'

'Well, she's not gonna find another one on Fifth Avenue,' said Deluthe with absolute conviction. 'You saw that place she lived in, all those unpaid bills. So the late sightings are bogus.'

Mallory glared at him briefly, a small threat to tell him that he must defer to her in all matters of police work and shopping. 'Stella has good taste.'

Charles stared at the glowing screen. 'This place was on the news tonight. There was a small fire on the top floor. The whole store was evacuated. Perhaps a—' He looked up to see the back of Mallory leaving the room. 'Well, I guess it was worth checking out.'

'Waste of time,' said Deluthe. 'The scarecrow always hangs them in their own apartments.'

'*Twice* isn't quite the same as always.' Charles picked up the deli bag and searched among the sandwiches for his own dinner. 'Oh, and he's got the hang of setting fires now.'

Suddenly, Deluthe was also leaving him, feet slapping the wood in the hallway, making a dead run for the front door.

It had never occurred to Mrs Harmon Heath-Ellis that cabs might be scarce in the hours after all the bars had closed. She crossed the small park and passed the fountain, hoping to improve her chances of hailing a car on Fifth Avenue.

A group of six people had gathered in front of her favorite department store. Suppose someone recognized her? Her social stature was too secure to worry about being caught in town during the loser's month of August. However, she did fear being discovered near her brother-in-law's hotel.

The socialite waved frantically, though the only cab, indeed, the only vehicle on the avenue, was stopped at a traffic light a block away. She glanced back at the people in front of the store, *her* store. They were wearing what must pass for evening clothes in that third-world country Middle America. The rubes were fixated on one window. Curiosity prevailed, and she walked toward the shabby little gathering. What was the harm? None of their social orbits could possibly intersect with hers.

The wealthy society matron looked over their shoulders and between their heads to see the lighted display. After all she had spent on haute couture, who was better qualified to critique the window-dresser's art?

Well, this was different. And it was inevitable, she supposed. This must be the next big thing, the new wave beyond heroin chic – *dead*.

'That's no manikin,' said the man directly in front of her.

Of course not. As any fool could see, this was a living woman playing the role of a department store dummy. It was an old idea with a new twist – literally. The model was slowly revolving at the end of a rope, allowing the public to view all sides of the blue suit and matching shoes.

'She *is* rather good,' said Mrs Harmon Heath-Ellis. 'This one doesn't blink.' Well, certainly the girl must blink, but not until the rope twisted her face away from the window. The model was quite pretty in a low-rent way. Her hair had not been styled by any reputable salon. The short spikes standing out on the scalp were so passé. Longer strands of blond hair trailed from the model's open mouth, and what sort of statement was that?

The window had been arranged with small kitchen appliances and utensils to create an interesting contrast with high fashion. Though somewhat nearsighted, the socialite recognized the designer by the cut of the light blue suit – quite respectable. Ah, but the rest – such tedious violence, no blood, no real drama.

An enormous woman in a muumuu – obviously an out-of-towner and Kmart shopper – was whimpering, saying, 'Oh, God, she's dead!' A man joined in this opinion. 'Hey, somebody call a cop!'

Mrs Harmon Heath-Ellis smiled benignly in the spirit of giving first aid to the ignorant and unwashed, the *tourists*. But now a man pointed to the glass, his mouth working in astonished dumbshow. The socialite stepped closer to the display window to see what she might have missed.

Her superior smile was frozen, and she was deaf to the oncoming screams of police sirens. Beneath the hanged model was a jar of dead flies encircled by flaming red candles. The woman looked up, and now she could not look away. What she had mistaken for a mole, a beauty mark, was a black fly crawling across the model's face and moving toward one wide blue eye.

The socialite was trembling, interior screams outshouting the sirens. She jumped at the screech of brakes and spinning red lights. Police cars disgorged men in uniforms and men in suits. There was one woman among them, but this tall blonde was hardly a civil servant. She wore a linen blazer of all too marvelous cut and line, a thing to die for. And now this young paragon of fashion pulled an enormous revolver from a shoulder holster and beat on the plate glass with the butt end of the gun.

Of course, the glass was holding up well. It was made to withstand such vandalism, and Mrs Heath-Ellis was about to tell her as much, for she was privy to every detail of her favorite—

'Hey, Mallory!' Near the far corner of the block-long store, a policeman called out, 'This door's open!'

Either young Mallory did not hear this man, or she did not care, so enraged was she, quite mad actually, beating, hammering the glass, electric-green eyes full of rage. With one last mighty swing of the gun, the glass wall shattered, and the young blonde was climbing past the shards, tearing her fabulous threads to get at the twisting figure on the end of the rope.

The policewoman was slender, and yet she was able to lift the dead weight as if it were nothing. She cradled the other woman's limp body like a babe in arms, then lifted it high until the rope slackened. She was fiercely concentrated on the model's still white face. And every watcher knew she was willing the hanged woman to live.

There was a hinged panel at the rear of the display window, but rather than simply open this door, the entire back wall was ripped from its moorings by a large man. Oh, and that face – brutality incarnate.

'Good job, Janos,' said another man, a less imposing figure with a bad suit, who climbed up to the raised floor, then quickly untied the thick knot of the noose. The rope fell away, and Mallory laid her burden down. The largest policeman, the brutal one called Janos, leaned over the prone body to remove the gag of human hair. With surprising delicacy, he pinched the model's nostrils closed and covered her mouth with his own. The young woman's body shuddered back to life in convulsions. Her hands rolled into fists that punched the air, batting at some phantom from an interrupted nightmare, and her mouth opened wide in a shrill scream. The large policeman gently gathered her into his arms and rocked her slowly. His voice was incongruously soft as he said, 'Hush now, Stella, it's all over.'

The small crowd of watchers went *wild*, screaming, cheering, whistling. The socialite was surprised by her own helpless laughter as she was engulfed in a hug from the heavy-set woman in the muumuu. Her head fell upon this stranger's generous breast, and she began to cry.

NINETEEN

Mallory looked less like a crime victim after removing the blazer torn by broken glass. The garment was neatly folded over one arm to hide her bandaged wound. And now her holstered revolver was on public display in a window on Fifth Avenue. She stood in full view of a sidewalk audience and watched the watchers. One of them picked up a small piece of glass from the litter on the pavement, and he slipped it into his pocket. Perhaps he prized this one above the other souvenir shards because of the small red stain. He was stealing a drop of her blood.

She turned to Ronald Deluthe. 'Take another look. You're sure he's not out there?'

The rookie detective shook his head. 'I don't see him.'

She pointed to three uniformed officers standing off to one side. 'What about them?'

This startled him. 'You think the scarecrow is a cop?'

'When I say look at everyone, that means cops too.'

'No, he's not there.' And now, sensing that she had no further use for him, Deluthe climbed out of the display window, giving the forensic expert more room to work.

Heller pulled down the rope that dangled from an exposed pipe in the chopped-away ceiling. 'Crude job for such a tidy killer.'

'And he's taking more chances,' said Mallory. 'Heller, you said this woman fought back?'

'Better than that. Dr Slope found blood and skin under her fingernails.'

Good for you, Stella Small.

'What about store security?'

'They got everything,' said Heller. 'Cameras, alarms, even guard dogs. But none of it was working, and the animals were locked in a utility closet.'

Mallory lowered her sunglasses. 'This store doesn't have a nightwatchman?'

'Yeah, they got one.' Riker climbed up on the raised floor of the display window. 'The watchman's a retired cop, sixty-four years old. Maybe he slept through the whole thing.'

Mallory turned back to the crowd of ghouls on the sidewalk. 'And maybe the old man's dead.'

'Well, that theory's my personal favorite.' Riker knelt down beside Heller. 'His basement office was wrecked. Broken glass everywhere, and there's blood on the floor. I didn't see any broken skin on Stella, so it might be the watchman's blood.'

Without a word or even a nod to Riker, Heller closed his toolkit and climbed down from the display window. For the past hour, these two men had not traded one insult, and Mallory wondered about this sudden rift in an old routine.

'Stella marked the perp with her fingernails,' she said.

'That's my girl.' Riker stared at the bits of hair on the floor. 'Not a very neat scalping this time, and you should see that basement office. The perp's not so fussy about cleaning up his messes anymore.'

Mallory nodded. The scarecrow was coming undone.

A crime-scene tape cordoned off ten feet of space in front of the basement office. John Winetrob, the personnel director, was not permitted any closer to the broken glass wall. This aftermath of violence was beyond his comprehension. He froze when a policeman passed by carrying a bloody shard in a plastic bag.

Detective Arthur Wang gestured toward a cardboard carton the height of a chair. 'Sir? Why don't you sit down?'

Before you fall down.

The man's shakes were easy for Wang to account for, but not only because of the crime-scene blood. The police were also making him nervous. The unshaven personnel director wore a suit, but no tie, and his socks were mismatched. Dressing would have been difficult at this early hour while a uniformed police officer, six feet tall and armed with a gun, had waited at his front door.

For the past ten minutes, Mr Winetrob had been talking nonstop, mostly inane chatter. Now he fell silent as the detective completed a cell-phone call.

'No answer.' Arthur Wang dropped the phone back into his pocket. 'The watchman isn't home, but I didn't think he would be. And he hasn't turned up in any local hospitals.'

'Thank you for trying,' said Winetrob. 'You don't really believe he could be dead, do you?'

Yes, that was exactly what Detective Wang believed. 'We're still looking for him, sir. We've got twenty men doing a sweep, floor by floor. If he's here – if he's hurt—'

'What if he didn't come to work last night? Now there's a thought.' The personnel director glanced at the broken glass wall of the night-watchman's office, then looked away. 'Maybe it's not his blood in there. You know, an old man like that, he could be at home right now, lying in his own bed, maybe— Oh, God. He could be having a heart attack. Can you send somebody over to his apartment? We must cover all the bases.' He raked one hand through his sparse hair. 'Yes – all the bases.'

'Of course,' said Wang. 'I'll send a cop to check it out – real soon.' Or maybe never. This errand would hit the bottom of police priorities this morning. The more important business was a look at the store's files. All the employees had been photographed, and this was the only helpful information Winetrob had given him so far – or so he believed.

Gently, Detective Wang helped the civilian to his feet and led him to an elevator that would carry them up to the personnel office. Later, Arthur Wang would wish that he had prioritized in a different fashion and paid closer attention to Winetrob's wacky ramblings, his hopes and fears.

When Deluthe had finished Janos's chore in the payroll department, he had been loaned out to Arthur Wang. Now he was posted at a secretary's desk outside the office of the personnel director. He had made short work of the first fifty photographs in the stack of employee files, and the man from Kennedy Harper's crime scene was not among them. More busywork. He glanced toward the open door. The senior detective was inside, drinking coffee and making notes on his conversation with Mr Winetrob. Wang noticed him and called out, 'Find anything?'

'Nothing yet, sir.' Deluthe closed another folder.

Arthur Wang walked to the door and tossed a file on the secretary's desk. 'That one goes in your stack. Put it back in alphabetical order, okay? When you're done, report to Riker.'

Deluthe opened the file of the nightwatchman and stared at the photograph. His eyes drifted down to the name, that vital clue to the man's place in the file cabinet. The line below it was a familiar East Village address. And now, with utter disregard for the alphabet, the young detective jammed the folder into the center of the large stack and left his job unfinished.

He had more important things to do.

In the back office of Butler and Company, Mallory was on the phone, terrorizing a clerk at the Odeon, Nebraska, Police Department. 'So what if your computer is down? What does that— Look, all I need is a photograph . . . Yeah, right . . . I told you that an hour ago . . . So pull it out of the hardcopy . . . Then *fax* it! *Now!*'

Fortunately, there had been no computer problems at the Nebraska Department of Motor Vehicles. Charles was looking at a monitor and their only likeness of the scarecrow. The image was not very good, but most license photographs were less than professional quality.

After relocating in Nebraska, Susan Qualen's cousins had changed their family name, and the boy they had harbored was called John Ryan. No doubt the cousins had called the boy by his initials, J.R. for Junior, the only name he was accustomed to.

Mallory sat down at the workstation. 'It'll probably take them an hour to figure out how a file drawer works.'

'Bad luck,' said Charles. 'How do you suppose ordinary people like the Qualens became so adept at changing identities?'

'Nothing to it. Idiots get away with it all the time.' She stared at her monitor screen. 'The scarecrow must've picked up another alias when he came east. He's not in any local databases. You know what that means?'

'He's been planning this killing spree for three years?'

'No, I think he only planned *one* murder.'

'The man who killed his mother?'

Mallory nodded. 'In Nebraska, Junior was a smalltown cop in uniform. Probably never got near a major investigation. So he comes to the big city. Figures he can find his mother's killer in a day – and without any help from us.'

Charles agreed. And when the boy failed, his last resort was forcing NYPD to do the job for him.

'The scarecrow hates police,' she said. 'He's very clear about that. So tell me, why would he become a cop?'

'Perhaps he had control issues.' Charles suspected that this was why Mallory had joined NYPD, but he could not complete this twinning image of her and the scarecrow. 'It's an interesting choice, isn't it? His emotional problems must have been very tightly contained while he was a police officer. The deterioration probably started after he moved to New York.'

He looked up to see Lars Geldorf standing just inside the door. Some tenant must have buzzed him into the building. Charles was unprepared for the change in him. The old man had aged another decade in a day.

Ignoring the unwelcome visitor, Mallory looked down at her keyboard. The retired detective walked a few steps into the room, then seemed at the point of falling down. Charles picked up a chair and rushed toward him, but the man waved him away and remained standing.

Lars Geldorf's eyes were fixed on Mallory. 'I heard about that poor woman – Stella Small. You think the copycat hangings are my fault, don't you? If I'd done my job right twenty years ago—' His shoulders sagged, and he braced himself with one hand pressed flat on the cork wall, then turned his defeated eyes to Charles. 'I think I *will* take that chair.' He sat down and waited out Mallory's silence. It was clear that the old man would not leave without a word from her.

She continued her typing, occasionally looking his way, annoyed that he was still here. Her eyes trained on the keyboard, she said, 'I can't discuss details of an active case. You *know* that.'

'Yes,' said Geldorf. 'I know.'

She could have killed the old man with only a few words, but she kept silent, and Charles saw this as the potential for kindness. Growing up in Special Crimes, she would have seen many of these old men coming and going, haunting police stations as confused ghosts, unable to come to terms with the end of things.

Mallory was done with Geldorf now, and he could make no mistake about that. The conversation was over, and yet he continued his vigil. After a time, his presence began to wear on her. She pushed her chair back from the workstation and swiveled round to face him. 'So you want me to tell you what you got wrong? Is that it?'

Yes, that was what he had come for. He had to know.

She strolled to the cork wall and what remained of the old murder case, then ripped down a sheet of paper. 'This is your report on the hanging rope and the duct tape. It's real short. "Common items. Untraceable." Wrong. The rope belonged to the building handyman. I got that information from the landlady's granddaughter.'

'The handyman was out of town when—'

'On a family emergency. I *know*. That's why he left his toolbox in the hall. The landlady promised to take care of it for him. But before she could drag it back to her apartment, the killer found it and stole the rope and the tape. If you'd talked to the handyman, you might've gotten a print from the toolbox.'

Geldorf had no comeback for this, but he would not look away from her.

She ripped two more sheets of paper from the wall. 'And then there's the locked door. *Locked* when the landlady called the police. *Open* when the first cop showed up on the scene.'

'I *caught* that,' said Geldorf. The light was back in his eyes, and he rose to a stand as he defended himself. 'That door was never locked. It was *stuck*. The landlady was old, pushing eighty. Tiny woman, no muscle. It was a hot night in August – and muggy. Wood swells in the damp and the heat. The door was stuck, not locked. And she admitted that when I—'

'Admitted what? That she was old? That you confused her? She never recanted her statement, and you didn't make any notes on that conversation. And what about Natalie's son? You never talked to him.'

'What the hell for? What good would it do to torture a little boy. He'd just lost his mother. When you've been on the job a little longer—'

'Natalie came to you for help, and you just strung her along, you and your buddies. After she died, you built your case around the easiest target, an innocent man.'

'I was *right* about the ex-husband!'

'No, you botched that too.' She paused a moment, waiting for him to challenge her, but he said nothing. 'And twenty years later, here we are, cleaning up the mess.'

Geldorf shrank down to his chair. His gaze lowered to the floor at her feet. She had won. He was finished.

Mallory hunkered down beside his chair and looked up at his face. If she had been a cat, Charles might have seen this pose as a prelude to a lunge, but he hoped for something better from her. For a moment, he believed that she planned to soften her words with some comfort for a vulnerable old man.

How foolish was that?

'Listen to me.' She gripped Geldorf's arm to shake him from his stupor of pity. He stared at her red nails, startled, as if she had just extended claws.

Mallory's half smile said, *I'm done playing with you.* 'Here's the best part, old man. This killer might be a *cop.* So go home and lock yourself in. If the police come knocking, don't open that door. It might be one of your mistakes coming back on you. Scary, huh?'

Arthur Wang finished telling the forensic expert about his conversation with Winetrob. He had intended it as a humorous story to break the tension in the nightwatchman's basement office.

'Sorry, Arty. Winetrob was right.' Heller pointed to the red smears on the cement floor. 'That's not the watchman's blood. I called the hospital to check for broken skin on the victim. When they removed Stella's shoes, they found cuts on her soles and glass fragments in the wounds. I got a partial footprint off one of the shards – real small, a woman's print. This is *her* blood.'

One of Heller's technicians nodded, saying, 'And Winetrob was right about the watchman not showing up for work tonight. The security camera has a record of everybody who uses the employee entrance. He's not on the film.'

'But the watchman isn't on vacation,' said Wang. 'I checked.'

'Then maybe Winetrob's right about the heart attack, too.'

Detective Wang produced a long piece of stiff paper sealed in an evidence bag. 'So who's been using the old man's employee card? Somebody punched in on the time clock last night.'

Heller turned to his assistant. 'Maybe the watchman's still here. Call out the cadaver dogs. We'll do another sweep of the store.'

* * *

Mallory ended her call with the Wisconsin detective, then turned to Charles. 'The scarecrow was planning murder when he left Nebraska. There's nothing wrong with the police computers. The damn clerk didn't want to tell me she couldn't find the records. The file was deleted from the computer. The hardcopy is missing too – prints, photos, everything.'

'Did the police talk to the relatives?'

Mallory nodded, then turned back to her computer monitor. 'They had to wait for a warrant, then they tossed the cousins' house. The only New York address they found was Susan Qualen's. Her cousins haven't heard from Junior in three years. They had a falling-out. They finally told him his mother's killer got away with murder. A bit late. When he came to New York, his Aunt Susan added her own poison.' Mallory's fingers flew across the keys, entering new parameters to narrow her search. Her eyes were riveted to the screen. 'Where are you hiding?'

'Maybe he doesn't live in New York,' said Charles. 'It's only a few minutes to New Jersey on the subway.'

She shook her head. 'He's living in the city. Deluthe saw him at Kennedy Harper's crime scene thirty minutes after we found the body. Either he works for NYPD, or he was picking up local radio calls on a police scanner. He's *here*.'

'I suppose that makes sense,' said Charles. 'His aunt said he came home, and that would be the East Village.'

'No,' said Mallory. 'Erik Homer had sole custody. Natalie never saw the boy after the divorce – not till the day she died. The scarecrow's home was always uptown with his father.'

'But his father was a bully,' said Charles. 'And he's dead now. The boy never lived with his stepmother, so he wouldn't think of that place as home anymore. Natalie was the parent he adored, the one he still obsesses about.'

Mallory abruptly stopped tapping keys.

* * *

302

Detective Janos listened to the theory on the missing nightwatchman, then nodded. 'Yeah, we know. Another guy was filling in for him.'

Heller's assistant glanced at the store's daytime security guard, then said, 'Can we take this outside?'

Janos followed the man out the door of the manager's office. When he returned, Riker was still watching the same videotape for the tenth time. 'This is crap.' The image was too dark to make out details finer than the profiles of shadows punching in on the employee time clock. 'No clear shots of anybody.' Riker glanced at the store's daytime security guard. 'I know, it's not your fault. You're sure this is the only tape of the new watchman?'

'Yes, sir. It rewinds every three days. So yesterday it—'

'Yeah, yeah,' said Riker. And that would explain the grainy images. The camera had clicked once every three seconds. The shadowy figure had the jerky motion of an old silent film. 'The time stamp on this video is too early for his shift. And why doesn't he punch in?'

'He's got his own time clock in the basement,' said the guard. 'No idea why he'd show up so early.'

Riker waved one hand to tell the guard that he could leave. 'Janos? What's happening?'

'The regular watchman wasn't scheduled for a vacation. And his payroll checks are getting cashed.'

Riker stared at the man on the videotape. 'So maybe the regular watchman pays this guy out of pocket.'

'That fits. Nobody's got a name for him.' Janos read notes made from interviews with store employees. 'We talked to a stockboy who does a lot of overtime. He says this new guy showed up one night, and nobody questioned it. He had the old man's keys on his belt and a security card to unlock the office door. That's the only place where you can turn off the alarms.' He looked up from his notebook. 'But the glass wall in the office was broken. So our perp wasn't the guy with the keys.' He turned to the man on the screen. 'Not that guy.'

'Okay,' said Riker. 'What about the regular watchman?'

'I'm on that.' Arthur Wang entered the room, a very worried man. 'Couldn't reach him by phone, so I sent a uniform to knock on his door. The place doesn't stink like a ripe corpse. But that's all the cop could tell without going inside. He interviewed the landlord. The apartment's been sublet.'

'Works with the vacation theory,' said Janos. 'Still, it's worth a look inside. The old guy might've left something to give us a lead. Let's get a warrant and toss the place.'

'It's in the works,' said Arthur Wang. 'So now we wait another forty minutes. The chicken-shit DA doesn't want to wake up a judge for a warrant.'

'No judge is gonna sign that warrant,' said Riker. 'Not unless that uniform forgets he talked to the landlord. The sublet angle is a paper-work nightmare.' He looked at Wang, and both men smiled in unison.

'But what if we *don't* know about the sublet tenant,' said Wang. 'Let's suppose the cop forgot to mention it when I talked to him.'

'Yeah,' said Riker. 'Let's just suppose that.'

'But it's still gonna take forty minutes to get a warrant.'

'Fine. I don't see the scarecrow stringing up another blonde today. I'll be at Charles's place with Mallory.' Riker looked down at his watch. 'Where's my ride? Has anybody seen Deluthe?'

Pssst.

The old-model humidifier emitted a light spray of insecticide every twenty seconds, flooding the room with poisonous fumes. No cockroach would ever brave this atmosphere. Yet there were roach traps on the floor, strips of sticky tape along the baseboards and fly paper on every surface, all the added precautions of a man with a phobia.

Ronald Deluthe sifted though the Polaroid photographs of Stella Small madly beating flies from her hair in a subway car. In another shot, a blue garment was slung over one arm as she actually smiled for the camera – while bleeding. Then she was climbing into a cab, unaware of the line of blood on the sleeve of her blouse. In the next photograph,

Kennedy Harper twisted on her rope, blurring the shot. Among the other Polaroids of the dead and dying, the prettiest subject was Sparrow, the vegetable woman in the hospital.

He glanced at the newspaper beside the telephone. *Backstage* was open to the columns for auditions. Two for tomorrow were circled in red ink. The mission was an ongoing thing.

Pssst.

TWENTY

Lieutenant Loman set down the phone and yelled loud enough to be heard all over the squad room, 'Hey, you bastards!'

Five heads turned his way.

'Has Deluthe been around this morning?'

'Blondie? No,' said one detective. 'I'd remember that.'

The East Side lieutenant closed the door of his office and returned to his phone call. 'No, Riker, he's not here. So, like I was sayin', the kid ain't the greatest cop material, but you got him all wrong. The brass didn't put him on any fast-track. The deputy commissioner hates his guts.'

'His father-in-law? Why?'

'Deluthe's marriage fell apart four months ago, and the wife's old man is out for blood. He ain't too subtle neither. Came right out and told me to crush his son-in-law. But I didn't want any part of it.'

'And that's why you unloaded him on me?'

'The truth, Riker? I forgot Deluthe was alive. He was only takin' up desk space around here. Wasn't just me – *nobody* noticed him much. Then, the night that hooker got strung up, he comes walkin' in here with a bad bleach job.'

'And *that* got your attention.'

'Oh, yeah. So how's he doin', Riker?'

'Good. The kid's doin' good.'

* * *

Pssst.

Ronald Deluthe listened to the police scanner as a dispatcher reeled off codes for domestic disputes and robberies. This address was not among the calls, and another few minutes would make no difference at all.

The insecticide permeated everything in the apartment including the closet and the clothes. There was no other discernible odor, though the body in the plastic bag was badly decomposed.

Pssst.

'Great!' Riker paced the length of the back office at Butler and Company. 'Now I got two AWOL detectives.' He leaned over the fax machine to read the last report from the Wisconsin State Police. 'So Mallory's on the phone with these cops, and then what?'

'We talked about the scarecrow.' Charles turned to the computer monitor. 'She was working on this machine, and then she left. Just got up and left.'

Riker glanced at his watch. 'We'll give it a few minutes. Maybe she'll call in.' He sat down at Mallory's desk and reached for the phone. While the detective waited on hold for Sparrow's doctor, Charles left the room to give him some privacy, saying, 'I'll make some fresh coffee.'

The office kitchen was only marginally more comfortable than Mallory's domain, though it housed fewer electronics. He loathed the coffee machine of chrome, plastic and computer components. The programmed brew was sterilized in his mind before it ever reached his taste buds. Unlike Geldorf, Charles was a Luddite by choice: he could work the machines, but he would not. Instead, he returned to his apartment, four steps from the door of Butler and Company, to light a flame under an old-fashioned coffeepot. The coffee was done by the time Riker had tracked him across the hall and into the kitchen.

The detective pulled up a chair at the table, and Charles set out an ashtray, inviting him to smoke if he liked. 'So how is Sparrow?'

'Bout the same. Still dying. They keep telling me that. She keeps hanging on. Then, an hour ago, the doctor thought she might be coming around. But he was wrong. A nurse confused a muscle spasm with a hand squeeze.'

Charles filled two large mugs with coffee. 'You check on her frequently, don't you?'

'Yeah.'

'But not just because she's a crime victim and a witness. You really like this woman.'

'We got a lot of history, me and Sparrow. She was one smart whore, and she made my job a little easier. All the dirt she ever gave me was gold. If she'd been on the payroll, she might've made lieutenant by now.' As an afterthought, he said, 'And she was good to Kathy.'

Charles wondered how Riker could say that. According to the prostitutes, Kathy had been left to fend for herself most of the time – with a little help from the Hooker Book Salon. 'Sparrow was an addict – hardly mother material. If she cared so much, why didn't she turn the child over to the authorities?'

'Because, more than clean sheets and three square meals, the kid needed somebody to love her. Sparrow loved Kathy like crazy. That was the best the whore could do – and it was a lot.'

Charles set the coffee mugs on the table, then sat down. 'But now Mallory hates this woman, doesn't she?'

Riker said nothing – and everything. The answer could only be yes. Charles held out a box of the detective's favorite pastries.

'Let me guess,' said Riker. 'A bribe?'

'Just one question. It's about the westerns and the prostitutes.'

Riker smiled. 'What a kid, huh? We only saw ten hookers last night. Figure most of them died or left town. That means Kathy was workin' whores all over the city.'

'And you think that was her only use for the books – trading stories for a support network?'

'Who knows?' Riker shrugged. 'Lou and I spent a lot of time trying to figure out the attraction. We didn't know about the Hooker Book Salon.'

'You don't think she cared much about the stories?'

'Well, she always liked cowboys and Indians. Saturday mornings, she used to watch old westerns on TV with Lou. That was their only common ground for a while. She loved Helen at first sight, but it took Lou years to get that kid to trust him.'

'You know,' said Charles, 'I always wondered why she never called him anything but Markowitz.'

The detective looked at his watch. 'I never did read that last western.' He looked up and smiled. 'So the Wichita Kid takes a bullet? Did I hear that right?'

'Yes.'

'I guess I always knew it would end that way.'

'If you only read the first six books, how did you—'

'I knew the sheriff would do his job.'

'But the sheriff loved the Wichita Kid.'

'That's why he had to kill him, Charles. That's what made Sheriff Peety a hero, bigger'n life. Now my job is a dirtier proposition. We give the bad guys a pass every day. They rat out their friends. We cut a deal, then watch 'em walk away.'

'But not killers.'

'No, that's the cut-off. Nobody walks away from that.'

'Except Kathy Mallory. Last night, you said she was wanted for murder and arson.'

'And the kid was posthumously charged,' said Riker. 'Case closed.'

'But Kathy didn't actually die.'

Riker drained his coffee mug. 'And she didn't actually kill anybody. So?'

The detective never noticed the comical look on Charles's face as he was left hanging one more time. This would be maddening to most, but he was a patient man. 'One more question? Are you disturbed by the parallels between Mallory and the scarecrow?'

Riker stared into his empty cup, considering his words carefully. 'It's an old idea that cops and killers are twins. What separates us – that's what happens after the killing is over. You think this freak has any remorse about murder?'

Charles shook his head. 'Not this man, no.'

'But when a cop's involved in a fatal shooting, we take away his gun – so he won't die of remorse.'

'So you don't see Mallory identifying with the scarecrow?'

'Never,' said Riker. 'I'm thinking now she knows what it was like to be Lou Markowitz.'

'Hunting the lost child?'

'Natalie's son, one sick puppy. Some days you got nowhere to put your hate.' Riker stared at his watch. 'Why doesn't she call?' He pulled a crumpled fax from his pocket and glanced at the text. 'So Odeon, Nebraska, was the last place the scarecrow called home.'

'We were discussing a definition of home when Mallory got up and left.'

Riker's fist banged the table hard enough to make the coffee mug dance to the edge. 'She *found* him! Mallory knows where the scarecrow lives. Tell me everything you talked about.' That was an order. 'Every damn word.'

Mallory stood on the steps of the East Village building, Natalie Homer's last address. She pressed the intercom button for the apartment on the parlor floor. There was no answer, and she heard no sounds within.

A man on the sidewalk was strolling toward her, regarding her with mild curiosity. He climbed the short staircase to join the detective at the front door. 'I live here. Can I help you?'

It was Mallory's impression that he actually had some sincere desire to be helpful, and now she coupled him with another Midwest transplant. 'Are you Mr White? Alice White's husband?'

'Yes.'

Mallory held up her badge and no more words were necessary.

Smiling, he unlocked his front door and opened it wide, never questioning her right to come inside. She wondered how these friendly Wisconsin folk survived in New York City. 'Is your wife home?'

Mr White consulted a note on the glove table in the hall. 'This says she's gone to the store.' He opened the large double doors to the front room and waved her toward a comfortable chair. 'Please make yourself at home. I'm sure she'll be right back.'

When they were both seated, he said, 'I understand Alice gave you the guided tour. So what do you think of our renovations?'

'Nice job.'

Mr White leaned forward, eyebrows arched, expecting more from her. Then he gave up and sat back, perhaps realizing that this was her entire store of small talk. 'Is there anything I can help you with?'

'I hope so.' Mallory pulled out the two sketches of the scarecrow, the poster boy for the average man, and laid them on the coffee table. Beside these portraits she set down the computer printout of another likeness.

'Oh, he's from Nebraska,' said Mr White, after reading the address line of the driver's license. 'I have a sister in Nebraska.' His forehead puckered as he stared at the picture. 'Terrible photography.'

Pssst.

Deluthe was slowly becoming accustomed to the poison. He knew better than to touch anything, including the off switch for the machine that sprayed the insecticide into the air. He hunkered down before the body on the closet floor. The flesh was covered with green mold and black, and so was a good part of the bag's interior surface. The age of the corpse was evident by the white hair, and he sexed the body by one mannish square hand pressed up against the clear plastic.

Next to the closet, an umbrella stand held a baseball bat, the New Yorker's favored weapon for defending hearth and home. However, the white-haired man in the bag had no bloody wounds, no apparent cause of death.

311

The young detective stood up and turned round, though he could not have said why. He looked about the room. Everything was just as it should be.

Pssst.

'Well now,' said Mr White. 'This could be most anybody.' He looked up from the sketch, which had been no more helpful than the driver's license. 'Sorry. You know I'm gone all day. It's my wife who knows all the neighbors on sight.'

'Maybe you noticed a stranger hanging around your building at night. He wears a baseball cap and—' Mallory turned her head toward the sound of a small bell tinkling over the front door.

Alice White was home.

Deluthe walked toward the closed bathroom. He could not remember if he had left the door ajar. Between the automatic sprays of insecticide, the room was dead silent. He was almost certain that he was the only living thing in this apartment. *Almost* certain, he drew his gun as he reached for the doorknob. His skin prickled and drops of sweat slid down his face as he conjured up a vision of Mallory standing over his dead body, making caustic remarks about his failure to call in for back-up.

Yet he opened the door.

A hand shot out and smashed into his face. His nostrils gushed blood. His knees were weak and threatening to dump him on the floor. The man in the bathroom was raising his other hand. Was that a gun? Deluthe raised his own weapon.

No, it was an aerosol can.

Pssst.

Deluthe's eyes were on fire. He had taken a direct hit of insecticide, and now he was partially blind, only able to discern a blurry white shape, a floating face, as he hit the floor, landing on his knees. *More* pain.

* * *

Mrs White entered the hallway, calling out to her husband, John? Did you see my note?' She walked into the front room and set her grocery bag on the carpet, then noticed that her husband had company. 'Oh, hello again. You know you're the third police officer I've seen today.'

'What? Say again,' said her husband.

'Early this morning, there was a young man in uniform. He came right after you left. I think he must have been a friend of George's. And then there was another one—' She stopped and turned to Mallory. 'George is one of our tenants. He used to be a policeman years ago.'

Mallory held up the sketches. 'Does he look anything like this?'

'Oh, no,' she laughed. 'George is sixty-five if he's a day. A very heavy man, and not so much hair.'

Deluthe moved back. Tears had washed his eyes, and now he could see the shadowy form of a man in front of him. When he aimed his gun, it was simply taken from his hand, for he had misjudged the distance of his assailant. Fists waving blind, he made contact with the other man's body. A savage kick to Deluthe's testicles doubled him over in pain, and a hard punch to his stomach took his breath away. He hit the floor and lay there, rolling on to his side, curling like a fetus and listening to the opening and closing of drawers, then the sound of something tearing. He tried to get his bearings in the room. Where was the umbrella stand, the baseball bat?

Next to the closet.

His vision was still blurred, but he could make out the dark rectangle of the open closet door. He crawled toward it and located the nearby umbrella stand by touch. As he reached up to grab the bat, he heard the running footsteps, gained his legs and swung at the thing rushing toward him.

He hit something. Yes, flesh and bone. The shadow man was down.

* * *

313

Mrs White looked at the sketches and the photograph.

'Take your time,' said Mallory. As if she had the time. 'Have you ever seen him before?'

'Well, he looks like lots of people. He could even be that young policeman. I told him George wasn't here. But the man he sublet the apartment to—'

'He works nights,' said John White. 'Same as old George.'

'So I thought he might be sleeping,' said his wife. 'And I told that to the officer.'

'The first one?' asked John White. 'Or do you—'

'Well, both of them,' said his wife. 'The second policeman was a detective. He asked if it was all right to leave a note under George's door.'

Deluthe's legs were pulled out from under him. He cracked the back of his skull when he hit the floor. The baseball bat was still clenched in his right hand.

The other man's weight was on top of him, and together they rolled across the rug and knocked up against the wall. The assailant was beneath him now, and Deluthe smashed his fist into the face that he could barely see. His opponent did not seem to feel the blows, a hand was closing on Deluthe's testicles, and he screamed in agony.

When had he let go of the bat?

Mallory was deep in denial. 'This man lives in your building, and you *never* got his name?'

'Well,' said Mr White, speaking for his wife, 'it's not like he's a complete stranger. He's been visiting old George for years.'

Once more, Mallory tapped the pictures on the coffee table. 'Could this be your sublet?'

'It could be.' Mrs White picked up one of the sketches. 'I'm not sure. It could also be one of those policemen. The detective – he's the one who wanted to leave a note. He came by just a little while ago, and

I sent him upstairs. Well, I had to run to the store, so the young man said he'd let himself out.'

Pssst.

Ronald Deluthe was lying on his side. He could taste the blood in his mouth as he ripped off the tape. His other hand was feeling around for the baseball bat. Blind fingers no sooner closed around the wood than it was twisted out of his grasp. His right arm was forced up behind his back, and he could feel muscle and bone ripping away from the socket. The pain was beyond anything he had ever imagined. Tiny points of shooting white lights were all that he could clearly see. His scream was muffled by another piece of tape covering his mouth.

'George's sublet is a very quiet young man,' said Alice White. 'We never hear a sound from that apartment.'

'Well, we wouldn't, would we?' Her husband smiled. 'It's on the top floor. So one day, I met him on the stairs. He had George's keys. He said the old man left town in the middle of the night. Some family crisis.' He smiled to reassure the skeptical detective. 'Well, he *did* have George's keys, and he seemed presentable. There was no reason to—'

'And you were afraid of him.' Mallory did not have to wait for a reply. It was in the man's face. And now she understood why no one had pressed the sublet for so much as a name to call him by. 'Take another look.' She held up one sketch. 'Imagine him with a baseball cap and a gray canvas bag with a red stripe.'

'Oh, that's the sublet, all right,' said Mrs White. 'You never see him without that bag of his.'

Mallory turned her eyes to the ceiling, as if she could see through all the floors of the building. 'Is there a back exit?'

'We have a door to the backyard.'

'That's it? No fire escape?'

'No.'

'So if he wanted to get out, he'd have to—'

'You'd see him out there in the hall,' said John White, who now finished sentences for the detective as well as his wife.

'Give me your keys.' Mallory held out her hand. 'Now!' Later, she would not remember screaming at this man to make him move faster. *'Keys!'*

When Deluthe regained consciousness, his hands were bound. He tried to lift his head. A rope was pulling tight around his neck, and his body bucked against the heavy weight of the man on top of him.

No breath. Eyes bulging, heart hammering.

Panic was magnified to monster-size primal fear. His legs kicked out, then thudded on the floor. His struggles ceased. His prone body was lighter now. Head swimmy, muscles relaxing, fear gave way to euphoria, and he closed his eyes. The heavy weight that had straddled him was suddenly lifted, and gravity ceased to hold his body down. He floated up into an ether of midnight black.

All sensation ceased.

The door closed. The room was dead quiet.

Riker yelled, 'Yes, you *can* go faster! You're with a damn cop!'

Charles pushed the gas pedal to the floor and never flinched at the near miss of a cab and now a truck coming out of a side street.

The detour was a long one, twisting round the gridlock traffic of a broken water main on Houston. They were driving ten miles of bad traffic to travel one as the crow flies.

TWENTY-ONE

The landlord had disobeyed a direct order to remain downstairs with his wife. He had silently followed Mallory to the top-floor apartment, and now it was too late to threaten the man – and unnecessary. John White quickly backed down to the lower landing when she drew her .357 Smith and Wesson, a cannon among revolvers. She favored it above all others for its drop-dead stopping power.

Pssst.

The door was ajar by the crack of a bare inch. She kicked it dead center, and it flew back with a bang and the sound of plaster crumbling where the knob had crashed into a wall. Fresh wet blood was splattered across the rug, and some of it stained a baseball bat. Mallory only glanced at the body on the floor. Ronald Deluthe had a rope knotted around his neck. She entered the apartment, aiming her gun at every piece of furniture that might give cover to the scarecrow. The bathroom was empty. She kicked open another door – no one there.

Upon returning to the front room, she found John White crouching on the floor and holding the wrist of the fallen detective. Deluthe's left arm was twisted in an unnatural attitude. His nose was smashed to one side and still gushing blood, the only sure sign of a beating heart and life.

'I've got a pulse,' said White, 'but it's thready.'

Mallory knelt beside the unconscious man, then put one finger between the rope and his neck. It was a tight fit. His oxygen had been completely cut off, but his lips were not yet blue. The scarecrow could only be a minute away.

John White was also working at the rope, but to a different purpose; he was trying to clear the man's air passage, saying, 'I was a volunteer paramedic back in Wisconsin.'

Mallory was not listening, nor did she watch as White performed mouth-to-mouth resuscitation. She stared at the open closet and its contents for a moment, then reached down and ripped back the lapel of Deluthe's suit jacket. His shoulder holster was empty.

The scarecrow has a gun.

She was rising, moving quickly toward the door and the inconvenient obstacle of Alice White. Mallory pushed the woman aside, shouting, 'Call 911!'

'I did. You told me—'

'Call *again*! Tell them an officer's down!'

The last staircase at the end of the hall would lead her to the roof: and Mallory was running toward it. She had climbed to the door at the top of the stairs when she heard a scream from the apartment below. Apparently, Alice had noticed the moldy corpse on the floor of the closet.

Riker spoke into his cell phone, 'Repeat that. An officer down?'

Charles was pulling over to allow an emergency vehicle to pass, when the detective yelled, 'Follow that ambulance!'

Mallory's revolver preceded her through the door of a small rooftop shed. Her eyes had not yet adjusted to brilliant sunlight when she took aim at the sound of footsteps. And now, in perfect focus, the profile of a young girl's head was lined up with the muzzle of the gun. The teenager had not yet seen the detective or the weapon, but she was shaking, and her face was a study in dumb surprise as she bolted for the rooftop door.

Mallory rounded the shed to see the back of a man's bloodstained shirt and jeans. He used Deluthe's gun to shade his eyes from the overhead sun. There were scratches on his face, the work of Stella Small. The scarecrow's right arm hung useless at his side, and she guessed that Deluthe had also done some damage before he was taken down.

Only steps away, a smaller man with carrot-red hair was huddled on the tarpaper ground amid a wash of white linen pulled down from a clothes line, perhaps in the belief that wet sheets could protect him from bullets. On the other side of a low brick wall that separated one roof from the next, an elderly woman tended a coop of carrier pigeons. She was deaf to the whimpers of the little man in the sheets and blind to the one with the gun.

At the sound of a nervous giggle, Mallory glanced back over one shoulder to see the children standing behind her, three boys in staggered sizes, and these television babies showed no fear of either weapon.

The scarecrow was facing her now, dazed and weaving. Blood dripped into one eye from a gash in his brow.

A massive head injury – a bonus.

She could hear the children creeping forward to watch the show. None of them had the sense of sheep to get out of harm's way. Mallory left her back vulnerable when she whirled around and yelled, 'Get inside!' Her gun produced no effect on the boys, but her eyes were promising something nasty if they did not move and *right now*.

They shrank back behind the shelter of a door made of wood, not fire-code metal. Bullets would rip right through it. The smallest child had been left behind. He was walking between the guns.

Thou shalt not get the sheep killed.

That had been Louis Markowitz's prime rule and Mallory's hardest lesson, for it tied into a bizarre concept: when she pinned on the badge, she agreed, if need be, to *die* for the sheep. This had been a difficult pitch to a child of the streets, who possessed an ungodly instinct for survival.

But a deal was a deal.

319

The scarecrow's gun hand extended slowly. Mallory's finger touched lightly on the trigger. She could drop him any time she liked, but fast as she was, he might get off one round. His every movement told her he was not left-handed. The shot would go wild.

One dead sheep.

All the children were targets, the one in the open and the two behind the door. Or he might blow away the pigeon lady, or the little man under the sheets. Mallory lowered her revolver to end the threat that would make him fire.

His gun slowly drifted toward the shed where the children were hidden but not protected. In sidelong vision, Mallory caught the motion of a wind-whipped flowery dress before she saw a terrified woman creeping toward the lone boy in the line of fire. Mother courage. The woman gathered the little boy into her arms, and the scarecrow paid no attention to her running backward with the child. His eyes were fixed on Mallory. His gun hand was on the rise.

She was faster. In a stunning flash, the muzzle of her revolver pointed at his eyes. 'You really want this bullet, don't you?'

The threat was meaningless to him. This was not the cornered animal she had anticipated, but something even more dangerous. Perversely, she raised her revolver high to aim at the noonday sun, and then, pushing perversity to the nth degree, she taunted him, saying, 'I know more about your mother's death than you do.'

Magic words.

His gun was lowering, buying her time to reassess his injuries. The right arm was certainly broken. All his weight listed to the right leg, and she knew the left was about to fold. One eye was clotted with blood, and one eye was attentive as be awaited the rest of her story.

Just like the old days – just like a whore.

'And I even know what *you* did that night.'

The scarecrow's one clear eye flickered with surprise. His left leg buckled, but he remained standing. He seemed unaware that he was aiming at the shivering pile of wet laundry. The little man in the sheets ceased to cry and laid his head down in a faint.

And the scarecrow was still waiting for his story.

'You found one of the stalker notes,' said Mallory. 'You found it on the floor the night she died.' She had guessed right. He was nodding. 'And you had a lot of time to read it – two days and two nights. Flies in your hair, roaches crawling in your clothes. The stove burner was on. The heat was suffocating.'

His gun was getting heavier, and his aim was drifting again. The old woman was his accidental target. He was tired in every part of his body and tired of his very life. Yet Mallory held his attention. 'You were in the bathroom when he came to kill your mother.'

The pigeon lady was oblivious to the weapon, but her birds were restless, sensing tension in the air as a threatening storm. Their wings batted against the wire doors of the cage, and a shower of downy white feathers drifted from the coop in an eerie August snowfall.

Mallory walked toward him, slow stepping. 'You heard something.' She circled around him, drawing his body and his gun away from the old woman. 'You opened the bathroom door – just a crack. The man was bending over your mother.' Now she was positive that he had *not* seen his mother strangled to death. The six-year-old child had believed that his mother was still alive while he watched a man mutilate her and hang her. If a fireman and a doctor could not tell the living from the dead, what chance did a little boy have?

The pigeon lady was on the move again. Mallory kept track of her in peripheral vision. The old woman crossed the roof, walking into the line of fire to pick up a heavy bag of birdseed.

Mallory backed off softly, slowly.

Easy now.

A hand tremor made his gun shake. He was sliding into profound shock and aiming from the hip.

'You watched him hang her – without a sound, no screams. She never—'

His head was shaking in denial.

Impossible. Mallory knew she could not be wrong about this part. Yes, she *was* right. She had simply not pushed this idea far enough. 'You never made a sound. You – just – *watched.*'

The man's head tilted to one side, as though some supporting string had been cut. His face contorted into a soundless scream, and the blood-clotted eye cried red tears. He was bleeding inside and out.

The birds were screaming, wings in a racket, beating the wire of the coop, frantic to get away.

'You *watched* that bastard kill your mother! You *let* him do it to her!' Of course he did – only six years old, traumatized and paralyzed, and now she played to the guilt of the innocent child. 'You never called for help. You never even *tried* to stop him.'

The doors of the pigeon coop flew open and dozens of birds escaped before the wide eyes of their keeper. In tight formation, they flew across the roof in a roar of wings and cries, diving close to the scarecrow, then veering upward. His eyes were wild, following the flight of birds into the sun.

'You couldn't reach her up there on the rope.' Mallory could see him as a small, shivering boy, crying to his mother, no clue that she was dead. 'How could you leave her – if she was still *alive?*'

He dropped his gun and never noticed its loss. On the next roof, the pigeon lady stared at the sky, arms fluttering in her own attempt at flight.

'After two days – the bugs and the heat – you couldn't take any more. You left your mother all alone in the dark. You knew what the insects were doing to her when you closed that door and walked away.'

His bad leg buckled, and he folded to the ground like a piece of collapsible lawn furniture. And there he made a stand of sorts, on his knees, as though his legs had been cut to stumps. Mallory stepped closer to kick his gun, sending it flying to the far side of the roof.

He was helpless. Both eyes were open now and looking in on some interior hell. She knelt down before him, facing him in the position of prayer. He raised his head a bare inch. Later, she would remember his eyes with an imagined film of dust, as though he had already been dead for some time – for years and years. It would have been a kindness to put a bullet in his skull – an act of mercy.

Resurrection time.

In the absence of kindness and mercy, she planned to rebuild him as her only witness to the murder of Natalie Homer. 'I know it was a cop who killed your mother. And you're going to help me nail that bastard. It's revenge you want, and I can get that for you.'

No, that was not what he wanted, *never* what he wanted. Mallory could see her error now, a very bad mistake.

Natalie's son was waiting for his bullet, staring at the revolver with a great hunger. He had foreseen this moment long ago as a little boy in the heat of August, waiting so patiently to be punished. And he had laid this out so clearly in the mad restaging of a crime that he believed was his alone. Three hangings, one endless shriek, *Catch me! Kill me!* He had even warned his victims and sent them into the arms of the police as his messengers, extensions of a scream.

Mallory could see all the way to the bottom of his madness, the rest of the damage done to a small child. 'You thought your father sent you away – because he *blamed* you.'

No response. The scarecrow was shutting down what remained of his mind. Mallory tried to touch him, and he shrank back, a reflex that she understood too well. Her hand froze, suspended in the forbidden act of reaching out. She was always clutching air – touching no one. Yet she tried again, gently grazing his battered face with the tips of her fingers.

A shadow blocked the sun. She heard the sick sound of the bat cracking his skull, breaking it open. There was time to catch him in her arms, and they fell together.

Ronald Deluthe stood over them, listing to one side. The baseball bat dangled from his right hand as he sank to the ground, where he sat bolt upright, legs splayed out, his eyes slowly closing.

The scarecrow's weight was on top of Mallory. His blood was on her face and in her hair. As she lay beneath the corpse, only her eyes were moving, slowly turning to Ronald Deluthe. She watched as his upper body pitched forward and his head hit the dusty tarpaper between his spread legs.

Mallory had lost her weapon. Her gun hand absently stroked the scarecrow's hair, then came away with bits of red bone and flesh. But how could this be? She had yet to tell him how his mother had really died – that there was nothing he could have done to save her.

Charles Butler's Mercedes pulled up in front of the apartment building and double-parked alongside a row of police units and their spinning red lights. An ambulance was at the curb, where two men in hospital whites stood beside an empty gurney.

Riker was the first one out of the car, yelling, 'What happened? Where's the wounded cop?'

'It's my fault!' An unnerved civilian rushed up to him, arms waving, as if this might help to gather his thoughts. 'I'm sorry. I thought he was unconscious. I just took my eyes off the poor man for a minute. My wife was feeling a bit queasy, and I thought she was going to faint. You see, she saw the body in the closet. And when I looked back – well, the man was gone.'

Riker barreled through the shed door, gun drawn, eyes going everywhere. He saw the little redheaded man rolling in wet sheets and moaning. On the neighboring roof, a confused old woman was staring up at the sky where her lost birds had gone.

He found Deluthe beside the shed, slumped over and holding a baseball bat in a one-handed death grip. Mallory lay a few feet away – underneath a corpse.

More sirens were coming, and she listened to them, as if from a great distance of miles and miles. The scarecrow's flesh was deceptively warm, and so was his blood. It dripped from the broken skull to soak her and stain her.

Riker rolled the heavy weight off her body and met with some resistance, for Mallory's hands were pressed to the dead man's face — still trying to make human contact.

TWENTY-TWO

Civilian conversations blended with the static of radio calls from police units, and yellow tape cordoned off the sidewalk in front of the apartment building. An ambulance and a meat wagon were parked at the curb, side by side, doors hanging open, awaiting the living and the dead. The man from the medical examiner's office zipped up the body bag on his gurney. A cigarette dangled from his mouth as he accepted a light from the homicide detective. 'Dr Slope's standing by to crack the old man open. So what's the story on the other corpse?'

'There's only *one* dead body,' Riker corrected him. 'This one.' He looked down at the remains of George Neederland, the missing department-store watchman.

The ME's man looked up to the sky and a departing police helicopter. 'Your guys just took another body off the roof. What's the—'

'Repeat after me, pal. There's only one dead body at this crime scene.' Riker turned to see another reporter approaching the police barricade. Nearby, a news van was unloading pole lights and camera equipment. He turned back to face down the meat-wagon man. '*One* body. If the press hears a different story, Dr Slope's gonna fire your ass. I'll make *sure* he does.'

In a less threatening mode, Riker turned to thank Alice White for the wet washcloth she pressed into his hand. He grabbed Mallory by the arm and forced her to stand still while he cleaned the red smears from her face. Then he stepped back to appraise the rest of her stains.

'Damn, you look worse than Deluthe. You're sure none of that blood belongs to you?'

Mallory turned away from him and walked toward a crime-scene technician, calling out, 'You! Stop!'

Riker strolled back to the ambulance crew. 'You're right, guys. No wounds on Mallory.' He turned to watch his partner issuing orders and signing the evidence bags for her crime scene, unaware that her bloody clothes and hair were making the civilian onlookers sick.

A paramedic hovering over Deluthe said, 'He's coming around again.'

There was no need to shield the youngster from the reporters and their cameras. His own mother would not recognize that swollen band-aged face. More bandages covered his scalp. He was being stabilized with injections and portable machines to keep him out of the danger zone of deep shock.

Riker waited until Deluthe's eyes flickered open, then continued the lecture where he had left off ten minutes ago. 'When you found Natalie's address in the watchman's file, you should've come to me. *Never* go after a perp without back-up. And that *door*. That was a major screwup, kid. When you saw the open door, you should've known the scarecrow was still in the building.'

The young cop was coughing. It was a fight to get the words out. 'Is this your way of telling me I'm fired?' The lame smile made his lip bleed again.

'Naw,' said Riker. 'I wouldn't waste time teaching you how to stay alive – not if you were on the way out.'

The medic unhooked the monitor. 'Okay, he's stable.'

'Give us a minute,' said Riker. When the two paramedics had walked around to the other side of the ambulance, he said, 'One more thing, kid. We're promoting you to a stone killer – just for a little while.' He pointed at the uniformed officers seated inside the ambulance, both men he trusted. 'Waller's got your ID and your badge. He'll field all the questions at the hospital. Just keep your mouth shut.' He turned around to look at his partner in her bloodstains. 'Oh, and Mallory's taking the credit for beating the crap out of you. But we'll clear that up tomorrow, okay?'

Before the ambulance doors had closed on the baffled Deluthe, Charles Butler joined Riker on the sidewalk. 'Shouldn't Mallory see a doctor?'

'Right,' said the detective. '*You* talk to her.'

'There's something – not quite right with her.'

'Oh, yeah?' Riker turned to watch her moving about the scene like an automaton. 'How can you tell?'

Charles certainly caught the sarcasm, but he was selectively deaf to detrimental remarks about Mallory. 'Under normal circumstances, she's compulsively neat. She'd never tolerate a smudge on one of her running shoes. Look at her now. She doesn't even see the blood on her clothes and her—'

'Yeah, she's not quite the little fanatic today.' Riker smiled. 'But that's a good thing, isn't it? Progress?'

Charles sighed. He pointed to the rectangular bulge in Riker's pocket. 'Are you ever going to give her that book?'

'I will – when the time is right.'

Mallory was walking toward them. Charles made himself scarce before she could order him behind the crime-scene tape again.

Riker grinned, so happy to see her alive and walking around in any condition. 'You missed your chance to tell Deluthe how bad he screwed up today. I filled in for you.'

'Did you tell him he killed an unarmed man – the *only* witness to Natalie Homer's murder?'

'No, kid, I saved that part for you. Wait'll he gets out of the hospital. He won't be expecting an ambush.' This was a joke, but she seemed to be considering it. 'So, Mallory, I hear you reamed out Geldorf.'

'He had it coming,' she said.

'Sure. That's why you told him the scarecrow was a cop. You'd need a pretty good reason to give up a detail like that. You figured the old man was on the perp's kill list, right? So you warned him. That was your twisted good deed for the day.'

He could see that she was not about to admit any such human frailty. Maybe it was all wishful thinking on his part, a fantasy of what he wanted her to be. He looked up at the clouds that threatened rain. 'Not very satisfying this time, is it, Mallory?'

No, he guessed not.

She raised her face to his, and he saw his Kathy, only ten, all played out at the end of a bad day, and he wanted to kill somebody to make her world right again. His hate was growing, going out to the man who murdered Natalie Homer. That worthless bastard had done so much damage. Twenty years later, the dead could not be officially tallied until Sparrow was taken off life support. And then there was Mallory, altered in ways that worried him.

Riker reached into his pocket and pulled out a brown paper bag containing a book. 'Here, a consolation prize.' He handed her the final installment in the saga of Sheriff Peety and the Wichita Kid. 'You might like the inscription.'

He had marked the page with a matchbook so she would find the brief message from her biggest fan, a love letter written before Louis Markowitz and Kathy had been properly introduced.

Riker walked away as she opened her present. He was heading for Mallory's car, planning to sabotage it so she could not drive home by herself. Also, she would not forgive him if he saw her cry, and he did not want that additional burden. He was still paying for all his old crimes against the child she used to be.

'Riker!' she called after him. 'We're not done yet!'

So much for his grand idea that she could be moved to tears. Perhaps his fantasy life was getting out of hand.

The decor of the Manhattan condo was expensive and spartan, though the living room had the smell of Brooklyn ghosts, Louis and Helen Markowitz. Their old house had reeked of the same canned-pine-tree air freshener. Riker supposed this was Mallory's idea of memento, for the room was bereft of family photographs or keepsakes. She must believe there was nothing here to give away any clue to her personality. Untrue. The white carpet had a low tolerance for dirt; chrome and glass gleamed from the toil of a cleaning fanatic; the dark leather chairs and the couch had severe right angles and hard straight lines. It was all black and white – no compromises – all Mallory.

And so it was easy to spot the small item that did not belong here. Evidently, he had not been the only one to rob a crime scene, and Mallory had been careless with her stolen goods. He knelt down on the rug and reached under the glass cocktail table to retrieve a delicate ivory comb. It was memorable for the elaborate carving and the look of money. Sparrow had worn it in her hair each time they met. And he had always been curious about this precious comb, this favorite possession of a junkie that should have been sold for a drug buy long ago. When Sparrow finally died, would the comb become Mallory's keepsake or her trophy?

He turned to see his partner enter the room, towel-drying her hair as she walked toward him in a long white robe. Mallory was resilient, and she cleaned up well.

Riker folded a cell phone into his pocket. 'Dr Slope cracked the nightwatchman's chest. The old guy's been dead about two weeks. Natural causes. You figure the scarecrow planned his last murder that far in advance?'

'No. He made friends with the old man years ago. He wanted to spend time in the building where his mother died. That place was his idea of home.' She accepted a glass of bourbon and soda from his hand.

Riker had been surprised to find the makings in her kitchen cabinet, and he wondered if she drank alone. Of course she did. She would never drink in public and risk losing control in front of witnesses. 'So that's what triggered the hangings? The watchman's death?'

'We'll never know – thanks to Deluthe.' Mallory stared at the pocket that hid his cell phone. 'What did you hear from the hospital?'

'If you mean Deluthe, he'll live. Just busted up is all.' Riker watched her finish the medicinal whiskey and soda. 'He's got a broken nose, a hairline skull fracture and a dislocated shoulder. Oh, and he's gonna have a wicked scar on his face, lots of stitches. But the doctor says he doesn't seem to mind that. In fact, he seems real happy about it.' He picked up the remote control for the television set. 'But if you mean Sparrow – the doctor says she'll be gone before morning.' He could not tell if this made any impression on Mallory. At least she did not smile.

'And now for the good news.' Riker switched on the television and killed the sound of the broadcast, preferring to give his own narrative. 'We got a very confused press corps with an inaccurate body count. They think the scarecrow's still alive, but badly wounded.' He pointed to the image of a teenage witness being attacked by microphones. 'That's all the girl could tell them.'

Mallory nodded. 'She was only on the roof for a few minutes.'

And the young girl was still shaking on camera as Riker leaned closer to the set. 'Here, watch this – her father's gonna deck a reporter.' The punch was thrown. 'Good job.' And now the picture changed to three small boys all talking at once. 'Oh, but these kids – they were great!'

'They didn't see *anything*,' said Mallory. 'Their mother took them off the roof before they could—'

'Yeah, but in *their* version, you shot the poor bastard's legs off. Then you pistol-whipped him and shot him some more. But they knew he was still alive 'cause they saw him try to crawl away from you. Bless their lying little hearts.'

'I need something to rattle a suspect.' Mallory stood before the rear wall of the incident room, pinning another array of photographs to the cork surface. 'We have to wrap Natalie's murder tonight.'

Understandable. Come the morning, every fact of the scarecrow's death would be public knowledge. 'All right,' said Charles. 'There were *two* stalkers. Only Natalie's killer would know that.'

She said nothing aloud, but he knew that smirk so well. *Yeah, right.*

'It's a matter of style,' he said, undaunted. 'The first stalker was the ex-husband. I'm sure Lars was right about that. So perhaps he could be forgiven for—'

No. One look at Mallory and he knew that forgiveness was never coming from that quarter. Charles unpinned one of the stalker notes and held up the aged yellow paper. 'Erik Homer was a wife beater, short on patience. I don't see him spending hours tracing individual letters of magazine script – just to make this beautiful for Natalie. Rather artistic, isn't it?' He read the words to her, ' "I touched you today." More like poetry than a threat. Not Erik Homer's style. When he met his second wife, the stalking ended, and Natalie had no more use for the police. That explains the two-week gap in her complaints. It was the second stalker who left her these notes, who loved her – and killed her.'

'All right, I'll buy that.' Mallory stepped back from the wall to give him a clear view of her rogues' gallery, five men as they had appeared twenty years ago. Lars Geldorf's portrait came from a newspaper archive. Head shots of two other detectives and one patrolman were made from Mallory's computer enhancements of the crime-scene Polaroids. And another patrolman's picture was taken from a personnel file. 'Next problem,' she said. 'We know the perp was a cop, but which one?'

'How can you be sure it was one of these men?'

'Because one of the uniforms called in the hanging as a suicide – and *three* detectives showed up.'

Apparently Mallory was picking up cryptic bad habits from Riker.

'Just guessing,' said Charles. 'You don't usually send so many detectives out for a suicide call?' What was he missing here? He stared at the pictures of the men in suits. 'So you've narrowed it down to these three because they all signed off on Natalie's stalker complaints? Is that it?'

'No.'

Of course not. Miles too easy.

'You're right about one thing.' Mallory pinned up a portrait of Natalie Homer smiling for her photographer. 'He loved her. He was obsessed with her. She was the prettiest thing he ever set eyes on.'

And you are beautiful. Had he ever told her that? No, never.

'But he was nothing special,' said Mallory.

Far from special, far from beauty.

'Not in her class,' said Mallory. 'All he could do was watch her and follow her. He probably figured she'd laugh if she knew how often he thought about her – about the two of them – together. She was unapproachable, unattainable.'

As far away as the moon. You would never—

'He was my best suspect.' Mallory tapped Lars Geldorf's photograph. 'The old man has an attachment to Natalie that just won't die. He was on the top of my list.'

'*Was,*' said Charles. 'And now?'

'When Natalie's son looked through that bathroom door, if he'd seen a detective in street clothes, he wouldn't have known the hangman was a cop.'

Though relieved that Lars was no longer in her sights, Charles's good logic held sway. 'You're not forgetting that Junior saw that man a second time – two days later outside the crime scene. The boy had to know that all the men in that room were police.'

'Three detectives turned out for a suicide call,' said Mallory. 'And it wasn't the address that got their attention. One of the uniforms gave the victim's name. No patrol cop was ever dispatched to Natalie's apartment while she was alive. I checked. She always made her complaints at the station. You read Deluthe's interview with Alan Parris. The uniforms were in that room for two seconds before they shut the door and called in the report. They saw a scalped corpse on a rope. It was bloated with gas and maggots, face wrecked beyond recognition.'

'But they knew it was Natalie,' said Charles. 'They knew that was her apartment.'

'One of them did.' She tapped the photographs of the uniformed officers. 'Can you tell Loman from Parris?'

'That's easy,' said Charles, though he knew neither man on sight. 'Loman is the only one in the crime-scene photos. Parris wouldn't go back inside that room. Oh, I see. They *are* rather alike.' Even Lars Geldorf had confused one for the other. Both in their early twenties, the patrolmen had the same regular features, dark hair and eyes beneath the brims of their caps. 'When the boy was in the hall with Alice White, that second encounter should have reinforced his identification. But he saw two men in uniform.'

'It's the uniform he remembered best,' said Mallory. 'If the boy couldn't tell them apart, how do we—'

'I suggest you flip a coin,' said Charles, for logic could not take him everywhere.

Riker leaned toward the window by his desk in the squad room. News vans on the street below were double-parked at the curb. A few men with microphones assaulted the police entourage surrounding and concealing the wounded detective, whose head was covered by a white helmet of bandages. The rest of the reporters were looking up at the second-story windows, mouths open like dogs waiting to be fed. 'Nothing like a good hungry mob to jack up the fear.'

When Officer Waller and his partner came through the door, they were supporting Ronald Deluthe on both sides. Nursemaids could not have been more tender than these large men slowly walking him across the squad room and watching his face with grave concern. The dividing wall between detectives and uniforms came down when one of New York's Finest was wounded in the line of duty.

An angry rope burn circled Deluthe's neck, exposed stitches ran down one cheek like a dueling scar, and the dislocated shoulder was covered with a sling supporting his left arm. Riker saw the dead-white face as a sure sign that the boy had not taken any recent medication to block the pain.

Had that been Mallory's idea?

The wounded man's honor guard was dismissed. Riker did not want the uniforms to see what would happen next. When the stairwell door had closed behind the departing officers, Mallory unclipped a pair of handcuffs from her belt and manacled Deluthe's good hand to the one that dangled from the sling.

TWENTY-THREE

Jack Coffey sat at the table beside the lockup cage. He had used a pencil to jam the sash of the only window, and now the small room was hot and airless as he entertained the East Side lieutenant with a story about the three Stellas' reunion. 'So this theatrical agent – real scary, like a nun gone psycho – she's got Stella Small an acting job on a soap opera. But the mother and grandmother plan to take the girl home to Ohio.'

'Good idea.' Harvey Loman's feet tapped the floor as his eyes strayed to a clock on the wall. He seemed mildly crazed by this tale that went on and on.

'Well, the poor kid's been through hell,' said Coffey, pleased with the other man's agitation. 'And she's knocked out with sedatives. So the agent leans over the hospital bed and smiles with real sharp little teeth. She says, "Up to you, baby doll. It's a three-year contract with the hottest show on daytime TV." Now the agent acts real concerned. She says, "Oh, sorry, hon. Would you rather be buried alive in Iowa?" Then Stella's mother chimes in, "We live in. *Ohio*." So the agent says, "Yeah, yeah," like there's a difference.'

'Nice little story, Jack.' Loman's political smile was flagging. He took out a handkerchief to mop his brow and bald head. 'Now what the hell am I doing here?'

'We're closing out an old case of yours. Nobody told you? It's the Natalie Homer murder.' Coffey could read surprise in the other man's face, but nothing more.

'That wasn't my case, Jack. I was only a uniform in those days.'

'I know. I invited Parris too. He's on the way over.'

Loman winced with real pain, then mopped his bald head and brow with a handkerchief. 'Alan Parris?'

'Yeah,' said Coffey. 'Your old partner.'

The man you sold out for a shot at the golden shield.

Lieutenant Coffey rocked his chair on two legs, enjoying the moment, for he had always disliked this man. 'So, how come you never mentioned that old hanging? When you dropped off the paperwork—'

'I never made the connection to the hooker's case.'

'Both women were hung by the neck and gagged with their own hair. How many connections did you need?'

'The crimes scenes were nothing alike.' Loman stood up and jangled car keys in his pants pocket. 'I'm not gonna stick around for this, Jack.'

'I'm not giving you a choice, Harvey. You're on my list of material witnesses. So you stay till we wrap it.' Jack Coffey was smiling as he rose from his chair, daring the man to push his luck in this precinct.

Still smiling, the commander of Special Crimes Unit stepped into the hall and locked the door behind him.

The squad room was quiet and dim. All but one of the overhead fluorescents had been killed, and only a few independent lamps were left on, though all the desks were empty. The only bright light was focused on Mallory and the rookie detective. Ronald Deluthe wore a bloody T-shirt. His jeans and baseball cap, ripped from the wall of the incident room, were free of stains.

Riker stood by the window and watched the crowded sidewalk below. He saw Charles Butler's head above the crowd of normal-size human beings and that other species, the reporters.

Mallory was still instructing her star performer. 'Keep your face down.'

Well, that should be easy enough. Riker doubted that the boy would have the strength to lift his head. 'We should send you back to the hospital, kid.'

'He wants to do this,' said Mallory, speaking for Deluthe. 'So he stays.'

Riker was about to make another comment but let it slide for Deluthe's sake. In the aftermath of killing the scarecrow, this was almost therapy, though that was not Mallory's motive. She only wanted an authentically battered doppelganger.

'One problem,' said Riker. 'Even if they don't see his face, they'll recognize the hair. You can see that bleach job through solid walls.'

'I know.' Mallory resolved the problem with a mascara wand. After a few deft strokes, the fringe of hair beneath the bandages was turned to brown. 'Deluthe, you've got everybody's attention now.' She leaned down to his eye level. 'So no more *bleaching*.' And that was a direct order. 'You're not invisible anymore.'

Riker was startled. Empathy was not his partner's forte. She should have been the last one to work out the puzzle of Deluthe's bright yellow hair.

'I don't want to see any emotion at all,' she said. 'We're clear on that?'

'Yes,' said Deluthe.

Mallory dabbed at his bleeding lip with a tissue, perhaps perceiving fresh blood as a sign of overacting. 'When Janos brings you back to the squad room, I'll ask a few questions. Don't speak. Just nod.'

'Yes, ma'am.'

'A lot hangs on that nod.' Jack Coffey crossed the squad room to join them. 'We got nothin' else, kid. No physical evidence.'

They could not even justify an arrest warrant. And since there was no need to mention that Deluthe had dispatched their only eyewitness with a baseball bat, the lieutenant led him down the hall in silence.

'So you got your perp.' Geldorfs voice came from the stairwell door, where he stood with Charles Butler. 'Nice work!'

'Hey, Lars.' Riker returned the old man's broad smile. 'You know all your lines?'

338

'Oh, yeah. Charles briefed me. Don't worry about—'

Mallory made a motion to silence Geldorf as the stairwell door opened again, and Alan Parris was escorted into the room by Detective Wang. Riker studied the suspect with the eye of a fellow alcoholic. The ex-cop showed no signs of a recent binge, but fear could sober a man. At least Parris did not reek of booze. His new suit was another sign of fear, disguising him as a respectable taxpayer instead of an unemployed drunk.

'Mr Parris?' Mallory pointed to the door on the far side of the room. 'Could you wait in there? Thanks.'

Geldorf watched the man enter Coffey's office and take a chair near the glass partition. 'He's gonna be way too comfortable in there. You need a closed room, no windows, no air.' The old man was reborn, and all the annoying cockiness was back as he turned to lecture Mallory. 'You want complete control over him. You decide when he takes a piss, when he eats – *if* he eats.'

'It's not your call,' she said, reminding the old man that he was visiting Special Crimes Unit on a provisional passport. 'Parris thinks he's here for a friendly little chat.'

'No, he doesn't,' said Janos walking toward them. 'When he saw Geldorf, he panicked. Now he wants a lawyer. So we gotta kill an hour till—'

'The hell we do.' Riker strode across the room, entered the office and shouted, 'What's all this crap about a lawyer!'

Parris's voice was surly. 'You plan to crucify me for these hangings, right?'

'You don't watch TV? You don't listen to the radio? We nailed our perp this afternoon, okay? Now I read your statement, and I got some questions on Natalie Homer.'

'I wasn't—' Parris turned to the door as two more people stepped into the office. Mallory sat down behind Coffey's desk, then glared at Lars Geldorf, warning him to keep silent and wait for his cue.

'Parris,' said Riker. 'You were saying?'

'I wasn't the one who took Natalie's complaints. I was a uniform, not a dick.'

'But you *knew* her.' Geldorf stood behind Parris's chair and placed one gnarly hand on the man's shoulder. 'You saw her every day on patrol.'

Parris shook off the man's hand. 'She never even looked my way.'

'That bothered you, didn't it?' Geldorf leaned down to Parris's ear. 'She was so pretty. And here you got this gun, all this power, but she don't even know you're alive.'

'Back off,' said Mallory. Now everyone in the room, including Alan Parris, was united by a common enemy – Lars Geldorf.

The old man pretended to ignore her and reached into his breast pocket. He pulled out a Polaroid of Natalie Homer, a close-up of a dead woman with mutilated hair and flesh. 'Not so pretty now, is she? Not so high and mighty anymore.'

Mallory leaned over and snatched the photograph. 'I said that's *enough*.' Some of her anger was genuine. She disapproved of ad-lib remarks and unauthorized props.

'I want a lawyer,' said Parris.

'I don't blame you,' said Riker. 'This is bullshit. But you haven't been charged with a crime.' He turned on Geldorf. 'Not one more word.' This small gesture had endeared him to the smiling Alan Parris.

'Mr Parris – *Alan*,' said Mallory. 'You were a cop. You know how hard this job can be. So what can you tell me about her? Anything that might—'

'Nothing. Every time she came into the station, there was a crowd of dicks around her. They talked to her for hours. For all the good that did her.'

'You felt sorry for her.' Riker nodded his understanding, his commiseration. They were brothers now.

'Damn straight. She deserved better.'

'Tell me about the extra patrols in that neighborhood,' said Mallory.

'You checked in on her, right? Maybe you stopped by her place to—'

'Why *should* I? The detectives never asked me to.' Parris turned to Geldorf. 'You bastards liked her well enough, but you never *believed* her.' He turned back to Mallory. 'They only saw Natalie when she was really scared. I guess they figured that was just normal for her.'

'But you knew better,' said Riker. 'You saw her every day. You knew what she was going through.' She was always Natalie to Alan Parris, a first-name acquaintance and not a woman who had never given him the time of day.

Jack Coffey had left the door to the lockup room wide. And now Lieutenant Loman watched the back of a prisoner being marched down the hall. Mallory was right. No one else could have been as convincing as this young cop in bloodstains, chains on his wrists, chains on his ankles, faltering steps and now a stumble. Janos's massive arms reached out to catch Deluthe before he could fall.

'The leg irons are overkill,' said Harvey Loman.

Coffey stared at the sweat shining on the back of Deluthe's neck. The mascara hair treatment was running in a brown streak that mingled with the T-shirt's bloodstains. Then he realized that the game was not over when Loman went on to say, 'I can't see that pathetic bastard outrunning Janos.'

'Yeah, well, the DA's coming,' said Coffey. 'So we're going by the book, leg irons and all. We're cutting a deal with the perp.'

'Yeah? What's he offering?'

'A photo ID on the man who killed Natalie Homer.' Lieutenant Coffey rose from the table and slammed the door. 'So you remember that crime scene pretty well.'

'Like I could forget. That room was hell on earth. The stink and the bugs. But it was a different kind of freak show for the hooker.'

'Sparrow.'

'Yeah, all those candles, a different noose. And she wasn't even dead. I still don't see the connection, Jack.'

'It's the scarecrow – Natalie's son. I think you met him once, Harvey.'

Charles Butler entered the office and stood behind Mallory's chair. Since he had been given no further instructions, all he could do was loom over the proceedings, bringing his own discomfort to the party. And now they were five – too many people and just the right number, each one jumping up the energy level, the heat and the stress.

Mallory stared at the window on the squad room. 'He's coming.'

Five pairs of eyes watched Janos escort his prisoner to the desk beneath the only overhead light. From the distance of the lieutenant's office, only the chains, the bandages and blood were visible. The battered face was shadowed by a baseball cap. Mallory glanced back at Charles, whose face could not hide a thought. He was merely curious. He had no idea that the injured man was Deluthe.

She leaned toward Alan Parris, talking cop to cop, 'I've got one break on this case, a witness. You met him once.'

'Yeah,' said Riker. 'You chased him away from Natalie's door. Remember? He was only six years old.'

'One of those little kids in the hall?'

Riker turned to the glass wall and pointed at the wounded man being guarded by Janos. 'He was Natalie's son.'

'Oh, Christ!' Parris turned around for a better look at the man in handcuffs. 'That's your perp?' From this angle, he could only see the curve of Deluthe's cheek. 'So the kid went nuts.'

Mallory nodded to say, *Yes, it's all very sad. Yeah, right.* 'Natalie's sister hid the boy out of state. You can guess why.'

Parris shook his head as he stared through the glass wall, eyes fixed on the young man in manacles. 'Her son hanged those women. I can't believe it. *Bloody Christ.*'

Detective Wang entered the office and tossed a manila envelope on the desk. Riker picked it up and inspected the contents, pictures of three detectives and two uniformed officers as they had appeared twenty years ago. He laid them out on the desk blotter.

Predictably, Parris focused on the portrait of his own young self fresh from the Police Academy. He was about to say something when Mallory cut him off, saying, 'This won't take long.' She picked up the photographs and rose from her chair.

'Oh, yeah,' said Lieutenant Loman. 'I remember the little kids in the hall – one of them anyway.' He was staring at the evidence bags that contained a twenty-year-old film carton and a set of notes written to Natalie Homer. 'You know *why* I remember him, Jack? This tiny little boy – he reached inside the door of Natalie's apartment and picked up an empty film carton. He wanted a damn souvenir of that poor woman's murder. Cold, huh? I wish I could forget that kid.'

Mallory stood before the injured detective, looking down on his swollen face. When she spoke to Deluthe, her voice was loud enough to carry across the squad room. 'Take your time. This is what they looked like the year your mother died.'

Deluthe kept his head down and stared at the photographs as she held them up, one by one, angling them away from the glass wall of Jack Coffey's office. And now she fed Deluthe his cue, the first question, '*This* one?'

The young cop nodded.

'Are you sure?'

Deluthe nodded again.

In a departure from the script, Mallory bent down to him and lowered her voice. 'Don't talk, don't move. We've got some time to kill before I go back in there. I know you can't get that dead man out of your mind. You never will. He's part of you now – and what you did to him.' She nodded toward the large man beside him. 'Detective Janos volunteered to look after you for a while.'

343

Deluthe stared at her with fresh damage in his eyes. 'You think I'm a nutcase?'

Mallory nodded. 'We *all* go crazy.'

'Crazy is a place,' said Janos. 'You go, you come back.'

'Happens so often, we even have a protocol for it – the suicide watch.' She held up the photograph again. 'Now tap this picture and we're done.'

He stretched out his handcuff chain to do it.

Mallory counted to ten slowly. 'Nod one more time.'

He did as she asked, then lowered his head, eyes fixed on the floor, a genuine portrait of remorse.

'Good job.' She prized realism.

Deluthe slumped over, fists clenched, eyes shut tight. The anesthetic benefit of shock was wearing off. She turned to Janos. 'Get him back to the hospital.'

Mallory made a show of looking at one photograph on the long walk back to Coffey's office. Arthur Wang blocked her way, handing her the evidence bags with the notes and the original film carton with the Polaroid logo. 'The boss is done with these.'

Detective Wang opened the door to the lock-up room and handed Lieutenant Coffey a duplicate set of photographs. Mallory had only given him one line to say: 'It's the one on top.'

Jack Coffey stared at the picture for a moment, then laid it down on the table in front of Loman. 'The scarecrow picked you.'

'He picked you.' Mallory pushed Lars Geldorf's photograph across the desk, then turned to Alan Parris, saying, 'You can go now.'

The ex-cop quickly left the office, and Geldorf sank down in the vacated chair. He clutched the portrait of himself at age fifty-five and shook his head. 'This is crazy. *Crazy*.' There was a flicker of panic in his face when he looked past Mallory, raising his eyes to stare at the tall man standing behind her chair.

No need to turn around.

With only the eyes in the back of her head, she pictured Charles's wonderful tell-all face stricken with surprise – the real thing. No actor could portray shock and betrayal so well as an honest man with her knife in his back.

Welcome to my job.

She watched Lars Geldorf's face and saw the reflected sorrow of Charles Butler, who had finally understood his role tonight. He had been gulled into preparing this old man, his *friend*, for the close, the kill. And now he joined the list of the wounded as he walked toward the office door, eager to put some distance between himself and his assailant – Mallory.

Ah, but she was not quite done with him yet. 'Charles?'

He stopped. She knew he would. There was a bruised and battered look about him when he turned to face her. Was he wondering how far ahead she had planned for this moment?

'I'm sorry. I wanted it to be Parris or Loman,' said the queen of all liars, and only Lars Geldorf believed her. The door closed on Charles Butler, and the old man's sole source of comfort was gone.

The room was colder now.

'I never set eyes on Natalie's son,' said Geldorf.

'That's probably what kept him alive,' said Mallory.

The old man turned to Riker. 'Help me out here. I'm telling you, I never—'

'Lars – don't,' said Riker, deadpan. 'It's over. Why would the kid lie?'

'My apologies.' Mallory smiled. 'I thought you botched this case because you were such a lousy detective. In fact, you were the one who fed me that line.' She picked up the small square Polaroids of the old crime scene, then dealt them out across the desk like playing cards. 'I know why Parris isn't in these shots. He was only in that room for two seconds. And you?' She stacked the photographs into a neat deck. 'You're not in them because you took all the pictures that night.'

'I could've told you that!' said Geldorf.

She held up the empty film carton. 'This always bothered me. The scarecrow left one at every hanging. It had nothing to do with Natalie's murder — only her crime scene. This one's twenty years old. The boy found it in the hall while you were shooting pictures of his dead mother.' She dropped the film box on the desk. 'A little something to remember you by.'

'And now it makes sense,' said Riker. 'The kid's family always knew a cop killed his mother. We wondered how a six-year-old would recognize a cop in street clothes. We thought that narrowed it down to Parris or Loman — the uniforms.'

'The scarecrow set us straight,' said Mallory, lying as easily as she drew breath. 'When he watched you shoot those pictures of his mother, he knew you were police. And that was his *second* look at you.'

Geldorf sat back in his chair and grinned. 'You guys are good, but you can't scam the master. I invented this little game you're playing. You got *nothin'*.' He stood up and buttoned his jacket. 'Try this on some other sucker.'

'Not so fast, Lars.' The man was stunned when Riker put both hands on his shoulders and forced him back into the chair. 'We haven't booked you yet. The charge is murder.'

And that charge hung on a pack of lies told by a fly on the wall.

'All those sausages,' said Mallory. 'Too many for one person, remember? Natalie was making dinner for her son. The boy was in the bathroom while you were killing his mother. We always figured the perp was someone she knew.'

'Her ex-husband!' Geldorf shouted this in the tone of, *Are you blind?*

'No,' said Riker. 'He was Natalie's *first* stalker. Then he met his new wife and the harassment stopped. You were the one who left the notes under her door. You scared her right back to the stationhouse — back to you. What a joke. You and that beautiful girl. Even twenty years ago, you were twice her age.'

'You didn't expect Natalie to be home that night,' said Mallory.

'She was always at work when you stopped by with your *love letters*. She caught you leaving that last one under her door. That's why the boy didn't hear any conversation before you killed his mother. How could you explain a thing like that?'

Riker was on his way through the door, saying, 'I'll tell the boss it's a wrap.'

And Mallory continued, 'He said his mother reached for the frying pan and dropped it. Then she tripped and fell. That's when she hit her head on the stove. She was out cold, but you thought she was shamming. You pulled her through a puddle of grease, and then you rolled her on her back.'

Were Geldorf's eyes a little wider? Yes.

'She was coming to,' said Mallory. 'Were you afraid she'd scream? Is that why you wrapped your hands around her throat and crushed the life out of her?'

Jack Coffey was standing in the doorway. 'Is that when you panicked, old man?' He walked into the room and tossed a pad of paper to Mallory. 'That's Loman's statement.'

Geldorf craned his neck to read the upside-down lines of longhand on the top sheet. 'Loman? The other—'

'Alan Parris's ex-partner.' Riker strolled into the room, smiling. 'He rolled over on you, Lars. He claims you tried to bury this case, concealing evidence and—'

'I was *protecting* my evidence!'

'Well, it's your word against his.' Mallory looked up from her reading. 'And he's a lieutenant.' Though Loman's statement was worthless, only repeating Geldorf s own story of misleading reporters, she said, 'And that's it. We're done.'

Coffey cleared the evidence from the desk, sweeping it into the carton, packing up the debris of the day. The lieutenant paused to hand her a slip of paper. 'I don't recognize this witness.'

'That's the landlady's granddaughter, Alice White. She saw a man steal the rope and duct tape out of the handyman's tool chest.' Another

347

lie, another nail. 'She's on the way in for a photo ID.' Mallory picked up the photograph of Geldorf and casually dropped it into the box. 'She'll testify that Natalie's son was in that apartment for two days. Just his dead mother for company – and the flies, the roaches. No wonder that little boy went psycho.' In an echo of Susan Qualen, she said, 'Who do you call when a cop kills your mother? The cops?' She turned to Geldorf. 'He told us the buzz of the flies was deafening, but he was only six years old. I guess the noise got louder as he got older.'

'You have the right to remain silent,' said Riker, pulling out his Miranda card, preparing for the last formality that would allow their suspect to call for a lawyer.

They were cutting the timing very fine.

Mallory snatched the card away from her partner and handed it to Geldorf. 'Look, it's been a long night. You know all the words. Just sign the damn thing, okay?' She held out the pen, and Geldorf accepted it like thousands of felons before him. So natural to take an object when it's offered. But now he only stared at the card.

Planning to lawyer up, old man?

In a preemptive strike, she slapped the desk. 'Sign the card! Bring on the lawyers!'

They were coming to the closing shots – almost done, for Geldorf must realize that no deal was in the offering, and this was the sign of a case with abundant evidence. He began to shrink, shoulders slumping, hunching. His hands were rising, as if to beg. 'I loved that woman. I *grieved* for her. Natalie was—' He had lost his train of thought, his reason; he had lost everything. The old man bowed his head, and Mallory strained to catch the mumbled words, 'I was a good cop once. That's worth – something.'

She stared at him, incredulous. 'You were expecting a *deal?*'

'I don't care if he was a cop.' Jack Coffey lifted the carton and feigned impatience. 'We're not gonna offer him any—'

'It's *my* case.' Mallory turned to Geldorf. 'I know what you're thinking, old man. All that embarrassment to the department. And saving the city the cost of a trial – that should be worth something, too, right?'

Geldorf nodded.

Jack Coffey dumped the carton on the floor, saying, 'Keep it simple, Mallory. I'm not giving him the moon.'

She leaned forward, eyes trained on Geldorf. 'This is the best deal – the *only* deal you get. The state won't request the death penalty. No cameras, no media circus, and the real story never leaves this room. If you waive a trial, we can probably get the DA to push your arraignment through night court – quietly.' In fact, the arrangements had already been approved. Sentencing would follow in the morning. 'All the standard perks for an ex-cop, and you'll do fifteen years in prison.' A life sentence for a man of seventy-five.

She pushed a yellow pad across the desk. 'Make up any version you like. Call it a crime of passion. Say you once loved a woman to death. You've got six seconds, old man. Take it or leave it.'

'Time's up!' Jack Coffey's fist came down on the desk, and Geldorf jumped. 'Now we book him. *Right now!*'

Lars Geldorf picked up the pad of paper, and his hand trembled as he began to write out his confession.

Mallory followed her partner across the squad room, not willing to let him out of her sight, not yet. He was one of few people who mattered to her, but that did not mean she trusted him. Riker sat down at his desk far from the pool of fluorescent light. The ember of his cigarette glowed in the dark as he dropped his match in a dish of paperclips.

'How's Sparrow?' This was a test. According to her paid informant, a nurse, Riker called for updates every hour.

'It's almost over,' he said, just a matter of hours.'

Mallory bit back a comment that he would not like, and they sat in uneasy silence for a while, watching his smoke twist and curl. 'You wanted Sparrow's case so bad,' she said. 'Just keeping faith with a snitch? Or maybe you thought Frankie Delight's murder would come back to bite you.' She wanted it to be one of these two things, something cold, less personal.

Riker shrugged. 'There was more to it, but that's between me and Sparrow.' He rose from the chair and stubbed out his cigarette. 'I'm heading back to the hospital. I wanna be there when—'

'No you don't,' said Mallory. 'I *know* she's out of the coma. You weren't planning to tell me that, were you?' Mallory stared at him until he met her eyes. 'It's *my* turn at Sparrow.'

What a kick in the head, huh, Riker?

After all he had gone through on that whore's account, now he must stand back, virtually handing a helpless woman over to her worst enemy. And yet he could not raise a challenge. Her claim on the dying prostitute was so much stronger than his.

He nodded, and their deal was done.

Mallory watched from the window on the street until Riker emerged from the building. Reporters converged on him with cameras and microphones – star treatment. Sergeant Bell came running out the front door to rescue him with a press release of lies, waving the paper as bait. After the mob had deserted Riker for fresh meat, he stepped into the street and let two cabs go by unhailed, for he was a man with nowhere to go from here.

A lamp switched on at the back of the squad room. The chief of Forensics sat in a small patch of light, hands folded, waiting.

Spying, Heller?

The criminalist stared at her across the span of five desks. How much had he overheard? As Mallory strolled toward him, she could see that his eyes were red and sore from lost sleep.

'Warwick's Used Books.' He simply put these words out in the air between them, then solemnly awaited her reaction. Mallory was stunned and feeling threatened. He misunderstood her expression. 'So Warwick *was* a suspect. I *knew* it.'

Mallory settled into a chair beside the desk. Dancing with this man was a tricky business, but she would not admit that she was mystified.

'I can't give up any information on him.' Always best to mix lies in equal parts with the truth. 'The scarecrow wasn't Warwick. Does that help?'

Heller's face lifted and brightened, flesh deepening in the folds of a wide grin. 'Well, I guess you won't need this.' He handed her a sheet of paper. 'Too bad. I called in a lot of favors to get it.'

She scanned the brief synopsis of a psychiatric history: As a child, John Warwick had stood accused of murdering his twin sister. An eyewitness had cleared the boy, but not before the police had spent six hours wrenching a false confession from a terrified eight-year-old grieving for his twin and crying for his mother. Gangs of reporters had stalked the family, increasing the trauma of a guiltless child. And John Warwick had spent the rest of his childhood in a mental institution, clinging to the fictions of cops and newspaper headlines, irretrievably lost in deep pain and unable to believe in his own innocence.

She dropped the bio sheet on the desk, unenlightened and unimpressed. From what she remembered of the bookseller, he was not capable of killing even one of the thousand flies left at each crime scene. This connection of Heller's was so pathetic. Something had clearly gone awry in his good brain. And this foray into Warwick's past was outside the scope of Forensics.

Mallory smiled, for she was always happiest in the attack mode. 'You shouldn't have messed in our business, Heller. If Warwick had been a solid suspect, you could've queered everything.'

'I had to know,' he said. 'That bastard Riker couldn't trust me to keep the book quiet. It should've been recorded on my evidence log.' There was no animosity in Heller's voice — far from it. He was one happy man.

The book.

Mallory was making linkages at the speed of a computer. Her machine logic flickered and faltered, for the paperback western had shown no trace of damage from the fire or the hose. Yet this book must be what Riker had snatched from the watery floor of Sparrow's apartment. And his other gift to her was the innocent deniability of a crime. He had risked everything to hide a dangerous connection between a whore and Markowitz's daughter.

'*Homecoming*,' she said, 'by Jake Swain.'

When Heller nodded, Mallory knew this man had solid proof against Riker, and no machine logic could have guided her to the next conclusion: her partner was Sheriff Peety in a bad suit.

Riker commanded such deep respect that no one could believe him guilty of a corrupt act, not even when guilt was proven beyond doubt. And Heller, of all people, had been unable to believe his own evidence, for how could Riker steal *anything*? The criminalist had denied his own religion of all-holy fact. He had stepped a hundred miles out of character to doggedly hunt down proof of Riker's innocence where none existed. And Heller had actually found something that looked the same, that shined like truth – though it was only faith.

Without another word between them, they left the stationhouse and parted company on the sidewalk. And there the young detective continued her silence as she endured a civilian's tight embrace and oft-repeated thanks. Mallory stepped back and stared at the smiling face of the next and final victim of the man who killed Natalie Homer. Susan Qualen had believed the press reports that her sister's only child was still alive.

And so the damage of a twenty-year-old murder would not end tonight. It would drag on well into the morning hours. Following Lars Geldorf's rushed arraignment and sentencing, Natalie's sister would be quietly told that the police had killed her nephew after all – with a baseball bat.

'So sorry, ma'am,' Jack Coffey would say.

TWENTY-FOUR

When Charles closed his tired eyes, he saw a tiny thief who ran with whores and lived by guile, surviving on animal instinct to get through the night – an altogether admirable child. Louis Markowitz's hero.

'Charles?'

His heavy lids flickered open, and Kathy grew up before his eyes. She was so lovely, and he wanted to tell her that, for how else would she know? The tragedy of Kathy Mallory was some malady that had no name but was akin to an aspect of vampirism. This sad insight had come to him by simple observation. She did not look for herself in mirrors, nor in the reflections of shop windows, never expecting to find herself there. He turned to the antique looking glass above his mantelpiece. Literally a magic mirror once used in a stage act of the last century, it was full of wavy lines and smeared realities.

'Charles!'

'Yes,' he said, without turning round.

'I want you to keep an eye on Riker tonight.' Mallory walked back and forth across his front room, impatient with a cell-phone caller who had put her on hold. 'You'll find him in that cop bar down the street.' She was still in motion as she resumed her phone conversation. Red designs in the weave of the mirrored carpet seemed to track the floor behind her.

Charles stared at the ancient glass, his gigantic nose, her wonderful eyes. He was fascinated by her form elongating and twisting, her legs bending back to form the hocks of a padding cat. Beast and Beauty were trading places. The reversal went far beyond their positions in the backward space of the mirror room, where she continued to walk to and fro. Her human face was gone, distorted and stripped down to the bestial aspect of Mallory in the panther cage, badly wounded by her life, elegant paws bleeding as she paced. *She* bore the scars, *he* felt the pain. How insane—

'Charles?'

The SoHo saloon was crowded with cops and one civilian. Charles Butler had lost his jacket and tie somewhere between one death and another. His white shirt was wrinkled, sleeves rolled back, and his face was showing the wear of long days broken by catnaps.

Riker stared at his own tired image in the mirror behind the bar, then quickly looked away, saying, 'Thanks anyway, but I'm taking a cab tonight. So pull up a glass. I hate to drink alone.' Of course, this was a polite lie, for the detective did his best binge-drinking all by himself.

Charles obliged him and ordered two rounds of Chivas Regal. 'So Sparrow is dying. And you're not going to the hospital?'

'No.' He prayed that Sparrow would be long dead before an old enemy turned up.

Awe, Mallory, what a gift you have for payback.

It made her the ultimate cop. She was the paladin everyone wanted, a perfect instrument of vengeance. In Riker's view, people should be more careful about what they wished for. Absent all humanity, its bias and fragility, the law was a sociopath.

Their drinks had appeared on the bar in front of them, and Charles had been left hanging again, awaiting some explanation for this failure to visit the deathbed of a whore. Riker cut the man off before he could ask one more time. 'So tell me, how did Sheriff Peety outdraw the Wichita Kid?'

'The usual way. The other man drew his gun too late.'

'Impossible,' said Riker. 'Drunk or sober – even with the damn sun in his eyes – that gunslinger was the best man.'

'Yes, if you mean faster. And that day—' Charles's eyes were in soft focus now, and Riker knew he was projecting book pages on his cocktail napkin and quoting verbatim when he said, '"That day, the gunslinger was a young god, walking out of the whirlwind of dust, growing larger, step by step. His birthright was dominion over all other men."' He shuddered, then tipped back his shot glass, as if to kill a bad taste. 'Terrible prose. You're right – Wichita was fast with a gun, but Sheriff Peety was bigger.'

'What?' And now Riker was left to dangle while his barstool companion sipped his drink, taking his sweet time. Charles's expression worried him. It was almost a Mallory smile.

'A hero bigger than life. Your words, Riker. Well, he was Wichita's hero, too – always had been. The boy *loved* the man. So you might wonder – did Wichita deliberately draw too slow? Or did he lose that gunfight in his own mind before he drew his weapon? Perhaps, at the end, he still believed that Sheriff Peety was a great man, the better man. Maybe that's how the sheriff won . . . Or maybe it was a suicide.'

'Thanks, Charles. That might drive me nuts for another fifteen years.'

'Happy to return the favor.'

Riker recognized his own twisted signature in this exchange, and he smiled with the grace of a good loser. 'Okay, you get one free question. Anything you want. Shoot.'

'You said Kathy was posthumously charged with arson and murder.'

'Right.'

'Though she didn't *die*, and she didn't *kill* anybody. But I've still got a corpse and a fire. Does this have anything to do with why Mallory hates Sparrow?'

'Yeah.'

Charles waited for the rest of the explanation. And he waited. Now the two men engaged in a contest to see who could outcreep whom with the most insipid smile.

Riker broke down first. 'Okay, this is the deal. It took me a long time to piece this story together. You can't repeat it to anyone. And when I'm done, you'll wish I never started. Kathy Mallory's death is gonna drive you crazy till the day you die.'

'Word of honor, I'll never tell.'

'Charles, are you sure you understand? When you know the truth, you have to eat it.'

'Agreed.'

'Some of it's guesswork.' Only two people knew the real story. One was a gifted liar, and the other was a dying whore with a scrambled brain. 'Fifteen years ago, Sparrow did a drug deal with a really scurvy character. She was trading stolen VCRs for heroin.'

'The VCRs that Kathy stole?'

'Yeah. So the hookers told you about the great truck robbery? Well, I'm guessing the drug dealer picked the location for the meet, a place with boarded-up windows and no back door. No neighbors either. The buildings on both sides were torn down, and this one was due for a midnight demolition.'

'Pardon?'

'The owner was planning to torch the place for the insurance money. He had accelerants stashed on every floor, kerosene, paint thinner. But that came out later – after the fire.'

'The fire that killed Kathy?'

'That's the one. I figure this dealer—'

'Frankie Delight?'

'Yeah.' Riker wondered what else Charles had pieced together with the help of the Hooker Book Salon. 'Frankie was gonna double-cross Sparrow. So he would've been the first one to draw a knife.'

'The one that made that huge scar in Sparrow's side?'

Riker nodded. 'And she won that fight, but she left her knife behind. I've got a witness who saw it buried in Frankie Delight's dead body. An ambulance picked up Sparrow three blocks away.'

'And Kathy?'

356

'She saw the whole thing. Another whore can place the kid in Sparrow's hospital room the next day – one real tired little girl And that's when Kathy was sent back to the crime scene to get the murder weapon.' This was the picture Riker wanted out of his head – that child pulling a knife from a corpse.

'Lou and me, we're in the car when we hear a call on the radio. A dispatcher's sending all available units to investigate a puddle of blood on Avenue B. We would've blown it off, but then another call placed a little blond girl at the same address – following a blood trail into an empty building. We got there just in time to see the flames. That's when Kathy came out the front door. One look at us and she runs back inside – back into the fire.'

'But that's not—'

'Not *normal*? No, you wouldn't expect a kid to do that. But she was carrying a knife with Sparrow's initial on the hilt and probably a good set of prints. If the kid was caught near Frankie's body with the murder weapon, her favorite whore would go to jail.'

'So she ran into a burning building, *knowing* she could die?'

'Naw, we never figured that – not for a second. This kid had a world-class survival instinct. Lou figured she was heading for the roof, maybe counting on a fire escape.'

'Could Kathy have staged her own death?'

'That was one theory, and she was that smart. But there was no fire escape. That morning, the owner sold the iron for scrap. We tried to follow her into the building. Then the first explosion blew out the boards on the downstairs windows. Cans of kerosene and paint thinner were goin' off like bombs. And now, there's no way in, no way out.' He recalled the open doorway as a wall of fire. Flames had boiled out of the ground-floor windows like the tail burners of a rocket. 'I thought the building was gonna take off and fly away. The back door was boarded up. The firemen didn't even try to break it down. All they could do was contain the blaze to one building.'

Riker slapped his hand on the bar. 'Bang, bang, bang! All the accelerants were blowing up in sympathetic explosions – all the way up to the top of the building. Then the roof went up in a ball of fire, and we knew the kid was dead . . . Well, *I* did.' It had taken more than Armageddon to convince Lou Markowitz.

'The fire marshal showed us the kid's shoes – proof that she made it up to the roof. They were still laced, blown off her feet in the final blast. One shoe was clean, thrown clear. The other one burnt black. The arson team figured she was at the center of the last explosion, and they didn't expect to find her in one piece.'

'So Kathy was presumed dead?'

'Well, they didn't know her name. All they had was one of her books, half fried . . . and her shoes. Later, a snitch tied the western and the kid to Sparrow. Two cops showed up in Sparrow's hospital room and told her that Kathy was dead.'

'Except that she wasn't.' Charles ticked off the points on his fingers. 'Boarded windows, no back door, no fire escape, no neighboring roof. How did she escape?'

'Kathy wouldn't tell. She *never* will. She *knows* it still drives me crazy. Damn kid never misses an opportunity to get even.'

'With a concussion,' said Charles, 'she might not remember.'

'But that won't explain how she got off the roof alive. Who knows? Maybe she flew. That was Sparrow's favorite theory.'

'I like it. If a shoe can be thrown clear, why not a little girl? With something soft like garbage bags on another roof—'

'No, Charles, we checked. No soft landing. And remember, this building was an island – twenty feet to the next roof. We caught Kathy that same night – no cuts, no bruises, not a mark on her. If you think about it long enough, it'll give you a headache.'

'All right.' Charles covered his eyes with one hand. 'You thought she was dead, but that was the night you found her – which suggests that you were still looking for her.'

'Right.' Riker slapped the mahogany. 'We were in this same bar, me and Lou.' He looked up at the television set mounted on the wall.

'Watching TV. The lead story was a little girl with green eyes who loved westerns. The kid was famous for two minutes on the news.' And she would have gotten more air time if a city garbage strike had not stolen her thunder.

'Suddenly the place gets real quiet. I turn to the door, and there's Sparrow. Well, this is a cop bar, and she's lookin' every inch a hooker. Just begging for a twisted arm and a short flight through the front door. I tried to get rid of her. Junkies are always messing with your head, and Lou was in a bad way. I didn't think he could take anymore. But now I see the blood leaking through her clothes and a hospital bracelet on her wrist.'

'And that's when you guessed she'd killed the drug dealer?'

'No, they hadn't even found his bones yet. It was the next day when they brought him in tagged for a John Doe. The autopsy turned up a thigh bone chipped twice by a blade. Dr Slope figured the knife cut an artery and it bled out. He even diagrammed the angle of the strike. That put Sparrow on her knees when she sank her knife into Frankie Delight. And it fit with the wound in Sparrow's side. The shock would've brought her down.'

'But *Kathy* was charged with the murder.'

'Charles, you're gettin' ahead of the story. So we're in the bar with Sparrow, and we wanna take her back to the hospital. But the whore won't go. She's sweatin' and she's got the shakes real bad. Lou figures she's strung out from withdrawal pains. So he empties out his damn wallet. It was maybe eighty dollars, a fortune to a sick junkie. And he slides the money down the bar. Now Sparrow says, "Her name is *Kathy*, and I'm tellin' you that kid is unnatural. She could be *alive*." And Lou says, "No, Sparrow – only if you believe in Superman comic books. Kathy was just a little girl . . . She didn't fly away . . . She died."'

Riker held up his glass and stared at the last drops of liquid gold. 'There's not much difference between me and a junkie. As long as I got my booze, I'm an okay guy. But take it away from me?' He shook his head. 'Much as I like you, Charles, I'd slit your throat for the next drink. With Sparrow it was heroin. Well, she's too bloody to work the street. No money to score her next needle. She's dope-sick, *dying* for a fix, but she pushes Lou's money back across the bar and says, "You gotta find the kid. She might be hurt."'

'So she *knew* Kathy was alive.'

'No, she didn't. That's the kicker. Sparrow was going on faith. And *that's* what the whore was buying when she gave the money back. She had to make Lou believe in Kathy, too. Because the kid *might* be out there alone in the dark, maybe hurt real bad.'

Riker drained his glass. 'That night, Sparrow was more of a man than I was. Well, she's got our attention. She says this drag queen commissioned the kid to steal parts off a Jaguar. Sparrow only found out 'cause Kathy had to ask what a Jag was before she could rob one. Now this happened way before the dicks tell Sparrow the kid is dead. She's still in the hospital and thinkin' ahead to her next needle. She tells Kathy about this rich yuppie who trolls East Village clubs and whores every weekend. And *he's* got a Jag. Well, it's Saturday night. I'm three sheets to the wind when Lou grabs my arm. And off we go with Sparrow.'

Three fools with absolute faith in comic-book heroes.

Riker could still see Lou Markowitz driving through the wet streets at a crawl of ten miles an hour, haunting every place where they had ever seen Kathy, chased her and lost her. It was insane to believe that the child had escaped from that fire. Yet they drove on through drizzling rain. 'We knew she was dead, but we couldn't stop looking for her. How crazy was that?'

As if it were happening all over again, Riker watched his old friend tune the car radio. Rock 'n' roll did not suit him that night. Lou picked a station that played bluesy music from an earlier era. There were pauses between the sad notes and phrases, like a conversation with the sorry man behind the wheel. 'And then we found the Jag. Lou pulls over to the curb and cuts the lights.'

The three of them listened to a sweet ripple of ivory keys tapering off in the low notes. Three pairs of eyes were trained on the sports car parked across the street. Piano chords dropped into spaces of silence, like footsteps of a child. And then, as if Duke Ellington had orchestrated the moment – along came Kathy. The golden head was bobbing and dodging behind the garbage cans. Out on the open street now, barefooting down the pavement, homing in on the Jaguar's trademark hood ornament.

Baby needs new shoes.

In and out of the lamplight, her small wet face glistened through the rain and the smoky gray cover of steam hissing up through a subway grate. The child was coming closer. Sparrow sank low in the back seat. Lou Markowitz and Riker slumped down behind the dashboard and watched, fascinated, as a little girl worked bits of metal in a lock. No crude coat hangers or broken windows for this kid. She opened the door with the finesse of a pro.

Once the child was inside the Jaguar, the two policemen left their vehicle, moving quickly, silently. It was a fight not to laugh out loud – or cry. When Markowitz bent down to the open door of the Jaguar, the little girl was sitting on the front seat, calmly dismantling the dashboard toys, tape deck and radio, using Sparrow's knife as a screwdriver. Lou leaned in close, saying, 'Hey, kid, whatcha doin'?'

The little girl smelled of sulfur and smoke; that should have been a warning. How indignant she was, and so angry, pointing her knife and yelling, 'Back off, old man, or I'll *cut* you.'

Lou's right hand flashed out, and startled, Kathy looked down to see that her tiny fist was empty.

'So then, Lou says to the kid, "Pretty fast moves for a fat man, huh, Kathy?" He pulled her out of the car, but she got away from him. Ran straight into Sparrow's arms. And then, what happened next – well, the kid never saw that coming. It was brutal. The whore drags Kathy back to Lou, and she's saying, "Baby, if you don't go with the man, how am I gonna get *paid*?"'

'So she did accept the——'

'Not one dime. At the end of the day, that whore showed a lotta class.' The detective lifted his glass in a salute, not noticing that it was empty, for he was still looking at Kathy's face, the confusion in her eyes. Her world was collapsing all around her, above and beneath her. 'The kid's survival was geared on running. Sparrow made sure she had no one to run to – no one who cared.'

And *that* was the moment when the little girl died, her bones going to liquid as she was sliding to the ground, trying to save herself by grabbing Sparrow's skirt, then collapsing and crying at the whore's feet. 'Kathy risked her life – and this was her payback. Sparrow just walked away. No goodbye, nothin'.' Riker looked down at his glass for a moment. 'So Kathy thinks she's been sold for money, right? That's all she's worth to the whore, another damn needle – and *still* she tried to run after Sparrow.'

'Because she loved her?'

'Because that whore was all she had.' Riker could hear the small needy voice crying, begging Sparrow to come back, *please, please.* So much pain – the child's and his own. Oh, the panic in Kathy's eyes when Sparrow turned a corner and disappeared.

'And then the kid went wild. All the guns and knives came out. I mean that literally. She drew on us with a damn pellet gun. God, how she hated Lou. He'd run her ragged, took everything away from her – first her books and then her whore.'

'Well, that explains the early animosity,' said Charles. 'Why she never called him anything but Markowitz.'

'Yeah, she blamed him for turning Sparrow against her. He spent years paying for that. So did I. That brat never forgets, *never* forgives.' Riker pushed his glass to the edge of the bar. 'So now we're headin' for Brooklyn. I'm in the back seat, and the kid's up front with Lou.' He recalled every detail of that drive, the smell of rain-washed air, the suburban lawns littered with bicycles and tricycles. The car radio was cranked up all the way, breaking the peace in a rock 'n' roll celebration.

362

Dogs barked to the high notes, and the lights of fireflies winked in sync with the beat of a golden oldie by Buddy Holly.

And a feral child was manacled to the dashboard. Kathy was a hellmouth of obscenities, a small storm of energy fighting against her chains, though she must have known she could never break them.

'Now it gets a little spooky.' And the music had changed to the Rolling Stones. 'But it helps if you know that Lou's wife could hear lost children crying on other planets.' The old green sedan pulled up to the curb in front of the house, where Helen Markowitz was framed in a square of yellow light – waiting. Suddenly, she was drawn away from the window and moving toward the front door with a sense of great urgency.

The car and the music should have reassured her that nothing was wrong. Bad news was so seldom announced by loud rock 'n' roll. And Lou's wife could not have seen the baby thief in the dark of the car, nor heard one small angry voice above a chorus of wailing rockers, steel guitars and drums. Yet Helen was clearly on a mission when she burst through the front door, flew down the porch steps and ran across the wet grass.

The little girl was screaming death threats at the top of her tiny lungs while Lou Markowitz grinned broadly and foolishly. His life was complete. His wife was busy ripping the passenger door off its hinges, and Kathy was almost home.

TWENTY-FIVE

The long summer fever was over. The heat was dying off in cool wet gusts of air and rain. The two men stepped out on to the sidewalk and stood beneath the awning.

'Louis must have told Mallory about the murder charge,' said Charles. 'When she joined the police department, he would've—'

'Yeah.' Riker was on the lookout for a cab to carry him home. 'He told her that much. Now she thinks it was Sparrow who pinned the murder on her. Lou couldn't set her straight. She would've wondered why he didn't make a case against the whore.'

Charles kept silent for a moment and listened to the steady rain. 'Mallory will never have any peace.'

'Neither will you . . . . Me either.'

Disregarding Riker's plans to take a cab, Charles opened the door of his Mercedes and guided him into the passenger seat, then politely looked the other way while the man wrestled with a drunk's problem of fastening a safety belt.

Charles started the engine, then pulled into traffic. 'Did Sparrow tell you she was defending Kathy when she got stabbed?'

'No, we couldn't ask her anything about that night. Guilty knowledge. If you know about a murder, then you're part of the crime. But it wasn't hard to work out. Frankie Delight was outmatched, a real flyweight. But good as Sparrow was in a street fight, she was never the aggressor. She would've kicked off her high heels and run when that knife came out. But she's got the kid with her, and little legs can't run

364

as fast as a barefoot whore. So we figured Frankie stabbed her while she was shielding Kathy. I know he made the first cut, 'cause the whore was on her knees when she put her shiv in his leg.'

Charles vividly recalled the photograph of Sparrow's scar. He could see it now – not a slit, but a gaping hole dug into her side. Yet she had found the strength to drive a knife through a man's clothing and muscle.

Riker read his mind and said, 'Sparrow's knife was razor sharp, and she got damn lucky when she hit that artery.'

Charles nodded absently, listening to the rain on the roof. 'Mallory's at the hospital now, isn't she? That's why you didn't go. She wouldn't allow it.'

His friend wore a look of surprise, perhaps wondering what he might have said to give that away. One hand on the armrest, he tapped his fingers to the beat of the windshield wipers.

'So,' said Charles, 'you're planning to let her bludgeon a dying woman? Oh, not with her fists – but you know what's going on in that hospital room. You *know*.'

'I can't tell her the truth. And neither can you. I had to pick a memory she could believe in. I'm gonna let her hold on to Lou.'

So she would never discover that Louis had ripped out her ten-year-old heart with a conspiracy of lies. 'And she goes on hating Sparrow until it's too late?'

'It won't be long now.' Riker rolled down the window and sent his cigarette flying into the rain.

Charles sensed a door closing here, and he picked up the thread of the previous conversation. 'Lucky the wound was in Frankie's thigh. I suppose that made it easy to blame a child.'

'You make it sound like we framed the kid.' Riker almost smiled. 'It wasn't even our case. Two other detectives closed out the paperwork. The death was self-defense, but connected to felony arson. Sparrow would've gone to prison.'

'So you kept silent, and Kathy took the blame.'

'Well, the kid was guilty on the arson charge. Kathy decided to get rid of *all* the evidence. She soaked the body with kerosene. Very thorough. All the medical examiner had to work with was some charcoaled meat and bone. So a nameless, dead kid took the blame for everything.' Riker yawned. 'Case closed.' And then his eyes closed.

Twenty minutes passed in silence before Charles pulled up to the curb at Riker's address. Rather than disturb his sleep, Charles gathered the man into his arms, then carried him through the door and up the stairs to the apartment. He laid the detective down on an unmade bed, then removed the revolver and put it away in a drawer. After slipping the shoes from Riker's feet, Charles followed the last of Mallory's instructions. He entered the bathroom and flicked on the switch for a plastic Jesus night-light.

On the lonely ride home, he thought about Riker's version of events and then the way it had really happened. On one point, he and the detective agreed. The drug dealer had made the first strike before his artery became a fountain of spraying blood. Sparrow's wound had come first – but not while shielding a child. That woman had been laughing when Frankie Delight put his knife in her side – Mallory's own words, the testimony of an eyewitness.

Caught by surprise, Sparrow had fallen to her knees, crippled with blood loss and shock, then a sudden drop in blood pressure and the resulting lightness in head and chest – the weakness of limbs. He could see her hands trying to plug that hideous hole. Perhaps there had been time to pull a weapon, but no strength to drive it home. And the dealer would have been on his guard against reprisal.

There were *two* chips in the thigh bone of Frankie Delight, an act of violence powered by rage and fear. Only a ten-year-old girl could have taken him down by stealth and surprise. Charles could see the small thief stealing the knife from the hand of the fallen prostitute, then driving it into a man's thigh once – twice – getting even. How surprised the child must have been to see Frankie Delight fall and die, wondering then, how could such a wound be mortal?

The little girl had killed a man for Sparrow's sake, then risked her life in trial by fire, and Kathy's reward was not the ongoing love she needed so badly, but betrayal and desertion. That was the only scenario to fit every fact and explain why the prostitute remained unforgiven.

Charles knew what was happening in Sparrow's hospital room. The dying woman, though deep in coma dreams, had been defeating the death sentences of her doctors for days. And this will to live suggested the stuff of her dreams, unfinished business. All this time, Sparrow had been waiting for Mallory.

His car rolled to a stop, and he closed his eyes in pain, not wanting to imagine this reunion, a chanted litany of hateful acts and trespasses, music to die by.

And so he turned his mind to the last riddle, expecting to make short work of it: how had Kathy escaped the fire?

Logic could not carry him everywhere, but damned close. He liked Sparrow's theory best. The child must have been thrown clear in the explosion. He envisioned Kathy surrounded by fire and running past the corpse of Frankie Delight as it burned brightly head to toe. Kathy's feet barely touched the ground, all but flying to gain that staircase before the flames could eat her. Behind her, the boards were awash in roiling liquid fire. He could hear her scream the only prayer a child knows to ask for pity and mercy, 'Mama!' Or had she called out for Sparrow? The flames raced up the stairs with her, singeing hair as she climbed higher and higher. Bombs were going off on the floors below.

Bang! Bang! Bang!

Kathy pushed through the rooftop door and saw the sky and – then what? No fire escape, no way out. She raised her arms like thin white wings. And what happened next? The whole world exploded under her feet. She must have been thrown clear, but how to account for her lack of injuries? How far could one throw a child without harming her? Given the probable force of the blast, the speed of propulsion, and the sudden impact – the child lay dead or badly broken in every logical scenario *all night long.*

Over the ensuing years, Charles would come to understand the persistence of whores, their book salon and the maddening quest for the end of a story. The problem of the escape would never be solved — unless one counted the last words he would write in his journal toward the end of a very long life. Because he had never betrayed his role as a keeper of secrets, an eater of sins, his children and grandchildren would be forever confounded by his homage to Sparrow's faith in comic-book heroes, a single line at the center of the page, 'Kathy, can you fly?'

EPILOGUE

Detective Mallory shuddered so slightly that the doctor beside her failed to notice. She dug her fingernails into her palms to bring on the pain – to stay awake and focused, to see this thing through.

Payback.

Rain drummed on the window of Sparrow's hospital room. The lights were low, and Father Rose hovered over the sickbed, armed with his magical rosary beads. Mallory watched him don his surplice to perform the sacrament of last rites – a waste of precious time.

The young intern affirmed this idea, saying, 'I don't think she knows what's going on.'

Mallory stared at the woman on the bed, eyes rolling, mouth drooling. Sparrow seemed smaller now, as houses do when children revisit them later in life. 'How can you tell if she's awake?'

The doctor shrugged. 'Does it matter? There's a big difference between awake and aware. She only has a few hours, I'm sure of that much. Her organs are shutting down.'

And the physician did not want to be here at the end. Why linger over his failure? He left the room quickly – escaping. Mallory listened to his footsteps hurrying down the corridor, outrunning death. Only a priest would be attracted to Sparrow now.

'Do you heartily repent your sins?'

'Father, that would take years. She's a whore.' Mallory opened the door as an invitation for the man to leave, and soon. The priest

369

stared at her in surprise, as though her hint might have been too subtle. 'Speed it up,' she said. 'I haven't got all night – and neither does Sparrow.'

Father Rose bent over his parishioner. 'Can you give me a sign of contrition?'

'She's sorry,' said Mallory. 'I saw her eyes move.'

'You're heartless.'

'I know that.'

'She's dying. Why can't you leave her in peace?' The rest of his words to Sparrow were close to mime, inaudible and ending with the sign of the cross.

'You're done. Good.' Mallory walked across the room and stood very close to the man. 'Father, leave now.' She held up her gold shield to remind him that she was the law. 'I've got official business here. I'm not giving you a choice.'

She would have liked him better if he had put up a fight, but he turned his eyes to Sparrow's, and every thought in his head was there to read when he shrugged. The priest was already writing off the whore as a corpse. What more damage could be done to her now? What comfort could his presence bring? *None.*

He left the room quietly, and Mallory shut the door behind him, then jammed a straight-back chair beneath the knob to keep it closed. There would be no more visitors tonight.

She walked back to her old enemy on the hospital bed, the woman who had betrayed her and, worse, *abandoned* her. Now the whore was the one who was utterly helpless, unable to lift one hand in defense. Her skin was as pale as the sheets.

'Sparrow? It's *me!*'

There was no response beyond ragged breathing and the endless demented motion of blue eyes that saw nothing. Could Sparrow hear? Could she understand the words? There was no way to tell. The only certainty in this room was death; it was coming.

The young detective leaned over the woman, bending low enough for her lips to lightly brush a tuft of hair near Sparrow's ear, then whispered, 'It's Kathy.'

And I'm lost.

Mallory settled into a chair beside the bed, then opened an old paperback book – the last western. Her head was bowed, eyes fixed on the page. 'I'm going to read you a story,' she said, as one blind hand reached out for the comfort of Sparrow's.

COMING NEXT …

If you've enjoyed this episode in the
Detective Kathy Mallory series, turn the page
for a preview of her next case.

DEAD
FAMOUS

PROLOGUE

Johanna could hear cat's paws madly thudding on the bathroom door, and the animal was crying in a human way – so frightened. Or was he merely hungry? She had fed the poor beast, but how long ago? No matter. The cat's cries receded, as though her front room had decamped from the hotel suite, floating up and away with utter disregard for gravity.

And time? What was that to her?

The whole day long, Johanna had not moved from her perch at the edge of a wooden chair. She sat there, wrapped in a bathrobe, as the sun moved behind the window glass, as shadows crawled about the room with a slow progress that only a paranoid eye could follow. One of the shadows belonged to herself, and the dark silhouette of her body was dragged across the wallpaper, inch by inch, extending her deformity to a cruel extreme.

Inside her brain was the refrain of a rock 'n' roll song from another era. 'Gimme me shelter,' the Rolling Stones sang to her, and she resisted this mantra as she always did, for there were no safe places.

Perhaps another hour had passed, maybe three. She could not say when night had fallen. Johanna unclenched her hands and looked down at a crumpled letter, as if, in absolute darkness, she could read the words of a postscript: *Only a monster can play this game.*

ONE

The black van had no helpful lettering on the side to tell the neighbors what business it was about on this November afternoon. Here and there, along the street of tall brownstones, drapes had parted and curious eyes were locked upon the vehicle's driver. Even by New York City standards, she was an odd one.

Johanna Apollo's skin was very fair, the gift of Swedes on her mother's side. And yet, from any distance, she might be taken for a large dark spider clad in denim as she climbed out of the van, then dropped to the pavement in a crouch. Dark brown was the color of her leather gloves, her work boots and the long strands of hair spread back across the unnatural curve of her spine. Her torso was bent forward, her body forever fused into a subtle question mark as her face angled toward the ground, hidden from the watchers at their windows. They never saw the great dark eyes – the beauty of the beast. And now the neighbors' heads turned in unison, following her progress down the street. Dry yellow leaves cartwheeled and crackled alongside as she walked with a delicacy of slender spider-long legs. Such deep grace for one so misshapen – that was how the neighbors would recall this moment later in the day. It was almost a dance, they would say.

And none of them noticed the small tan car gliding into Eighty-fourth Street, quiet as a swimming shark. It stopped near the corner, where another vehicle had just taken the last available parking space.

* * *

The young driver of the tan sedan left her engine idling as she stepped out in the middle of the street. Nothing about her said *civil servant*; the custom-tailored lines of her designer jeans and long, black leather coat said *money*. And the wildly expensive running shoes allowed her to move in silence as she padded toward a station wagon. She leaned down and rapped on the driver's window. The pudgy man behind the wheel gave her the grin of a lottery winner, for she was that lovely, that ilk of tall blondes who would never go out with him in a million years, and he hurried to roll down the window.

Oh, happy day.

'I want your parking place,' she said, all business, no smile of hello – nothing.

The wagon driver's grin wobbled a bit. Was this a joke? No man would give up a parking space on any street in Manhattan, not *ever*, not even for a *naked* woman. Was she *nuts?* He summoned up his New Yorker attitude, saying, 'Yeah, lady – over my dead body.' And she raised one eyebrow to indicate that this might be an option. The long slants of her eyes were unnaturally green – unnaturally cold. A milk-white hand rested on the door of his car, long red fingernails tapping, tapping, ticking like a bomb, and it occurred to him that those nails might be dangerous.

Oh, shit!

One hand had gone to her hip, opening the blazer for just a tease, a peek at what she had hidden in her shoulder holster, a damn cannon that passed for a gun.

'Move,' she said, and move he did.

Kathy Mallory had a detective's gold shield, but she rarely used the badge to motivate civilians. Listening to angry tirades on abuse of police power was time-consuming; fear was more efficient. And now she drove her tan car into the hastily vacated parking space. After killing the engine, she never even glanced at the black van.

It was her day off and this covert surveillance was the closest she could come to an idea of recreation.

The routine of the van's driver was predictable, and Mallory was settling in for a long wait when a large white Lincoln with rental plates rounded the corner. This motorist was less enterprising, settling for double-parking his car across the street from the vehicle that so interested Mallory – until now. The driver of the rented car became her new target when he craned his neck to check the black van's plates. His head was slowly turning, eyes scanning the street, until he located the deformed figure of Johanna Apollo walking down the sidewalk in the direction of Columbus Avenue.

Mallory smiled, for this man had just identified himself as another player in the mother of all games.

The company uniform was stowed in Johanna Apollo's duffel bag along with the rest of her gear. She never wore it when meeting the clients. The moonsuit was far more unsettling than the sudden appearance of a hunchback at the door.

A man her own age, late thirties, awaited her on the front steps of a brownstone built in the nineteenth century. He wore a flimsy robe over his pajamas, and, though his feet were bare, he seemed not to mind the cold. When Johanna lifted her head to greet him, his face was full of trepidation, and then he nearly smiled. She could read his mind. He was thinking, *Oh, how normal*, so glad to see her conventional human face. He adjusted his spectacles for a better look at her warm brown eyes, and he took some comfort there, even before she said, 'I'll be done in an hour, and then you can have your life back.'

That was all he wanted to hear. Relieved, he sighed and nodded his understanding that there would be no small talk, not one more chorus of *I'm so sorry*, false notes in the mouth of a stranger.

Johanna followed him into the house and through another door to his front room. It was decorated with period furniture and smeared with the bloody handprints of an intruder. She recognized the spots on the wall as a splatter pattern from the back-strike of a knife. The chalk outline sketched on the rug was that of a small, lean victim who had died quickly, though her blood was spread thin all about the room, giving the impression that the attack had gone on forever. She wondered if anyone had told the husband that his wife had not suffered long. Johanna turned to the sorry man beside her. It was her art to put disturbed people at ease; she did it with tea.

'You don't have to stay and watch. Why not wait in the kitchen?' She pulled a small packet of herbal tea from the pocket of her denim jacket. 'This is very soothing.'

The client took the packet and stared at it, as though the printed instructions for steeping in hot water might be difficult to comprehend. He waved one hand in apology to say that he was somewhat at sea today. 'My wife usually handles these—' Suddenly appalled, he lowered his head. His wife had usually handled the messes of their lives. How could he have forgotten that she was dead? His hands clenched tightly, and Johanna knew that he was silently berating himself for this bizarre breach of etiquette.

The murder was recent, and she would have guessed that even without the paperwork to release the crime scene. Judging by the growth of stubble on the man's face, only a few days had passed since his wife's death. Unshaven, unwashed, the widower walked about in a stale ether that the bereaved shared with the bedridden. His head was still bowed as he edged away from her and ambled down a narrow passageway. Upon opening a door at the far end of this hall, he raised his face in expectation, perhaps believing that he would meet his dead wife in the kitchen – and she would make him some tea.

Johanna knelt on the floor and opened her duffel bag. One hand passed over the hood and the respirator. No need for them today. She pulled out a protective suit and gloves for working with blood products in the age of AIDS – even the blood of children, nuns and other virgins. Her employer had given her the basic vocabulary of the job: *fluids* and *solids* and *hazardous waste*, though she had never seen the common debris of brains and shattered bone, feces and urine as anything but human remains. She had also been encouraged to remove photographs of the victim before she began, and this was another trick to dehumanize the task. But Johanna never disturbed the wedding portrait on the wall, and the bride with downcast eyes continued to shyly smile at the chalk outline of her own corpse.

Johanna sponged the stains on the cream-white wall and charted a thief's progress around this room, going from drawer to pulled-out drawer. She knew where he had been standing when a policeman had barreled through the door with a drawn gun. The bullet had been pried out of the wall, but the hole remained. The thief must have had the knife in his hand, and the officer must have been very young, untried and nervous.

She filled the hole with a ready-mix plaster. A small brush and a few deft strokes of tint made it blend into the paint. Below this patch were red drops of *hazardous waste* from a murderer. He was wiped away with one wet rag, and, though no one would ever know, she placed it in a separate bag so the blood of the innocent woman would not mingle with his. Next, she replaced the contents spilled from the drawers, then went on to the problem of a torn lampshade and resolved it with a bit of mending tape. Last, she pulled out a hairdryer and moved it across the wet areas where she had spot-cleaned the rug, the couch and the drapes. Some of her services went beyond the job description, but she wanted the widower to find no trace of murder, no damp ghost of a stain that he might commit to memory.

No more than an hour had passed, as promised, and now the client inspected her work. She watched his fearful eyes search the wall for the bullet hole, but there was no sign of it anymore. And, by his wandering gaze, she could tell that he had forgotten the exact location of that scar in the plaster and his wife's chalk silhouette on the floor. The room seemed so normal, as though no violence had ever taken place here — and his wife had never died — so said his brief smile as he wrote out a check.

Four months ago in another city, her first crime scene had required less work, and she had been her own client on that unpaid job. The armchair had absorbed most of the FBI agent's blood, and so it had been a simple matter of furniture disposal after mopping up the puddle on the floor and the red drops spattered on the wall. In that room, death had been a drawn-out affair, for Timothy Kidd had not struggled enough to spend all his blood at once, and there had been ample time for him to be afraid.

However, that event had occurred in a previous life lived by another version of herself, though the dead man did remain with her as a constant presence, a haunt. And so it was neither odd nor coincidental to be thinking of Timothy when she emerged from the building to find an unpleasant reminder of his death.

Marvin Argus was waiting for her on the sidewalk. His trench coat flapped open in the wind, exposing a dark-gray suit with a slept-in look. She guessed that he had taken the red-eye flight from Chicago to New York, and there had been no time for a change of clothes after landing, that or his fastidious grooming habits were deteriorating. Perhaps there had been some urgency in tracking her down today.

No, that was not it.

Argus had found time to carefully style his sparse brown hair so that no strand could escape the gelled fringe of bangs covering his receding hairline. The effect was juvenile and so at odds with his forty-year-old face.

'Hello, Johanna.' He smiled to show her all of his perfect teeth, acting as if this meeting might be a happy chance encounter and not an ambush, not a defiance of the court order to keep him at a distance.

Did he seem a little jittery – just on the verge of a tic or a twitch? She looked through him, then passed him by on her way back to the black van.

He walked alongside her, keeping his tone light, fighting down all the high notes of runaway anxiety. 'You're looking well.'

'Still alive, you mean, and you're wondering why.'

'No, seriously, I think physical labor agrees with you,' he said.

'But I suppose this new line of work is your idea of penance.'

Much could be read into that clumsy little barb, perhaps some desperate situation coming to a head. Johanna's bent posture had made her a student of footwear, and now she gleaned more from his shoes than his words. The black leather was, as always, fanatically shiny, but both laces had been broken and repairs effected with knots. The man was coming undone.

Good.

She raised her face to his, not bothering to hide her contempt. 'You don't look well, Argus. You seem a little shaky today. Under a lot of stress?' Did that sound like a taunt, like getting even? She hoped so. 'And you're losing weight.'

He dismissed this with a wave of one hand, saying, 'Long hours.' He drew back his shoulders in an effort to appear larger and less the nervous rabbit. Eyebrows arched, he folded his arms to strike a condescending pose, exuding an arrogance that invited every passerby to punch him in the face. 'I met your boss today.' Argus staged a pause. 'We had a long talk about you.'

'Really?' That was unlikely, for Riker was tight with his words. And so she could surmise that this lie was an implied threat. Yes, Argus would want her to worry about what he might have shared with her employer. She stared at him, wondering, *How frightened are you?*

'That guy Riker, he's a heavy drinker, isn't he? Yeah,' said Argus. 'Couldn't help but notice. You can tell by the eyes, all those red veins.' He was still pressing what he believed was his advantage over her. A few seconds of silence dragged by before he realized that she was not at all threatened, and neither was she inclined to banal conversation. The man looked up at the sky, unwilling to meet her steady gaze anymore.

'He tried to grill me on your background.' The old familiar pomposity was back in his voice. 'I could tell Riker was an ex-cop by his interrogation style. They never lose that, do they? On or off the job, they can never have just a normal conversation. I figure he doesn't know the first thing about you, Johanna. That or you fed him some fairy tale – and he *knows* it.' Argus smiled, awaiting praise for this insight. Failing in that, he flicked imaginary lint from the sleeve of his coat. 'Of course, I didn't tell him anything. Not who I was or what I—'

'So you lied to him. You think Riker didn't pick up on that?' She swung her body up into the driver's seat and slouched deep into worn upholstery that received the hump on her back like a cupped hand. She faced the windshield.

Marvin Argus rushed his words. 'Does your boss know—'

'I told Riker my history was none of his damn business.' She slammed the door and put the van in gear.

Argus reached up and gripped the door handle, as if that could prevent her from driving away. He yelled to be heard through the rolled-up window. 'Johanna! About Timothy! Did *you* believe him – while he was still *alive*?'

If the man had held on to the van another moment, he would have lost his hand when she pulled into the street. Johanna pressed the accelerator pedal to the floor and sped toward the broad avenue at the end of the street. She passed through a red light amid the screech and squeal of braking cars and a cabdriver's hollered obscenities.

Marvin Argus had grown smaller in her rearview mirror, only insect high when she rounded the corner.

Have you read every case in the Kathy Mallory series?

Mallory's Oracle

Crime brought them together. A killer tears them apart.

Book 1 in the Kathy Mallory series.

When NYPD Sergeant Kathy Mallory was an eleven-year-old street kid, she got caught stealing. The detective who found her was Louis Markowitz. He should have arrested her. Instead he raised her as his own, in the best tradition of New York's finest.

Now Markowitz is dead, and Mallory the first officer on the scene. She knows any criminal who could outsmart her father is no ordinary human. This is a ruthless serial killer, a freak from the night-side of the mind.

And one question troubles her more than any other: why did he go in there alone?

The Man Who Lied to Women

Some lies can get you killed.

Book 2 in the Kathy Mallory series.

No one in New York's Special Crimes section knows much about Sergeant Kathy Mallory's origins. They only know that she can bewitch the most complex computer systems, can slip into the minds of killers with disturbing ease.

When a woman is murdered in Central Park, it appears to be a case of mistaken identity. Mallory goes hunting the killer, armed with under-the-skin knowledge of the man's mind and the bare clue of a lie.

Mallory holds on to the truth: everybody lies and some lies lead to death. And she knows that, to trap the killer, she must put her own life at risk.

Killing Critics

When art imitates death.

Book 3 in the Kathy Mallory series.

An artist is murdered, in a stylish, surprising and deadly act of perform-ance art. The murder almost goes unnoticed, but it reminds NYPD detective Kathy Mallory of an older, more brutal crime investigated years before by Mallory's now dead adoptive father.

As soon as Mallory starts to work on the new crime, old ghosts rise up, and the word comes down from on high to close her down, to shut her out the case.

But for Mallory, rules exist only to be shattered . . .

Flight of the Stone Angel

Revenge is a reason for living.

Book 4 in the Kathy Mallory series.

Seventeen years ago, a six-year-old girl disappeared from the small town of Dayborn, Louisiana.

She vanished the day of her mother's murder, and all assumed that she, too, was dead.

Now, Kathy Mallory has returned home. She has left her badge and her police issue revolver behind in New York City. She is no longer a cop. Just a daughter in search of a very personal revenge.

Shell Game

There's a shooter in the crowd.

Book 5 in the Kathy Mallory series.

At a sell-out festival of magicians in Manhattan, in front of a live audience and eight million television viewers, a death-defying trick goes tragically wrong.

NYPD detective Kathy Mallory has learned the hard way that things are rarely what they seem. But she is the only cop who believes the death is not an accident.

Hiding behind the smoke and mirrors is a ruthless killer who will soon strike again.

Dead Famous

How fast can you run?

Book 7 in the Kathy Mallory series.

It's the highest profile acquittal in recent history – and when a serial killer starts taking justice into his own hands, interest hits fever pitch.

NYPD detective Kathy Mallory finds herself in a race against time to save the remaining three members of the jury before the Reaper gets to them first.

And before the radio shock-jock Ian Zachary plays the next round in his deadly ratings-grabbing game of 'hunt the juror'.

Winter House

It was dark when she stabbed him the first time.

Book 8 in the Kathy Mallory series.

When a known serial killer is found at Winter House, with shears sticking out of his chest and an ice pick in his hand, NYPD detective Kathy Mallory is called in to investigate. At the scene of the crime seventy-year-old Nedda Winter immediately confesses to the killing, claiming it was self-defence. Case closed.

However, Nedda is in fact the most famous lost child in NYPD history, missing for almost sixty years, thought to be kidnapped following the massacre of her family . . . with an ice pick.

And a remarkable story begins to emerge, of murderous greed and family horror, abandonment and loss, revenge and twisted love.

Shark Music

They search the highway of death.

Book 9 in the Kathy Mallory series.

The mutilated body is found lying on the ground in Chicago, a dead hand pointing down Adams Street, also known as Route 66, a road of many names. And now of many deaths.

A silent caravan of cars drives down the road, each passenger bearing a photograph, but none of them the same. They are the parents of missing children, brought together by the word that children's gravesites are being discovered along with the Mother Road.

Detective Kathy Mallory drives with them.

The Chalk Girl

A child covered in blood. A body in the trees.

Book 10 in the Kathy Mallory series.

She appeared in Central Park: red-haired, blue-eyed, smiling, perfect – except for the blood. It fell from the sky, she said, while she was looking for her uncle, who turned into a tree. Poor child, people thought. And then they found the body in the tree.

For NYPD detective Kathy Mallory, there is something about the girl that she understands. And she will lead to a story of extraordinary crimes; murders stretching back years, blackmail and complicity and a particular cruelty that only someone with Mallory's history could fully recognise.

In the next few weeks, Kathy Mallory will deal with them all . . . in her own way.

It Happens in the Dark

Forty seconds from alive to dead.

Book 11 in the Kathy Mallory series.

The killer had just forty seconds to act, in total darkness, surrounded by a theatre full of people.

NYPD detective Kathy Mallory knows that even the most impossible of crimes have an explanation, if only you look in the right place. And after three deaths in three nights, she needs to find that place soon.

But when everything about the scene of crime is rigged for dramatic effect, and the suspects are actors, judging the difference between appearances and reality can be deadly . . .